"Help me!

She could feel her fear rising up into the top of her throat. She had to get him to take the pillowcase off. If he didn't, she would die. If he wouldn't, she would know he was going to kill her. She had to be able to see and to breathe.

"Please. Please, Nate. Let me see."

"Shut up. Don't call me that."

"What? Don't call you what?" She wanted desperately to please him.

"Nate. Don't call me Nate. And speak up. I can't hear you." She couldn't believe this. He wanted her to talk plainly with a pillowcase on her head?

"Take the pillowcase off. Please."

Charlie shrugged. What the hell difference did it make now? She knew what he looked like. This had been one awful day. He untied the knots around her neck and slid the filthy pillowcase off. He couldn't believe this was the same pretty waitress he'd dated. Her eyes were underlined by streaks of mascara and her face was puffy and covered with red splotches.

Verbena's eyes traveled around the small rustic room. Except for Charlie's things and a new layer of dust, the cabin had changed little since the last time Molly and Mickey had played house there. She saw no furniture; no closets and none of the comforts of a real home, just log walls, rough panel floors and a large hearth. The patchwork quilt in the corner and a little bowl of chokeberries next to the big fireplace didn't belong to the man she knew as Nate, so someone else had once lived here. As for her abductor, she wasn't sure what to say to him next. The last few hours had changed everything she thought she knew about him, and she had to find some way to get this stranger to let her live.

"BEAUFORT FALLS is an engaging page-turner of a first novel. Mari Sloan propelled her considerable writing skill onto the pages of BEAUFORT FALLS with the same spectacular propulsion as the atom bomb!"

"Snakes, spirits, spiders and balls of flame cannot stop the classically evil character J. D. Parsons as he misuses religion, manically dominating his small daughters. His young and beautiful dead wife Eliza returns from the grave to this deep-south region of Alabama searching for her lost baby. Her ex-lover, Charlie Callahan, is gender-challenged but doesn't let that get in the way of his terrifying hobby, the taxidermy of human heads."

"These diverse characters interact in the slalom ride of stunning developments in BEAUFORT FALLS. Masterful descriptions provide a realistic backdrop for the secrets that explode along the riverbanks of this sleepy little town. The matter-of-fact portrayal of life for the children in the local psychiatric hospital makes the neglect of them believable."

"Mari Sloan's well-written character portrayals are multi-layered in the style of Raymond Chandler's THE BIG SLEEP. She successfully presents cherubic children and a wolf-like, wild dog, along with the sense that right overpowers might in the end. The novel concludes with a one-two punch of a finish that is worth the wait, but you'll want to race ahead to the last line. Don't do it! It rockets along like a stagecoach on the loose with a surprise at every turn! THIS BOOK IS A MUST-READ!"

Nancy Rodgers started her writing career as a proofreader and has written for newspapers since 1995. Currently she is writing a column portraying the humorous, sometimes touching, side of life for The Farmland News in Toledo, Ohio. She is also an award winning, free-lance photographer who has had pictures accepted by the Perrysburg Messenger, The Rossford Record Journal, The Point and Shoreland Journal, the Bowling Green Sentinel Newspaper and the National Catholic Chronicle."

BEAUFORT FALLS

MARI SLOAN

BEAUFORT FALLS in its original form was published by Light Sword Publishing copyright April 2007 by Mari Sloan.

This edition of BEAUFORT FALLS has been re-edited and modified in its content for It's ME! Ink Press, copyright October 2007 by Mari Sloan.

BEAUFORT FALLS, Second Edition, by Mari Sloan
First Printing by It's ME! Ink Press.
ISBN # 978-0-9798583-0-7

Printed in the United States of America.

Cover design by Mari Sloan and Alvin Kalelski.

Photograph provided by Mike Rash.

BOOKS ARE AVAILABLE AT QUANTITY DISCOUNTS WHEN USED TO PROMOTE PRODUCTS OR SERVICES. FOR INFORMATION PLEASE WRITE TO BEAUFORT FALLS, PO BOX 4361, THOUSAND OAKS, CA 91359

DEDICATION

Sometimes things come easy, then other times--they don't. My life has been a series of stops and starts, and in many ways, this book has been also. One person has been my support, my business manager, my creative partner and my soul mate. This person encouraged me to take an insane risk to get the job done right. This book is, again, dedicated to the one I love--my husband, Alan.

ACKNOWLEGEMENTS

First of all I would like to thank my editor, Margaret Kelly, for her hard work, suggestions and support. I also would like to thank and recognize Mike Rash for the photo used in the cover art, and Kevin MacLeod and Tim Parker for music used on the web page and in promotional book trailers. Tim was also the first person to actually read BEAUFORT FALLS in completed form, and to tell me that it is worth publishing. My warmest thanks and heartfelt appreciation for the hordes of friends and relatives who bought BEAUFORT FALLS, the first edition, and let me know that they enjoyed the story. They make writing worth the effort.

Hellnight

It began softly, a whisper on the thick Southern breeze, part of the transition from twilight to dusk barely discernable amid the deepening chorus of nighttime katydids, crickets, and the occasional mellow croak from a territorial bullfrog.

Where is my baby? What did you do with my child?

John Duke Parsons rubbed his eyes. It was gone now, but he glanced behind him nervously, squinting into his rear view mirror, mouth slightly open. It usually happened here.

"Oh, my Lord of Hosts, be my solace and my guide," he prayed anxiously.

The words calmed him as he passed the old Armstead farm, and then Perkins Hardware. He'd never gotten this far before. Those lazy kids better have his supper ready for him. Preaching the country circuit paid only pennies, but it was enough to keep the bottle filled. Longingly, he felt for the half-empty fifth of Early Times he'd shoved under the passenger seat of the vehicle. It wouldn't do to get caught drinking. His reputation was already down the tubes.

It wasn't going to happen tonight. He was going to make it. He grinned and reached for the bottle; he was almost home. Then he felt the shiver. The moon tucked behind a racing cloud and he heard the noise. Actually, it was a voice, a small voice, and it sounded like it came from his own mind. He pulled the top of the bottle of whiskey from its brown paper bag and gulped a huge swallow of the fiery liquid. That was better. He almost couldn't hear it now.

Where are my babies? What are you doing to my children?

Not now.

Where is my baby? What did you do to my infant child?

He was moving faster. The darkness moved closer to the road, large tree limbs scraping the ground. He applied the brake, and the truck slowed. It was going to be all right tonight. He was going to be fine. It wasn't going to happen tonight.

Grinning, he took a second big swig out of the open bottle. He settled into the seat, relaxing. No way the bitch was going to tell him what to do.

"You're dead!" He sneered. "Dead! You can't hurt me, you stupid whore." Arrogantly, he shoved the bottle into the seat beside him.

The road seemed almost friendly. The moon was back and the sky was filled with stars. In less than ten minutes he would be sitting at his kitchen table, hot soup ready for him, if Molly wasn't lollygagging somewhere. Damn kid would forget her head if it wasn't attached.

The truck was moving a little faster. Nothing to worry about, but the road was once again dark, shadows moving menacingly across the bright line on the asphalt highway. Clouds moved in quickly. It was time to be home. He pressed the accelerator and then squinted at his speedometer. *Sixty?* That was too fast. No way to be going that speed on this road, not in the old Ford pickup. The speedometer must be broken. He took his foot off the accelerator and waited for the old heap to slow down, but it didn't.

Instead, it picked up speed. He slammed both feet on the brake pedal and fumbled under the dash desperately, searching for the emergency brake. He could feel the brake engage, but the vehicle didn't slow down, it moved faster, barely missing century old willows that lined both sides of the little road.

Stunned and groggy from the booze, John Duke Parsons realized that he was going to die. Strangely enough, he did not appeal to his Lord of Hosts for help, but instead screamed a name; shrieked it with all of the stored hatred that could consume a soul and render a once handsome man into a twisted rack of jutting bones. Moving at more than one hundred miles per hour, the truck plowed into the ancient water oak, and after the last tinkle of shattered glass, the only sound was a soft low laugh.

Beaufort Falls

Chapter One

Soup

Beaufort Falls was not exactly what you would call a "happening" town. It was east of Mobile, west of Panama City, south of Montgomery and north of the Gulf; in other words, right in the middle of the flattest part of Alabama. This was the country everybody left to go somewhere else, leaving the town with two filling stations, a school and fourteen churches, but few residents. It was a dry county, but it did have a pool hall. You could play pool and, mostly, folks brought their own beer or whiskey, which they drank in the cabs of their old pickup trucks in the parking lot. Beer was available only thirty miles to the north, in Sicily, from a package store right next to the new Woolco. The road to Sicily was the widest one out of town, not to mention the most frequently traveled.

The town existed only because the Census Department was too lazy to remove it from the maps. To be considered an official town there had to be at least two hundred inhabitants. The last census listed its population as one-hundred-sixty-two permanently mired citizens, some of whom actually liked living there. The rest waited for their ship to come in so that they could join the exodus. Most of them would die while still in Beaufort Falls.

Actually, there was no falls in Beaufort Falls, but there was a river, only five minutes away from downtown. The Conecuh River was an uninspired little eddy that meandered through a hundred miles of depressed farmland, providing water for a series of old river oaks draped with romantic Spanish moss. Under the trees and covering the riverbanks grew wild tangles of blackberry and primrose, a haven for snakes. Along the river itself were places where bass hung out in the deeper pools of water, frogs serenaded each other, and an occasional body would be found tangled in the underbrush. That didn't happen often. But it happened.

Most often, it would be the body of a child who strayed too close to the water, or a kayaker who never learned how to turn his boat right side up after it flipped. During spring floods, or worse yet during any of the malevolent hurricanes that tore through South Alabama going to or from the Gulf, the bloated bodies of dead livestock also drifted to resting places under the twisting trees. Life could be a struggle in Beaufort Falls.

Struggling was what J.D. was doing at the moment. As the only mechanic at the number two service station on Main Street, he jockeyed a motor into position to be dropped into the engine compartment of a Chevy. The engine-puller he used to lift the heavy piece of machinery was missing a nut, so it hung sideways. He lowered it, moving carefully. Ever so slowly it swung to the right and left a noticeable scratch on the car's fender. J.D. Parsons eased it to the left, his clenched jaw highlighting the long red scar across his left cheek. He said nothing. Reaching under the dangling engine, he braced himself against the frame of the vehicle. Using his shoulders as leverage, he managed to lift the engine clear without further damage. It then settled into position without further problems. There was a rustling of skirts and J.D. stopped what he was doing and looked toward the bay entrance.

"J.D., are you busy?"

Exactly in the middle of the open bay doors stood a little woman, the sort you describe as "solid," not heavy, but definitely not slender. Chin-length, bright-auburn hair, a touch too bright to be natural, framed a square face with blue eyes that blazed a strange shade of blue. She wore makeup and a tailored skirt, a strong contrast to the clean faces and simple shorts worn by almost everyone else passing the shop.

"Verbena, seven. I'll see you at seven."

A shadow of annoyance crossed his face as he turned his eyes toward the woman; the expression on his face ice cold in spite of the sweat that rolled off his forehead and down his neck. He turned and began inserting the bolts, reattaching the engine to the frame of the vehicle. The woman stood and watched him for several minutes, then left. He never looked up. Two hours later he straightened and began removing his tools. He placed them into his toolbox carefully, ratchet head on the top shelf, right slot; 3/4" socket to its left; and no crescent wrench. John Duke Parsons had no need for a tool that did not have its own specific purpose.

Oh, thank you Father in Heaven, for this task you have allowed me to complete. He placed his 1/2" wrench in the drawer, right side up. Precisely, he folded his work rags, frowning at those with spots of oil on them. *May I be a vehicle for your justice and a sword for your righteous vengeance.* He pushed the engine-puller into its usual corner. *And may all of your enemies be removed from this earth that you have made.*

He never tried to start the car. He knew it would run. Quietly, he closed the double doors to the garage, put the padlock in place, and walked down the small town's main street.

In the little house three blocks away on Sycamore Street, two little girls were working frantically.

"Molly. Molly. Please help me!"

The smallest, her large blue eyes beginning to tear, almost dropped the enormous kettle of water she struggled to lift out of the huge kitchen sink. Molly, as dark as her sister was blonde, put down the onion she was peeling and came to help.

"Tessie, I told you not to get water. You're still too little. You could slide down and get hurt!"

"I am *too* big enough. I'm strong! Besides, I don't want him to be mad."

Together they lifted the heavy kettle and placed it on the burner of the gas stove. It was obvious that they had much experience working as a team. While the older one, at least eight, cut the vegetables; the younger, a tiny tike of five, scraped them off the glistening-clean counter onto a plate and then dropped them into the kettle.

"We need more celery."

A blur, the little one ran out to the backyard to the carefully nurtured kitchen garden.

"Here, Molly."

One grubby hand clutched half a celery stalk, roughly broken and dripping mud from its roots.

"Tessie! You know we can't spill dirt. We don't have time to clean it up. He'll be home any minute."

The little girl made a soft small sound.

"Now, now. Don't cry, little dear." Very adult-like, Molly took the little face in her hands and kissed Tessie's cheek. She wrapped her sister into a tight hug.

"But now we have to hurry. Get the dustpan. Run!"

Little feet scurried to the back kitchen porch.

It was too late. J.D. stood in the doorway of the kitchen, watching his two children. He looked at Molly impartially, evaluating her as if he were examining a paid servant.

"The supper, Marguerite? Where's supper? You know that Verbena will be here at seven. You do nothing all day. Where is supper?"

Molly said nothing, but stood stiffly at attention with her hands clasped behind her back. Just at this moment, Tessie popped back from the porch, carrying a dustpan almost half her size.

"And Elizabeth? What have you done, Elizabeth? Does my work mean nothing to you? My hours spent cleaning up after you and your sister? What is this?"

Jaw clenched, he strode over to the counter where the freshly pulled piece of celery stalk left large clumps of mud on the shiny white tile.

"I'm cleanin' it up, Father. I'm sorry..."

Tears slid down the end of her small nose. Molly stood quietly, tensely at attention. She made no move to intervene.

He turned, then reached and caught Tessie by her left ear. Molly's hand slid cautiously toward the kitchen knife. Moving very slowly, she eased toward it, then slid it into her small palm, an odd gleam in her strange dark eyes. There was no hint of innocence in their intensity; just a fierce, feral protectiveness; a mother wolf, defending her pup. Tessie yelped, and Molly took two steps forward, knife clutched tightly, the silver blade glistening, its edge honed from frequent sharpening. There were two loud raps at the front door. J.D. let go of Tessie and Molly stepped back, still holding the butcher knife behind her back.

"I'll take care of this later."

With one last evil look, he moved toward the front door, which opened as Verbena bustled in noisily.

"Look what I brought you, little angels." Reaching into a brown paper bag, she brought out matching purple satin ribbons and tied one in each child's hair.

"Why, you sweet little things, just the picture of me and my sister when I was your age." Suddenly, she noticed the knife in Molly's hand, held loosely now. "You're fixing supper? Let me help."

J.D. lost patience with her meaningless nonsense. He took her arm firmly and escorted her back into the living room. Molly could hear the two of them through the shuttered half-door separating the two rooms.

"No supper yet? They're just children, J.D. Let's go out." She heard Verbena shifting restlessly on the old velvet couch.

"'One that ruleth well ruleth his own house, having his children in subjection with all gravity; for if a man know not how to rule his own house, how shall he take care of the church of God?' First Timothy, 4-5, Verbena, we'll eat here. We'll wait."

Molly added chicken stock to the pot while Tessie whimpered softly by her side. It was better not to think about later. Methodically, supper began to take shape. She hummed softly to herself.

"Our fathers chained in prisons dark, were still in heart and conscience free," she sang brightly, her child's voice finding great comfort in the solemn words. Leaning over the stove, she stirred the bubbling cauldron vigorously.

"How sweet would be their children's fate, if they, like them, could die for thee."

On the counter in front of her, she set four bowls. She added a sprinkle of salt to two of them. The remaining two received a heaping spoonful of *Fly No More* Wasp and Hornet Killer. A half-smile on her face, she turned and stepped into the living room, where Verbena was still chattering gaily. Molly looked at the pair on the sofa. Verbena was half turned, facing J.D., who was doing his best to look interested, and neither saw her standing in the doorway. No one heard her speaking. Her voice was far too soft, too low, to be heard by anyone who was busy talking.

"Wherefore if thy hand or thy foot offend thee, cut them off, and cast them from thee: It is better for thee to enter into life halt or maimed, rather than having two hands or two feet and to be cast into everlasting fire. "

Sweetly, she announced, "Dinner is served."

Chapter Two

Reap What You Sow

Molly glanced up from her position seated on the ground. Sweat rolled down her neck and she wanted to scratch her back, but her hands were covered with South Alabama's red soil. The hot sun felt good on her arms and face, but it soon would be well into the nineties.

"Molly, how much longer?"

She looked over to the nearby garden fence where Tessie was standing; leaning would be more accurate. The kid was serving out her sentence for having dirtied the kitchen last night, and she couldn't help but be grateful that a six-hour timeout was deemed the "proper consequences," and not an all-night prayer session. If Verbena and J.D. had not driven themselves to the emergency room between convulsions, she knew her knees would have been sore from kneeling this morning. Fortunately, after dinner the pair had shared illegally obtained moonshine made by a friend of Verbena's, so no one investigated the supper stew. A partially empty mason jar of the nasty liquid was transported to the Beaufort County Sheriff's Department to be analyzed, and troopers were looking for a mysterious "Tommy Smith," the supposed maker of the stuff.

Sometimes it seems like a guardian angel is looking after me. What on earth made me do anything so stupid? What doesn't kill you makes you strong. All I need is for him to get stronger.

Punishment Parsons's Family Style was tedious. Since six AM, Tessie had been standing by the garden fence, and she would not be allowed to leave that place until twelve. Her instructions were to recite the several bible verses that she knew, hoping she would see the error of her ways and be more careful in the future. She was allowed to sit on the hard ground once an hour, for three minutes, and if caught not reciting or seated at any other time, her punishment would be extended by an hour. She was not to cry, not to complain, but to benefit from this experience in proper respect and humility. If Molly did not enforce the punishment, she too would face a "timeout."

At six, when the punishment began, Tessie had been shivering from the cold. Now she was hot and thirsty, and had to go to the bathroom desperately.

"Molly. I hafta go. I hafta pee. Please. Please let me go."

Molly looked both ways. She knew that she would receive more than a timeout if she let her little sister leave, but she had no choice. If Tessie peed her pants she would get a caning, and after the last one, she had screamed in her sleep for a month. The dreams were even worse than the strange things that had been happening since her mother died, or more accurately, since her father almost died in the accident. He was in a coma at the local hospital for over a month, and had a long, ugly, red scar on his face as a lingering memory of the experience. She liked the scar. It made him more real, and let people know what he was really like. *Let him be ugly so that people can see he isn't good.*

"Molly?" Tessie really needed help.

"Over here, Tessie. Just pee behind the rock here, and hurry."

Tessie wobbled as she trotted over and squatted to pee, but she didn't argue. In a flash she was back at her post, serving her last twenty minutes.

Remembering three years ago was like trying to vacuum cobwebs out of a dusty corner. It was only a few weeks after Mom had died that Father was in the wreck, and at first all she could remember was looking at the twisted carcass of the truck the next day, before the city removed it to the scrap yard. She and Tessie stayed with Ma'm-ma, her mom's mother, for six months after the accident. The woman cooked cookies. She hugged people. With a sigh, Molly tossed a large rock toward the rock pile near the fence.

"I won't feel guilty," she growled. "I do wish he'd died. We were happy with Ma'm-ma. We're not bad. He is."

Three more rocks, thrown forcefully, followed the first one.

"I hate him. He's bad to my baby."

My baby? She frowned, confused by her own words. *Tessie isn't my baby.*

"Us." She corrected. "He's evil and he's bad to us."

Exhausted, she stopped flinging rocks and stretched out flat on the soft cool ground, squinting at the fierce sun directly overhead. After a little while, it reached the proper place in the sky and she knew that they were allowed to leave.

"Tessie, it's over, Honey. We can go eat lunch now. It's twelve." Tessie collapsed onto the ground next to the fence, and they both spent several quiet minutes before trudging back to the house, shoulders slumped and eyes weary far beyond their tender years.

The girls found J.D. flicking the last little flake of dust from the newly waxed silver Cadillac that had replaced the old truck destroyed three years ago in the collision that almost took his life. The car was a bonus–a secret settlement extracted from the city, which decided it would not fight J.D.– who claimed that the big tree should never have been so close to the side of the road and so conveniently in his path. For J.D., the car was a victory, an affirmation that he was unjustly harmed, and that the loss of his itinerant preaching circuit was not due to being pried out of the wreckage dripping cheap whiskey. Instead, it was the fault of the city. His ugly scar and violent nightmares proved it, and now he had the Caddie.

The mayor of Beaufort Falls came up with the solution to the lawsuit problem. Naturally, the city had no intention of allowing anyone to win a lawsuit against it; that would set a dangerous precedent, but John Duke's persistence and his violent threats concerned those involved. Also, the lawyer was a big-city type, one of those legal leeches that showed up at accidents and chased ambulances, and he had no business meddling in Beaufort Falls' affairs. In desperation, after a nasty confrontation with J.D. at the local grocery, the mayor convinced the police chief to release the Cadillac to J.D. for an "inspection," which never occurred. They classified it as "acquired city property." It had been seized from a drug dealer, who preferred not to return and reclaim his vehicle after four pounds of marijuana were removed from its hubcaps. As an added bonus, the city paid to insure it, which delighted J.D., not that he would ever allow a scratch on it. The settlement worked out well for everyone involved except the lawyer, who never got his foot in the door to the court system of sleepy Beaufort Falls. Discouraged, he returned to the more active courts of Montgomery and Birmingham for causes to pursue.

The girls approached the car and were very careful not to touch the newly waxed surface. Failure to follow the procedure for getting in and out of the vehicle could result in "consequences," ranging from punishment like this morning, to just an ugly scowl if Father was in a good humor. Today, he was in a good mood. He smiled as he finished fondling the side mirror, and gave the driver's side window a final swipe of the chamois cloth.

"Rejoice in this day that our Lord hath made*"*.

Tessie brightened and teetered toward her dad.

"Sing, Father. Sing a song. Please."

He looked at his smallest child, and for a moment his face softened; then like a dark shadow, his features returned to their usual rigid cast.

"I've got something better. Get in the car."

Tessie, standing closest, reached up carefully, and touching only the door handle, pulled mightily on it, trying to open the heavy door without touching any other part of it. Molly moved in quickly to help her, and, feet scraping only the floor, hands touching only the seat, the two girls positioned themselves carefully in the front. Their Father folded himself in beside them, and pumping the pedal only once, turned the key. Like a great gray ark, the vehicle pulled out majestically, moving along the main road toward town.

Briefly, Molly skimmed over possibilities. What sort of treat might be in store? A hamburger at Bob's Hamburger Heaven? Ice cream? Only a year ago, when the Ten Commandments remake was released, they went to a movie on a Saturday afternoon just like this. She remembered the hours that followed as J.D. lectured to them, pointing out all of the errors and fallacies in the film they had just seen. Nothing good can come out of a treat today, she thought morosely, but Tessie was positively glowing. It required great willpower for the baby not to bounce on the seat, but long familiarity with the effect of "bounciness" on her father trained her to sit quietly. Still, Molly could see she was excited. She hoped they weren't going to be disappointed. Tessie deserved a treat, and Molly was hungry. She knew Tessie was, too. It was with a sick lurch that she recognized their destination.

"Standing on the promises of Christ my King..."

As they pulled into the parking lot, they could hear the liquid notes of the gospel hymn. A few people surrounded a large table loaded with pork roasts and barbecued chicken, and the girls looked at it with longing, but it was not to be. J.D. strode past the food as if it did not exist, going straight into the church, and the girls followed quietly. They knew better than to ask about lunch. Verbena waited for them on the front row, and she moved several people over to make room for them. J.D. reached for his half of the hymnbook, and Molly took one from the pocket on the back of the pew in front of them. Dejectedly, the children sang along as the congregation finished two more revival songs. Usually, Molly loved this part of any religious service, but today all she could think about was the growling of her empty stomach and the tired look on her little sister's face.

When the musical part of the service ended, a plump, red-cheeked man, dressed in faded overalls, approached the pulpit.

"I'd like to thank you kind people for coming to the Pulpwood Primitive Church of God Revival Meeting today, and we have a full program of foot-stomping, toe-tapping hallelujah planned. Yesterday, Sister Evelyn saw the light and broke through to the other side, and she done spoke to every one of them angels whilst she was there, too. And brother Elvis brought the true test of faith for us all. The serpent, which is the bane of mankind, is the servant of our blessed Lord."

Molly felt a twinge of fear. She'd been to hundreds of revival meetings in her short life, and only two types of meetings really scared her; meetings where people hopped around shaking and babbling in a foreign language, and meetings where there were live snakes. The language thing could be tolerated. It was supposed to be the language of Adam and Eve in the garden, and the "loosening of tongues" was frightening mainly if it happened to someone close to her, but not the snakes. She was terrified of snakes. In a service like this often they were everywhere, slithering and sliding between the pews, shaking the little rattles on their tails. With a worried look, she scanned the pulpit area. Sure enough, she saw a basket on the floor.

"Oh, blessed family in God, let us pray."

In the seconds before the preacher began the prayer, she heard a faint little rattle surface from the round wicker basket at Reverend Callahan's feet.

Her throat tightened, and she kept one eye open during the prayer. Quietly, she mouthed her own little prayer.

"Oh, Jesus, please don't let me pee my pants if that man lets those things loose. Oh, Jesus."

She repeated the words over and over until the booming voice of the preacher ceased, and all eyes were open once again.

The sermon was exactly what she expected. All persons who did not march up to the altar and take the Lord Jesus Christ as their personal savior that second were condemned to an eternity of flames and molten rock that was hotter than the inside of a volcano.

"The wages of sin is death."

Callahan chanted loudly, and as the volume crested, people on all sides began moving toward the front, shaking and trembling and babbling whatever guttural sounds surfaced

26

from their innermost souls. Only her father stood still, strong and impassive, by her side. Verbena had been part of the first wave and was now kneeling, sobbing, at the altar, her head resting on the rail. Two fat women from the beauty parlor were swabbing the soggy makeup from her face with tissues. Molly glanced down at Tessie. Strangely, the tike had fallen asleep on the pew, and only the confusion of the noisy multitude moving forward kept her father from observing her lack of proper piety. Horrified, Molly noticed the preacher pulling the basket of snakes toward him, closer to the mass of repentant sinners at the altar rail.

Oh, God, please don't let those snakes get out.

Molly knew that her father must be able to hear her thoughts. They echoed through her head, crushing any other coherent thinking.

"Come on." J.D. pushed Molly roughly toward the aisle. "Get your sister and come on."

Suddenly, Molly was as afraid of his catching Tessie sleeping as she was of the snakes. He had a strange, cold, look on his face. She grabbed Tessie by the arm, and the baby woke with a quick little jerk, big blue eyes seeing the chaos in front of her and reacting, bewildered, but obeying Molly as the older girl pulled her to her feet. They both followed their dad as he moved to face the front altar, stopping directly in front of the basket of snakes.

Trembling, Molly watched as the Reverend moved the half-open container to the altar, only an arm's length from them. Molly could hear the rustling noises as the reptiles moved freely within the cavernous walls of their container—a reed sarcophagus, a modern imitation of the basket used in biblical times to bury the dead. She glanced at her sister. The small child, no longer sleepy, examined the interesting vessel with an expression of rapt attention. Because it was taller than

Tessie, she couldn't see the evil hidden inside. Suddenly, the writhing mass began moving, and a chestnut-brown, speckled head darted a forked tongue over the edge.

The preacher pulled away from the sinister snout, but held his ground, clearing his throat and gathering his courage. His congregation pulsated with excitement as it waited for him to reach inside and pull out one of the highly venomous Rocky Mountain rattlesnakes. Anticipating the grand finale, the crowd around the altar moved back a few feet.

Faith would make him strong, but only he knew how little faith he truly possessed. Preaching was only another of the many one-way roads he traveled, only to find a dead end where he had anticipated a future calling. He felt lucky the world couldn't read his mind while he spoon-fed them the expected exhortations, and he hoped he could pull this off one more time. Even this poorly paid stroke to his ego was at an end. The new circuit preacher started next weekend with a new spiel and a fresh panacea for the masses. Snakes were out. Glitzy costumes and the bus tour were in. "Just one more time," he prayed silently, but before he could reach for the obligatory snake, fate intervened.

"And so it shall be at the end of the world: the angels shall come forth, and sever the wicked from among the just," he chanted. "And they shall cast them into the furnace of fire: There shall be wailing and gnashing of teeth."

Suddenly, Tessie reached toward the basket, her cherubic face with the gold curls a picture of innocence. The entire congregation held its breath, and waited to see what would happen next.

"No, Tessie! No. No. No!"

Molly wanted to stop her, but she couldn't move, couldn't speak. J.D. did nothing. He stood motionless and expressionless, a pillar of ice, frozen beside the preacher who suddenly saw a new way to work the crowd.

"Suffer the little children to come unto me, for of such are the kingdom of Heaven." Reverend Callahan took Tessie's hand.

A voice inside Molly's head was screaming, and tears began to run down both sides of her face. *No, Jesus! Don't let her do this! No. Please no! I will be good! She will die. Please no!* A buzzing like a swarm of a thousand bees deafened her, and rendered her powerless to intervene.

"She is pure and innocent as driven snow. Oh, ye of little faith, she will not be harmed. God will give her power over the vilest beasts of the earth, and he will protect her, as he does all of his chosen ones."

Tessie showed no fear. "Snakes."

She saw the first one come sliding over the edge of the basket. She reached for it, catching it in one grubby little hand. It shook its rattle lightly, more in play than in any sort of excitement, and it squirmed through her fingers onto the planks of the church floor. Instantly, a pathway opened to let it make its way to the freedom of the open doors. "See the snakie?" She smiled at the preacher. He moved like a man in a trance.

Suddenly, a peace came over Molly. She heard a voice, faint at first, but growing louder and drowning out the awful buzzing in her ears. It was a voice she recognized, one full of warmth and love; one that promised pancakes on Sunday mornings, bedtime stories and happy laughter. It was her mother. She could even smell her perfume, White Shoulders. The last bottle of it had been tossed away two years ago, but she could smell its heavy scent all around her.

I will not let them hurt her, Molly. It was a whisper, but Molly heard her plainly.

"Mommy?" She questioned.

Suddenly, the minister lifted Tessie. He carefully avoided all contact with the mass of serpents and placed her in the basket, where she stood with the wiggling knot of copper-brown vipers all around her. There was a warning rattle from at least a dozen snakes, but none of them pulled back to strike her, not even the several which narrowly missed being crushed by her little feet. As if in a daze, she smiled, then stroked a fat brown rattler gently. "Pretty snakie. So pretty."

J.D. moved closer to his child and the snakes.

"Behold our Lord God of Hosts, and the wonders which he has wrought. Glory be to the Lord My God."

J.D. chanted now, exhilarated, caught up in the fever of revival, confident that he was one of the chosen.

Tessie looked at him strangely. She no longer gleamed with child-like innocence. Her features changed subtly, became womanly; more like the young woman she would someday become, or maybe like the young woman who had given birth to her, dead now. Snakes were crawling all over her little body, up her arms, out of the collar of her dress, winding around her legs, her waist, and her neck. She reached to the side of the basket, and in both hands scooped up the largest snake of all–a fat diamond-back creature–at least three inches thick, and probably three-and-a-half feet long. She lifted it over the rim of the basket, stretched toward J.D., stood on tiptoe, and reached toward him with the huge reptile. Suddenly, the expression on his face changed. His eyes widened, and all of the blood drained from his features. He moved back quickly, but not fast enough. As the snake struck him, he spit one word into the highly charged sanctuary, a word that profaned all that he held sacred–the ultimate curse.

"Eliza!" He shrieked. "God damn your soul, Eliza!"

The creature hanging from his forearm actually seemed to grin. The congregation scattered as the rest of the snakes poured out of their prison to freedom, leaving Tessie smiling sweetly alone in the basket, singing softly to herself.

"I gotta mansion. Jest ova tha' hilltop. In that great land where I neva' get old."

Molly stared at a place far beyond the ugly basket, past the vestibule and the image of Christ hanging behind the altar, her face shining with her tears. "I love you, Mommy," she whispered.

Chapter Three

Way Out There

J.D. reached under the thin blanket and pulled up the hemmed end of something that looked like part of the sheet. The flimsy gown wrapped around his neck tied with a cord and had no back, and he realized that he was still in the hospital.

Still here? No. Here again.

The walls blurred and the stripes waved into themselves. In the corner, he saw her. *Smug bitch. Just sits there and grins at me like a cat.*

He struggled to get out of the bed but could not; something kept him from being able to move his arms and his legs. She moved closer to him, her long blonde hair blowing in the breeze. Wait. There was no breeze; that was an air-conditioning unit directly above the bed. Could not happen...

Horrified, he could feel her next to him. Instinctively, he cringed, pulled back. She was beautiful, slim and sinewy, with full breasts and that maddening grin, beautiful and angry. She touched him, and her finger became bone, white, glistening, bleached bone, carpals and metacarpals, and it burned; scorched like a thousand bonfires consuming his arm.

Out, damned demon! Get thee out of me! Oh, Father, who art in Heaven, remove this unclean beast from me.

He shrieked, kicking and struggling to break his restraints, but he was firmly tied to both sides of the hospital bed.

"Mr. Parsons. Mr. Parsons, it's just me. I'm here to change your IV. Don't be afraid. I won't hurt you. I'm Sally Cline, your nurse. If you stop fighting, we'll take those restraints off, but you have to leave your IV line alone. We're trying to help you. What you're seeing isn't real. It's a result of the snakebite and the antivenin. You're lucky to be alive! That snake had quite a bite, and the cure wasn't much better for you. I've never seen anyone else react so badly to that medicine."

Her face came into focus for just a second and J.D. relaxed, but then he heard Eliza's low laugh. Behind the nurse, he could see just a wisp of silk, that fucking kimono she'd ordered from the catalogue, in the pale green that always drove him insane; the silk she wore on that last night, the night that turned out so badly, the last night of her brief existence. It was what she always wore whenever she returned to taunt him, to tell him that he would never escape her.

With great effort, he focused on the face of the young nurse, a cute little woman with a pert nose and short brown hair. Suddenly, her features melted, became liquid, then melded into the creature he didn't want to see, its eyes hard. Its mouth began to move. From very red lips and sharp, pointed teeth, it spit out words, their hoarse staccato cadence pummeling his so-sensitive ears.

Where is my baby? What have you done to my children? Where is my baby?

The crimson mouth moved independently of the words, oddly out of sync with any other part of the sensuous body.

I'm not afraid of you! The words screamed through his reverberating brain. *You killed that baby. Not me. The acid poison of your womb, the rock-hard clenching of your evil thrusts, you evil bitch--you killed that ugly little rat! Not me.*

'The wages of sin is death'...death to you, you Whore of Babylon. Death for you and all of your spawn!

His arm burned. He pulled at the restraints that held him to the narrow bed. With great difficulty, he focused on his arm, which, in spite of the IV and the bandaging, was securely attached to the railing of the cot. It was on fire! He could see flames arc along the bandaging, consuming the white gauze, pouring smoke into the room, filling it with fumes. He choked and gagged, totally alone with the specter of her. Her. The red mouth held his attention. It stayed centered directly above him, even as he struggled and writhed on the bed. He could not get away from her. He could not save himself from the fire. The flames licked around him, hungry for him, waiting for him. He would die in torment, in great pain. Tears scalded his cheeks, their hot moisture eating away the flesh of his gaunt cheeks and leaving the bone exposed. Even without a mirror he knew that his skull must be bare, all of his skin evaporated by the fierce heat.

You are a liar. Liar! Yet you shall be brought down to the nether world, to the uttermost parts of the pit.

Then the laugh began, shrill at first, and then sharp, pitched like the crisp tinkling of a small bell, slicing his brain with its cold precision, deepening gradually and becoming louder. The sound filled all of the small spaces in his head with harsh, guttural, manic noise, wiping his cranium clean of all activity. The last thing he heard before he went limp was a final sneering chord.

He had to get out of the hospital. She was going to kill him here.

A different kind of laughter escaped from the little pink trailer in the other part of town, where Molly giggled and pulled her foot away from Verbena, who kept trying to paint her toes.

"It tickles. It feels so funny."

"Be still." Verbena laughed, too. She loved taking care of these two sweet little girls. Without children, and in her forties, her biological clock definitely was starting to wind down. Tessie sat squeaky clean after a bubble bath, wrapped up in a huge beach towel at the foot of the soft double bed, waiting for her turn to have her "toesies turn red." On the counter next to them, the remnants of pepperoni pizza waited for the three of them to finish. Later, when Verbena tucked them in, Tessie reached out of the thick covers and hugged her tightly.

"Thank you, Beeny. Thank you." The little arms reached all the way down into Verbena's heart and tied themselves around it.

"Sleep, sweet little ones," she mumbled, as she tucked the covers around the two kids and exited quietly, to make up her own bed on the couch in the living room of her small home. Later, as she drifted off to sleep, she dreamed of little feet with tiny toes, and imagined happy voices begging her for pony rides, while she took freshly baked cookies out of a brand-new oven. When she awoke early the next morning, she remembered that she would have to give them back, and her stomach responded with a dull ache.

Chapter Four

Trouble In Paradise

Anna Johnson pushed the glasses up from the bridge of her nose and leaned back in the ancient wooden chair. Family and Children Services didn't have prime office space in City Hall, and Anna and the other twelve county employees, who made up the entire staff, shared three dim florescent lights and a series of desks left over from the old high school. By squinting, she was able to make out the words, large and small print, from the set of encyclopedias that was left behind when the new high school was built. The little bit found in the reference book, and a leaflet advertising the revival from the parking lot of the church, were all she could find to provide facts to assist her with the difficult decisions ahead of her.

Written material on the Primitive sect of the Charismatic group of Church of God churches proved impossible to find, not surprising since it represented some of the poorest people in Alabama, and some of the most secretive. No one in the congregation would speak with her. The only reason she knew anything at all about the revival meeting in which Tessie interacted with twenty or thirty Rocky Mountain rattlesnakes, was due to the obligatory report made by one of the ambulance technicians who picked up the unconscious J.D. at the church. Church members left him at the altar; however, Molly, like the little trooper she was, walked a mile to a neighbor's house and had someone call 911. No one stayed to help him because he obviously lacked faith–that was all she could figure. No one who had faith, according to the information she studied so intently, was ever bitten.

"The frenzied stomping, the shaking and waving of hands, and the chanting tend to disorient the snakes, and instead of striking, they glide harmlessly away, even after being handled. Also, there is a complete lack of the enzyme activators that signal fear, which most often is a trigger for aggression with animals, who equate fearlessness with superiority, and flee rather than confront a fearless adversary, even when attacked by them. Even the most zealous members of a congregation seldom interfere with a large rattler on his way out of the area, and they allow them to slither away to freedom.

Although rare, there are instances of the faithful sustaining bites, or sometimes drinking poison, to prove their faith in the powers of God to protect them from harm or to heal them. It is more difficult to understand how ingestion of normally lethal substances fails to even make the parishioners ill, but it may be that the substances are not mixed in deadly dosages. It is known that when someone is stricken or affected by either snakebite or poisoning, medical help is usually refused."

–Encyclopedia Britannica, 14th edition, Oct. 5, 1971

"That certainly is not what is happening with that sick asshole responsible for those two little girls," she mused reflectively.

When the ambulance arrived, the Reverend Charlie Callahan materialized from a side door and ordered them "off the Lord's property." According to him, God would take care of his own. Once they established that he had no legal jurisdiction over the fallen man, they brushed him off, loaded J.D. into the ambulance, and headed back to the hospital, sirens wailing. When medical records indicated he had accepted previous medical treatment, and with no one else to forbid treatment, they assigned the comatose man a room and began emergency measures to save his life. Day three now, he still raved and screamed and writhed on the bed, not approaching any sort of coherency, even though most of the danger from the snakebite had passed. After two more days like this, they would carry him upstairs to the mental section of the facility where he would be maintained as insane, no longer a medical emergency.

Thirty minutes after J.D. arrived at the emergency room, Verbena Rogers appeared, crying hysterically. From her, the technician who brought him into the medical center got a tearful account of the afternoon's events, including the news that the Reverend Callahan placed the five-year-old child in a basket full of snakes. "J.D. was bitten," Verbena told him, while "stepping up to rescue his baby." The admitting clerk for the hospital asked Verbena a few more questions.

"Why did you leave the man and the children at the church?" As part of his job, it was his duty to call the police, if needed.

Unfortunately, Verbena sobbed too loudly to be able to answer him. They finally sedated her, and later, after she calmed and convinced them that she was "scared shitless of snakes," they sent both girls home with her, pending the decision of the county as to where they would stay until J.D. was better. They called Anna ten minutes after the little group left. After establishing that Verbena was a "close friend of the family," and the girls seemed to know her, Anna decided to leave them with Verbena until she could contact the elderly grandmother who lived in another town, fifty miles away. Better they stayed with someone they knew than to stay with strangers. She hated leaving frightened children with people they didn't know.

Almost everyone in the hospital knew J.D., and many agreed that a permanent new placement for the children might be a good idea.

"Crazy as a bedbug."

"Strange."

"Downright odd."

"An alcoholic several years ago."

These comments now were part of the case file.

"A good father? I don't know." No one but Verbena seemed to think he should be the only parent for two precious little girls, and everyone found the children charming.

The doctors, who had treated him during his last hospital stay, refused to answer any of her questions, but when hospital records indicated that he and his girlfriend were in the emergency room. with alcohol poisoning just the week before, Anna knew that she had to conduct a formal investigation. Two such incidents that close to each other were rare, and in a small town almost always indicated that something serious was wrong. She found Verbena's protestations that he was "a wonderful father" suspect. It was obvious that the woman was "smitten" with him, although looking at the grimy patient in Room 146 who was screaming and fighting the restraints that tied him to the arms of his bed, she couldn't understand how anyone could be so attracted. Verbena brought the little ones in every day to visit, although much of the time J.D. didn't even seem to know they were there.

In the twelve years that Anna had worked as the only Child Welfare Protective Services Caseworker for the Department of Family and Children's Services, Beaufort County, she'd made some tough decisions as to the best placements for hundreds of needy kids, and it never got any easier. None of the other workers had the sort of responsibility that made her particular job so difficult. The facts were not easy to uncover, and sometimes they were hidden intentionally. Other times, when she was meeting with people who had never reported an incident before, they did not know what was important enough to tell her, and, of course, she wouldn't know enough about the child's situation to know what to ask. Lately, she felt like nothing could surprise her. Only last year, she pulled two children out of a well, where they were placed intentionally, because they had been thirty minutes late getting home from school. If anyone else in the department had shown any interest at all in her job, she would have gone on to another position without regret. Her memories of tight little faces relaxed in a smile, or laughter, where once there had been lines of worry, kept her going. None of the tikes were old enough to carry the burdens that had been placed on their narrow shoulders by uncaring adults. She agonized over the times she'd been wrong, and it never got any easier. Sighing, she placed the literature in the file folder and picked up the phone.

"Nate, what can be done about those church services? Can we arrest that man for putting that baby in that basket of snakes?"

She didn't hesitate to get the Reverend Charles Callahan picked up and put somewhere he could do no more harm. That man was a menace. She felt a familiar surge of irritation as she listened to the county sheriff quoting laws and ordinances that gave the church almost unlimited power to do whatever it wanted with anyone who professed faith in its doctrine.

Several minutes after his conversation with the beleaguered county worker, Sheriff St. Claire decided that they might have a case after all. There had to be some way to take care of that bible-thumping son of a bitch, and after examining the facts as he knew them, he thought he might have found it. Since J.D. was not a member of the church but a visitor attending a revival meeting, he would not have actually implied agreement with Callahan's actions. As long as J.D. could not press charges himself due to his condition, it was the duty of the county to do so, and promptly, before Callahan left the area. The Sheriff had a four-year-old niece and the thought of snakes twining around little blonde-headed Tessie started to make him itch. It was about time that some of the "insane" around Beaufort County were held accountable for their actions. With a grim smile of satisfaction, he reached for his holster and sidearm, and strode out of the little shack used as a police station on Main Street to take care of this arrest personally.

Meanwhile, Molly sat quietly beside J.D., who slept for perhaps the first time since he had entered the hospital. Massive doses of thorazine and morphine were responsible for this miracle. The staff grew very tired of the screams and moans and exhortations that had been a nonstop onslaught since J.D.'s admission. Lead nurse Wilson made the changes just an hour ago, administered the medicine, and took the chart with her to note the new treatment at the nurse's station.

Molly reached over and touched her father's extended hand, which poked through the railing close to her chair. Her face changed slightly, forehead wrinkling, as she gazed at her father's face sleeping so peacefully, no longer contorted with rage or pain. Her features acquired an intense look not found in a child her age, which puzzled the nurse who darted into the room carrying a tray full of medicines and needles. Hurrying, the "Meds Lady" looked for J.D.'s chart, which was missing from its customary place in the chart holder at the end of the bed.

"Has anyone else been in here?" she asked the little girl, who turned a calculating gaze her direction.

"Anyone at all? Any hospital staff?"

Molly looked to the end of the bed, where the metal frame that normally held the chart gaped like a hungry hole.

"Someone like a nurse?" Molly answered innocently. "No. No one. No one for hours." She turned her back on the anxious angel of the medicines. "No one at all," she mumbled quietly, to no one in particular.

Grimacing her annoyance, the nurse took a syringe from the tray, and measuring .5 mg. thorazine, she mixed it with an equal portion of morphine and quickly injected J.D. for the second time in less than thirty minutes. Molly smiled, a satisfied look on her no-longer-childlike face, as the woman bustled off to the next patient.

"And ye fathers, provoke not your children to wrath," she mumbled softly. After a quick intense glance at her father's peaceful features, she walked calmly out to the waiting room to wait for Verbena and Tessie to return. Five minutes later, the monitor alarm sounded and a small crowd of doctors, nurses and orderlies formed in front of Room 146. Molly ignored them, humming softly, waiting for the elevator door to open.

Chapter Five

Reality Bites

A lone egret pulled one leg out of the cold water which ran red beneath its feet, and attaching no significance to the scene beneath it, lifted snowy wings and glided gracefully toward the rising sun. The river ran shallow here; too shallow to cover the large belly of the fallen lawman, no longer dressed in crisp uniform browns but ingloriously stripped to his birthday suit. His badge and his weapon were missing too, as was his head. Not far from the body, half covered in the tangle of honeysuckle and blackberry thorns lining the red clay riverbank, a heavy axe, the sort firefighters or bush clearers use, lay half buried in the mud.

On the other side of the riverbank, forty feet away, in front of a leaning log cabin, the Reverend Charlie Callahan groaned softly in his sleep. Covered with soft river silt, wet and soggy overalls clinging to his thighs, his hand jerked, bumping the bucket next to him. Nearby an empty whiskey bottle rested on its side, half covered by leaves and grass.

Oh, Lord, forgive the transgressions of the weak, the poor sinner who has fallen from grace.

The beginnings of a prayer slurred unintelligibly from puffy lips; a bruised face provided evidence of participation in a recent fight. Startled by the words, a skinny green lizard scooted down a tall pine tree and lightly brushed the back of the neck of the errant child of God.

"Git off'a me, you venomous scourge. May the walls of Babylon rise up against you and all of your filthy kind!" With a dull roar, the preacher roused, lurching forward, and tipping the bucket onto its side.

Sheriff St. Claire had seen better days. His glassy blue eyes and matted curls, crimson with blood, were never going to exude authority again. In fact, the half-open mouth of the bodiless face would never issue another order to anyone. Callahan recoiled in horror.

"Oh, my God!" He stared at the head, transfixed, unable to move from the spot. Slowly, he backed away from it and vomited violently against the tree. He stifled an urge to run, to run as far away from it as he could, to leave it and its damning, leering features far behind.

For thirty minutes he looked at it, glared at it, cursed it, and willed it to leave or to be one of his frequent hallucinations, a vile act of the devil sent to torment him in his affliction of drunkenness. It didn't go away. Finally, he approached it, and with his index finger he touched a blood-matted, silver lock of hair. It was real.

By sheer force of will, he grabbed it by its hair and hefted it back into the bucket. It made a sick *thunk* as it hit the galvanized tin bottom. He grabbed a dark blanket from the cabin and wrapped the bucket in it, hiding the mess, and then he opened the trunk of his old Impala and shoved it in.

Where is the rest of him? he wondered. He barely remembered any of the events of the night before. He had to leave this place. Now. Re-entering his cabin, he found St. Claire's uniform, underwear, and sidearm neatly folded in the chair in front of his smoldering fireplace. *How did it get there? Where was St. Claire?* The man's head was in a bucket in the trunk of his car, but he had no idea where the rest of him might be. What did he remember? Moving slower than cold molasses, he forced himself to recall the night before.

Late yesterday afternoon, the sheriff had pulled up in front of his cabin and summoned him outside.

"Charles Callahan, you are under arrest for the attempted murder of young Tessie Parsons, and the willful assault on her father, John Duke Parsons, currently in the Beaufort County Medical Center, not expected to live. Come out of the building with your hands up."

"Nate, you've been seeing too many of them T.V. shows. For the love of God, I haven't killed anyone. Come inside and let's talk about it. Besides, last I heard they were fixing to put J.D. in the mental ward. I don't believe he's in any mortal danger from anyone right now. And little Tessie ain't hurt. God protects little children and Irishmen."

He remembered watching Nate shuffle from one foot to another, his gun held unobtrusively by his side. Finally, after several minutes of looking foolish, he holstered his gun and came inside, took a seat at the old table, and shared a cup of coffee with him.

"Charlie, I'm curious about them snakes. How was it that child was able to sit in that basket of big rattlers and not get bit?"

Charlie felt the hand of God upon him to witness to this interested layman. Explanations took time, so not much later a bottle appeared, and events became fuzzy after that. Did he kill Nate? Did he hack him up with that big axe that he always kept by the fireplace? Cut his head off? If so, where was the rest of him? And why wasn't there a mess in the cabin? There was no sign of a fight. Nothing was out of place. The room was neat as a pin, uncharacteristically so. Wincing, he looked at himself in the mirror. He was filthy, caked with mud and vomit, the very picture of a guilty man. Some mild sense of self-preservation clarified his dulled brain.

"I have to clean up," he told himself softly. Still trembling, he peeled off his dirty clothes, climbed into the rusty tub, washed his body and hair, and removed all trace of the night before. When clean, he threw the sheriff's underwear into the still-smoldering fireplace, pulled on the former lawman's uniform, and strapped the gun and holster around his middle.

"Not bad. No one'll stop me now."

It was amazing how much he looked like Nate St. Claire when wearing the fallen officer's uniform. In too much of a hurry to search the woods for the rest of the body, he climbed into his Chevy, and then remembered that he was quite possibly going to be a wanted man in an hour or so. Grabbing a screwdriver from the floorboard, he stepped out of his car, moved around to the back of the police vehicle parked next to him, and removed its license plate, fastening it onto the back of his car, replacing his own. "That'll buy me a little extra time," he commented to no one in particular, as he tossed his old tag into the woods next to his cabin. Without a backward glance, he drove away, carefully obeying all speed limits, so as to attract as little attention as possible. Forty miles away, he stopped for coffee at a local truck stop near Sicily.

"Coffee on the house for our fine officers of the law," the counter attendant told him cheerfully. Leaning over his cup, hiding his features as best he could, Charlie shuddered. Pretending to be a dead man was unsettling, but right now it was his only chance at a new life. Once again, he wondered where the body could be. He imagined that if anyone found it, he and the rest of Alabama would be informed immediately.

"Anything else, Sir? I think we have a leftover cinnamon bun that would be okay to give you, if you would like it. "

Smiling, a passing waitress slid a small plate onto the edge of the counter.

He realized the young woman looked at him with an expression of respect– admiration even–and for the first time he realized that playing lawman had additional perks he hadn't even considered. He wondered how long he could continue the role, but for the moment it didn't seem to matter. Resurrecting Nathan St. Claire was going to be more fun than he had ever imagined.

At the hospital, the staff resumed a half-hearted effort to save J.D. 's quickly diminishing existence. Only the head nurse fought like one inspired, ordering more tubes and machines and medications pumped into the totally limp man, who was barely clinging to this world. His heartbeat was light, his breathing almost nonexistent, and the staff wanted to disconnect him from the machinery that was keeping him alive; but, as their supervisor reminded them, they'd already made enough mistakes for one day. Now they must operate "by the book," and no one was allowed to cut him free without written consent from a legal relative. Verbena adamantly refused, and they quickly discovered she had no legal standing in his life anyway. She took the children back to the trailer, left them snuggled in her bed, and then returned to the hospital to spend the long night by J.D.'s side.

Close to dawn, the effects of the drugs began to wear off and he rallied, surprising them all. With a sigh of relief, they pushed the equipment back down the hall to the storage closet. Verbena thanked God for the repeated miracle of life, celebrating the routing of the Angel of Death over coffee in the hospital cafeteria, accompanied by an army of weary nurses who were grateful to have Nurse Wilson off their backs. Life was returning to the usual bustle and hurry of normal hospital routine, and that was good news for all of them.

Rubbing her eyes fiercely, Molly woke as the first soft light of dawn filtered in through the dirty trailer window. For the second time that week she felt panic, wondering where she could be and what might have happened. Vaguely, she remembered being at the hospital, lots of flashing lights, and a voice in her head laughing; a mean, cruel laugh she did not recognize. If only her head would stop hurting, she would be able to think and recall what had happened. Something evil, she sensed. Something else very bad had happened, but she couldn't remember it. Tessie moved in her sleep, snuggling closer, like the little snuggle-bug she was.

Snuggle-bug. Molly wrinkled her forehead and focused her thoughts, trying to impose discipline on her disobedient mind. *Someone else long ago had used that word, used that word for Baby Tessie. She used to be a snuggle-bug. Mommy had called her a snuggle-bug, but Mommy was dead. Was Mommy cold in the ground?*

An icy wind battered the gravestones of her final resting place; soon it would be her birthday. They always bought flowers on Mommy's birthday. Even though it was Halloween, they always bought flowers. How would they get flowers this year?

Maybe Daddy will be in the ground, too, this year. A shiver ran through her, as she remembered what she had told the nurse in the hospital. Why did she do that?

I'm going to Hell. Images of flames and little red devils raced through her aching head, and a raw knot choked her throat as she remembered lying to the nurse.

"I'll burn in Hell forever," she croaked, barely able to speak, tears rolling down her little face.

How could I be so awful? How long is forever? she wondered.

No wonder I hear mean laughs. The devil is going to drag me into Hell.

Her little body shook as she pictured a skinny red man pulling her along a rocky trail, ready to throw her off a cliff into a deep pit, like the picture of the volcano crater she had found last week in the new set of Encyclopedia Britannica at school. The sobs began, but a sweet, familiar voice whispering from the grave wrapped around her, tenderly.

Little children never go to Hell. Jesus loves little children. Don't cry, my sweet little worrywart. It was Mommy. She could feel her gentle fingers stroking her hair, touching her face. She calmed, and the pain slowly faded away.

"Mommy won't let me go to Hell," she mumbled, and putting her arms around her little sister, she coasted back to sleep. *Mommy won't let me burn.*

Quietly, relentlessly, the water worked at the obstacle in its path. It tugged gently at a foot, pushed a leg further into the swiftly moving current a little further out in the channel. Thunder sounded in the distance. A storm, happening a few miles upriver, channeled more water into the almost-empty riverbed. Long tendrils of Spanish moss fluttered from the low limbs of the gnarled trees as the wind picked up, becoming a menacing whine as the streaks of lightning moved closer. Thunderstorms were rare this time of year, but not unknown.

Soon, trickles of water eroded the wet ground beneath the earthly remains of the former Beaufort County Instrument of Justice, and the headless body began its last journey, floating majestically downstream, bumping into logs and trash, just another remnant of life's messy passage. Bobbing and weaving from bank to bank, it moved rapidly as the scenery changed, leaving the flatlands and becoming the red clay cliffs surrounding the merging rivers closer to the Gulf.

Finally, it eased into a dark little indentation in the riverbank; a cold little cave known only to the wild foxes and varmints in the desolate countryside where, decorated by a shiny tinfoil candy wrapper and a cellophane cigarette pack, it came to rest. The wages of shoddy police work is death, and the Sheriff of Beaufort County was most certainly dead. Secrets of the river are carried to the grave.

Chapter Six

Serious Events

Shivering from a blast of the cold October wind, Molly pulled the hood on her knit windbreaker over her head. Looking behind her furtively, she slipped into the woods.

Please God; don't let him catch me gone.

She had very little time. Since getting out of the hospital, J.D. had made life even more difficult for them, each morning handing her a new list of tasks to be accomplished before he came home from work. He never raised his voice, never lost control with either of them, but his arsenal of punishments reached a new level of ingenuity. Nothing they did satisfied him, and Tessie was having nightmares once again.

Today's list included cleaning the oven, a job required on Monday of each week, and one Molly particularly detested. It required wearing heavy gloves far too large for her, and using lye. If she got any of the caustic chemical on her clothes, it burned a hole in them, and she would get a beating with Father's leather belt if that happened.

She looked toward the woods directly across the street from the house. Bright patches of sunlight flickered across the path, filtering through the limbs of the still-leafy trees. It was not leaves that Molly wanted, but wildflowers, Goldenrod and

Aster and Thrift. She couldn't ask Father for flowers for Mommy's grave this year, and her mom's birthday was today.

It was also Halloween. Molly pushed aside thoughts of the fun it would be to wear a costume and go from door to door begging for candy, like all of her third grade classmates. That had never happened before, and it wouldn't happen tonight. Instead, Father would send them to bed an hour early and turn the light out, pretending that no one was home. This was their long-standing ritual for Halloween, which was regarded as an "evil, pagan custom," and one to be ignored. The only good thing about it was that evening prayers would be considerably shortened.

Abruptly, the path ended, and she looked into the meadow, her secret flower shop, but something was very wrong. Instead of acres of goldenrod, she found a gaping hole in the forest. Where formerly grass and flowers mingled with the fading greens of fall, she now found bare red dirt. A huge bulldozer, parked by the new asphalt road, waited to gobble up the rest of her special hideaway. Confused and frustrated, she stepped into the field, sinking ankle deep into the wet mud. Now she'd done it. Almost forgetting her mission, she turned and ran back through the woods, dropping globs of mud with each step. It would take her at least thirty minutes to clean it all off her shoes and wash, or hide, her socks, and she didn't have time to spare. In her haste, she tripped over a large rock, sprawled forward, and flattened a single bright blue flower almost hidden by the drifting leaves.

"It'll have to do," she muttered.

Hurrying, she added bright golden and red leaves to her bouquet, compliments of a low-hanging maple tree, and rushed back to the house. There she found Tessie sweeping the front porch, the broom three times as big as she was.

"Look, Tessie! We have Mommy's flowers."

"They're beautiful."

The little girl was too small to even remember her mommy, but Molly did. Tessie was only two years old the night that their mommy left them and never came back. Molly was the one who'd found her in Mr. Evan's pasture the next morning; her long blonde hair cushioning her face, eyes staring straight ahead, her head tilted at a strange angle, possible only because her neck was broken. Mommy loved getting flowers on her birthday, and Father would always buy them that one time a year. Sometimes, he would take Molly with him to pick them out, and let her buy a little bunch of flowers to be from her alone.

But there were no flowers on that birthday, the Halloween that was Eliza's last night on earth, no flowers and the terrible storm. In Molly's last memory of her beautiful mommy alive, she wore a shimmering green wrap and held Tessie in her arms.

"My little Molly Mommy, I have something to ask of you, something that may be very hard for you to do. Will you try to do it for me?"

She was only five then. Looking up from her play, she nodded solemnly. Mommy looked so serious.

"If anything happens to me, you must never let anyone separate you and Tessie. You're family, and you must never be apart. You're Dupartes, the last of the Dupartes, and you two girls are very special."

"Isn't Daddy a Duparte?" Molly asked, wondering.

He seemed so different, so not shiny and beautiful like Mommy. He never laughed or hugged her or cuddled like Mommy, so not being a Duparte must be a sad thing.

"No, my Honey-Bunny, my little Kitten Child. He's not a Duparte, but this sister of yours is, and you must always look out for her. Promise me?"

She looked into her mommy's blue eyes and saw tears. *Why would she cry?* She knew it must have something to do with the sounds she often heard coming from the bedroom where her parents slept. She wasn't allowed in there, and the room scared her. Bad things lived in it. She could feel their eyes staring at her from the darkness.

"If I go away, my little one, I'll come back and get you and this little tadpole. You'll have to take care of her until I get back. Can you do that, my sweet little girl?"

She said nothing. Tears trickled down her cheeks. Shoulders trembling, she wrapped her arms around her mommy, sobbing.

"Never go away." Molly clung desperately. Eliza took her by her shoulders and held her apart from her.

"Molly, this is very important. You must do as I say. I can't stay, and you must be very grown up and care for yourself and your sister until I can come back. I'll come back and get you and Tessie when I can. Promise me now. Please, Honey." Both of them were crying now.

Through her tears she remembered looking at the yellow-haired child and knowing deep down inside that she could never let anyone hurt her. *But how could she stop them? Who would hurt her anyway?* She could see the worry lines etched deeply on her mother's face, and so she knew it might be possible. *Who would hurt a two-year-old angel? Who would hurt her?*

A sharp noise jolted Molly's attention back to the present. Anxiously, she looked upward. There were a few clouds in the sky, and the sound she heard meant that there was a storm occurring, maybe headed in this direction. She needed to finish her tasks very soon, or there wouldn't be time to take the flowers. Very bad things would happen if they didn't take the flowers. She wasn't sure just how she knew, but she was absolutely sure of it–very bad things. She heard the familiar humming in her head, a sound like horseflies buzzing around something dead.

Wincing, she tried to block the memory of the dead dog from her mind. It was not working. She could see the flies crawling out of the black dog's nose. She could see it like it was all happening again, like she saw it in her nightmares.

Several months after her dad's release from the hospital following his accident, they were on their way home from a weekend tent revival meeting held in Arkadelphia. They were riding in an old Chevy truck, lent to them by the City of Beaufort Falls, pending settlement of the lawsuit, and it was very hot, so hot that waves of sunlight reflected from the front windshield of the vehicle. She felt sick. She had to pee so badly that it took all of her energy to not pee in her pants, but she knew better than to ask. Baby Tessie, only three then, started to cry. Her father's mouth tensed into the hard line it took when he was very annoyed. She gulped, choking back the hurting that started low in her stomach when he got that look. Anything could happen when he got that look.

"Father. Pee. Please?"

Tessie had to go, too. Tears flowed silently down her little round cheeks. J.D. looked to both sides of the road for a place to pull over. A slight clearing appeared ahead to the right, so he pulled the car over and coasted to a stop. He came around to Tessie's side of the car and he bumped her knee on the door as he pulled her out the vehicle. He set her down on a little path leading into the woods, and Molly could see the little girl trying very hard to choke back her tears. She ran for the nearest bush, and Molly followed.

When they reappeared, they found J.D. staring into a drainage culvert designed to keep the superhighway dry during periods of heavy Alabama rain. Molly wrinkled her nose. A familiar, unpleasant, heavy odor wafted from the ditch, and she knew she had smelled it before, in the pasture on the day that changed her life. J.D. noticed them.

"Come here," he ordered. They approached slowly. "Now! Come here." Molly came close to the edge of the ditch and stopped. Half covered by mud, the carcass of a black dog stared up at them, its body bloated from the heat, lying with all four feet extended, a grimace baring white teeth as the lips shrunk back from the bones of the face. She saw maggots crawling inside the split belly area; loops of intestine exposed, gleaming white, in contrast to the animal's mummy-like dark skin.

The slightly sweet odor mingled with a cloying fragrance she could not identify. Her father walked over to the nearby pine thicket, and, using his pocketknife, trimmed a long branch, and poked at the dog and prepared to lecture.

"The wages of sin is death," he began, "and corruption of the flesh is the eventual reward for evil."

Long arm extended, he caught Tessie by the back of her jacket, pulled her forward and held her over the rotting creature in the ditch. She struggled, pulling herself back, trying to hold onto him to get away from the terrifying caricature of what might have once been a loved family pet.

"Please, Father. Please. No!"

She reached frantically for him, kicking her short legs and sobbing, anything to get away from the horrible creature as big as she was, and so distorted; so unlike the living, breathing doggies she knew.

J.D. hesitated, looking at Tessie differently. She'd stopped kicking, and her innocent little face had changed, its features hardening into those of an adult woman; her eyes glazed and her mouth contorted.

Molly rubbed her head. The buzzing was worse, but she knew she couldn't avoid the memory that surfaced next.

Somehow, her father no longer held a three-year-old child in his arms. He gripped a woman instead, a woman who looked very much like the mommy she missed. Involuntarily, stepped toward them. Then she realized that waves of anger surrounded this mommy, and her father. recoiled from its touch. He tried to disengage, but the apparition who was not Tessie now held onto him.

I will lay thy flesh upon the mountains
And fill the valleys with thy foulness
And the channels shall be full of thee.

Its voice reverberated from within her head, hurting her ears and chilling the inside of her. She needed to run away from this creature, so much more horrible than the poor, decaying, carcass beneath it. Its red eyes flashed, sparks flying from them, and it burned, searing her father's arms and legs. She saw him struggle to get away, the flames consuming him. She wanted to scream, to move her leaden legs, to fall, to leave, to go somewhere she would not be burned by this wicked thing, but she couldn't move. The sky darkened and clouds covered what had been a sunny sky.

From the rigid body of the apparition, the voice began again. Molly could see its lips moving stiffly, each word forced through clenched white teeth, like the dog that now cooked in the ditch. She heard hissing and popping sounds, like meat cooking on the grill. Shadows from the fire all around them illuminated Tessie and J.D., the creature that replaced her little sister shining like an angel of death.

And when I extinguish thee, I will cover the Heavens,
And I will make the stars thereof black,
And I will cover the sun with a cloud,
And the moon will not give her light.

All the bright lights of Heaven I will make black over thee.

And then the storm hit with a shrieking violence that drowned out all other sensation around them. She never remembered what happened after the lightning and the wind began, only finally sitting bundled in a blanket in Verbena's little trailer. She remembered seeing men in uniforms everywhere, and hearing them talk about a fire, a forest fire, and they finally brought Tessie in and put her down beside her.

Several days later, J.D. came to pick them up. He thanked Verbena for her kindness, and soon, almost as a matter of habit, he began taking her out. No one ever talked about that night. When she thought of it her head throbbed, her vision blurred, and a sound like the wet whining wind of a hurricane deafened her; immobilized her until she could manage to reattach herself to reality; something that would happen just as the pain and fear threatened to overwhelm her. She turned to face the voice that snapped her back into the present just now.

Oh, no, not Verbena again. She felt awful when Verbena stopped by. Not long after the alcohol-poisoning incident, their father told them that Verbena "was not a proper Christian," and they could no longer talk to her. She couldn't tell the kind woman that, not after all the nice things she had done for Tessie and her. Molly could tell Verbena didn't understand that J.D. intentionally avoided her now. She stopped by almost every day, only to be told that J.D. was "busy," or "not home," or "would call her later," a later that never came. She didn't have time for Verbena today. Smiling weakly, she offered the same excuses again, and accepted the same confused responses from her father's former sweetheart. Lying to her was wrong! She felt a familiar anger as she watched the woman leave, her shoulders slumped and her steps uncertain and slow. Submerging her feelings about injustices beyond her ability to correct, she began cleaning furiously, hoping to be able to sneak out later to do what needed to be done tonight.

As the fog lifted, it was easy to count the gravestones in the small cemetery, only sixteen in all, most of them with the family name Duparte deeply etched on grimy white marble. A rusty ironwork fence and the litter of fallen leaves indicated that many years had passed since a gardener had lovingly tended this family cemetery, but it wasn't a hopeless place. Despite the tendrils of gray Spanish moss trailing the limbs of two huge water oak trees, the light fragrance of honeysuckle wafted romantically in the soft breeze, and a large pale moon danced through the tree limbs, casting silver shadows on the white marble.

The children weren't afraid of the graveyard, even though the hour was late. Molly held Tessie's hand and clutched a bright bouquet of autumn leaves, reds and golds, surrounding a wilted blue flower; their stems tied with a wrinkled, purple-satin ribbon. Suddenly, Tessie stepped on a thorn.

"Molly, stop! Hurt my toe! Stop!"

"Tessie, we can't stop here. Father will catch us. We have to put these on Mommy's grave, or she'll be sad." The littlest one began to sniffle.

"My feet are cold and they hurt! We forgot our shoes."

Molly looked down at her sister's little feet. Sure enough, she'd been in such a hurry to slide out of Tessie's window, she hadn't even thought about getting the poor little girl's shoes. Her own were still hidden under the front porch steps. Tessie began to whimper, little sobs with a gasp between, hard to hear as the breeze began to pick up. Molly looked up at the sky, and the moon was partly hidden now, as wisps of fast-moving clouds skirted its edges.

"We have to hurry. If Father catches us, the storm will come."

She knew their mommy wouldn't let him hurt them, but she didn't want to endure the storm. Molly pulled Tessie along, dragging her through the weeds around the deserted gravestones. Soft as the touch of a Gulfport ocean breeze and heavy with the scent of mimosa, suddenly a burst of warm air surrounded the children, soothing the cold little feet that were in such a hurry to reach their destination.

A pale little woman stepped out from behind one of the stones, watching them intensely. Although tiny, her stance was that of a creature determined to have her way. Looking at them with longing deeply consuming every part of her essence, the spirit moved toward the children, and as she stepped closer the clouds broke, allowing a glimmer of moonlight to illuminate the two little ones, now standing quietly in front of her.

"Was Mommy pretty?" Tessie asked.

"Oh, yes, honey, she was so pretty. She was little, and she had long blonde hair, just like you."

"Do I look like Mommy?" The smallest child put one hand on the gravestone, and reached right through the little woman watching them.

"You look just like her." Tears began to slide down Molly's nose. "Just like her," she repeated, almost whispering. Reverently, she placed the bedraggled bouquet on the mound of weeds and dirt in front of the stone.

"Eliza Duparte Parsons. Born 10-31-1954. Died 10-31-1975. May God have mercy on her soul."

She read aloud for Tessie, who was still too young to be able to read it herself.

"Was she bad?" Tessie asked, looking up at Molly anxiously. Father never talked about her mommy and she suspected he thought she might be evil.

"No. No, she was never bad. She loved us very, very much."

Molly put her arms around Tessie and held her close. No matter how hard she tried to protect the little girl, she couldn't keep her from all hurt the way she had promised her mommy that she would. Something new always reached beyond her small powers and made Tessie cry. Tenderly, she stroked the little girl's shining curls, and she wanted desperately to let Tessie know that someone had once loved them, but she didn't know how to communicate it to her.

The Watcher felt Molly's thoughts, sadness and longing softening her nearly transparent features, but then her face changed, grew hard as she remembered injustices yet to be avenged. Her eyes went cold blue, far more frigid than the icy wind that had suddenly picked up, causing the babies standing in front of her to shiver.

I won't let him hurt you, Eliza promised her children. *He'll never hurt you like he hurt me. Never.* Calming, she watched as Molly placed the wilted little bundle of flowers on the bare earth in front of the marble gravestone that marked her final resting place. Frustrated, unable to communicate with her girls, Eliza faded and disappeared as if she had never been present at all, leaving a trace of her perfume lingering, as the wind quieted to the former soft breeze.

Chapter Seven

Which Way To Go?

Charlie Callahan reluctantly returned the wallet full of credit cards to his back pocket. He had no choice. With the biggest manhunt in Beaufort Falls' history currently in full swing, he couldn't use any of Sheriff Nate St. Claire's lovely credit for at least a few months, long enough for everyone to stop looking for him. It helped that they couldn't find a body. From the information he picked up off the six o'clock news, he gathered that most of the county searched for "Sheriff Nate." Actually, about half the people who knew him and Mrs. St. Claire believed the sheriff had just made a run for it. Mrs. St. Claire was renowned for a tongue sharp enough to slice and dice the best of them. In spite of her wailing and loud lamenting, and her insistence that every available lawman in a six-county area look for her "poor murdered Nathan," almost everyone expected that he'd left on his own and had enough sense not to be found.

She ordered a beautiful funeral from Beaufort Falls Mortuary, scheduled the church, and summoned all of her relatives to comfort her, but no one could find his body. Most inconveniently, the insurance refused to pay, but the revenue from her trust fund more than provided an adequate income. When Assistant Sheriff Bobby Cox found that someone had made inquiries from nearby Sicily as to the sheriff's credit card balance, he just smiled.

That clever Ole Fox, he smirked.

Rumor had it that for the last year Nate had been "seeing" a young woman who worked in an office there. He would disappear occasionally for a weekend, only to return looking cheerful and well laid. Bobby wasn't about to mess this up for him, if he actually managed to escape the two-hundred-fifty-pound harpy who screamed orders and made life miserable for the fifty or so workers who combed the countryside for any hint of foul play. So far, the only thing they'd established was that he had made a visit out to arrest Charlie Callahan, also missing, but Charlie didn't have an army of relatives to insist upon a search for him.

Oddly enough, Bobby didn't feel certain that Charlie was actually missing. The boys examined every inch of the lean-to log cabin, and only Callahan's clothes were gone. Groceries and canned goods stocked the cabinets, the bed was neatly made, and a large stack of firewood sat to the left of the large fireplace, ready to warm him when he returned from wherever he went. Bobby believed he probably got wind of his imminent arrest, and just "disappeared" when he saw the cop car. Everything was in its place, and there was no sign of any kind of a struggle. In this part of the country, people who didn't want to go to jail had plenty of room to hide.

He heard Arlene St. Claire's stringent whine interrogate the last of the returning searchers. For the last ten hours, more than a hundred and fifty volunteers had combed the riverbed and marshy flatlands surrounding Callahan's reclusive cabin. They'd discovered enough water moccasins, raccoons, and swamp vermin to wipe out the city, but no sheriff.

"No Ma'am," he could hear, as one of the searchers responded to the sheriff's wife, politely. "We ain't seen no part of Nate. Yes, Ma'am. We sure did look real good."

The kid was wet, reeked of river mud and was shivering, but Mrs. St. Claire continued. With a resigned sigh, Bobby picked up his cap and his badge and decided to go rescue the poor young man.

"Ernie?" he asked. "Kermit Wilson's kid?"

"Yes, Sir," Ernie replied courteously.

"Ernie, run over and get Mrs. St. Claire and yourself some of that hot coffee we have brewing over next door at the Community Center. Bring us back a couple of doughnuts, too, while you are there."

The kid took off like a scared rabbit, and Bobby turned to face the hopeful widow-to-be.

"He's out there somewhere," she shrilled, large fake tears streaking expensive makeup, which was carefully applied and artfully destroyed.

Deputy Cox grimaced, images of the dancing elephants from the recent re-release of the movie Disney creation Fantasia tiptoeing through his weary mind. The movie had totally enchanted his children, and he'd watched it with them three times. Tuning her out, he turned and rubbed his eyes. According to the timesheet that he filled in a few minutes ago, he hadn't slept for forty-eight hours. It was time to call this madness off, he decided. Sheriff Nate was fine, and no one except that old maid social worker gave a hoot about what had happened to Charlie Callahan. Let him rot out in the swamps by the river.

"Fuck this shit," he mumbled to himself. Reaching around Arlene St. Claire, he took a cup of coffee from Ernie, who'd reappeared.

"Ernie, you look like hell. Go home and get some sleep." He reached for the intercom button. In his most official voice he announced: "All personnel who are not scheduled for regular duty are now dismissed, the manhunt is over. Alma, radio the site and tell them to wind down operations. I will be out there in twenty minutes to commence shutdown."

Struck speechless, Arlene St. Claire's mouth moved, but no sound emerged. When she found her vocal chords again, her words were not pretty. Her small eyes became slits in her fleshy face; she responded like a woman obviously used to getting her way.

"You will *not* stop hunting for my husband. He's an important man. I'll have your badge within a week!"

"Ma'am, if I had my way, you could have it right now."

Wearier than ever before in his life, he reached for the thick packet of forms that still needed to be filled out before he could go home and tucked them securely under his arm. Arlene stood, seething, almost bubbling with rage. He took his keys from the hook on the wall and turned to face the angry woman. He made sure she was the only one to hear his next words.

"Arlene, we've been neighbors for a long time, and my family has known yours for almost half a century," he spoke softly, sympathetically. "We both know Nate isn't dead. When he gets tired of that little floozy in Sicily, he'll come home like the old dog he is, tail between his legs, whining for you to forgive him. It'd be a lot better for everyone not to make such a fuss."

Like the collapse of a hot air balloon, the anger left Arlene's puffy face. For the first time, the lines around her eyes, the sadness and the fatigue and sheer frustration, were those of an old woman who now would almost certainly spend the rest of her life alone.

"I hope you're right," she muttered as she turned and left. The biggest manhunt in Beaufort County history was over, and no one but the bored news staff in nearby Sicily was sorry to see it gone.

With a deep sigh, Molly wiped the polish across the leather of the shoes one more time. She was locked in the small space of the kitchen pantry, a walk-through closet area that normally held nothing but groceries and provisions, and the fumes from the strong colorant made her dizzy. She'd lost track of time. She might have been here an hour, maybe six hours, but she knew better than to leave before her father came to get her.

Around her, in neat stacks, sat fourteen pairs of carefully polished shoes. She would polish them again, and again, and again, until she completed her "punishment." Her own muddy shoes, which she had been caught hiding under the stairs, now looked brand new.

After her punishment, she would finish her normal chores, and the lye, minus the heavy gloves that usually protected her hands, waited on the kitchen counter. Preferring not to anticipate that task, she returned to polishing shoes. She examined them for scuffmarks using the small flashlight that J.D. had left for her, and while the battery was dim, it still managed a little light. Grimacing, she glanced at her bruised, sore knuckles, stained with polish. Its oily resin should give her some protection against the caustic oven cleaner, she hoped.

"Molly, you okay?" Tessie's little voice sounded worried.

"I'm fine, little angel. Stay away and don't get caught talking to me."

She heard a little bump and realized the child must be sitting right in front of the padlocked entrance to the closet.

"Is he gone?" she asked. They both knew who "he" was.

Tessie didn't answer. Molly heard the soft sniffing sounds the little girl made when she cried.

"I'm fine! Stop crying! Did he do anything to you?"

She didn't think he would have. They'd made it back inside, and she'd already tucked Tessie into her bed, when J.D. caught her groping under the porch step looking for a place to stash her muddy shoes.

"Did he do anything to you?" She no longer felt tired.

"Did he do anything to you?"

Tessie didn't answer. The silence, enhanced by an odd off-season surge of heat and humidity, forced walls, already only four feet apart, to close in on Molly. Their unyielding surfaces threatened to crush her and press her into them. She couldn't breathe, couldn't think. She had to get out of there. She tried to fight her panic, tried to go limp, but it didn't help. Like hot gases from a crackling fire, energy possessed her and she pushed upward with all of its surging power, collapsing the oak shelf above her that formed her roof. Cans and boxes tumbled all around her. Screaming her rage, she threw herself against the locked door. "You will die, John Duke! You will die!" She couldn't remember anything that happened during the rest of that day.

Chapter Eight

The Eye Of The Devil

J.D. stood in the doorway of the little house on Sycamore Street. He held a legal document in each hand, looking first at one, then the other. His right hand held the carefully worded complaint drawn up by his lawyer, accusing Beaufort Falls County Medical Center of:

"Willfully and wantonly committing such negligence as to cause irreparable harm to one Mr. John Duke Parsons, entrusted to its care during a state of unconsciousness. Through crass indifference to his pain and suffering, lack of training and supervision of its staff, it did on Occasion One administer snake bite antivenin to said victim without testing for possible allergic reaction to it. On Occasion Two it administered double injections of powerful medications and ignored his piteous condition, almost costing him his life."

The other document read:

"Beaufort County Department of Child and Family Services, Protective Services Division" in its upper, left-hand, corner.

Hands shaking disapproval, he tucked both documents into his dark wool, worsted suit jacket's inner pocket.

Why would Family and Children's Services want to investigate me? he questioned, looking around the immaculate living room. *I haven't done anything wrong.*

Well, he was ready for them. No matter what the reason, they would have no choice but to find him an exceptional parent. There was not one speck of dust or dirt in the house. Two freshly scrubbed children stood politely in front of the coffee table, on which a large King James Version of the Bible was prominently displayed. He examined them carefully; hair brushed, faces clean, freshly ironed white blouses, clean white socks and freshly polished black loafers. Yes, they presented exactly the image he wanted portrayed.

Only Molly knew the sustained effort that preceded this visit by Miss Anna Johnson, Protective Service Caseworker for Beaufort County Department of Family and Children's Services. A close look at the child's expressionless little face revealed large dark circles under her eyes. Not nearly so visible were the red welts left on her calves and upper thighs, or the darkening bruises along her skinny shoulders, held resolutely squared, posture perfect.

J.D. glanced at her with an annoyed frown. Leave it to Molly to provoke him and cause him to leave marks on her legs right before this most important visit. Skirts made so much more favorable an impression than those common cotton pants, but he had no choice. Just as he had no choice but to chastise her for the appalling mess she created in the pantry, and the incineration of fourteen pairs of perfectly serviceable shoes. It was a good thing the neighbor called the fire department, or the entire house might have gone up in flames. As it was, he would never get the charcoal stains off the porcelain surface of the bathtub.

He played with the idea of having the children attend school barefooted for several days to atone, but it didn't seem like a good idea with this visit impending. It was no accident, however, that the handsome loafers each child wore were a size too large, and Molly's shoes were painfully narrow on her uncharacteristically wide feet. He smiled as Molly shifted uncomfortably in the new shoes.

I pray for them: I pray not for the world, but for them, which thou hast given me, for they are thine. Composing his thoughts, he prepared for the difficult visit ahead.

Anna scanned the police report in front of her, trying to get a feel for the Parsons' family structure. This new report puzzled her. Nine-One-One got calls every week from this household, and they were very serious ones—poisonings, fires, threatening events—but J.D. Parsons was just the sort of serious parent she always hoped she would find. Even if it made her late for the home visit, it was up to her to figure everything out, and years of experience taught her to be ready for the smallest clues. Bifocals balanced precariously on the bridge of her nose, she continued reading.

"Upon arriving at the scene, we found smoke pouring out of the open front door of the domicile, and a visibly upset small child outside, seated on the curb next to the mailbox. Inside, we found an actively engaged conflagration located in the bathroom in the bathtub. It had been purposefully set, and the most likely perpetrator, an older child, was approaching the scene of the fire with an armload of magazines and leaflets. Already burning were shoes and a leather shoeshine kit. Protective Services was notified and said that the minors were to be remanded to the county for investigation into their home situation."

She'd arrived to find Tessie sobbing uncontrollably, and Molly sitting quietly on the porch, an inscrutable expression on her face.

"What a dark child that is," she'd mumbled softly to herself. The little one was a ray of sunshine, but the older kid bristled with hostility. Sighing wearily, she reached for her purse. She got so tired of being the one responsible for determining the futures of other people. The world was so screwed up, and she sure as hell couldn't fix it. Turning back to her notes, she refocused on her reading.

When she had contacted J.D. briefly, a week ago, to question him about the incident, he'd refused to let her inside the damaged little house, but he'd given her his full attention. He'd motioned her to a seat in the swing on the old-fashioned porch, while he and the two children had stood directly in front of the door. Molly was "odd," he'd told her, had been since the death of her mother several years before. When asked if he'd tried counseling or had someone professional talk to the child, he'd confided that the pastor of his church had spoken with her, and until the other day, he'd thought that she'd gotten better. He'd repair the bathroom, he'd told her, a look of bewildered exasperation on his face.

He had reached down and put his arm around the stony faced child, who'd showed no reaction whatsoever to his caress. As soon as he'd let her go, she'd moved quietly away from him, almost an arm's length. When the little one had wrapped her arms around his legs, he'd picked her up and kissed her cheek, and she'd smiled with delight. That had been such a pretty picture, she'd remembered. She'd questioned him about his reaction to the damage. Most parents would have been tremendously upset to come home and find the house on fire.

"I only care that my children are safe," he'd told her earnestly.

"The Lord God protected them," he'd told her.

She sensed that something had to be very wrong to create the resentment she felt in the older child, and it was her job, and her obligation, to stop it before someone in the household was permanently harmed.

Molly tried to erase the images that were racing through her mind as she stood stiffly at attention, waiting for the visitation. Over and over she saw it, over, and over, and over, again–his anger. His face had been contorted with suppressed rage, but his voice was almost a whisper. He'd slid his hand around her throat, almost gently at first, then applying pressure to the small space below her Adam's apple. He'd leaned over her, his leather belt in his hand, and he'd trembled in anticipation of applying it to her bare skin.

"You'll remember this," he'd hissed.

Naked and afraid, she'd thought she would die. Inside her head, she'd heard the voice she knew she could turn to for comfort and solace. *It will pass, little one. It will pass. He will die horribly. It will pass.* The whisper started inside of her mind, as it always did.

She'd turned her head and waited for the first blows, the ragged sting of the leather on her skin, not wanting to give him the satisfaction of seeing her cry, but he'd surprised her. He'd moved away from her and called out, softly, sweetly...

"Elizabeth, come here. Marguerite has been bad." Her sister had come to the doorway and peeked in.

"Bad?" she questioned. Puzzled, she'd tiptoed in and stood close to the two of them.

"I want you to see what happens when you are bad." He'd lightly pulled one of Tessie's blonde curls, tenderly, playfully, a half-smile on his face.

Molly had cringed. She couldn't let her sister become involved. It couldn't happen to Tessie. It could *never* happen to Tessie. Her indifference melted and she'd fallen onto her knees before her father. Groveling, lying flat on the floor, she had embraced his feet.

"Please, let her go. I don't care what you do to me. Just let her go. She didn't do anything. I was wrong. I was evil. I will do *anything* for you. Just let her go."

"Molly is hurt?" Tessie had asked, looking up at her father.

"Molly is fine." He'd looked down at the crying child almost underneath his feet, a look of total satisfaction on his face. "She's learning how to be a child of God. She's paying for the error of her ways. Go and play now, an hour of TV for you, little angel. Go and watch TV. I'll be in soon to change the channel for you." Tessie had darted back into the living room alone, excited by her treat. Coldly, deliberately, he'd stepped on Molly's outstretched hand, his weight crushing it into the hard surface of the wood floor.

"I'll be back," he'd told her. "You have lessons to learn." The rest of the night had been a blur to her.

J.D. shifted in his sleep. Moaning slightly, he moved over onto his side. The visit had gone well, but to his disappointment, Anna didn't immediately close the case. The social worker insisted that he make an appointment to bring the girls to the department office to meet with the staff child psychologist, particularly since it was obvious that Molly might have severe emotional problems. He had been restless when he went to bed, and now he couldn't sleep peacefully.

Suddenly, he found himself in the middle of a dream. He ran in this dream, ran as fast as he could, but still he kept falling behind. Shiny black crawly things engulfed him, flowed around him on both sides, moved over him like the relentless waters of a moving river. He heard her call him, soft and low and cruel. The last thing he remembered before the blackness of deep sleep was a wisp of green silk.

In another part of the house, Tessie also moaned, a little chortle of delight. It was so pretty with its shiny black body and its long, irregular, pointy legs. Mommy gave it to her. She told her where to find it. The pretty lady was Mommy. She had long blonde hair and she loved Tessie, Molly said so. She shivered, cold in the dark basement, but then she felt the lady's warm arms around her again. Her attention returned to the spider.

It raised one long leg and she could see the underside of its fat belly. Such bright red, like a splash of bright lipstick! Fascinated, she reached toward it with a chubby finger. After a second's hesitation, it danced up onto her hand. *What if it was cold?* she pondered. A breath of chill air whistled from the broken window directly above. *What would keep it warm?*

Stacks of clean laundry covered the table to her right. She reached into a basket full of socks. Perfect! A black sock! Clean and nice! Her father's sock would keep it so warm and snug. Gently, she fluffed it open and let the big spider crawl inside.

I'll just carry it upstairs where it is warm. She smiled at the thought that her friend would be safe and snug in the kitchen upstairs where it was comfy. *You'll like it with us.* She smiled joyfully as they climbed the stairs. She could hear the pretty lady singing. Mommy was so happy.

"Shall we gather at the river? Where so many saints have trod. The beautiful, the beautiful river...."

Her child's voice trilled the grown-up words and she carefully placed the sock near the warm air vent on the kitchen floor. It would be warm there, warm and safe, she thought, as she crawled into her bed. Tomorrow she would check on her new friend.

Chapter Nine

Things Are Never What They Seem

The Reverend Charlie Callahan, or Nate St. Claire, as he now called himself, pulled the shriveled head from the formaldehyde bath in which it had soaked for the last month. When it had become so pungent even he'd noticed it, he'd removed it from the trunk of the car, and brought it inside the small apartment he'd rented, using the former sheriff's identification and credentials. He consulted his new bible, the large edition of *Taxidermy as a Hobby,* seriously overdue at the Sicily library but no one contacted him to request its return.

It surprised him that he slipped into his role as Nate with so little trouble. No one questioned him. No one from Beaufort Falls appeared on his doorstep, begging the supposed icon of the community to return. Using Nate's Visa card to charge his supper at a neighborhood diner the first time terrified him; but he'd almost starved living in his car for several weeks, too afraid to say more than a word or two to anyone. Before long, he'd learned to lie comfortably, boldly even, his confidence bolstered by the purchase of another big fireman's axe just like the one he'd left behind in Beaufort Falls. He kept it safely under his thrift-store bed, waiting to protect him from intruders. He'd grown a beard that gave him a rugged look, and had lost several pounds during the period of time he'd spent without regular meals.

A couple of weeks working as a day laborer for Manpower toned up the soft flab he'd accumulated as a "Man of God," a role he'd left behind after realizing that he probably coldly murdered the man whose head was now his best friend. Oddly enough, although he still couldn't remember anything that happened during the night the sheriff was murdered, just the thought that he might have killed the man gave him a new respect for his own abilities. He'd lost the loser look that had influenced his every action in Beaufort Falls, and somewhere during this transition, he'd lost his aversion for the grisly object from the pail.

Now. You are starting to look right spiffy. Okay--to the right a little. Let's comb those wavy locks just so. You clean up right nice for a fat old guy. Grimacing, he stepped back to admire his work.

You're not just fat, but you're a Negro sheriff now, that's for sure! As the head seasoned, not only did the skin pull tight across the cheekbones and jaw-line, but it also turned rich ebony-black. Jowls and folds formerly fat now turned into flaps of something that resembled leather, tough and coarse to the touch. It stared back at Charlie with glassy eyes, opaque and sightless now for eternity.

Charlie finished styling the hair, pulling it back into a short ponytail which he tucked close to the back of the neck, and then he slid the entire skull into a thick plastic bag slightly larger than the circumference of the head.

Where's that heat gun? He reached under the bed and brought out a tool often used by painters to remove paint from walls. Carefully, he focused it on the bagged head, and switching it to low speed, he watched with satisfaction as the plastic shrank.

"I think you're ready for your new home, old boy." Lovingly, he placed the leering caricature toward the back of the top shelf of his bedroom closet.

"Too bad you can't come with me, Old Man."

Whistling cheerfully, he dressed for his date. He remembered the first time he'd seen Verbena in Sicily, and he wondered what she would wear for him tonight.

Verbena rearranged the hairnet and straightened the skirt of the uniform she wore as a counter attendant at the DeLight Donut shop a few blocks away from the apartment Charlie had rented after being homeless for weeks. Moving away from Beaufort Falls and starting a new life had saved her.

One Friday, she'd realized that she'd left for work an hour ahead of time, just so she could watch J.D. walk past the corner of Sycamore and Wright Street. Suddenly, she knew she could never get over the need she felt for the man in any place where she saw him every day. Even worse, she remembered how sweet it felt taking care of his little girls, and the feel of Tessie's arms around her neck was a much warmer memory than any caress ever given to her by the man of her dreams. J.D. satisfied his needs in a most direct and basic way. Still, he'd remained the most exciting man she'd ever known, and sex with him, even lacking affection, was sex. *There sure ain't a bunch of men lined up here, waiting to take me out.*

She'd built an entire fantasy about J.D., herself, and the two children, beginning with the thought that she would move into the little house on Sycamore and take care of him and the girls, fold his clothes, and cook his meals. They would all go to the movies on Saturday afternoon, laughing and happy and...

"Ma'am. Could you help me please?" Charlie had recognized Verbena as one of the women at the revival meeting where the baby had crawled into the basket with the snakes, and although it frightened him a bit, this would be a good test of his new persona. Would she recognize him? And why was she working in Sicily now? He'd thought she had a good job at the beauty parlor in Beaufort Falls. She was a pretty little thing, with her rounded hips and large, full breasts, very attractively displayed in the tight pink uniform. *All women should wear pink. It's such a soft color.*

Reluctantly, Verbena had left her dream and turned to wait on the customer. She'd seen a man in the last glow of middle age, late thirties, but weathered and strong. Something in his eyes let her know that he thought well of her when he looked at her. He'd worn a faded flannel work shirt and overalls, and obviously was on his way to some sort of a manual labor job. He'd looked vaguely familiar, but then, this was a donut shop and men came in every day and eventually they all became familiar to her. "What can I get for you, Big Guy?" He'd grinned good-naturedly.

They all liked being called that. She loved working in fast food. Humoring spoiled old women in the beauty shop seemed a bad dream to her now. For the first time, she actually could please her customers. She went home at night now physically exhausted, but mentally intact. Bringing sweet rolls to hungry men sure beat redoing some old hag's fingernails until she finally decided which color matched her new dress. If she didn't feel bone-weary lonesome, it would be a good life. Thirty-five years old, and her chosen vocation consisted of working in a donut shop. Yeah, life sure was grand.

"Other than your phone number?" Charlie hadn't been able to believe he could be so bold. He'd smiled gamely. He hadn't used a line that corny in years. In fact, he hadn't talked that way to a woman in years.

Verbena had taken a longer look at him. He'd radiated good health. He'd seemed to have most of his teeth. He wasn't bad looking. Why not? What did she have to lose? It wasn't like she had a dream that might actually come true.

Later that evening, he'd arrived on her doorstep with an armload of roses and the evening paper, so that they could select a movie. She'd smiled her approval at her unlikely Galahad. Finally, she'd found a man who knew how to make her feel like a woman.

"You like Elvis?" she'd questioned, as she fixed them each a gin and tonic. Charlie wrinkled his nose a little as she handed him the drink. Gin always smelled like pine trees to him, but a woman handing him liquor seemed like a good thing.

"It's a shame about the King, isn't it?" he'd asked her, making casual conversation on that first date. Verbena shoved her favorite eight-track tape into its drive, and the liquid voice of the man who died at Graceland had filled the small apartment. *"Love me tender, love me true."*

Charlie sighed. It'd been a long time since a woman thought of him in any sort of a romantic way. Verbena liked him; he could tell. She'd already changed into "something more comfortable." He'd drink pine trees all night long, as long as she dressed like that. Leaving the past, he grinned as he got ready to meet her at nine, hoping she still had that filmy little nightie nearby tonight.

Another person was busy weighing options just then, too. Mrs. St. Claire examined the credit card statement with its long list of charges, all signed for by "Nathan St. Claire."

At the other side of the receiver, a worried customer service representative asked, "Should I send photocopies of the signature? Do you think it might be a forgery?"

"No," she answered wearily. "No. I think it's probably him. I'll just pay it."

Scribbling the address and phone number for the liquor store on Eighth Street in Sicily where he'd purchased a fifth of Early Times, she decided to have him found. *I've given him some time to get tired of the floozy.* He'd also charged a dozen long-stemmed, pink roses. *I'll have a detective find him and then I'll pay him a visit.*

A lousy man was better than no man at all. It'd been a long time since the old coot had bought her roses; but then, she usually bought her own flowers and would take care of that right now. Hmmm, she never bought her roses that cheaply.

A sad little woman stood in the shadow of the steps in front of the house on Sycamore Street. Tears ran down her pale cheeks, down a pert little nose, splotching a green silk kimono. The huge moon passed silver shadows all the way through her fragile form. Tessie climbed the porch steps, and the woman reached for her with arms that passed through the little girl. Tessie hesitated, and Eliza smiled.

"Lady?"

"You're a good little girl," Eliza whispered, her voice more the soft force of an autumn breeze than any form of spoken speech.

"Tessie. Time to come inside. Too late for you to be outside." Turning toward Molly, who waited for her just inside the house, Tessie continued up the steps. Molly took good care of her.

The little ghost followed her youngest daughter up the stairs and then stood on tiptoe and peered into the house, straining to see the rooms inside. Looking past the two girls, she continued to search; finally stepping back onto the porch, remembering.

My children. But he's not here. My little son never lived in this house. He took you away from me. Rubbing her temples, she struggled to recall the events of the night that she lost her baby boy.

John Duke won't tell me. He hates you. You aren't meant to be. But you're mine. Wherever you are, you are my little child, and anyone who hurts you will die. Anyone who hurts any child of mine will die. Horribly!

Dissolved by her warm tears, her image faded briefly, and then intensified, clear again, as the vague features hardened into an angry scowl. Above her, tiny wisps scuttled ahead of huge storm clouds, moving in quickly from the West.

Her face twisted with hatred now, blue eyes blazing red, huge orbs spitting flame into what had been calm air.

I hate you, John Duke. You'll die! You'll die soon, and you'll die in agony! All trace of the soft spring breeze was gone now, and a cold wind screeched as it raked the siding of the house and displaced shingles on the roof. It was time to find J.D.

Unaware of his ethereal visitor, John Duke frowned as he placed his clothes for the next day carefully on the end of his bed, his nightly ritual. First his clean work shirt, then pressed jeans; carefully ironed by Molly's little arms that barely reached the top of the tall ironing board. Clean underwear and his polished shoes; something was missing? Where were his socks? Molly knew to put them with the other clothes where he could find them. He could barely control his irritation as he scanned the kitchen looking for his socks.

He found them in front of the heat vent by the door to the basement. Damn careless child. He would take care of this later. Angrily, he snatched the offending garments and methodically folded them, placing them on top of the rest of his clean clothes.

Another mother was very busy inside in the dark womb of the soft sock. Thousands of babies were being born. Black widow spider babies are special. Each is born with its own little system already intact. Each has a little mouth and its own little poison sac, ready for use; a tiny adult ready for the challenges of spider life, ready to exit the dark tunnel and engulf whatever happened to be lying in its path. Mommy spider was quite pleased. She lifted her pointy leg and the crimson spot on her underside faded as the last of her life passed into the many vigorous young. They scurried over and around each other, ready to leave the nest. J.D. finished his prayers and climbed under his crisp white sheets. Soon the exodus would begin.

The spirit watched, as he coasted into a restless sleep. He moaned fitfully, and she remembered a little of what had occurred on the night she'd lost her little boy. The labor pains woke her up, and although she'd expected to hurt, these pains engulfed her, immediately intense, different from anything she had ever imagined. All of her short life, she'd waited to become a mother, and the excitement reassured her, even though each contraction felt like her body ripped itself apart.

Even though she knew it wouldn't help, she'd screamed for help. She knew that no one would hear her, so far out in the woods away from everyone in the old cabin. Other mothers once slept on the cotton-wadding pallet she'd found there, but it was her bed now. They'd also screamed for mercy, only to hear their cries reflected back to them by the ancient walls.

The cabin was her prison, and she'd had no friend or relative nearby. Her time of trial was now, and she'd known that she'd need help with this birth, but just as dozens of black slave women before her, she knew she would face her ordeal alone.

"John!"

She screamed; then screamed louder. She didn't expect a response. He'd locked her in the cabin soon after he'd discovered her secret shame. Every few days he would reappear with food and water, and would empty the pail she filled with her waste. Her husband knew her secret and he wouldn't come to help her now. She would bear her shame alone. He had seen her with her lover and she had no way to defend herself. The only saving grace was that the child she carried could be John's.

She'd hidden her pregnancy from him as long as she could. He'd just begun to treat her normally again, although he would not even trust her to get groceries for them at the corner store. When he'd realized that she was with child, he'd immediately counted the days. She begged him to consider that he had also been with her, many times, during that month. "The baby is yours!" she'd shouted, crying, and she'd followed him around the house until finally, she'd forced him to speak. Shuddering, she remembered his response. He'd looked at her as if she were a roach on his clean carpet.

"If a man be found lying with a woman married to a husband, then they shall both of them die. You, your lover, and all produced by your union shall die."

"But the baby? The baby is innocent," she'd begged.

"A bastard shall not enter into the assembly of the Lord; even to the tenth generation shall none of his enter into the assembly of the Lord." She'd expected another beating, but instead he looked at her coldly and walked away. "I will know if the child is mine," he'd told her later, and three months before the birth he'd taken her to the cabin and left her locked up and alone.

Now, in the darkness of the woods, her labor was tearing her weakened body apart. "John? John, please! You have to come and help me. Help the baby!" She'd been so thirsty. Her screams finally tapered into a hoarse croaking. He wasn't coming. She could tell. Then she'd heard footsteps coming toward her from outside. He was going to help her. Her baby would live!

"Mommy?" A voice from the hallway diverted her attention from her past pain. The dark, serious, face of her oldest daughter peered at her from the open door to J.D.'s bedroom.

"Mommy? Is it really you?"

Molly could see her? It wouldn't do for her to come into this room with the tiny spiders ready to make their way into the world. Unlike Tessie, the older child wasn't protected by the innocence of ignorance. Molly worked so hard, tried so hard to live in the impossible reality that J.D. established for the children.

She's such a sweet, sad, little girl. Overcome by a wave of tenderness for her lonely child she moved toward her, and then remembered that she could not touch her no matter how much she wanted to hold her in her arms.

Molly, little sweetie, go to bed now. I'll watch out for you. I'll take care of you. I love you. Molly moved back, away from the door.

"Okay, Mommy." She turned and moved toward her sister's room, a smile on the child's prematurely old, little face. Eliza faded into the darkness as Molly told slumbering Tessie, "Mommy is here. She'll take care of us." Curled up together, they slept through the night.

Chapter Ten

Death, Where Is Thy Sting?

"Wasn't anything we could do," Nursing Supervisor Ellis put her arm around the exhausted lead nurse's shoulders.

"It's just that he's been in and out of here so often, I got attached to him."

Lead nurse Wilson had been shocked to find J.D. back in his usual room this morning when she'd begun her shift at six AM. During the day he'd grown progressively worse, and she'd stayed through the night, trying to save him from the deadly toxins that gradually overcame every one of his body's strong defenses. The swelling would soon leave the purplish lump of human remains, lying on the stretcher, waiting to make the journey to the morgue. An hour ago, it could not be identified as a man. J.D. would have been disgusted with himself. His trim one-hundred-seventy-five-pound frame puffed out a to a measured two-hundred pounds, all fluid trying to repulse the strong poison from the hundreds of little creatures that cheerfully bit him. They were now on their way to a malevolent existence threatening livestock and careless exterminators who spray basement crawl spaces or attic eaves. Everyone involved believed that only a miracle could save him after this accident, and it didn't look like one was on the way.

A miracle was what J.D. needed, all right. He hadn't given up on his fight with the evil creature with which he had wrestled for the last twenty-four hours. Unseen to all, he still fought hard to live, for he didn't know that they had pronounced him dead.

You can't kill me. I am an emissary of the Lord God of Hosts, and I will vanquish you to Hell from whence you cometh!

With a shrill laugh, the yellow-green vamp from Hades extended her talons: long red fingernails, hundreds and hundreds of long razor-sharp fingernails, each filed to a needle-sharp point. She danced around him on every side.

Aiiiiiiiieeeeeeeee.

Pain traveled through his body in waves. He could feel the little insects piercing every inch of his naked body, and now the heat returned, starting on his bare feet and climbing. Why did he still shiver? How could he be cold and hot at the same time? Was this Hell? He couldn't be in Hell, but a strong sulfuric odor overpowered his ability to inhale, making him struggle to breathe, making it very hard for him to gasp breaths from the putrid fumes.

Struggling to focus on the creature he could hear so intensely, the evil wraith who caused him such excruciating pain, he forced his eyelids to open a fraction. It was a she, of course, but a female form that surrounded him, undulating and weaving around him on all sides, moving in and out of his earthly form at will. She was beautiful. Her blonde hair floated freely behind her slim form, dressed in her alluring silk kimono, her skin soft and white.

Get thee behind me, Satan. Eliza, you art Satan, you unclean whore. You whore! You will not kill me, you filthy whore!

Immediately, she changed. Her white skin changed to parchment yellow, and then dripped from her lovely face, exposing white bones, hideous jagged teeth loosely fastened in her open jaw moved toward J.D., seeking his exposed throat. Her front teeth elongated. They reached and searched for the vulnerable dip right below his pulsing Adam's apple.

He flailed wildly, pummeling nothing, screaming and kicking the air. He was bleeding; he could feel it. He was bleeding from a thousand little holes in his body, but she wouldn't win. His universe exploded; he could hear and feel the percussion thuds on his skin, in his mind. He launched himself at her. He must remove her from this existence; he must send her back into the fires of Hell where she belonged. *I will not die. You will not kill me, you whore! Go back to Hell! Get thee behind me, you filthy whore of Beelzebub! Go back to Hell! Now!*

Blinking, he opened his eyes. He was lying on the floor, halfway underneath a cart in a hospital room, and a female orderly was screaming. She shrieked and stared at him with horror-filled, wild eyes. Backing away from him, she turned and ran out of the room.

Fifteen minutes later, the elderly orderly sat in a plush office on the top floor of the hospital. "I ain't go'in that room again. I don't care if'n you fire me. I ain't never worked no place where dead men comes back to life whiles I's putting um in de bag. I ain't never done it and I ain't intending to start now." It was obvious that she was nervous and had never been in this part of the building before, may not have even known it existed. Ashley Eugene Beaufort, III, sitting behind his massive oak desk, brushed aside her objection.

"Millie. Make sure this woman is assigned to Pediatrics."

Feigning patience, he fingered the legal document sitting in front of him. It was very inconvenient that the man had survived. It would cost money to defend the six-hundred-thousand-dollar lawsuit and unfortunately, his brother-in-law's insurance firm had dropped the Medical Center as a client last year, claiming the facility was "a bad risk."

"My *own* brother-in-law," he muttered. Beaufort Falls Medical Center was his legacy to protect; a gift from his grandfather to the community, at a time when it was a bustling mill town and nearby Sicily was a three-cow well. He'd owned the cotton mills, which faded into oblivion with the onset of polyester, and now almost all of the family money was sunk into this failing medical center. Grants were dwindling quickly and taking his yearly income as administrator with them. The center was far too much hospital for the fewer than two hundred residents in Beaufort Falls. As a result, people from Sicily, which had no hospital, traveled thirty miles or more to use its facilities. Most of them were none too happy about it.

This morning he had received unsettling news. The new mayor of Sicily called him to let him know he intended to call for a referendum to purchase or build a hospital for Sicily, and if the price was right and the finances were stable, he would consider buying and moving Beaufort Falls Medical Center and renaming it for its original founder. The Ashley Eugene Beaufort Memorial Hospital and Research Center–what a beautiful name! It was not a good time for a costly lawsuit.

Hmmm, well, one thing he could do. He could be sure J.D. never again left this hospital on his own feet. From what he'd heard, he would be doing everyone a favor. It would be a lot cheaper to pay a hit man than a lawyer.

"Sir?" A.E. Beaufort jumped. He'd forgotten the woman sitting in front of him.

"Sir? Can I go now?"

"I want you to submit a detailed report to your supervisor of everything that took place in that hospital room before you leave the building today. Are we clear on that?"

The tired old woman looked down at her feet. Who would she be able to get to write the thing for her? But she dared not cross this man. He was obviously the one in charge.

"Yes, sir, I will. May I go now?" She shuffled her feet, still sitting, waiting to be dismissed, but he had already forgotten her and was looking through papers on his desk. Hesitantly, she stood, and when he didn't object, she left.

With no one else to take the two Parsons kids in, Anna found herself once again bringing home strays. Anna tried calling their grandmother, but she was told by someone answering the phone that the old woman was "unavailable until further notice," meaning either that she was sick, or that she had no intention of trying to act as a substitute parent once again for a son she admittedly did not like. What was there not to like about J.D.? From what she could tell, he tried his best to be a good and proper parent. Still, Anna ran into this so often she didn't even question it; just packed up a few belongings for each of the kids and loaded them into her beat-up old Ford.

Damn it. I wish there was at least one more person working protective services. As always, after a few minutes of driving the two little waifs toward their temporary new home, she softened. The little blonde was choking back tears, and the older one, while a hard case, was fidgety and nervous.

"It'll be all right." She knew she lied. Nothing ever went right for the children. Their father was almost certainly dead. What would happen to these kids when they reached the Children's Home in a few days? The least she could do for them would be to make it as painless as possible.

Usually, the children would have spent this time in a foster home, awaiting disposition as to the fate of their father, but none were available right now. The little one clung to her sister like glue, and the older one looked like fate had shoved a ramrod up her rear. It would be nice to receive a little appreciation for her kindness, but she didn't expect it. That was good, since Molly's sullen expression did not indicate any on the way.

The odd thing was, they seemed to have a fine father. What would cause the older one to have such problems? It was certain she had started the fire earlier in the week. What had caused the man to have a hundred spider bites while asleep in his own bed? No one could be that unlucky. She didn't buy the story that the smoke from the earlier fire drove creatures out of the walls and caused it. To her knowledge, nothing like this had ever happened before. Either there was a curse on the man, or someone actually wanted to kill him. No one could be in and out of the emergency room as often as he was without some reason. It just didn't make sense.

She had to admit that for all his sternness, J.D. was a very attractive man; tall, dark, and serious. She'd always liked men like that. Something was wrong, but he seemed to work very hard raising his two little girls. He took them to church and kept them neat and clean. He kept a spotless house, they were well fed, and he attended every parent-teacher conference. She did her homework. No one thought that he neglected them.

The oldest really had problems, but she remembered his young wife.

Eliza was wild, and from a family known for its emotional excess. No one ever understood why someone like him would take up with a janitor's daughter. The Shanty Irish were meant to be avoided, not married. Although the oldest looked like him, it was obvious she'd inherited her mother's mental instability. Now, the younger one? She was a sweet kid, and she adored her daddy. Everyone could see that. She hung all over him. Her dad? He would make someone a fine husband when he actually got over the loss of his wife. In spite of her instability, he seemed to have adored her.

With a sigh, she looked at Molly, perched nervously on the edge of her seat, a deep frown on her tight little face. That one was going to be trouble. After years of experience, she could tell when she was going to regret a good deed. If it weren't for the little one, she would already be headed to the County Shelter, which was inadequate even for the stray dogs that inhabited the south end of it. Children had been an afterthought there.

How long would it be before she had any children of her own? She wasn't even sure she wanted any, after taking in the county strays for so many years. Still, it would be nice to have a home with someone of a like mind; someone serious and God-fearing, a good man. How many years could she dream without finding anyone suitable? Quite a few, it appeared. Where was she when a man like J.D. was hunting a wife? What a shame they always seemed to be attracted to trashy good looks rather than to intelligence and breeding. What a shame.

A wife was not at all what Charlie Callahan had in mind, as he and Verbena made up for every chaste moment either of them had ever spent. From their first date, they'd made the best use of her efficiency apartment on the south side of the Christian city of Sicily, Alabama. He'd never thought it possible to be so horny, but this woman inspired wicked thoughts, that as a man of God, he'd pushed aside on a continual basis. She'd had him up and down, on every soft place in the apartment, and finally they'd done it on the kitchen table, where even his freezing rear, pressed close against the table's hard pink, plastic surface, didn't inhibit his performance one little bit.

Not to mention she did things he'd only seen done in magazines, during moments of awful impurity. Damn! His conscience bothered him briefly, but he knew he never was the man he should have been. His body seemed to have a mind of its own; a result of suppressing his desires since he'd lost his one truelove, he guessed.

Verbena amazed him. They could go at it for hours, it seemed, stopping only when they were too sore to do anything but grin at each other with that shit-eating, lopsided grin that meant only one thing; that the sex was good. What more is there to life than that? So she wasn't wife material. How could he take a wife anyway, when he used a phony name? She was well worth a dozen roses, a movie and Chinese takeout each visit. Oh yes! No matter what atonement he might have to do later, this was good! When he called out God's name now, he was in true ecstasy. No matter that he would probably burn in Hell. That was then, this was now.

He found himself making a thousand excuses rather than bringing her home to his apartment, though. He developed a real fondness for his best friend, the head, and he couldn't figure out how to explain the grisly keepsake. Finally, he told her that he was still living in his car, and showering at the YMCA. She accepted this explanation, and for some reason he couldn't figure out, didn't invite him to move in with her. Why? He didn't really care. Just so long as she didn't cut him off, he was fine with it. In fact, she didn't even ask him to save his money and stop bringing the roses. Women were funny sometimes, he guessed. As long as his trusty credit card held out, he could shower her with roses.

Smiling, Mrs. Nathan St. Claire continued packing her suitcase. Enough time had passed. It was time to remind Nathan of his husbandly duties. Safe in her industrial-sized purse, she carried the address of one Nathan St. Claire, living in Sicily, Alabama. Acting Sheriff Bobby Cox had called her earlier this afternoon, to discuss a strange letter he'd received from her erring husband. If she didn't do something soon, it appeared that Nate would remain in Sicily, maybe forever.

He'd asked Bob Cox to recommend him for a law enforcement position in the local county sheriff's office, reminding him of their long relationship, a friendship of many years, and begging him not to notify his wife. He couldn't come home, he told Bobby, because he was "in love." How dare he think he could be "in love," while married to her and using her charge account? She would see about that!

Was she sure it was him? Of course it was! He'd always been a fool. Bobby was worried because it was a typed message, and Nate never, to Bobby's knowledge, used a typewriter, but she knew why. Of course, he wasn't going to send anything in his own handwriting that could be traced to him. She'd finally managed to have a funeral for him, and the life insurance company was thinking of settling. He wouldn't jeopardize that, and he would have to be aware of it. It was in all the news reports.

How on earth did he think Bobby would go along with that? Bobby was the most honest young man she'd ever known! Only the fact that she had assured Bobby that she had Nate's address and was going to run up to Sicily and talk some sense into him, kept the young man from reporting him to the insurance company as a fraud. Damn it! It meant she would have to withdraw her claim, but she just wanted the old rascal back. It was lonesome without him. Boy, would he be surprised to see her! With a little smile, she decided to include that black negligee she'd bought on her last visit to New Orleans. Maybe next trip, she would even take him with her. It would do the old stuffed shirt some good, especially if he'd acquired a taste for young women. She could put out pretty good, when inspired.

J.D. slept peacefully at last, in his hospital cot. No one bothered him. No one checked to see if the machines were all doing their proper duty. No one changed his sheets, gave him medicine, took his vital signs, or added to his chart. He was the most solitary man in the hospital. Once you were dead in Beaufort Falls, they were willing to leave you alone. It seemed to suit him just fine.

Chapter Eleven

Suffer The Children

Molly wiped a tear away from her nose. No one would ever see her cry, especially not here. The bossy old lady had brought her here the first thing this morning, and all of the questions made her head ache. She was relieved when the woman questioning her handed her a piece of white paper and asked her to draw her family. She needed to be very careful. The questions were all so strange.

Did she wet her bed? Did she have thoughts that someone was telling her what to do? What did she dream? Did she like her father? Did she like her mother? Was her little sister bratty? What was her favorite color? Was she worried about her father?

She hesitated, and gave each one a great deal of thought.

"No, I don't wet my bed." She grinned weakly at the therapist, hired by the Beaufort Falls Department of Family and Children's Services to assess her mental condition.

"Of course, Father tells me what to do. That's his job, just as his Father in Heaven instructs him."

Highly intelligent, the worker notated on her form. *Exceptional use of adult language inappropriate for her age. Sounds like a little old lady.*

Carrie considered the child's choice of words as Molly continued. Mental status exams on a child younger than twelve were almost always a waste of time. The drawing and your gut feeling about the child were much more useful.

"I can't remember my dreams." That was the truth. Molly winced as she tried to remember the last convoluted progression of wild images and scary noises that woke her, only to watch a very real line of little spiders march through the house. She opened the front door for them and they all left, one by one, like tiny soldiers.

Visible agitation when discussing her dreams.

"Of course, I like my father. He is my father. My mother is dead. I liked her, too, when she was alive. Tessie is a very good girl."

Extremely flat affect when discussing her family. Investigate further.

"My favorite color is red."

Ahhh, now we're getting somewhere. Red. A fire-setter. Someone has seriously harmed this child. Red. She accented the word red with her yellow highlighter. Time to ask her a serious question.

Was she worried about her father? How could she answer that? The feelings that engulfed her were much stronger than worry. *What would happen to them if he died? What would happen to them if he lived?* Even more frightening were the waves of relief and anger that followed the cold fear.

If Father dies, can we go live with Verbena? Did she say that? Out loud? Her eyes got wide. Somehow, she knew that wasn't what she should say. She turned away from Carrie and tried to get her feelings under control before answering again. Carrie just sat there, no reaction. She must not have said it. *Good.*

"Father is very strong in the Lord. God will take care of him. If it's his time to go, he'll go to Heaven and live with God. Ma'am, do you know where Tessie and I'll go? Can we go live with grandma?"

She knew they sent kids to go live with relatives, just so long as they went somewhere good. Carrie didn't answer. The child was centered in reality. While someone had certainly trained her in religious responses, her worry was realistic.

Realistic anxiety, but lack of expression of concern for father. Investigate further. Unusual religious ideation.

Molly began her picture by drawing a box in the middle of the page. This would keep her within the lines. First she drew her father. He was very tall, and had a smile on his face. His hands were big, as were his feet. He was very thin, but not a stick figure. She dressed him in his Sunday best, but forgot his socks. His ankles went straight into his shoes.

Oops. Quickly, she added socks. Without success, she tried to erase the lines his ankles made through the socks. Well, he would just have black socks. That would work. His socks were black. She carefully centered the word "Father" under his feet.

She measured half of the space to the end. Now she would draw Tessie. Tessie had a big smile, and lots of curls. She had one long arm that reached toward Father. Why was that arm so long? Well, it was too late to change it. She was little, no higher than halfway to her father's knee. Smiling, Molly took the yellow crayon and spent time coloring in a head full of curls, adding big blue eyes with long eyelashes. She created a pale blue party dress for Tessie; she liked for her to be happy. With a final look of satisfaction, she drew pretty, shiny, black-patent-leather shoes onto her sister's feet. Now it was time for her to draw herself.

This was hard. What did she look like? She was dark and ugly, not at all like Tessie. She tried to visualize herself.

Finally, she drew a figure only slightly taller than Tessie, and gave it very straight brown hair. It was a stick figure and had a pointed nose and two brown spots for eyes. It stood very straight, stick figure straight, and one stick arm was hidden behind pretty Tessie. She placed a proper smile, a perfect half crescent, in its proper place, on its circle face. What color should her dress be? Carefully, she gave the figure a two-triangle red dress. That was fine, and at the end of her stick legs, she placed big, ugly, brown, shoes.

Now there was one more figure to draw. She began her masterpiece, a beautiful blonde angel with wings around Tessie and her. Its long blonde hair flowed all the way off of the border of the drawing. It was wearing green—a green robe—pretty and shiny, and silky. She labeled the angel "Mommy," and made her huge. The majestic figure took up the entire drawing, making even Father seem small. Two little wet spots appeared on the drawing, small flaws. Maybe they wouldn't be noticed, Molly hoped.

Carrie tried not to let her expression change when she looked at Molly's pictogram. In her thirteen years of assessing children, she'd never seen a picture like that. The angel put its wings around the children, but the face looming masterfully over the representation of the father was far from friendly. She'd never seen a child that age so able to portray emotion in a face. Its features were consumed with rage. Something exceptionally strange was going on in this family; something she'd never seen before. Frowning, she reached for her copy of DSM I, the diagnostic tool used to put a name to her misgivings. There. That was close. She penned a diagnosis into its proper space on her form.

"299.9x   Childhood   Onset   Pervasive
Developmental Disorder–Schizotypical"
Recommended Treatment:

Remit to West Alabama Regional Children's Psychiatric Hospital for 72-hour evaluation. Very disturbed child. Notify me of findings immediately upon further assessment. –Carrie Densley, MSW.

Chapter Twelve

The Halls Of Hell

*P*lease help me, Mommy. I'm so afraid. I'm all alone. I have no one. Please help me, Mommy. I tried to be good. I don't know what I did wrong. Please help me. The little girl was rolled into a tight little ball on the cot under the dim fluorescent lights that never went out. Around her, fourteen other little girls of different ages slept fitfully. The smell of antiseptic burned Molly's nose and did nothing to cover the odor of the other children. She was used to the sweet smell of the flowers from the meadow near her home, and the clean fragrance of Lemon Pledge. Some of these kids wet their beds, or worse, and having to breathe the stuffy fumes was making her ill. Most of all, she worried about Tessie.

The woman who asked her the questions looked at her picture and then told her that they had decided that she needed to go to a hospital for a little while. It was not a hospital where people were sick, but one where there were children who were sad or confused, and they would help her figure out some of the things that bothered her. They would take care of her. She didn't need to be frightened, and everyone was going to be good to her. No one would hurt her. She couldn't believe what she'd heard. She wasn't sick.

"Is Tessie coming with me? "

"No. She'll stay with Miss Johnson. She'll be fine."

Molly backed away from Carrie and eased over to the one-way window. Through its smoky glass she could see Tessie playing with Miss Johnson, the old lady who had brought them to the clinic. Tessie was laughing and making a house out of Lincoln Logs. The woman smiled and laughed with her, both of them seated on the floor, with Tessie's curly head next to her dark one. The bottom sill of the window struck just lower than her chin. Reaching, she pressed herself into the wall, scratching at the ledge with little fingers, trying to press her face into the glass. She heard an awful sound, like that of a wounded animal, and realized it came from her own throat. She never saw Carrie moving toward her. The blackness overwhelmed her before the counselor had time to react.

The ward orderly at West Alabama Regional Children's Psychiatric Hospital stopped to pull the covers around the little one. They always threw their covers off and then rolled up in that fetal position as if they could not get warm. *What was this one's name? Molly. That was right. Molly.* He'd tried to talk to her when she was delivered to his unit, but she wouldn't speak. She stared ahead, as if he didn't exist. Sometimes they did that. He didn't take it personally. They were scared, or hurt, or just crazy.

Children could be crazy, just like adults. He saw that craziness often, thinking of the girl who drew pictures on the wall with her own shit. Whenever he lost track of that kid, he found himself busy with a bucket and a sponge again.

Some people didn't think children could be nuts because they weren't completely formed, but he knew differently. This one? She was a cute little thing, and would be right pretty if she smiled. No chance of that anytime soon, from what he could tell.

The note on her chart told him to watch her for "suicidal tendencies." According to the story he'd just heard, she'd thrown herself at a window at the Outpatient Clinic while undergoing the Mental Heath Exam, and somehow she had cracked a sheet of inch-thick, impact-resistant glass. *How could that be possible? She was such a little thing, not more than about eight years old. It must'a already had a crack in it.* When they ran to help her, she resisted, began kicking and fighting, and then started screaming in some sort of strange language that no one understood. By the time they found the juvenile straight jacket, she'd passed out.

Moving along the narrow passages between the beds, he stopped at the new girl's cot. Curious, he examined her sweet little face. *Well, she ain't no trouble now. They don't mean no harm. They's just kids.* He finished his sweeping and moved on to the next ward.

As his steps faded into the distance, the occurrence began. At first it was just a breath of cold air, emerging from a dusty corner; then it strengthened into a gust, a sharp breeze, and finally into a raging whirlwind. Children woke, rubbed sleepy eyes, and threw little bare feet over the sides of the cots. They shrieked with terror as the wind picked up blankets, books and shoes, and slammed them into walls, pushing the beds into each other. A loud wail began, and soon it became a chilling, nonmusical, auditory assault that forced the children to press their hands tightly over their ears as they shivered and cried in fear; every child except one. Molly slept peacefully at last.

Irritated, Charlie pulled the pillow over his ears. If that fat woman didn't stop pounding on his door and leave, he didn't know what he would do. He had opened the door a little while ago, and told her that her that no Nathan St. Claire lived at this address, but she waved a copy of his lease in his face and demanded to be allowed to come inside. He'd slammed the door, but she wouldn't leave. Now, his neighbors were opening their doors and starting to look. Soon someone would be certain to call the police. Just what he needed, a policeman. Any kind of a recorded fuss right now would end any chance of being hired in the sheriff's department. This was a small community, and any disturbance would be noticed. Damn it. The fucking bitch was loud! With a sigh, he climbed back out of bed, put his pants back on, and went to the door.

"Go away. You have the wrong address."

"Open this door! You're hiding my husband. I know he's in there. I've got copies of his credit card charges and they list this address."

"Oh shit," he mumbled softly as he assessed his options. Not good. This woman couldn't tell anyone about the charges. "Who are you?" he asked, the chain door guard still fastened, and only his nose was visible to Mrs. St. Claire.

"I'm Arlene St. Claire, Nate's wife. I have to talk to him. I'm not leaving until I do."

It was obvious that the mountain of flesh in front of him didn't intend to move in any direction but forward, into his home. Reluctantly, he opened the door, and pretending indifference, he invited her in

"Ma'am, I have no idea who Nate is, but, if you want, you can come inside and look." Mrs. St. Claire stormed into the apartment, examining every object within eyesight for any sign of her departed spouse. After a brief hesitation, she followed Charlie into the kitchen, where he offered her a chair, and moved over to the counter to begin a pot of coffee.

"It's obvious that you and Nathan are roommates," Arlene began, still scanning the scenery for anything that might belong to her husband. Her confidence was only a little shaken by the lack of any evidence that another person lived with Charlie. She saw nothing that might be Nate's.

"I have to get a message to him," she continued. "He has to know that even though he's behaved horribly, I'm willing to forgive him and take him back, provided he returns soon. Otherwise, I'll be forced to remove him from my credit account and to report his theft of my money to the proper authorities."

Charlie handed her a cup of coffee. How could anyone live with this monstrous woman? Poor Nate. He felt a wave of sympathy for his friend, which was how he regarded the sheriff now, his friend–the Head. He confided in him, told him all of his secrets, his plans, and his hopes for the future. What was wrong with this woman? He was lucky that she didn't know the sheriff was dead. It was good that the body had never been found. Curious, but cautiously, he asked her,

"I've got no idea what you are talking about. I've never seen nor heard of anyone named Nathan anything, but I want to help you if I can. What puts you on my doorstep?"

Suddenly, Arlene couldn't find words. She'd never expected this to be so difficult. There really wasn't any sign of Nathan anywhere. What if the credit company had made a mistake and gotten the address wrong? What if he wasn't here after all? She had to find some sign that she was right.

"Pardon me, but I really need to use your restroom. May I, please?" She looked at Charlie anxiously. Shrugging, he pointed her toward his bedroom. The only bathroom in the small apartment connected to it, and the closest entrance from the kitchen led through there. He turned his back discretely as the large woman disappeared through the doorway.

What am I going to do? And what on earth am I going to feed her? he wondered, as he opened the refrigerator, looking for something to serve as a snack. He felt sure someone that size would be calmed by food. She had to leave convinced that he knew nothing about the sheriff, or anything else having to do with Beaufort Falls. He had to be sure he kept her there until she no longer associated him, or his address, with her husband.

He'd eliminated toast and stale pop tarts as possible edibles when he heard a scream, immediately followed by a soft thud. Rounding the corner that placed the closet out of his eyesight, his eyes scanned an unthinkable scene. Arlene had found her spouse, but only Nate was grinning. Arlene had fainted from the shock of seeing her husband's bodiless head leering down at her from the top closet shelf, and no explanation was going to remove the look of horror from her unconscious face.

"God help me, I'm fucked," Charlie moaned.

Resigned to the inevitability of fate, the reluctant killer reached for his kitchen knife. Only one action would protect his future, and it was somehow fitting that Arlene would join her husband. Everyone needed company. Let those be joined in death whom life had torn asunder, but what a mess this was going to be. Sighing, Charlie began examining alternatives for the disposal of her body.

At half-past twelve, a burly male nurse quietly entered Room 327 of the Beaufort Falls Medical Center. J.D. was asleep, his sharp face a picture of relaxed innocence in the half-light of the night hospital. Gently, with almost a caress, the attendant eased one hand beneath J.D.'s neck, sliding the other under on the opposite side, preparing to squeeze tightly. J.D. began to groan, then to thrash, flailing his arms at this attacker. The "supposed" hospital employee heard footsteps right outside the room.

"Everything all right in there?"

He froze, his hands still tightly fastened around J.D.'s neck. When there was no answer, the steps moved away. *Damn. I have to be quieter!* With a deep growl, the assassin looked to see what he could use to finish the job. He couldn't find a syringe, or any medicines. *What sort of hospital was this?* The only piece of equipment left in the room was a set of defibrillator paddles, forgotten after the last resuscitation attempt that was made on J.D. before his miracle resurrection.

Frowning, he turned the knob to its maximum setting and gently eased the paddles under J.D.'s loose hospital gown, placing them directly over his heart. *Good.* They were still plugged in. *Perfect.* He turned the switch and moved back, as J.D.'s sleeping body arced and stiffened, lifting him almost entirely off the bed.

"Code Blue! Get someone in here!" he shouted; hiding his face as he hurried away before anyone who might recognize him later could see him. Almost reluctantly, hospital personnel began to move toward the room. Keeping J.D. alive had become a real burden. What was wrong with that man that he couldn't just stay dead like anyone else? Rumor was that he was suing the hospital and could cost some of them their jobs.

"If that man lunges at me I'll put a pillow over his head!" the closest nurse's aide muttered, as she hurried to the room. Word had already gotten around that J.D. wasn't the least bit normal. Some patients just had no manners at all.

Stirring slightly in her sleep, Molly smiled, enjoying her beautiful dream. She was curled up in Mommy's lap with her arms around her. She felt warm and happy and Mommy brushed her hair. She felt the brushstrokes as they tickled her aching head, lovingly. "Mommy," she mumbled sleepily, "when are you coming home? I miss you." Her headache melted away at the loving touch.

Hours ago, the staff had replaced the fluorescent bulb and had finally managed to calm the little girls and get them all back to sleep. Molly never woke during the commotion or the cleanup, but remained in the fetal position, curled up in her cot the entire time, oblivious to all of the activity going on around her. Now all was quiet and peaceful and the attendant played solitaire in the far corner of the ward, never seeing the shadowy figure leaning over Molly, gently stroking her dark hair.

My little darling girl, I wish I could come home. You're so sweet and so brave. You must stay brave. I'll take care of you. I'm never far away. A few feet from them, a pair of bright eyes opened a few inches, and then a small head lifted off its pillow.

"An angel! The new girl's got an angel!"

The wide-eyed child didn't move for fear the shining, yellow-headed woman beside Molly's bed would disappear. The woman couldn't be real. The child could see the other side of the room through her shadowy body. Waves of light reflected from the apparition, shimmering light like little rainbows, spilling waves of pretty stars into every corner of the dismal ward. Gold and silver, and purple, and pink– dancing and sparkling, and bright!

The waif wanted someone else to wake up and see it, but if she moved, it might disappear. The sparkly stuff made her feel good, happy, warm and safe. The little girl smiled and wiggled a little closer to Molly's cot, hoping the angel would come her way, too. It felt good. She wished all of her dreams were like this one. It had been a very long time since she had felt this good. She coasted back to sleep, smiling, and eventually Eliza disappeared.

Chapter Thirteen

Valentine's Day

Grimacing, J.D. set the bouquet of roses carefully on the back seat of the car.

"Father, are we going to get Molly?" Tessie spoke quietly, not wanting to bother him. Since returning from the hospital and picking her up from Miss Johnson's house, he'd seemed distracted, only remembering her when she spoke directly to him.

"The virtuous child is seen and not heard," he instructed her. Coldly, he turned away and started the Caddie, eyes on the road, and Tessie ceased to exist in his frame of reference. The little girl squirmed in her seat, then turned to sit primly forward, her short legs sticking straight out, too short to bend over the front. She pulled the ruffles of the party dress out around her, fondling each stiff layer of lace carefully so as not to wrinkle a single tier.

"Damn Verbena." Face frozen in a scowl, J.D. pondered the idiocy that would cause a grown woman to buy a child a dress like that. Anna had called thirty minutes ago to remind him of the two-to six-year-old children's Valentine Day party, and after examining the clothes in the girl's large, almost-empty, closet, this was the only thing he could find that was even remotely appropriate. It was so important to appear appropriate right now. With Molly in the state psychiatric facility, and every move he made examined by nosy old women, he had to behave perfectly. Leave it to Verbena to buy something for Tessie so gaudy that he was ashamed to be seen with her while she was wearing it. It was only by the grace of God that it still fit her. While it was a little short, it still managed to cover her little rear end, which was going to suffer his handprints if she didn't act like a lady during this ordeal. He felt a glow of satisfaction as he thought of the flowers he had just purchased for the woman who had cared for Tessie this last month, while he had been hospitalized after his most recent "accident." A bouquet should win him some points with her. All women liked flowers.

That Miss Johnson is actually an attractive woman, well brought up and highly educated, the sort of person I should have married to raise my children and keep my house running smoothly, J.D. mused. Picturing her discreetly dressed trim figure and well-shaped ankles, he enjoyed a brief flash of prurient interest. Her hips held the allure of a woman who possibly had never bestowed her favors upon a man, a deeply passionate well of sensual delight, just waiting for a righteous husband to show her the ways to best please him. He pictured her standing in front of the little house on Sycamore Street, one hand on those marvelous hips and a wooden spoon in the other, overseeing the girls while they cleaned the front yard.

His pleasant daydream was rudely interrupted as he pulled up in front of the Family and Children's Services office, only to find every parking place taken and a gaggle of poorly dressed, downright ragged, women and their associated waifs gathered in front. He was the only man there, and it looked like it would be a long afternoon. Very correct in his impeccably pressed black suit, he picked up the flowers in one hand and took Tessie's with the other. She was busy brushing the folds of that silly red velvet dress with her other hand. He gave her arm a yank and pressed his fingernails into the soft little palm. *She'd better behave perfectly!* After tripping during the drop to the ground from inside the car, she followed him tentatively.

Reaching the door, he moved to the back to allow several thousand pounds of woman-flesh to press ahead. No sense in losing dignity by entering with that motley crowd. He and Tessie waited until they could enter alone. More than one set of heavily mascara-laden lashes batted his way before the coast was clear.

Anna saw them the moment they walked into the Recreation Hall. She'd remember this moment for the rest of her life. The tall stern man holding flowers, and the beautiful little girl, her blonde curls spilling over the white lace collar of the red velvet dress, poised at the edge of the crowd looking in but not a part of the scene happening around them. They were searching, searching for something–someone–not yet found. Suddenly, Tessie saw Anna and she looked up at her father, begging for his attention.

"Miss Johnson," she told him. "Miss Johnson is here!" She was positively shining with excitement and happiness.

"Quiet," he told her. The child composed herself quickly, patting her dress to be certain it was straight. This was his moment. Taking care not to outpace Tessie's little legs, he moved toward Anna, brought the bouquet of fragrant red roses forward, and presented them to her with a gesture worthy of a medieval knight.

"I never got the chance to thank you for taking care of Tessie for me. She seems to be very fond of you, and, as you know, my life has been somewhat disrupted lately." Tessie stood stiffly, as she had been taught, with her hands clasped tightly behind her back.

Look at me, she screamed silently. She hoped Miss Johnson would think that she was pretty, but she knew better than to voice her hope out loud.

Her goddess never looked her direction. Anna took J.D.'s outstretched arm and the two of them moved toward the large table of refreshments, loaded with paper valentines and silly cupids, none of them as pretty as the little lace and velvet angel standing alone. Suddenly, remembering her, J.D. turned.

"Tessie, go play with the other children; and make sure that you don't get into any trouble now. I will see to you later."

"She is such a sweet little girl. She was no trouble at all." Anna couldn't believe how handsome J.D. looked in his formal black suit, blue tie correctly knotted, his immaculately polished black dress shoes completing the image of a successful businessman.

Tessie stood motionless, dejected, as they walked away from her. After a minute, she moved to the side of the room and carefully settled into a large frame chair to wait. She was wearing the prettiest dress she had ever owned, and it seemed easiest just to stay put. It would be awful to get anything on it.

West Alabama Regional Children's Psychiatric Hospital also had a party. Molly stood by the table in the cafeteria, licking the pale pink icing off of a large, heart-shaped, cookie, first the left side of the heart, then the right, finally disposing of the hard pointed end in one decisive bite. Intent on her task, she didn't see the little boy behind her until she felt a tug on the back of her tee shirt. Turning, she found herself face to face with an elf. At least, that was her first impression. The kid had flaming red hair, freckles and pointed ears.

"Who are you?" she asked him, scowling. He said nothing, just grinned at her, an ear-to-ear pumpkin grin.

"Who are you?" she asked again, reaching toward him to return the tug. Faster than anyone she'd ever seen, he moved away from her, then stopped. She examined him carefully. He was her height, but painfully thin, wearing a green flannel pajama top and ragged overalls that swallowed his bony frame. He motioned for her to follow.

"Don't you talk at all?" she questioned.

Standing very still, he grinned even wider, smiling with green eyes like huge emeralds. Without thinking about it, she grinned back. He glided quietly toward the large kitchen attached to the dining hall and she followed. Ten minutes later, the two of them sat on a box of lettuce inside of the industrial-sized refrigerator, stuffing themselves with all of the chocolate pudding two little imps could enjoy. He noticed she was shivering. Carefully, he returned the pudding container to its exact place on the shelf, opened the big walk-in from its inside handle, and led the way back to the party.

Molly noticed that with all of the excitement and all of the children present, no one had missed them. The only trace of her adventure was a chocolate smudge on the corner of her mouth. Turning around to thank her benefactor, she found that he had vanished.

This isn't such a terrible place, she reflected, smiling. She had a friend, someone she liked very much. Later, her dreams were full of fun and laughter and mischief, all in the company of a small, funny looking, redheaded boy.

Late that night, Arlene St. Claire got her fondest wish as Charlie Callahan reunited the two old sweethearts, finding a place on his closet shelf where they could sit facing each other. She was much more attractive than her husband, having benefited by Charlie's recent education in taxidermy, provided by the city library system. The rest of her resided regally in the brand-new freezer, purchased only that week from Sears, who rushed it to him when he told them he had returned from a hunting trip and meat was spoiling even as they spoke. Sears prided itself on its quick response to customer needs and delivered it that very day. Looking at his darling heads from the comfort of his bed, he felt smugly satisfied with his work. Thanks to Verbena's prattling, he'd selected just the right hairstyle and makeup for Nate's "lady," and she looked quite grand.

"And I bet you just love the way she holds her tongue now, right, Old Man?" he quizzed the dead sheriff's head, playfully. He thought the blonde hair was a nice touch. Arlene was no longer gray. The saleswoman at the Be-Lite Drugs had been glad to help him select a hair color for his "girlfriend." "Drop Dead Bombshell Blonde" was a nice touch, he thought. It was a total improvement from the tired old bag who had almost broken down his door a few days ago.

Verbena had helped out too, far more than she ever would realize. They'd eaten dinner at her apartment, celebrating Valentine's Day with a minimum of sentiment and a maximum of good basic sex. Verbena wore a lacy red teddy with matching thong panties, and alluring lip-gloss that tasted just like chocolate-covered cherries. After an inspired thirty minutes of frenzied activity in every position either of them had ever imagined, Charlie popped his head up from his love goddess's nether regions and asked, "Where do you buy makeup?"

With tremendous difficulty, Verbena shifted gears, moving from fantasies of shiny blue-black Nubian slaves tenderly licking her vaginal folds, to a visual of her corner drug store.

"The drug store. Why?" she asked.

"Uh…no good reason. I'm just interested in things you like," he back-pedaled desperately.

She turned over and sat up. Curling her arms around her legs, she began silently compiling a list of cosmetics she could request. Naked as the day he was born, but considerably more impressive, Charlie jumped up and found a pencil and paper in the desk drawer next to her bed.

Verbena was now thinking Marshall Fields, but Charlie was more interested in product than brand names. Foundation, mascara, eyeliner, lipstick, blush…shit! This was complicated! Still, he knew something must be done to keep Arlene from turning the same dark color as her husband's face, and he would have to be the one to do it. No way he could ask Verbena to do this for him.

"Be sure it is all hypo-allergenic," she added helpfully. This was going to be her best Valentine's Day ever! When he left an hour later, clutching his list, she was positively giddy with anticipation. Presents! So they would be late. No one else ever bothered to shower her with gifts, much less things she really liked! Charlie was really a good sort.

Somewhere in the back of his thought processes, Charlie realized that Verbena expected these products to be given to her. He supposed if he only used a little, he could tighten the caps carefully and she would never know a dead woman used them first. He would only have to apply it once to Arlene, he guessed.

Several hours later, he was ready to reunite the happy couple.

"You like her, Old Man?" he asked. "I'll bet you do. I'll sleep now, and let the two of you catch up on old news in peace."

Giggling oddly, he turned out his bedroom light and settled into bed, relaxing as he snuggled into the contours of the old mattress. *"Good night, Sweet Lovers,"* strains of an old love song, wafted through his drowsy mind as he drifted into a deep and dreamless sleep.

There was a brief stir of air as a pale form materialized near his closet. He wasn't the only one viewing his handiwork, and he would have been horrified had he known this particular presence could return from his almost-forgotten past. Eliza didn't forget. Life isn't over for the living or the dead until all of the markers are called in. He owed her. Even more than John Duke, he was a force of destruction during her short time on earth.

She remembered how frightened she was when the man of God first put his arms around her, how revolted and repulsed. "Such a Godly young woman, " he told everyone in their small community, including her drunken mother, who willingly volunteered her child's services to help the preacher clean his filthy hovel of a house, and Eliza obeyed Charlie. One doesn't question an agent of God when one is only thirteen. "God chose you for me," he told her, and she believed him.

He clutched his bottle of whiskey in one hand and forced her thighs apart with the other. She didn't run. Where would she hide? Shrieking silently, she did whatever he wanted. She couldn't escape the pathological fascination she felt for him.

Later, she came to love him in the way that you love the first man who makes you feel desirable and needed. He never hurt her on purpose, and much later she realized that he felt great shame at having taken her childhood from her.

Even after she ended her affair with him, and it did become an affair after she grew old enough to choose, and after she married J.D., Charlie was still the only man she ever really loved and who loved her back. Funny how J.D. thought he was the first to have her. He was two years too late to be first.

When the tables turned, she had come to see Charlie for what he was, a tremendously flawed loser. He was a loser who loved her, though, and he never forgave himself for the ways he'd mistreated her, and failed her. She turned to him when J.D. hurt her, and met him whenever she could. A man who had stepped in and out of her life at his own convenience, he was never there when she needed him. He was a very remorseful man, one who cried buckets when he learned of her death but whose failure to believe in a future for the two of them caused it.

Charlie, you were always so crazy. He stirred slightly, and she reached a small transparent hand toward him to stroke his face, but her hand faded right through his features. *Heads. You collect heads. At least you found something you're good at. You always had the potential for unlimited evil. So strange, I see you perfectly now. And they don't care. They really don't.* She moved to the end of his bed, watching him sleep the rest of the oblivious, while her mind moved with the speed of someone who is no longer limited by time and space.

How lovely it is, when a plan comes together, she mused, and smiling grimly, she faded into the dawn's early shadows, leaving nothing to reveal that she had ever been there at all.

Chapter Fourteen

The Woods Are Lonely, Dark And Deep

The gaunt, white, dog winced as she lifted her hindquarters over the steel edge of the dumpster. She landed inside with a resounding thud, and began nosing through the garbage looking for a scrap of any kind of meat, eggs, or milk. The kitchen site was the best on the hospital grounds, and she knew it, but usually it was tightly closed. Quickly, she hooked a half-eaten piece of ham in her sharp teeth and made the leap over the side, clearing it by inches and picking herself up after landing in the sandy red dust. Scanning all directions first, she loped off into the woods surrounding the facility.

A few yards away, the pup waited. Like its mom, it was dirty white and it looked up at her with the blue eyes specific to its breed; but unlike her, its coat was streaked with sprinkles of gray and black. She passed the meat to it and the baby gnawed at it weakly, barely able to stand on its hunger-weakened little legs. The moon appeared, skirted by wispy cirrus clouds. Shivering, the pup reacted to a gust of cold, wet, wind by ruffling its soft fur. Momma circled it protectively, sheltering it from the chill with her thin body, digging the two of them into a burrow of remaining autumn leaves, no longer golden or muted reds, but dingy brown, dry and brittle, but warm. His belly temporarily full, the little guy whimpered, content, and the bitch licked his face and carefully cleaned his ears. She stopped suddenly, alert to the sound of feet moving toward them.

Molly giggled as RatBoy pantomimed a head-over-heels fall, rolling in the dead leaves along the forest path. Just ahead, the old slave cabin nestled quietly hidden from view; in the same place it had existed one-hundred years ago, when the hospital had been a prosperous plantation, its halls crowded with slaves and "white folks" alike. It was one room with a loft, its logs rusty-brown, the old chimney leaning to one side, covered by birds' nests and spider webs, musty with disuse. Cradled in one arm, Molly carried a bundle of sticks, which had been hidden under her cot for a week in preparation for their visit.

"We'll have a fire tonight." She still talked to her friend, even though he never talked back. "I don't think anyone can see the smoke behind all these trees." Mickey nodded his head and forced open the strong plank door to the cabin for her; then followed her inside as she placed her armload of kindling on the broad brick shelf forming the hearth.

She called him RatBoy and he didn't seem to mind. In fact, she loved the way he wiggled his ears and his nose when she addressed him that way. He had a little dance he did just for her. His arms bent at the elbows and held waist height, his hands cupped, he would hop a few steps while wiggling his ears and nose furiously. She would laugh until she wet her pants. He would grin proudly and take a deep bow. She couldn't remember ever laughing so much.

Even though the boys' and girls' wards were in separate buildings, they shared the classroom buildings, and she saw him frequently as she traveled the halls, changing classes. Unless a child was violent, or openly disruptive, no one kept close watch on any particular kid. The girls in her ward avoided her after the strange events of her first night, so she didn't encounter the usual hazing that most new children endured during their first week.

Except for her daily session with a counselor, a different one almost every day since the mental health interns made their rounds, school was the only demand on her time. Because no one was particularly able to learn, she found the lessons ridiculously easy. She finished her work quickly and never brought homework back to the ward. It was easy to sneak out after "lights out" and meet her friend in their accustomed spot at the back door of the kitchen. No one seemed to realize a child might want to roam the spooky-dark hospital grounds at night. The attendant in the wards never noticed that pillows replaced one of her little charges. Only the old Negro man, who swept and mopped each night under the fluorescent light, knew that she wasn't in her bed, and he didn't seem to care. She had no idea how RatBoy got free, but he was always there, waiting for her.

She was terrified the first time they crept away from the hospital in the dark, but he led the way. He knew everything about the hospital. Although he had a small flashlight, he seldom used it. Never tripping, or stepping in a hole, or making a wrong turn, he quietly and confidently led her into countless secret places, down passageways and into the attic, making footprints in dust that was only disturbed by them. She wondered how much of his life he'd spent at this hospital. Had he ever lived in a house with parents and sisters and brothers? She asked him, but he only looked up at her with those bright green eyes reflecting her question. He either couldn't, or wouldn't, talk. Not now, maybe not ever; but she could say anything to him. He always listened.

The slave cabin was her favorite place. They were not the first people to find refuge within its tarred walls. They'd found a patchwork quilt neatly folded in front of the hearth, and a well-worn Bible placed carefully on an old shelf. Just under the window, Molly had discovered a basket of tiny clothes, painstakingly hand-stitched for a baby, a little nightgown and cute little booties. The two of them played house; she was the mommy and he was the daddy. Laughing, she dressed a doll made of pine branches and paper to be their "baby" and he smoked "rabbit tobacco" from a corncob pipe. She made pretend meals out of poke berries and pebbles, and cooked them in the cold fireplace. Always, before they left, she folded the little clothes carefully and swept the cabin with an old broom that had been thrown away by the hospital cook.

"RatBoy, full of joy,

Eats my cheese

My funny boy..."

Molly sang, as she pulled treats out of her basket. Crackers and sharp cheddar cheese, welfare peanut butter and thick slabs of homemade bread; there was little that couldn't be pilfered from the kitchen walk-in cooler. They made it their first stop before diving out the door behind the kitchen. Her little redheaded procurer of treats reached behind the door for the quilt, shaking it carefully before arranging it in front of the large open cooking area.

"No. Not that close!" Molly pulled it away from the fireplace, but stopped when she saw the hurt look in her friend's eyes. He didn't need to speak. She could feel his thoughts. She said nothing, but instead touched his face with her palm. He pulled away from her and moved solemnly to the little window that faced the only clearing in the stretch of woodland. She moved behind him and put her arm around his skinny shoulders. Together, they looked out at the stars.

"You're my friend. You don't have to ever worry about anything I say. I'll always be your friend unless I tell you different. I love you. Now, let's eat, silly boy." Holding hands, they crossed to the repositioned blanket and finished unloading the basket, hands moving quickly as they stuffed their mouths with stolen goods. Molly laughed and giggled as Mickey clowned, pretending first to be a hunchbacked old man, then fat. He patted his front appreciatively. She could never be quite sure that he actually ate the food; most of it seemed to end up back on her plate, but he loved playing the game.

A pale figure moved in the shadows as Eliza watched her child having fun. When Molly smiled, she echoed her smile, and when Mickey began to dance, she leaned toward the two of them. She was happy that her child had a friend. The odd little boy reminded her of someone, but she couldn't quite decide whom. Puzzled, she shifted her thoughts back to her Molly.

I wish I could touch her. Visions of Molly as a baby, a two-year-old, dark-haired little whirlwind, toddling as fast as she could until she went sailing into the pile of raked leaves, flowed through what had once been her brain. She ached to be able to move from the metaphysical realm into the physical. Every part that was left of the young mother she once was wanted to return and be able to live again. *If I could just be able to be a small part of her life, if I could only...*

Just then she heard an eerie howl, a moaning shriek of such pain it demanded her full attention, instantly. Quick as an impulse, she centered fifteen feet away, to where a ragged female dog frantically nosed a limp little body, trying to revive it, to make it move once more. Finally stopping, it moaned its grief, stopping to return to the little form every few minutes as if it might have returned to life during the moments she was gone. Finally, standing still in the middle of the clearing, the dog looked toward Eliza. She returned its wounded gaze, and their eyes locked.

Erupting twenty feet into the air, the green-clad woman singed trees with the breath of her fury as flashes of memory, scraps of the seconds that she had known her tiny boy, empowered her rage. Inside of the cabin, the two children reached for each other as the sound echoed around them like a clap of thunder, very close. The apparition could feel the hot raw pain engulfing the mother dog, and it was the same as her own; searing her soul once again, just like the night she'd lost one child. A shimmering of sparks surrounded the confused dog, knocking her legs out from under her as if hit by a bolt of lightning.

Two minutes later, she shook herself, stood, stretched, extended her muzzle and inhaled the wet spring air. Turning to the rippling creek, she found a shallow pool of water and gazed at her reflection, leaping into the cold liquid gleefully, splashing, smoothing and cleaning her white fur with her tongue. Finally, with a satisfied sigh, she ambled off toward the woods, leaving the dead pup behind. Her last glance toward the cabin was distinctly human, clear-blue eyes examining her surroundings in a new way.

I'm alive again, and I'm beautiful, Eliza thought as she ambled into the forest.

J.D. sat up with a jerk and touched his forehead. The heat consumed him; his hair, his clothes–they were drenched with cold sweat. What was the dream? Sometimes he remembered it; at other times, he could not. He turned on his side and drifted fitfully back to sleep.

He was in a dark forest and he was afraid–very afraid. It was coming for him. He could hear the rustle of leaves, smell a deep musky fragrance, and he felt an immediate need to empty his bladder and run–run wildly, to climb a tree, dig a hole–anything to be somewhere else.

He squinted. The rustling stopped. Terrified, his eyes darted from side to side. He had to find out where it was. He had to find it. If he didn't, he would die. He moved two steps to his right. He heard a slight noise next to a large, water oak. Staring toward the darkness past the low-hanging branches of the tree, he saw a flash of white. Intensity mounting with each endless second, he searched grimly for the instrument of his death. Then he saw them. Deep, deep-blue eyes, hot with hatred, burning with the fires of Hell, they returned his stare.

Oh, God, don't desert your servant now.

His own scream woke him this time, and he discovered tears running down his cheeks. He didn't sleep again that night.

Mickey scanned the path to his lair furtively. It was a meeting of the high council and they'd all be there. It wouldn't do to be followed. Protection of the Princess would become difficult soon, and the walls of his world would come crashing down. When that happened, he must be prepared for the Time of Death. They all must prepare because it would be soon, and the next stage couldn't start without it. The Life Everafter must come. Half crouching, he pushed the overgrown bush out of the way, exposing the entrance to the cave, so close to the little tributary branch of the Conecuh River that ran behind the hospital that they could wash their feet from the back entrance to the cave.

Inside, he could hear the breathing of the other animals in his pack. As his eyes adjusted to the dim light, he made out the features of the other boys. To his right, Lion warmed his hands with a cigarette lighter, charring blonde hairs on his wrist as he toasted his cold fingers. His shaggy blonde hair needed cutting, but didn't detract from the noble majesty of his aristocratic face and broad shoulders.

Next to him Beaver chattered, hovering near his idol, interrupting his flow of words to gnaw on his beef jerky with his oversized front teeth. His plump middle further illustrated his love of good food, and several items in Mickey's knapsack were particularly for him.

Horse sat in the one chair, a throwaway found near the kitchen dump. The kindergarten-sized furniture teetered unevenly on three of the four legs, threatening collapse under his weight. Every bone in his body extended further than it should. Fifteen years old and six feet tall already, he ran like the wind, but his elbows showed through gaping holes in his sleeves, and his pants were a good two inches too short. Long cheekbones and a high forehead framed alert gray eyes that stared seriously at the entrance to the cave.

Seated cross-legged on the ground, little Fox grinned. Barely the size of a cricket and the youngest one of the ragged group, he drew pictures on the sandy floor.

Clearing his throat importantly, Lion rapped three times on a tall rock with a jawbone, the talisman for their family group. He had found it on the path the day of their first meeting, and it was an omen of events to come.

"I call this meeting to order. Rat, do you have provisions?" Mickey nodded. *It was funny how Molly didn't realize that she sensed his clan name from the clues he gave her. It was just as well. She didn't need to know right now.*

Solemnly, he moved his knapsack from his back and tumbled a dozen cans of food onto the floor, Spaghetti Os, Pork & Beans, Vienna sausages, and several large cans of roast beef stew. Silently, he reached inside and pulled out a package of excellent cheddar cheese and a bag of rolls, which he handed to Lion, who indicated that they should take seats next to Fox on the ground. Horse remained in the chair, but turned to face his leader.

"Let us eat the blood and substance of Rat's kill. May it provide fuel for our bodies and fire for our souls."

"At your service, Great Leader."

Horse and Beaver and Fox mumbled together while Rat watched with rapt attention. Just then, there was a noise at the entrance of the cave. Five sets of eyes turned toward it.

A large white dog filled the small hole, watching them intently. Its light-blue eyes searched each of their faces, and while they sat motionless, transfixed by her strong presence, she padded quietly into the circle and waited to be given a share. After a moment of surprise, Lion shrugged and reached toward her soft white fur.

"Nice Dog." Eliza growled, deep and low, showing sharp canine teeth in a most unfriendly grimace. Lion pulled his hand back quickly. "Rat. Feed our guest."

Mickey divided the cheese and bread in six portions, placing a share in front of each of the boys and one in front of the bristling dog. She quieted, and all of them ate. When finished, she stood, and, like a mythical goddess, she turned and trotted into the darkness. Lion continued the meeting, giving each boy his tasks for the week ahead.

"Beaver, you build. We need another three feet dug to enlarge the provision shelf in the back of the cave. Fox, you see. I want to know everything that happens, and I want a report on that dog before next meeting. Horse, you protect. Go to the library and find out information on martial arts. I expect instruction for us all. Rat, you do well. We need supplies to keep all of us fed for two weeks, and they need to be stored in the new area of the cave as soon as Beaver finishes it. Go brothers, and produce." One by one, they slipped out of the cave.

The river near Beaufort Falls sang in a new way. It trickled over the stones near its banks, gurgling and chuckling, splashing the rocks with renewed vigor, blessed with the energy of the season to come. Shrubs along the banks were covered with buds, eagerly awaiting their yearly renewal. Far, far from Alabama, in the Appalachian Mountains that fed the Chattahoochee River, which, in turn, fed the smaller rivers and streams that found their way to the muddy plains, snow was melting and beginning its journey, and the rains were beginning.

Soon, spring downpours would send the little river laughing and singing, frenzied, tumbling over its banks, into the fields, cleaning, scouring and washing debris from its most hidden recesses. In a dark cave on the side of a cliff the water was rising, working busily at the winter's unwanted accumulation of trash. Each day, Nathan St. Claire's decaying carcass eased a little bit closer to the entrance. It was only a matter of time. No secret is safe forever. The river was restless and judgment day was near.

Chapter Fifteen

Business As Usual

Acting Sheriff of Beaufort County, Bobby Cox, gently stroked one of two sheets of paper facing him on his cluttered desk.

Damn it! I've put this off long enough. Perplexed, he pulled a pencil from the holder on his desk and gave his ear a good scratch. This morning he'd received another call from his friend Joe Henry, and he really didn't know exactly what to tell him. Exhaling deeply, he scanned first one, then the other. One was a standard form from nearby Sicily, requesting a reference for a Nathan St. Claire, who was applying to be a deputy in the Sicily City Police Department. It contained all of the standard questions. How long did Nathan work for Beaufort Falls? What was his last position and salary? Was he on time? What was the official reason for his termination? Would Beaufort Falls rehire him if he became available?

Bobby wasn't sure how to answer these questions. How do you tell an agency that its potential hire used to be the sheriff at his last position and that he left his job and his wife without notice, allegedly for an office floozy, and never returned? But this was an easy problem compared to the other paper on his desk, a letter.

The former sheriff had supposedly sent the letter, but Nate had never typed a thing in his life. Bobby knew that he hated typewriters, calling them "those noisy, new-fangled, expensive, writing things that make your fingers hurt and head ache." The letter rambled for a good page and a half, talking about Sicily, losing weight, feeling better, and being happy. Skimming, Bobby zeroed in on its final paragraph.

"I've found a new love and a new start. I can't face the people in Beaufort County after leaving the way that I did. I'm giving Arlene the house and I'm moving here. Please do all you can to further my application?
Very sincerely,
Nathan St. Claire."

He'd never heard Nate call himself Nathan, either. "Nathan?" He used to laugh at his given name. "Sounds like some sharecropper from South Georgia," he'd always shrug his shoulders and laugh. "My ma didn't do me no favor by giving me my granddaddy's white trash name." Bobby couldn't count the number of times he'd heard Nate say that.

Nothing was right about the letter, but Bobby didn't have the time or the staff to send a man to Sicily to look for the lost sheriff. It would take a body to make him send a man out of town right now. He had a working department of five deputies. Bubba was on his honeymoon right now and Carl had broken a leg in a boating accident last weekend, showing off in front of Sally Sue Lowen. That left three men and him to handle all complaints. Reaching a decision, he reached for the referral form. He didn't owe Nate or Nathan, or whoever this was, a damn thing.

"Honest answers are what they are going to get," he muttered, as he filled out the form.

Last Position: *Sheriff*

Length of service*: 14 years*
Reason for termination: *Left without notice.*
Rehire Status: *Would not rehire.*
Why? *Left without notice.*

Let him put *this* in his pipe and smoke it. His life went to shit when he got stuck as Acting Sheriff. His pay didn't increase, and every time a cat climbed a tree in the county, someone called him at home. Let him suffer, too. Maybe if he didn't get hired he'd come back and finish what he'd started here. Bobby whacked a stamp on the corner of the envelope and shoved it into the mail drop.

Two weeks later, Charlie stared in horror at the polite letter of rejection from the Sicily Police Department. It never occurred to him that they would refuse him a job. Temporary jobs were few and far between right now, and he was overdue on his rent. For some reason, the agency that placed him in temporary positions was handing him more excuses than work. His only consolations were his two friends in the closet and faithful Verbena, and even she was asking to see "his place" lately. Maybe he should change back into Charlie and disappear. No one gave a shit about the fucking Sheriff of Beaufort County here. Time to lose that name.

Groaning, he pushed the refrigerator out of its place, and, feeling underneath, he removed the torn wallet he had taped to its bottom. Driver's license, social security card; Charlie Callahan's old life remained intact and waiting for him. Using lots of duct tape, he placed Nate's identification in the spot and carefully re-taped it. His only hesitation came as he included Arlene's useful credit card.

"Days of living in high cotton are over," he sighed. He would have to give up Verbena, too. He couldn't afford her or the car until he could get new plates for it. He was a fool not to have kept the original ones registered in Charlie's name.

Fortunately, it was parked out of sight in the alley behind the apartment. He would also have to shave his dark beard and his collar-length hair. An hour later, the smooth-cheeked bald man who left his apartment to pick up a paper at the corner looked nothing like the former resident of the apartment. Charlie was back.

Tessie looked toward the woods, longingly. Since they'd sent Molly away, there never seemed to be a break from the chores. She worked all day Saturday if her father was at home. She watered the new plants growing in the garden, washed dishes and floors, and folded laundry. Her sixth birthday came and went. No one noticed. Increasingly, she found herself alone while J.D. worked extra hours or took Anna to social events "not appropriate for a little girl." They never stayed out very late; Anna made sure of that, citing how inappropriate it was to leave a child that age alone, but J.D. answered her concern with a list of tasks for the little girl to complete.

"Idle hands are the devil's toys. As long as she is busy, nothing will happen to her. This is a small town, Anna; she is fine here. Nothing ever happens here." Reluctantly, looking backward toward the woeful little child in the doorway, Anna always followed him without further protest. No one noticed that Tessie's hands no longer looked like the hands of a child. They were chafed and red. Dark circles around her knuckles from pulling weeds matched the new circles under her china-blue eyes.

One night when Anna and J.D. returned from Bingo at the Moose Club, Tessie was asleep on the sofa, curls soft across the cushion, her mouth half open and cheeks rosy, looking just like one of Michelangelo's cherubs. Anna looked from the beautiful child to the spotlessly clean living room and into the sparkling kitchen, where white counters shone hygienically bare.

How does he do this? She wondered. *He works all day. He must come home and clean and care for this little child until the wee hours of the night.* It never occurred to her that it was impossible. He spent the hours he was not at work courting her.

Tessie moved in her sleep, throwing one plump little arm out toward the back of the sofa. Half awake, she opened sleep-glazed eyes and saw Anna. Instinctively, she opened her arms and reached for the spinster social worker, and Anna's heart melted. Gathering the baby into her arms, she felt a rush of maternal concern as the child wrapped herself around her tightly.

"John, you must be sure this child gets to bed on time. It's not good to come home and find her sleeping on the sofa like this. What a sweet little face she has." J.D. returned from his inspection of the kitchen. For once, Tessie had done well. He found a well-swept floor, water in the cistern, and not one smudge on his kitchen counters; everything was just like it should be. He did so like clean kitchen counters. He barely glanced at Tessie, but the glow coming from Anna was hard to miss. He saw that his little waif had captured her heart.

"Oh, Lord, I thank ye for your blessed gifts
To aid a wretch like me.
A tool for your undying grace
I will so strive to be."

His deep, low voice gave the words added impact. Anna turned and smiled at him. Such a good man. So Godly, and so beleaguered at every turn by misfortune and pain.

As he walked Anna home later, he hummed this old hymn and smiled. How easily this educated woman fell prey to his charm. God was on his side, all right. Now if he could just extract righteous justice from the hospital as easily.

On the top floor of the Beaufort Falls Medical Center, in a section marked Non-Medical Services, South Office Annex, A.E. Beaufort, the Hospital Administrator, was discussing his options. After several furtive glances toward the door, he leaned forward and spoke softly to the heavyset man who was wearing a dapper fedora hat.

"You can guarantee the solution to my problem?"

"$1200 in advance, Mr. Beaufort."

"It'll look like an accident?"

"Of course. We do it all the time. You'd be surprised how many people in this part of the country get run over by a tractor."

"You're sure? I mean–he won't end up back here at the hospital? You're sure?"

The would-be henchman smiled wickedly.

"When we get through with him, he…"

A.E. interrupted him. "I don't want any of the details. I mustn't know anything about it. Here." He handed the large man a thick roll of twenty-dollar bills.

"Just do it."

Spike pocketed the bills, grinned at A.E., and left without speaking another word.

What kind of man am I becoming? A.E. moaned, resting his aching head on his desk and covering it with his outstretched arms. *But God help me, if that man ends up in this hospital again, I just might have to kill him myself.* Hopefully, Beaufort Falls Medical Center would never see John Duke Parsons again. It almost felt like community service.

Chapter Sixteen

Encounters

Verbena ducked back behind the wall at the end of the alley. Grimacing, she craned her neck trying to see the face of the bald man leaving the apartment that the rent receipt listed as belonging to her sweetheart. He was about the right height and weight, but nothing else about him was the same. It was pointless. Whoever was striding toward the bus stop moved far too fast for her to see anything but the back of his shiny head. *Could Nathan have a roommate?* The rent receipt she'd sneaked out of his wallet carried only one name, his. *Whoever you are, you'll have to wait for the bus.* Feigning indifference, she moved toward the bus stop.

There were plenty of differences between this man and the man she had dated for the last few months. First of all, the man had no hair. Her sweetie's thick, dark cinnamon-colored hair reached the top of his collar, and she knew he took great pride in it. Her beau always wore a denim jacket, but this man hid his body in a khaki trench coat and carried an old-fashioned umbrella.

The man she knew walked tall; this man slumped and moved furtively. Although he covered the ground quickly, he was hesitant; he looked both ways when he reached the street and her man had exuded confidence. He appeared to be planning to catch a bus, whereas Nate owned and drove his car, which was conspicuously absent from the street in front of the apartment. Most of all, he stopped at the paper stand and bought a paper. The man she knew never read anything. She always ordered for him in restaurants. She wasn't sure he actually knew how to read.

When she reached the bus stop, she pulled her coat up around her face and moved to the side in order to get a good look at the man's features. She stopped, shocked. It looked like Nathan. It really did look like Nathan's face. He scanned his paper and didn't see her yet.

"Nathan?" Her voice echoed the uncertainty that she felt. "Nathan?" She moved closer to the man. He reacted, almost dropping his paper, then turned away as if she'd never spoken. "Nathan?" She reached for the man, grasping his shoulder. He pulled back, putting distance between them.

"Ma'am, you must have me confused with someone else."

What the hell was this? It was Nathan. His voice gave him away. She was sure this was Nathan.

"Nathan? Are you okay? This is Verbena. Verbena! You know me. I'm Verbena."

Something was very wrong. They'd spent hours together, extremely intimate hours. She even knew which side of the bed he liked. It wasn't possible he didn't know her unless something very bad had happened to him. She searched his eyes, looking for some sign of recognition, but they were cold and veiled, the eyes of a snake. Verbena started to shake. This was too much. *How dare he pretend not to know me? How dare he?*

"You're Nathan. What's your game? You know me. Why are you doing this? Why?" Her face was flushed and her eyes sparked flames. Her chin set, she demanded the truth. "Why are you doing this to me?" The man appeared flustered for the first time.

"Ma'am, I don't know who this Nathan is, but he isn't me. I can prove it." Fumbling in his pocket, he pulled out an old wallet and pushed a valid, current driver's license toward her. It was in the name of Charles Carlton Callahan, and it had his picture.

Unmistakably, this was the picture of the man she faced, but the resemblance to her Nathan was amazing. Just then the bus arrived, and Charles Callahan pocketed his wallet and rushed aboard. As it disappeared into the morning traffic, Verbena looked down into the gutter that the man had just crossed. There was a glint of silver, a key. *The key to the apartment that the man, whoever he was, just left?*

Smiling for the first time, she stuck it into her pocket. She didn't dare do it right now, but she would get to the bottom of this mystery if it killed her. If that wasn't her Nathan, then her man was in trouble. If it was, he wasn't going to treat her like that. She would find out the truth.

Shivering, the man sitting in the last seat of the bus displayed none of the certainty he had summoned when confronted. He had just lived his worst nightmare, that he might be seen by Verbena. Hands still shaking, he turned to the want ads. There must be some sort of job he could fill quickly. Rent was due. *Wait, here was something. On the edge of town out by the river, but at this point, distance didn't matter.*

"Ward Security Guard. No experience needed, will train. Contact Personnel at TU-2-4859, or apply in person between the hours of 8 AM and 4 PM, West Alabama Regional Children's Psychiatric Hospital, 1126 Stony Cave Road, Sicily."

He reached for the pull cord and prepared to change buses. The one he needed went to the other side of town.

A pair of bright-green eyes peered through the underbrush. Without speech, Mickey had developed his other talents. Concentrating, he brought each of his brothers into focus. He could always see; he just couldn't speak.

Lion did well this morning, presenting his report with the quiet dignity that made him the leader of their pride. He stood in front of twenty-nine children, all dressed in various stages of cleanliness and order, reflecting the different levels of mental competence of the children in Mrs. Ledbetter's Special Education, Level Six, class. Some fidgeted, others stared straight ahead; only the teacher looked at Li, and she listened attentively. Reaching into his friend's well-organized mind, Mickey smiled as he felt the confidence Li felt as he read his pages.

"And in conclusion, the fall of Rome was unavoidable and predestined, as inevitable as the fall of leaves in the autumn to make way for the new growth and renewal of spring."

Mickey grinned as he watched Lionel react to the strange words he'd added to his dry writing. He loved playing with his powers. He couldn't read or write much, but he could see into minds and he knew what thoughts made the people he monitored happy or sad, or afraid.

"Why, Li, you're a poet!" The teacher reacted warmly. Shaking his shaggy, blonde, head, the usually composed child folded his paper, placed it on Mrs. Ledbetter's desk, and returned to his seat. Shifting his attention, Mickey felt for her reaction. He felt surprise and joy. That was good. She liked it when her students were poetic.

Mickey knew many things about her. He knew that she was lonely since her husband had died a year ago, and he sensed the frustration she felt trying to teach children with so many differing types of mental disturbances. Her job offered her little reward, and she was so easy to please. Basking in her radiating warmth, Mickey moved on.

The desks in Level Three were smaller and closer together, and the students there were much more animated. Miss Bell struggled to handle her active group, and her harassed look indicated that she soon would reach her breaking point. A skinny little girl pulled at her sleeve, blubbering loudly. Kids moved everywhere, pushing and pulling on each other. Loud noises erupted from a corner. An argument progressed to the fighting stage, and Sally Bell stepped on the crying child's foot as she rushed to pull the angry boys apart. Completely discouraged, the ragged little one sat down on the floor and sucked her thumb vigorously. To her right, at the ancient blackboard, another child licked, then carefully chewed and swallowed a piece of chalk.

The books stayed in a stack in the corner, gathering dust. There weren't many, one book for every two students, but it didn't matter. None of the third graders could read. The books were cast off from the public school system, and Miss Bell felt lucky to have them. She couldn't take a chance that anyone would tear or destroy even one, because some classes didn't have any books at all. Such was school in the Alabama State Mental Health System. In the middle of all of the confusion, Fox worked. Freddy sat in a desk much too large for his little frame and scratched numbers on a sheet of paper. Boring. Time to move on.

After a few minutes of mental searching, he located Horse in the institution library. He was the only child in the large room, sunlight coming in a picture window on one side of an old wood table. Shelves held the discarded books of three generations of generous Alabama citizens; books too good to be trash, but not wanted by their original owners. Someone had taken care to make this part of the hospital almost pleasant. In the corner by the window stood a tall rubber tree, and the shelves next to it held issues of *Botany for the Beginner* magazines. Bright travel posters decorated the walls, and a thick green throw rug felt comfy to feet used to wood floors or concrete walkways.

Harry grimaced as he struggled to trace a diagram from a dusty book of ancient martial stances. His large fingers wouldn't respond, and his markings were clumsy and crude, with large smears from frequent erasures. Mickey felt his tension and his frustration and weariness. Carefully, he took Harry's hand in his own and gently guided his lines. Harry didn't react. He felt Mickey often, and he never knew why sometimes he could draw, and other times couldn't. Normal wasn't a functional concept here, and not one little inmate harbored the slightest concept of what posed as reality in the rest of the world. What *was*, was reality. Mickey relaxed as Harry felt pride in his sketch. Time to check on Barnes.

Beaver was in trouble! Good. The chubby legs managed to get him into the closet in time, and the group of five angry Ward-Sixers flew by, looking for their prey in the huge, empty, Recreation Room. He would be fine. He had better sense than to come out anytime soon. Mickey focused on the boy's round little face. His eyes were squeezed tightly shut. It was funny how Barnes thought that if he closed his eyes no one could see him. That was one funny little kid and...

Suddenly he felt the powerful force that began when he first came close to the strange white dog. It pulled him, hurt him, and confused him. His mouth opened slightly, and he felt pain and tears glide down his thin little cheeks.

Ayeeeee.

He saw her a few yards away, also watching from the woods. She was watching his Princess, just as he had been watching his Molly. *What was this feeling?* It filled his head and then his heart; warm, burning, the sweet heat of love, an emotion rare for him. Her gaze locked with his, and he fought its fascination, fought a need to embrace it, to wrap it around him and submit to its blazing radiance. No one saw into his soul--until now. He felt a shudder from the creature, a cool current and a glimmer of surprise as it reacted to him. *What in him triggered this reaction in this powerful creature?* He tried to see into its mind. He couldn't make out coherent thoughts; its feelings were too intense and something about them diffused his natural ability.

It looked away, looking back toward his Molly, who sunned herself in the small clearing. Sorting through the tumultuous emotions left in the wake of contact with the animal sitting quietly on its haunches close by, he focused on one word. *Angel. The dog was an angel. And it loved his Molly, just like he did, and it would protect her.* Trusting his instincts, he crept away, brushing the leaves from his old knapsack reverently like a prayer shawl, full of the holy calmness of a pilgrim leaving a great cathedral. The Time was near.

With a grubby hand, Molly wiped tears off of her cheeks. Struggling with the words, she reread the folded letter taken from its secure place in her pocket.

"I exhort you, my child, to turn away from the ways of iniquity and return to the fold, to the God who has made you and will embrace you as his own, once you repent of your evil sins. He will release the demons that possess you, and you will be a paragon of virtue like your sister, Elizabeth. See how diligently she works in school? If you are good, we will come and visit you, but only if I receive a good report on you from Miss Johnson. "

Underneath, uneven and painfully printed, were Tessie's words.

"Molly. Get well. Please come home. I love you.

"Tessie"

The section of the paper containing these words looked scuffed and smudged. Molly choked back a little sob as she pictured the effort it must've required for her little sister to write those words. Tessie had just started first grade and she knew what a stern taskmaster her father could be and how many times Tessie must've printed the words to have them be that perfect. She would see Tessie again soon! She'd be very careful not to get caught out of the ward at night.

She felt a pang of regret as she thought of the times she and RatBoy had spent at the cabin. If they ever caught her, she'd never be allowed to see Tessie, but she couldn't give it up. She needed her friend, but Tessie needed her. She knew that. Tessie needed her and that was more important. The two of them would have to be very careful and she'd have to be good, pay attention in the school, and find all of the right answers to Ms. Densley's questions during her therapy sessions. Everything would work out.

From her place in the woods, Eliza felt Molly's hurt, her frustration at being so far away from her little sister and not being able to help her. The animal growled softly and moved toward the clearing. Hearing the noise, Molly looked up to see a large white dog staring at her intently. Its blue eyes blazed love and concern, and Molly couldn't pull away from the warmth. She felt drawn to touch it, but she didn't want to scare it away. It appeared just like a ghost, out of nowhere. *You'll be my beautiful white Ghost*, she thought, aching to have a creature to love and call her own.

"Doggie." Calling to it quietly, she fumbled in her pants pocket for a cookie, left over from her evening meal. "Doggie. Please come here. A cookie for you." She needed to touch this dog. It couldn't leave her. Her feelings poured out onto her small face, open for the birds and the small creatures of the forest to see. Eyes narrowed, every ounce of her being concentrating on not making any sudden moves, she placed the cookie on the ground and moved back several feet.

"Come, eat your cookie. I won't hurt you. Please come eat your cookie." She begged, pleaded with it to stay. She couldn't be left with her loneliness again. She needed the heat this animal radiated. "Please. Oh, please."

The dog approached her slowly and ignoring the cookie, stood directly in front of the trembling child. Gently, a tender caress, it placed its cold nose on Molly's wet little cheek; then with its long pink tongue it began washing her tear-streaked little face. Molly wrapped her arms around it and buried her head in its thick white fur, at peace.

Mine, thought Eliza, images of this child, another child, a baby and a sad little dead pup all merging into each other, like scenes from a silent movie, confusing, in bright color, and hurting her head. She didn't know why they were hers, but they were. She belonged with this child and this child belonged with her, but she couldn't tell why. Nothing was as it should be and she needed to make it right. She would take care of her little ones somehow. She snuggled with the girl until suddenly the child pulled back and spoke to her.

"You have to go away now, Ghost." Molly realized that it was getting late and she needed to get back to the ward before someone missed her. "I'll be back tomorrow. Please be here tomorrow."

Knowing she had no choice, she released the warm dog. When she looked into Ghost's pale-blue eyes, she saw intelligence that surprised her.

"Please be here." The animal stood, not moving, and watched her leave.

In another place, and another city, two partly prepaid assassins encountered difficulties.

"Who the hell said nothing runs like a Deere? Damn, fucking, tractor won't start worth shit!" Spike pumped the accelerator desperately as he watched J.D. stride across the pasture, totally unaware of the danger the two men posed. Virgil propped his meaty frame against a pine tree and calmly gnawed the end off of a piece of saw grass as he waited for instructions. Bellowing rage, Spike stormed off the tractor and stomped into the woods, followed by his grinning sidekick. John Duke Parsons never noticed.

Chapter Seventeen

Star Light, Star Bright

"When the wind blows out here it gets mighty cold and dark." The old black man lingered, outpaced by the long legs of his trainee. Young folks never took time to be sure everything was in place. This one was no different. As they left the outside entrance to the kitchen, Homer Harris stopped, took a deep breath of the chill air, and then hurried to catch the new employee.

Something was different about this man. He smiled, but without warmth in his eyes. He seemed impatient, and you just couldn't hurry around children. Not his children, anyway. The ancient orderly thought of them as his, the children of Ward Ten, lost little souls each with a character different from any of the other hundred or so kids at the hospital; his precious little charges, his little angels.

Charlie stopped and looked back. It was bad enough that he didn't get a permanent shift and was going to be the "swing" shifter with a different ward every night of the week. Only five minutes earlier, and he would have been the one with the steady assignment. His only consolation was that several nights a week he pulled outside guard duty and wouldn't have to sit with those squalling brats. After only two nights, he thought he must've heard every sort of noise a child

145

could make, and none of them were pleasant. The ward smelled, too; the foul odors of piss and sweat permeated everything; bed linens, bathrooms, even the children. Didn't anyone make sure any of the kids took a shower? His worst nightmare was the thought that he might have to carry one of the pathetic little urchins to the toilet and then change wet sheets. It brought back memories he thought he'd buried years ago, thoughts that repelled him and tore at his heart with equal intensity.

There were five brothers in the Callahan family, and he was the oldest. His mother, the only woman in the household, cooked and washed and cleaned herself into an early grave, not making it past his thirteenth birthday. After that, it was his job to feed the brood and keep them safe from his dad and the demon bottle of whiskey that ruled the man's every mood.

He loved his brothers and somehow managed to get them all out to school, even though his education stopped before his first year of high school. When he took this job, he'd depended on his love of kids to make it easy for him, but he'd never seen so many sad little ones in one place before, and the wailing; all they seemed to do was cry. He preferred spending his time outside unless they needed something.

Who was going to make him do anything differently? Not that frail old man who threatened to have him fired if he found one of his little darlings wet. Wouldn't he shit his pants if he met Nathan? He could just see the introduction now.

Why, Mr. Bo Jangles, meet my friend the former sheriff of Beaufort County, Mr. Nathan St. Claire. By his side, you will find his lovely wife Arlene. Stifling a giggle, he stopped to wait for the old man to catch up. What was the old man's name? Homer, that was it. *Why, Homer, I do believe you had a heart attack! Wet yourself, did you? Well, I suppose we might muss a set of sheets a bit with you.* As he waited, he pictured

Homer's head on the shelf as part of his collection. It was small and dark, much like the shriveled, wrinkled, old skulls headhunters brought out of Africa to sell to tourists.

"What ya thinkin' 'bout, young man?" Homer limped the last few yards. He seemed to have a thousand aches and pains lately. Just his normal work left him out of breath.

"What a pretty night this is," Charlie answered.

"Yas Sir, they mus' be a thousand stars in that sky." The old man grinned at Charlie. There were so many things left to show him before dawn when the night shift ended and he would return to the tumbledown house that he shared with his sister and her five kids. There was so much to teach him and so little time. *So very little time,* he thought again, as he watched Charlie hurry away from the ward toward the beckoning light of the guard shack.

Sometimes he thought he saw as many tiny hearts broken in these halls as there were stars in the cold winter sky. Why did the young never see what was important? Why were they always in such a hurry, running and speeding up the flow of their life juices, always in a panic-driven rush to grow up, to be independent, to marry, to make more children, to grow old, and to die? The faster the time stream of life flowed, the sooner it was all over.

What's tha hurry? Couldn't they see that death weren't tha enemy, but time, time that neva had 'nuff seconds or minutes to feel it all anyways? Time what lost its seconds 'lentlessly, movin' towards tha end soon enough without da idiots done racing' towards it, stampin' and killing' most everythin' in tha path? What was ta say tha little ants crushed beneath yo feets didn't have a purdier soul than your own? Who should be tha judge? Sighing wistfully, he watched as Charlie walked quickly down the little path to the gate. No way around it. He'd have to keep up with him. It was his job.

Several hours later, the dog's eyes glowed dark red as she watched Charlie shuffle his deck of cards one more time, while he hunched over a battered shelf inside the frame shed next to the gate. This had been a difficult night for the animal. She couldn't sleep.

Whenever she closed her eyes, bright images poured through her brain overpowering her senses, images of a woman and a redheaded man, laughing and singing. She knew somehow that the redheaded man in her dreams was the man from the guard shack, but he was not the man who frightened her the most. There was another man, dark and evil, who would take her into a dark room where he would hurt her. When the images ended, she would wake up trembling and whining, to find herself in the strange body covered with white fur.

Sometimes, she would dream of the other man, the man with the sharp features in the black suit, and she would feel the sharp sting of this man's whip on her skin.

"Pay for your sins, heathen whore! I won't have you flaunting your body and imbibing spirits, allowing any trash on the streets to have his way with you. I'll inflict the scourge of Babylon upon you until you repent and are fit to receive God's mercy once more. 'Out, foul demons! Get thee out of this young woman.'"

His eyes, laden with lust, gazed at her as she tried to cover her naked breasts to protect them from his small riding whip. She knew he would be on her next, shoving her face into the cotton wad mattress as he pushed into her from behind. When he finished, he'd pull up his pants and leave without a parting look, quickly, as if ashamed of his actions, never forgetting to turn the key in the lock that kept her imprisoned in the small cabin.

She would feel the baby move in her and wondered about its future. She felt sad that it was coming into a world that she couldn't control, sad that it already felt the violence that would become its legacy. *Poor little tike*. This was not the way she imagined she would become a mother, but all of her dreams were as ashes blown away by a hurricane of fury and mistrust.

Tonight, she felt the great fear and returned to consciousness to find herself part of a four-legged body in flight, legs flailing and throat in mid growl. Watching the man in the guard shed made her nightmares worse. He was different now, evil and crazy, and she smelled his insanity with her new nose. It was a ripe sweet scent, like the smell of something long dead. She liked her enhanced senses and her ability to see and hear and smell better than any human creature. She ran faster than the wind, and her sharp teeth could tear into tender flesh.

Her reverie was disturbed as a rabbit hopped into the clearing about five hundred yards from the sentry station. Automatically, she focused her attention on the unaware creature. She felt her muscles tense under the soft white fur, and every nerve in her canine body ached to lunge in the animal's direction.

Hungry as she was, she didn't hunt, but the desire to chase and kill was a part of her now, and she felt it struggling with the human soul that had merged with the carnivore's powerful body. She could almost taste the warm, salty, blood of the rabbit. Only through a great act of will was she able to resist the urge to begin the chase with an easy meal so close to her. She turned her back on the clearing and re-centered her gaze on Charlie.

She knew this man. She'd known him in another life and once had loved him. Why did he reek of death now? A cancer grew in him of a most insidious nature and it consumed him, changed him into the sort of animal that Eliza refused to be. Confused, she snuggled into a nest of leaves and watched him until daylight, until he left the little building and made his way to the kitchen to claim his share of the breakfast being dispensed to a hundred young patients. Another long night was over, another night where the watcher was also the watched.

Chapter Eighteen

Domestic Bliss

Scowling, Anna reached for her glasses and focused on the inter-office mail envelope. CONFIDENTIAL. MEDICAL RECORDS ENCLOSED. Nothing made sense. She should be satisfied with this case. According to the reports, the Parsons child was making steady progress. Since her incarceration, nothing strange at all had occurred with the family, but the littlest child had become more and more peculiar. And J.D.? She just couldn't figure him out.

He seemed attentive to her every wish. He sent her flowers every Thursday. He smiled appropriately, complimented her appearance, took her to a movie every Friday night, to the Lion's Club Bingo game on Saturday, and acted in every way like a doting admirer, but something seemed to be missing. It felt rehearsed. Sometimes, she turned suddenly and found him watching her. For some reason, it sent shivers racing up her spine and not the tingly type either–they were the Alfred Hitchcock, something is just not right, nasty kinda shudders–like the ones you get right before the hero gets a knife in the back.

He and Tessie acted like a parody of the Cleaver family, and she found herself cast in the role of June Cleaver, right down to the apron. Last Sunday night, she felt his hand on her waist, and he had actually tied a frilly apron around her. It was pink and covered with incongruent ruffles, stiff with starch. Worried about the little tike who never seemed to eat, she'd brought the two of them a tuna casserole, and from some kitchen drawer he'd produced the silly thing. After fussing with the bow, he'd moved away and examined her critically. She'd laughed and posed suggestively, putting one hand on her hip, but he'd frowned. He was some serious character, all right. Determined to break the spell, she'd approached him and reached to touch his cheek, but his frowning face remained intent on whatever vision he had seen of her clothed in his frilly apron.

She heard a crash behind her and turned to find little Tessie wearing two huge oven mitts trying to put the casserole back together. Poor little imp, she should never have tried to put the heavy dish in the oven by herself. At six years old, she was too little to pick up a heavy dish and far too small to be operating the oven by herself. She really needed to talk to J.D. about what tasks were appropriate for a child that age, but J.D. raised such a fuss whenever she did that, she found herself hesitating each time she wanted to intervene.

Avoiding the mess on the floor, she'd hurried to comfort the child, who tried so hard to please her dad.

"Father. I'm sorry. I'll fix it. Please don't be angry." When she'd gathered the child into her arms Tessie didn't relax into her embrace, but instead continued to stand stiffly, her eyes glazed like a deer caught in the headlights of a quickly approaching vehicle. She'd refused to be comforted, but instead continued trying to rake the fragments of the dish and food into a pitiful beige-gray mound of broken glass shards and lumps of tuna and cheese.

"It's okay, Honey. It's okay. Don't worry. We'll go out for hamburgers." The child had looked for her dad hopefully, but

Anna realized J.D. had left the room. Thinking he'd gone to the kitchen for the dustpan to clean up the mess, she'd looked for him, but he wasn't there. She'd found him on the front porch, staring off into the clouds of dust hovering above the small-town street.

"John. Your child is too small to be cooking. That dish was far too heavy for her to lift."

"Oh, she's strong enough. She's just clumsy, like her mother and her sister. That whole family was a shiftless bunch of drunks, not one of them worth training."

"John, she's only six years old. I don't care about the food. Let's go out for hamburgers, my treat." She'd rather pay the bill for all of them than watch J.D. force the little girl to play grown-up and prepare a meal. He'd continued staring into the distance for another moment. When he'd turned to face her, she saw that his eyes were as cold as the irritation in his measured tone as he answered.

"Tessie is fully capable of taking care of this house and all of the lovely things our Maker has given her. I don't believe in rewarding children for bad behavior, but if that's what you want, that's what we'll do." He'd walked around her, re-entering the house, and she'd felt his sternest disapproval even as he obeyed her request.

Two hours later, she felt grateful to be back at her own home and out of his presence. He'd barely touched her as he untied the apron before they left for Bob's Hamburger Haven. It was no treat for Tessie, either, who had watched her dad anxiously the entire meal. Methodically, he'd ordered a sandwich, fries and a shake for each of them, and she and Tessie had eaten silently while he made polite small talk with the owner of the nearby diner. As soon as they'd finished eating, she'd excused herself immediately, not even walking back to the little house with them. She'd needed to figure out what was wrong with that picture. Suddenly, she'd felt very sorry for the little ray of sunshine who lived with her own dark cloud; her own very, very, dark cloud.

Lionel scratched his head and turned to Horse, who squatted at his right. In this position, they met eye to eye. Tall lanky Horse stood almost twice as tall as the clan leader.

"Something is strange. What do you know about the dog, Harry?" He readjusted the wire-framed glasses over his ears, and pressed one finger into the mud paw print that was so close to the large boot print that belonged to the new ward security guard.

"Why would she be following this man? She's important. We have to know what she knows."

"I don't know. Maybe she likes him. Maybe he's feeding her?" Li remembered the blazing blue eyes and the sharp teeth that had almost connected with his wrist when he'd reached to touch her soft white fur.

"I don't think so." The prints were fresh. He looked behind them nervously. Usually, he felt safe when he was with Horse, but not today.

"We must know everything. I want you to keep an eye on her. I have to know where she goes, whom she's interested in. She's the key to the mystery, the portent of things to come. She's the key. She's our key and the end is near. Soon we'll have our home."

Rat, Beaver and Fox sat on a tree limb nearby. Barnes smiled, thinking of a scene from a movie that had made the rounds of the hospital last month.

"Will we make Irish stew?" In the movie, a peasant woman had peeled potatoes and shaved carrots and dropped large chunks of beef into a broth so thick and rich that they almost could have smelled the thick aroma from the steam escaping over the large cook pot on the screen. It'd been particularly attractive since the whole hospital was in the middle of a budget cut, and the last three days a hundred hungry children had dined on canned mackerel cakes, the least favorite food served in the large cafeteria. When the friendly woman on the screen had reached for a bucket and poured dollops of heavy cream into the cooking mixture, there had been an auditorium-wide, audible sigh. Li smiled at the chubby cheeked, younger pack member.

"Yep. We'll make stew."

"Can we have a cow? I want a cow. I know how to milk a cow." Li left the prints and walked over to sit by little Fox, who had shimmied down from his lofty perch. Freddy was the baby of the group, and Li's favorite. He put one arm around the little boy and playfully stroked his sandy cowlick with the other, trying vainly to smooth it into place. Fox had lived on a farm before his parents had left him at the gate of the hospital one night and then disappeared. When authorities had investigated the address Freddy gave them, they'd found a deserted old farmhouse and not much else. No trace of anyone or anything alive remained at the place that the kid insisted used to be his home. Freddy loved animals, any animals.

"Of course, Freddy. We'll have a cow, and some chickens, and maybe a pig." The small boy glowed with excitement.

"And I'll take care of them. Just me. I'll be their keeper."

"Yes, you will, Freddy. Just you." Just then the wind kicked up, and Li could feel the energy of an approaching storm.

"Come on, Guys. We have to get back now. The rain is coming." He looked for Rat, but Mickey was nowhere to be found. He'd disappeared just before they found the print; just vanished into the evening mist, as was so often his habit. It didn't matter. He'd be at the cave with a knapsack full of food by the time they arrived. Only Horse remained behind, following the paw prints, looking for the white dog. They had to know what she knew. It was part of the plan.

Several hours later, the elderly ward security guard pulled the wool blanket a little tighter around the child and the large dog. It would be hell to pay if anyone caught that animal in the hospital, but his children needed their creatures sometimes. That was a mighty clean stray. It had to belong to someone around here.

Funny, it almost looked like the dog had its paws around the child, the way the two of them intertwined. The creature's soft white fur completely surrounded the kid, who snuggled in next to its belly like a baby held by its mother. Usually, it would be the kid hanging onto a pet, little arms wrapped tightly around it so that it couldn't escape. The child's face looked so sweet as she slept peacefully tonight. Peace was good; she often thrashed around in her cot during awful nightmares. No one else would be in for a while. He'd be sure that the dog left before the morning crew came in. Let the little angel sleep in peace for one night.

Chapter Nineteen

Winds of Change

"**I** won't be threatened by a malingering malcontent who doesn't even have the decency to die when it is time to do that gracefully! Two-hundred-thousand dollars? No one's worth two-hundred-thousand dollars!" Seething, A.E. looked from one stack of papers to the next. The first stack listed three hospital admissions:

July 29th, 1978 alcohol poisoning 1 day ...$325.00
July 30th, 1978 snakebite 14 days ...$2,178.00
Sept 3rd, 1978 spider bites 23 days ICU $3,497.00

In the next stack sat copies of fourteen letters requesting payment, seven to *Allied Health Indemnity,* and seven addressed to John Duke Parsons. These were not unanswered. There were two letters from the insurance company stating that it wouldn't pay because the hospitalizations occurred following "suspicious circumstances." Also, John Duke replied to the ones addressed to him, invoking "the wrath of God upon their heads" for "operating a human slaughterhouse," and stating that their doctors and nursing staff were "avatars of death."

"What the hell is an avatar? Whatever his damn problem is, we sure ain't no "avatars of death." The hospital administrator scratched his head, perplexed; but it got worse.

"A representative of Beaufort Falls Medical Center is hereby requested to be present in Civil Court on Wednesday, March 28, 1979 to state why it should not be liable to pay the sum of two-hundred-thousand dollars to Mr. John Duke Parsons in compensation for his suffering, anguish, and near death at the hands of the medical staff of said facility on numerous occasions. Failure to contest will result in a judgment in favor of the plaintiff, payable immediately upon request."

He supposed he should be grateful that they had reduced their demands from the original six-hundred-thousand dollars, but it should never have gotten this far. What happened to the two thugs he'd hired to take care of this problem for him? Frowning, he opened his bottom desk drawer and reached under a stack of forms and papers to extract a ragged telephone book marked "personal and private."

"Spike. I paid you to do a job. Why wasn't it done?" There was a long silence.

"Uh. No one by that name." Click. Dead wire. A grim look on his face, A.E. dialed again.

"Don't hang up on me or I'll make a trip down to 351 Belmont Street and we can talk in person." Silence. The blood rushed from Spike's face as he realized that A. E. actually knew where he lived.

"Boss. We had some problems. Do we have to talk about it now?"

"Sonny. Who's that you're talking to?" A voice sounded sweetly from the kitchen of the small house. Spike covered the mouthpiece of the telephone before he answered.

"No one, Mom. No one you know."

"144 Second Street then. Six-thirty tonight. Be there or get ready for a visit. I want answers." A. E. had said all that he needed to say.

The sound of the phone hanging up did nothing to relieve the rush of hot acid reflux in the bottom of the bumbling assassin's stomach. Trembling, Spike dialed a well-memorized number.

"Oh shit. I sure hope Virgil has a bright idea. We're fixing to be royally fucked," he mumbled, horrified at this new turn of events. Then he heard a familiar noise over his left shoulder.

"What is that, Sweet Boy?"

"Nothing, Mom, nothing at all. I'll have your supper ready for you early tonight. Okay?"

He and Virgil had spent the advance given to them by Beaufort months ago, and now A. E. expected them to produce results. He felt walls closing in on him from every side. This wasn't going to be easy.

"I hate you!" Molly flung herself at the wiry girl, but no matter how hard she tried, she couldn't catch her.

"I'm gonna tell! I'm going to tell! Molly has a doggie! Yucky Molly smells!!! Yicky, icky Molly and her dumb old doggie smells! I'm gonna tell! I'm gonna tell!" The mean little girl positively shimmered with glee as she out stepped larger, stronger, Molly at every turn.

Tears of frustration stinging her cheeks, Molly gave up chasing her. No matter how hard she tried, she couldn't get along with the girls around her in the ward, not since her first night when she had felt her mother's presence, and the entire ward had awakened to the loud disturbance that she'd blissfully slept through. She didn't understand why they avoided her, but she didn't care. Mickey was company enough for her, but to her amazement, the girls resented her solitary stance, and when no other events occurred, they began to tease her.

Two nights ago Debbie had discovered Ghost sleeping peacefully by Molly's side. Spitefully, she'd poked the animal in the ribs, resulting in sharp teeth pinning her little wrist to the bed. Her shrieking had wakened every other child, but fortunately did not catch the attention of the ward security guard, who'd been out taking a bathroom break about that time. Since then, Molly had lived in constant fear of being found out and no longer having the comfort of the big white dog who protected her in this new and strange place.

Debbie stopped, a tantalizing few feet away. She wasn't really about to tell yet. This was too much fun. She and her friends had searched for a month to find something that would upset Molly, and this was the first time she'd reacted to any provocation they'd provided. She expected at least another week or so of fun before reporting her. Besides, there was something strange about Molly and that dog, and she wanted to figure it out. She would swear that sometimes at night when she watched them, the dog looked almost human, but she knew that couldn't be possible. She wanted the mystery solved before Molly was forced to live without the nasty creature. She had plenty of time.

Molly wasn't sure she wanted to catch her. If she beat the crap out of this annoying little creep, she'd snitch on her for sure, but she had to put some fear into her. She had to, right now.

"Debbie, if you say a word about Ghost, she'll find you. You know she's a killer, a wild dog, and has super powers. If you say a word about her or bother me in any way, she'll wait for you along the path and tear your throat apart; just like the rabbits she eats every day. Sweet tender little rabbits, yum, yum, yum."

Debbie stopped and looked ahead of her. She and Molly were on their way to the soccer field for gym class, and the path led straight through the woods near the river. She didn't want Molly to see the effect her words had on her.

"Nah! That dirty old dog couldn't hurt a flea."

"She'll tear you apart like a little bunny, but if you act nice, I'll ask her to leave you alone." Molly warmed to the part now. For the first time she felt control of the situation shifting her direction.

Debbie stopped, frozen in her tracks. Out of nowhere the dog appeared, and it wasn't the same animal she saw sleeping with Molly. Its blue eyes blazed into hers, and she wasn't able to pull her gaze away. It loomed huge, its gaunt frame undulating in melting white waves, and the winter chill suddenly felt as hot as an August summer day. Touching her forehead, she felt beads of sweat pouring off her scalp. Then the animal smiled. Its red mouth stretched as big as a watermelon, exposing sharp fangs, hot saliva dripping from its lolling tongue trailing flames like moving fourth of July sparklers.

Suddenly dizzy, Debbie felt her bladder release and her eyes bulge, a sharp intake of breath stopped her heart from beating, and she waited for the inevitable ending of her life.

Eliza stared at the child, feeling her power once again growing within this new and strange body of hers. She felt no remorse. The child was going to hurt her child and didn't deserve kindness, or concern. She was learning how to curb

161

the dog impulses now, to understand more of the changes that took place when she'd returned to the realm of the living to suffer once again its limitations as well as its pleasures. She liked her body, and she liked the animal that once possessed it, and she hoped she would be able to restore it someday when she no longer needed this form.

She was frustrated and uncertain as to what she could still do and what was now impossible due to her physical frame, but she still possessed power. That was good. She and her children faced great evil from several fronts, and she could feel it all around her. She wished these minutes of clarity lasted longer. As soon as her power faded, her awareness would, too. It would come again, but now she was already feeling the fuzzy aura of her canine hostess return.

Molly watched as Debbie sank to the ground. Directly ahead of her, almost as if on cue, she saw her dog. What was wrong with Debbie? Ghost just stood quietly, looking at Debbie. She walked around the scared child and put her arms around her pet. She could tell that something about Ghost terrified Debbie. Molly decided one last threat was appropriate.

"Say anything to anyone and she will hurt you. Do you understand me?"

Unable to speak, the girl nodded silently. Molly and Ghost turned and left her in the dust of the path, unable to move. Debbie missed practice and spent the next two days in detention, happy not to be required to walk the dark path for the rest of the week.

She also kept her distance from Molly, especially at night. Her medical chart noted the onset of nightmares and disturbed sleep, but she knew better than to share her experience with the intern who visited her weekly, to provide "therapy." Nothing good ever resulted from honesty in this dark place, and there were many levels far worse than Ward Ten; places she didn't visit even in her worst nightmares, places worse than sleeping in the same room with a terrifying demon dog. Debbie kept her problems to herself.

Chapter Twenty

Secrets Revealed

"I never knew a naked man could be so ugly."

"Smells like shit, too!" The younger scout poked what was left of Nathan St. Claire's penis with the nail end of the pole he'd used to retrieve trash during the Spring River Clean-up.

"Don't expect me to ever touch that pole again," the bigger kid snickered. In spite of his bravado, he looked like he might have to make a run for the bushes again. An hour ago, when they'd first seen the bones of the half-decayed hand extending out of the cave and they'd pulled the rotting body out into the open with the stick, he'd puked his stomach half-empty immediately.

"Wonder what happened to the head?"

"Don't expect me to wade into that hole looking for it!" It was too much for him. He backed away so that his buddy wouldn't see him lose what little was still left of his lunch.

Actually there really wasn't much of an odor to what was left of the once-proud sheriff of Beaufort County, reduced now to bones and leathery shreds of flesh floating in the rapidly moving current. Still, it was getting dark and it was scary standing around next to a dead guy. The younger boy looked at the sky anxiously.

"Do you think they'll be here soon?" It didn't seem such a great idea now, staying behind while the rest of the troop hiked two miles down the road to call the authorities. It could be hours before they got back. It didn't help that they were only a couple of miles from the hospital where they locked up crazy people.

"Do you think maybe one of those psychos from that hospital did this?"

"Dunno. Could be a nutso in the bushes right now just waiting for it to get dark." Now the big guy was getting nervous too. Best to do something. He was the oldest. He had to take charge.

"Eddie, pull some of that brush over here. Maybe we ought to make a fire. It's starting to get cold." March still got chilly at night in Alabama.

"Sure, Mike." The time moved quicker with something to do. Never turning their backs on the body, they moved away from what was left of Nate. Mike fumbled for his kit, an emergency pack he had an opportunity to use for the first time, and taking out matches, he lit a pile of small sticks arranged strategically underneath a large stack of dry limbs. Soon they had a blaze going big enough to be seen for several miles.

"Who do you think that dead guy is, over there?" Eddie furtively glanced in direction of the gently floating carcass.

"Some bum. Some jerk who wandered too near the hospital."

"I wish they would hurry."

Conversation stopped and they huddled closer together, waiting for a rescue party that was taking its own sweet time. Eddie hoped they wouldn't be singing songs with the angels before their buddies returned. He couldn't think of a single one of them that knew how to tell east from west. It was going to be a long night.

Eight miles away, Verbena eased the key into the lock. She was careful and waited until she saw Charlie leave for work, waiting until she was certain he actually boarded the bus and had time to be far away. She felt sure the man she confronted several weeks ago was her Nate, but she couldn't get rid of a few persistent doubts. What if she'd made a mistake and the man who called himself Charlie caught her and called the police? What reason would her Nate have to change his name and his appearance so radically? What if someone else was home? She couldn't force herself to knock first and check. In her presently agitated state of mind, she couldn't think of a good story.

For weeks she'd wavered back and forth as to what would be the best plan. First J.D. didn't want her, and now Nate. What was so wrong with her? She was no raving beauty, but she knew she was good to people and she couldn't imagine anything she'd done to cause a man to take the trouble Nate obviously was taking to avoid her. He must be in other trouble too. In the end, it was this thought that decided her. If he was in serious trouble maybe she could help, if she only knew what it was.

Shit. She'd forgotten to put on the gloves. She didn't want any trace of her presence left in the apartment no matter who was living there. Awkwardly, she took her hand off the doorknob and pulled on sheer plastic film cosmetology gloves. Good thing she got a new pair every time she colored her hair. Was there anything else she was forgetting? If anyone was in there she was sure they could hear her heart beating by now, it was pounding so loud and so hard.

Very slowly, she opened the door. So far all was quiet. She stood in the doorway and scanned the kitchen and living room area. She could see the open door to the bedroom, and no one was in sight. Unless someone was in there, asleep, or in the bathroom, she was alone. She waited motionless, straining to hear the sound of water running or human movement. She decided to cover her bases.

"Hello? Anybody home? Your door was open."

No answer. Relaxing a little, she stepped into the apartment and stopped, uncertain as to where to search first. For some reason she didn't understand, she opened the refrigerator. It was standard bachelor fare; a gallon of milk, a stick of butter, three eggs and a bottle of Early Times whiskey. On the very bottom shelf she found a takeout box of some sort of moldy Chinese food.

At least he isn't dating, she thought somewhat self-righteously. *What next?* She looked at the cheap Salvation Army coffee table placed in front of a torn, brown, leather couch. There was nothing on it but a big book, a very thick book.

Taxidermy as a Hobby? From the Sicily library? What strange reading. For some reason she crossed to the kitchen and opened the cabinet under Charlie's sink.

Cleanser, dishwashing liquid, formaldehyde? She glanced at the walls. There were no trophies hanging anywhere. She expected to see a stuffed trout or a deer head complete with antlers, but she found bare, clean white walls.

Maybe Charlie's making money stuffing animals for hunters? It seemed reasonable. Most of the men in rural Alabama hunted or fished for recreation and they bragged about their "kills." A skilled taxidermist could make good money and all it required was the ability to endure pungent odors and handle dead animals. She was glad she had never known that he did this while they were dating. She couldn't bear the thought of his touching her with hands that had handled dead things.

Yuck! Disgusting! Wonder where he keeps the rest of his equipment? Curious now, she opened the closed bathroom door. Sure enough, there was a large galvanized zinc tub and heavy rubber gloves stacked neatly in one corner. At least he had gloves. That made his choice of part-time work a bit more acceptable. None of this explained the sudden change in his personality.

Why did he act so strangely? Was that really Nate? Did he have a roommate or maybe a twin brother who looked just like him? In the small bedroom she sat down on the bed to consider alternatives. If two people lived in this apartment, they slept in one bed. Nate didn't act like "that" sort of man, but you never knew. She'd heard that some people liked both sexes.

Thank, God, the bed is made. She sat on a clean, green, gabardine bedspread. At least it looked clean. She realized how little she knew about the man she'd trusted with her body. She needed to know if there were two sets of clothing in the wall-length closet that faced the bed.

Almost afraid to know the truth, she slid the closet door open. Her eyes traveled across half of a closet full of clothing. As well as the old jacket she remembered, there were several suits, a pair of overalls, several pairs of jeans and a couple of flannel shirts. She also found the beige trench coat the stranger had worn on the day she had questioned him at the bus stop. Even so, it was obviously clothing just for one person, since no effort had been made to separate the space or any of the items.

Her eyes traveled to the top shelf. Four glassy eyes looked down at her. Reeling, she staggered, coming to rest on a large chest freezer sitting close to the bed. Every horror movie she'd ever seen came pouring back to her in a series of bright scenes, giving the entire experience an aura of unreality. There was only one reason why a person with two severed heads in his closet would have a freezer in his bedroom. She eased the lid upward a small bit, peeked inside, and then ran gagging for the bathroom.

Charlie couldn't believe his own stupidity. Of all evenings to forget his ID Pass! He'd already been warned, and now he had no choice but to return and get it. Tonight he had no time to waste. He needed to rush to get to the hospital and make his report before that orderly came back and made him look bad. He was just doing his duty and the dog had attacked him. With a little luck, he would get the orderly's job when they fired the old idiot. He'd waited around for several hours this morning before anyone told him that the Ward Supervisor didn't come to work until 3 PM. Assholes! Beyond irritated, he turned the doorknob to his apartment and realized that it was already unlocked. Did he leave his door open, too? What if someone had let themselves in?

Then he heard a voice coming from his bedroom. He froze, horrified. After a few seconds he walked in quietly and found Verbena seated on his bed, hunched over the bedside extension phone.

"Heads. Yes, sir, there are two heads. Whose? I don't know. They're kinda brown and wrinkled. Please hurry," Verbena was whispering although she wasn't sure why. "It looks like they're looking at me. Yes. They're cut off at the neck. Please, please, hurry. 1235 Elm Lane. Please. I feel sick, and that's not all! There is a …" She felt someone else in the room and looked up to find Charlie staring at her from the doorway.

"You fucking bitch!" His face was red, its Irish features contorted with suppressed rage. "You damned, meddling, bitch!" Every drop of blood drained from Verbena's face. She dropped the phone, turned and looked for a place to run, but there was no place. Charlie blocked her only exit from the room. Briefly, she considered pretending she had seen nothing, but realized he'd heard her desperate call to the police.

"Nate," she stuttered, choking on her words. "I was worried about you. I came to see if you were okay. You weren't here," she continued lamely.

"How'd you get in?"

"The key. The key you gave me."

"You lying bitch. I never gave you a key. You've never been in this apartment. How'd you even find me?"

"You dropped it. I just came to return it to you. You weren't here." Tears ran down her cheeks as she cowered, trembling, clutching the telephone. She knew she was a dead woman. Charlie moved close to her.

"Give me the phone. You've caused enough damage. Damn it, you bitch, we don't have much time." He reached for the phone but Verbena refused to give it up. Yanking the cord from its socket in the wall, he pulled the receiver out of her hands. Then, as she tried to run, he forced her back onto the bed. The heavy black telephone clanked loudly as it hit the wood floor.

"Stop it! Don't hurt me. I love you, Nate." Verbena spoke softly, as convincingly as she could, as she struggled to push him off of her.

"Bullshit! You have no idea what I'm capable of. Cooperate and I won't kill you right now."

Verbena fought valiantly, but he was just too much stronger than the little woman. Grunting, he twisted both of her arms behind her back and tied her hands together tightly with the telephone cord. He looked for a place to secure her while he decided what to do next. Removing a pillowcase, he covered her head and tied her to the cast iron bed.

Verbena's last semblance of bravery collapsed. Whimpering, she lay trussed like a rabbit, snared close to its hole. She could almost feel the cold bite of an axe on her neck, but Charlie was busy. He had too much to do very quickly to worry about her right now. The police were undoubtedly on the way and he was moving. It was too bad he wouldn't have time to empty his freezer. He was about ten minutes away from having his picture posted in every post office.

"Sorry, Old Man." Roughly, he scooped up the two heads and tossed them onto the floorboard of the back seat, tossing clothes and toiletries in over them. Opening the huge trunk to the old car, he placed the metal can of formaldehyde, the gloves, and his reference book inside the large tub and put them inside, next to his big wood axe and his hunting knife. Last, he wrapped the frightened Verbena in his bedspread and shoved her in too. He heard sirens approaching as he drove away.

Chapter Twenty-One

The Catalyst

The slogan on the side of the dilapidated step van read *Sicily Wholesale Produce, The Best without the Pests,* but it was a sad-looking vehicle as it pulled onto Main Street in Beaufort Falls. There were dents on top of dents, and the bumper cleared the ground by only a few inches. The transmission groaned and its brakes squealed as it pulled into the loading zone in front of *Ma Everett's Kitchen.* While his nephew went inside to conduct his business with the restaurant owner, Homer walked around to the back of the truck. A pair of bright blue eyes waited for him, and when he opened the back panel, Ghost hopped out and loped northward, easily dodging the few supper-bound motorists on the half-empty street. Vaguely, within the mind of the dog, Eliza stirred restlessly. She knew where she was headed, but could not remember why. Homer watched the dog leave, sorrow and regret etched into the dark furrows lining his ancient face. *She's gonna miss ya, white dog, but yo gonna git her inta big trouble. Her 'n me too.*

Last night the new ward orderly, the one that rotated among the wards, had found Ghost curled up with his favorite little waif and he'd attacked the dog with a broom, only to find himself pinned to the floor with the animal's teeth at his throat. *Dat fool was a goner. I'm lucky the animal likes me.*

When Homer had dropped his mop and run to rescue Charlie, the dog had obeyed him and released its captive. After a second's hesitation, the animal had allowed the old orderly to put it into a kitchen closet. It was as if the dog knew that Homer would protect it and that it was part of a plan.

Homer's nephew ran a produce business, and his truck made a stop at the hospital first thing every morning delivering fresh fruits and vegetables all the way from Sicily to sleepy Beaufort Falls. Homer knew that the dog could not stay anywhere near the hospital; Charlie would make sure it was hunted down and exterminated. When he got back, Charlie was gone, but he knew he only had a few hours to send the dog on its way. A report would certainly be filed, since an entire ward full of sleepy children witnessed the attack.

Poor little Molly. When he had left she was a sodden little lump of misery, curled up alone on the small cot. He'd promised her he'd make sure the animal wasn't hurt and it looked like he was able to keep that promise. Be darned if it didn't look like it knew where it was going.

Ghost broke stride to sniff the corners of a couple of streets before turning up Sycamore. Halfway up the street she stopped, her sensitive ears craned forward. Faintly, she heard the shrill shriek of a small child.

"Father, it hurts! Please, don't hurt me. I'm sorry. I didn't mean to break it. It fell." The white fur on Ghost's back bristled.

"Owww! Please, please stop it! I'll be good. Owww!"

At the last cry of pain, Ghost launched into motion, a white blur moving up the street at mach-one speed. Entering the back yard of the little house by clearing the fence in one leap,

173

she found J.D. holding Tessie three feet off the ground by her long blonde hair. He held a small riding whip in one hand, and welts on the baby's back indicated that he had been using it.

"I won't allow you to follow in the footsteps of the evil woman from whose womb you were born. I'd rather see you food for the worms than..." He never finished the sentence.

Ghost lunged at him, throwing him backward onto the ground, and then the dog made a sincere attempt to remove his face. She was a twisting helix of fury. Like volcanic gases, a faint impression of the woman Eliza wafted high above the avenging animal. She wore pale green satin and her eyes burned like lumps of dry ice. Gently, the apparition caught Tessie, placing her on the grass nearby, well out of harm's way. Suddenly another voice echoed from the gate.

"Tessie. Are you okay?"

Anna couldn't believe what she'd just seen. It wasn't possible. It couldn't happen. She had to get the child out of there and call an ambulance and the police. She saw J.D. strike his child with the whip, but before she could move, the dog appeared from nowhere. Tessie saw her idol appear at the gate and moved toward her.

"Miss Johnson! It's okay, Miss Johnson. It's Mommy. It's my mommy."

Almost as quickly as she appeared, Eliza evaporated. Ghost turned and left the now-motionless J.D. lying in the Alabama dust, the man's blood dripping onto the dry ground. Tessie ran to the creature and threw her arms around the animal's shoulders, bright splashes of the crimson liquid rubbing onto her long blonde hair. Scarcely breathing, Anna waited for Ghost's reaction. She didn't dare startle the beast, but she needn't have worried. Tenderly, the canine curled her long body around the child and began to lick the welts on the little girl's back. It was obvious she'd attacked to protect the child and wouldn't harm her now.

Anna eased into the house to make her emergency calls, keeping an eye on Tessie and Ghost through the open window. She'd been doing this too long. She had no idea what she'd just seen or how to describe it to anyone else, and she had trouble phrasing her request for assistance.

"Send an ambulance and the police to 1256 Sycamore Street right now. This is Anna Johnson with Protective Services and I'll explain when they get here."

When she returned, Tessie sat calmly on the ground and the dog was gone. She wrapped her arms around the six-year-old cherub and then checked her carefully for injuries. The only marks on her were stripes on her little back from the blows Anna saw inflicted upon her by J.D. How could anyone hurt this little one? She swore she would do everything in her power to keep it from ever happening again.

J.D. groped for consciousness from behind the mists surrounding him. It was her! He saw Eliza. She mocked him, laughed at him, and tore him apart with the harlot red lips of that big dog. Dimly, he realized he was being loaded into the ambulance once more, and he felt the familiar lurching as the vehicle sped toward the hospital emergency room. He had to tell them not to take him there. He couldn't return there. Moving bruised and torn lips he mumbled; more like whispered.

"You can't take me there." They didn't hear him. He had to make them hear him. "You can't take me there!" Good. The pimple-faced one in the back heard him now.

"What, man? Not go to the hospital? You crazy? You look like one near-dead bastard right now." Once again J.D. forced words out of his mouth.

"Some other hospital."

"What? What other hospital? You're headed for the only hospital in any direction for a hundred miles."

"Yeah and ain't old A. E. going to love this delivery," his partner grinned back at him. They'd delivered J.D. once or twice before.

"He looks pretty bad this time." The younger one looked a little worried.

"Nah. He never dies." They weren't even careful or in much of a hurry as they wheeled him in.

Miles away, Ghost shook the cold water out of her fur as she ran along the river bank on her way back to Sicily. She couldn't quite remember what had happened, but she knew it was horrible. She would have to be very careful. Somehow she knew there'd be a price on her head. Only Molly would see her. Only Molly. When the moon crested she paused, assumed an eons old stance and howled mournfully, pouring centuries of anguish into her tortured cries. She knew it was the beginning of the end.

Chapter Twenty-Two

Go In Pieces

*T*here seems to be no end to surfacing body parts today. Joe Henry, Sheriff of Lee County, Sicily, Alabama, scratched his ear as he poured over missing person reports, trying to find a man matching the approximate size of the body found by Boy Scout Troop 505 on the river, a little while ago.

He was a tall man, thin, bordering on scrawny, but he looked comfortable in the prosperous office of the bustling City of Sicily Police Department. It was the pride of the area, a new government building funded by citizens eager to do their civic duty, protecting themselves from the influx of big city crime creeping in from Atlanta and Birmingham. It had all the new bells and whistles, including a special laboratory room for developing official-looking black and white photographs and for running fingerprints. There was even a fine slide projector and a screen for viewing films that showed the boys how all the new toys should be used.

In the corner sat a complicated machine that was supposed to help them match fingerprints from all over the state, but no one had summoned the courage to touch it yet. It was still in its original packing box. Joe figured that sooner or later it would be up to him to unpack it and figure out how it worked.

Right now, he had a patrol car in route to investigate the discovery of some sort of "shrunken heads" downtown. Probably some dusty old antiques brought out of Africa during the big game era. Well, he'd know in a few minutes. The loud ring of his phone pulled his nose out of the folder of reports.

"Boss, there ain't too much here. The door was wide open and it looks like there may have been a struggle in the bedroom. The phone is torn out of the wall, the bed's mussed and a lamp is overturned. Someone was in a hell of a hurry to get out of here. There're clothes on the floor and some things from the closet have fallen off the top shelf. No heads though."

"Give it a good search. You know, like that film we saw last week. Move all the furniture and look underneath. Check for loose boards on the floor. Look in all the cabinets. Do me proud, now."

They were good boys but they definitely needed to be told what to do.

"While you do that, I'll look up the registration on the apartment. Call me back before you leave."

"Yes Sir."

He heard mumbled directions being given before the phone clicked and the connection went dead. He'd call directory assistance in a minute. 1235 Elm. Right now, he was examining a report that looked promising.

Nathan St. Claire

6'1", 245 lbs. Caucasian, ruddy complexion, blue eyes, grey hair, scar on right upper torso,

Disappeared around November 15, 1977 while on official duty for Beaufort County

Foul Play not suspected

That was in Beaufort Falls, not far away. The size and timing were right. Too bad there wasn't enough skin left to identify any scars. Disappeared on official duty and no foul play suspected? That was curious. He reached for his phone but as he did, it rang.

"Hey Joe, we found something! You'll never guess!"

Shit. He hated games.

"What, Roy?"

"A fucking sheriff's uniform, a badge and a gun! Stuffed up under the refrigerator! And a wallet!"

"Let me guess. Sheriff Nathan St. Claire?"

"How'd you know? And the landlady is standing here and she says the apartment is registered to St. Claire. He told her he was tired of being a sheriff so he moved. Also for her not to tell anyone he was living here. What gives?"

"I don't know. Do fingerprints. You remember how? Get Al down there to do 'um. He's done 'um before. And talk to that landlady. Find out if he had any friends, visitors? Be sure and look under and inside everything before you go. Everything! Don't miss anything! Did you get everything? Did you remember the camera? Touch nothing until you take some pictures. I'll hold the line while you check one more time."

He heard Roy quizzing his team.

"Al, did any of you monkeys look in that freezer in the bedroom? That's a damn strange place to put a freezer." It was really starting to be a mystery. If the body they found was Nathan, he couldn't have rented an apartment, not with the time the body had been buried in that cave, and he was the only missing person for months who met the description.

People just didn't go missing in Alabama much. Maybe someone used his ID. It looked like he might've met with foul play after all. It was time to start an investigation and it looked like he was going to be very busy for the next few weeks.

Maybe he should call his friend and colleague Bobby Cox in the Beaufort Falls Office.

He heard shouts in the background over the crackling telephone connection. Roy returned, his voice radiating excitement.

"Boss, you ain't going to believe this! There's a headless body in the freezer and it's one big fucking woman. I have to get off the line. We've got to call a doctor for the landlady." He heard a click as the conversation terminated suddenly. Sheriff Henry shook his head as he placed a dead receiver back in its cradle. When would his boys develop some manners and learn to say goodbye?

Not far, but what seemed a million miles away, Verbena squirmed, trying to find a soft spot on the rough panel floor. She could no longer feel her hands or her ankles and she was finding it increasingly difficult to breathe through the pillowcase that still covered her head. Six hours ago, Charlie had unloaded her just like the other items from the car, and she had no idea where. She thought she might be in a wooded area and it had to be night, because she could hear the screech of an owl in the distance, and the plaintive howling of a lonesome wolf or dog. It smelled musty, little used, but she also smelled pine bark, strongly. She was afraid, not just of Charlie, but she kept hearing little feet patter across the floor close to her, and had no idea what sort of vermin might be sizing her up for a meal. Other than the night noises, it was totally quiet. Charlie had left and she had no idea when, or if, he would come back.

Meanwhile, Charlie was only a few thousand feet away. This was one night he was seriously late for work, and he had no time to spare. In spite of all the disaster he'd already encountered, he still had matters to settle. He didn't want to bring attention to his late arrival, so he waited a couple of hours before dropping by the office. To his horror, a Lee County policeman was at his supervisor's elbow as he approached. He turned quickly, hiding his face, but he listened carefully as the policeman continued questioning his boss.

"There wasn't any chance any of the inmates could have escaped for a short time?"

"The inmates here are children!" The administrator decided to end the conversation. "None of my children here are responsible for your headless corpse that you happened to find washed up close to here. I'm sorry your Boy Scouts were traumatized, but it's hardly anyone here's fault. There's no child here strong enough to kill a six-foot-tall man. And there are no missing homicidal maniacs that are running around killing women in Sicily here, either. Now please, I've got work to do. Next." A very irritated Ward Supervisor turned to face Charlie.

"Yes."

"Uh. I can catch you later. Nothing important."

Stuttering, Charlie just wanted to get out of there. Unlike anyone else in Sicily, he knew who the headless corpses were and he wanted the secret kept forever. What a time for Nate's body to surface! He'd forgotten his best friend had ever been more than just a head. Ducking his shoulders, he practically ran for the door. Suddenly he needed to get back to the old slave cabin where he had left Verbena and his things. Should he run again, or dig in? What a mess! The assholes could keep their job, but he had to stay somewhere. He couldn't go back to his apartment now. What was he going to do with Verbena? He really didn't want to kill her. Even though she had enough information on him to put him away forever, he'd shared some mighty good times with her and couldn't stand the thought of hitting her with the axe. Verbena wasn't sure whether she was more afraid or grateful when she heard footsteps come into the cabin.

"Help me." Her lips and throat were so dry she barely could mouth the words. The feet approached her and stopped.

"Shut up, bitch."

She could feel her fear rising up into the top of her throat. She had to get him to take the pillowcase off. If he didn't, she would die. If he wouldn't, she would know he was going to kill her. She had to be able to see and to breathe.

"Please. Please, Nate. Let me see."

"Shut up. Don't call me that."

"What? Don't call you what?" She wanted desperately to please him.

"Nate. Don't call me Nate. And speak up. I can't hear you." She couldn't believe this. He wanted her to talk plainly with a pillowcase on her head?

"Take the pillowcase off. Please."

Charlie shrugged. What the hell difference did it make now? She knew what he looked like. This had been one awful day. He untied the knots around her neck and slid the filthy pillowcase off. He couldn't believe this was the same pretty waitress he'd dated. Her eyes were underlined by streaks of mascara and her face was puffy and covered with red splotches.

Verbena's eyes traveled around the small rustic room. Except for Charlie's things and a new layer of dust, the cabin had changed little since the last time Molly and Mickey had played house there. She saw no furniture; no closets and none of the comforts of a real home, just log walls, rough panel floors and a large hearth. The patchwork quilt in the corner and a little bowl of chokeberries next to the big fireplace didn't belong to the man she knew as Nate, so someone else had once lived here. As for her abductor, she wasn't sure what to say to him next. The last few hours had changed everything she thought she knew about him, and she had to find some way to get this stranger to let her live.

"What should I call you? I always called you Nate. I guess you never were a sheriff, right?" she smiled weakly. Suddenly feeling pain from her hands, she grimaced and squirmed on the hard floor.

"If you untie me I won't run away. Besides, I have to go to the bathroom really bad. At least loosen it. I can't feel my hands or my feet."

What was he going to do with her? He looked over in the corner at his axe but he knew he could never kill someone who was looking right at him. Sighing, he leaned over and untied her feet. She tried to get up but couldn't.

He walked over to the tinderbox beside the hearth and found an empty ice cream carton in the trash, waiting to be burned.

"Pee in this. There is no bathroom. And don't worry about being modest. I've seen your ass."

He waited until she managed to squat over the little carton and then he removed the wire from her wrists.

"Don't try to run."

She said nothing, but looked around the little cabin anxiously, searching for the two grisly objects that could easily be predictors of her own future. Charlie saw her looking for them, and it brought his dilemma home. He was so tired. The last time he had lived through such an awful twenty-four hours, he'd discovered a severed head at his feet. He couldn't sleep with Verbena loose, but he was just too tired to kill her. He'd have to scare her. He hoped he was up to this.

"Did you know that you are wanted by the law?" Shock appeared on her puffy face.

"Me?"

"You bet." A cruel smile crossed his tired features.

"I've just been out gathering information. You and I are being billed as 'the new Bonnie and Clyde'. They found some of that makeup I gave you in my apartment. And I listed you on my lease."

"Why did you do that?" Now Verbena was genuinely puzzled.

Yes, why would I do that? Charlie's sluggish mind scrambled for an answer that would convince Verbena.

"Uh, before I went insane I thought I'd ask you to move in with me. The landlady insisted on having everyone who might live in the apartment listed. Of course, you saw the freezer. It became impossible later."

Verbena relaxed a little. This was good. He still cared about her so maybe he wouldn't kill her. Thoughts of the grossly huge, blue, headless woman in the freezer encouraged her to work those feelings for whatever they were worth. For a second she pictured her own head on that shelf and she remembered she wasn't home free yet, far from it. She softened her voice.

"What happened to you, honey? You were so sweet."

Damn! Damn nosy woman. Why wouldn't she just let it be? He was so terribly tired. Vaguely, he remembered a special from Channel Six a few weeks before. He'd been running the TV in the background while he restyled Arlene's hair, looking for a better do, something to flatter her features.

"Uh, food additives. I think I had a really bad reaction to MSG." Verbena remembered the box of moldy Chinese food in the refrigerator. She hoped it was very, very, old.

"Did you know Chinese food is full of it?"

"Yeah. I found that out."

Verbena looked too comfortable all of a sudden, so he'd better turn this up a notch. He walked over to the corner and picked up his axe, testing its edge for sharpness. Her reaction far exceeded his expectation. She could feel her feet now and she lurched to a standing position, looking wildly for a place to run. *Ack!* He didn't want her doing that. *Was everything going to screw up today?*

"Okay. Calm down. I'm not going to hurt you. We're way out in the woods and if you behave, you'll be all right. You will not go out of this cabin. You will not make loud noises. I'm part Indian and I sleep with one eye open. If they catch you, they're going to find you guilty of accessory to murder and they'll fry you like a piece of bacon, so you and I are in this together. They're looking for us both. Just sit down and be quiet while I try to figure out a way to get us some food."

He put the axe down and she sat back down on the floor and began assessing her options. *That lying bastard! He isn't Indian! With that red hair and pale rosy skin he'd only seem more Irish if he held the Blarney Stone in one hand and a side of corned beef under his arm.* She needed to get him to leave her untied so she could escape at the first opportunity, but she'd have to hide out, too, until she found out how deeply she was involved. What a crappy situation, but at least she knew she was involved in two murders before the police came knocking at her door.

She wore the gloves in his apartment. Well, at least most of the time except for the moment at the front door. *Wasn't a doorknob the first thing they checked? Oh, hell. And where were the gloves now?* Did she lose them when she was struggling with what's his name over the phone? *What was his real name?* She supposed it must be Charlie like the license he showed her, Charlie Callahan, she remembered, but who really knew? What an awful mess she'd gotten herself into. If she got out of it, she'd change her life and do something for others, live quietly, have a home with friends around. She sniffled quietly as she started making plans to take control of her life once more.

Chapter Twenty-Three

The Tides Are Changing

"Miss Johnson! Miss Johnson!" Tessie's sweet voice echoed down the hall of the social worker's three-bedroom, brick house. Anna stopped working on her reports and looked for the sunny face, anticipating her arrival with a shiver of happiness. After only a week, she couldn't imagine how she had ever lived without her.

This morning she woke up to find the little lass had fixed a complete breakfast of oatmeal and toast for the two of them. Even the thought that a six-year-old child used her stove horrified her, but Tessie had turned the gas off and held the pan with an oven mitt, huge on her small hand. When she tried to explain to the tike that she shouldn't use the stove, Tessie's nervous, phony, smile saddened her. She wore that smile, Anna realized, whenever she feared she'd made a mistake.

Since then, the child found something every few minutes that delighted her, and her laughter made the large empty house into a home.

"Look at Tiger! Look at Tiger! Come now! Look!" Anna left her work and walked outside to see her fat tomcat hanging precariously from a limb, showing off for the kid. Even her pet loved attention from Tessie, and Tessie was bubbling. Soon Anna was laughing too, as she reached up and helped the old cat down. This child was so much fun to have around. After a minute, she left Tessie dressing the cat in doll clothes leftover from her own, long-distant, childhood and she returned to her work.

This had to be done right. In the state of Alabama, the courts seldom removed a child from its natural parent. Even the strangest abuse could be justified as the parent's prerogative, and children were like property until they were eighteen. J.D. had several things going for him. Tessie never missed school, or church, and J.D. was active in events at both places. He appeared to be an almost perfect parent. "Spare the rod and spoil the child," reflected the attitude of most of the farmer citizens in the area and Tessie behaved perfectly. She tried to be realistic about her chances of winning a new life for this child. Slim at best, she would be vilified for attempting to place the kid in her home. A few weeks ago, she might have been the first one to criticize a social worker for doing what she now knew had to be done.

She knew what she had seen. The sick expression on J.D.'s face, as he'd swung the baby by her hair, disgusted her. As long as she lived, she'd never forget that scene. She wondered how many times in the years she'd dealt with abusive parents and their innocent children, she'd had missed the same sort of ugliness. It frightened her how glad she'd felt when the dog had attacked J.D. She'd reached for the rake and would have gone after him herself if the dog hadn't suddenly flattened the man, but would any court in the land see it like she did? She needed a powerful argument and it needed to be substantiated by at least one more case somewhere in the state. After saving money for ten years, her life held little that mattered for her to spend it on. She'd hire a lawyer if she needed to.

As to the strange, shadowy-green light that hovered above the dog; that would remain her secret forever. She didn't even believe she had seen that herself. She couldn't explain it, and she couldn't explain it away. It must have been some sort of lighting effect from the position of the sun coming through the trees. She took great pride in her powers of observation and never discounted anything she actually witnessed; it was there. She didn't have the slightest glimmer of an idea of what it had been.

Whatever plan she instigated to remove Tessie from the custody of the man she now saw as abusive, she had some time. Reports from the hospital indicated that J.D. would live, but he'd undergo extensive surgery on his face before he could be released. This gave her at least a couple of weeks to get things started.

Meanwhile, the stars twinkling outside made it a perfect night to go out for hamburgers, and she could picture the bright smile on Tessie's face when she told her. She'd work on this after her little ward drifted off to sleep. Having a mission to fulfill took ten years off her age. If she could do anything to prevent it, the little angel would never have to be afraid again

"Spike, we have to get hold of that dog. I never seen nothing like what it done! Right for the throat! Made that son of a bitch's face into mincemeat! What an animal!"

Spike put down his beer and gave Virgil "The Look." He reserved "The Look" for the times when his partner was more of a moron than usual. The two men sat in the last booth at Bubba's Beer Hall and Biker Bar, and Spike did his best to maintain a low profile. He wore his black leather jacket and his dirtiest pair of jeans. Virgil, of course, was dressed to the

T's in his favorite Hawaiian shirt and perky Bermudas; standard issue garb for him, even though it was barely March.

"Look, Shitbrains, when'll you get it into your head that Beaufort paid us in advance to make sure that turd never entered the doors of Beaufort Falls Medical Center again, and right now he's resting comfortably in his usual room there, in no danger of imminent death." He liked using big words. He also liked it when Virgil looked in his direction with that clueless look on his face.

"What does 'imminent' mean, Spike? You know I got kicked out of school in fifth grade."

"Never mind, Einstein. What does matter is that we do something, and do it now. That ass of an administrator's got my home address, and my mother's not a healthy woman. We can't do anything while J.D.'s in intensive care. There're nurses all over the place."

"And we would have offed him with the car if he hadn't been beating the shit out of his kid in the backyard. Then the dog showed up and that nosy old maid." Tired of Virgil's whining, Spike continued the story.

"Yeah and we could've gotten him with the grenade except it was a left-over from World War Two and didn't work, and we could've picked him off as a hunting accident except you forgot to fill out the registration for the rifle, and we might have shot him with the archery set except you are one hell of a lousy shot. Maybe he'll just drop dead of natural causes and we can run over and claim the kill." The sarcasm was lost on Virgil.

"Wouldn't we get arrested if we did that?" Spike had taken about all he could from his fellow assassin.

"Just shut up and listen, you fucking idiot. We have to kill him now and it has to look like an accident. He can't see with all those bandages. As soon as they move him into a regular room, I'm going to make sure he falls out of his bed on his head–*hard* on his head.

"That would do it! And then we won't hafta give the money back!"

Virgil smiled brightly now, grinning from one cauliflower ear to the other. Spike sighed. It was useless explaining anything to Virgil. He was about as sharp as a box of rocks, but he tried anyway.

"Virgil, hit men never give refunds. It's part of the unwritten code. You do the job or you die. Got it?" He finished his beer and looked for the bartender. He wasn't sure that he wanted another one, but the most unpleasant part of his evening was still ahead.

"Die? Well shit, Spike. No one could try harder than we are. It's not our fault…"

Spike let him drone on; right now he was barely listening. He had to decide what he was going to tell A. E. in a little while. It wasn't going to be easy. A. E. wasn't happy and that was an understatement and a half.

Meanwhile, the air crackled with excitement at the Sicily Police Department. Glossy eight by tens were drying, strung on a clothesline across the new lab, and Al used the new slide projector to examine a half-dozen different sets of swirls and whorls, enlarged to the size of small cats, on his projector screen. Suddenly, the entire department came to an abrupt halt as Joe slid the telephone receiver into its cradle. He returned, his face grim

"Not enough tissue from our John Doe to match with the prints you got from Nathan St. Claire's service record. However, the coroner says there is an alternative method of identification. Drag those service records out one more time."

He enjoyed the attention he suddenly received from his boys. He kicked his feet up on the good-looking new desk, leaned back in his swivel office chair, and continued his impromptu briefing.

"I just got off the phone with my colleague Bobby Cox in Beaufort Falls. He's the one who took over Nathan St. Claire's job when St. Claire disappeared.

Seems he's had some misgivings about the sheriff's disappearance from the start, but the man had a reputation for womanizing and even his wife thought he was chasing young snatch over here in Sicily. Funny thing was, she disappeared a while back too, but no one thought anything about it.

She told her neighbor that she was going on vacation and not to worry if she wasn't back in a few days. Somehow, she'd gotten the insurance company to settle, but it was messy, and they all thought she just needed a rest. They don't owe any money on the house, so no one thought a thing about it. They don't have kids, or close relatives, and while people liked the sheriff, seems like no one much cared for her. Bobby says they all just kinda forgot about her until today. He feels right bad about it. Chuck, how ya coming on those service records? Anything else distinguishable about Nathan St. Claire?"

Squinting, Chuck looked up from the manila file. "He got hit by shrapnel while he was in live ammo training at Fort Dix. Seems they had to put a steel pin in his left leg."

"Bingo!" Joe grinned. Our corpse has a steel pin. We've found Nate. Now to find out who our killer is. Al, what about those fingerprints from that apartment?"

"Well, none of them match any criminals we have on record. Sure would help if the Motor Vehicle Department or some other civilian authority would take fingerprints too." Al looked a little sheepish. This was an important job they gave him, and so far he wasn't sure at all just what they wanted him to do.

"What! Are you nuts? Only the communists would make people do that!" The deputy running the projector grinned, pleased with his insightful remark, and the rest of the boys started to snicker.

"Did any of them match the ones we have from Nathan St. Claire?"

"Yeah. One on the holster to the gun we found under the refrigerator."

"That's great! Any from anywhere else in the apartment?"

"Uh, no. I thought that was kinda weird since the apartment lease was in his name."

"Okay. Given the time frame on our John Doe from the river, do you think it very likely he rented that apartment?" Several of the guys were laughing and Joe didn't want Al feeling even more embarrassed. He raised one hand indicating that they were to be silent and examined the lot of them sternly.

"This is how police work is done. Give Al a few minutes to help me put the pieces together." Al shifted his weight to his other foot and answered his boss.

"My thought is that whoever killed Sheriff St. Claire probably used his identification to rent the apartment." Joe grinned and reached over slapping Al on one brawny shoulder.

"Exactly! My thoughts exactly! Now, let's try to figure out who the killer is and who else's been in that apartment. When I was talking to Bobby Cox, he told me that the last time anyone saw Nate alive was right before he'd left to go on a call out by the river to talk to an itinerant country preacher named Charlie Callahan. Seems this Callahan is a shifty sort of character who holds those church meetings where everyone plays with snakes, and Nate was really upset with this man because he put a little kid in a basket with the snakes. The kid wasn't hurt but her father was, and Nate wanted the man arrested for assault. Unfortunately, Callahan never served in the military, so we have no prints for him, but let's go through what prints you found anyway. How many different sets of prints did you find, Al?"

"Well, there were a bunch because we didn't find the gloves we were supposed to wear on a crime scene until we got to the bottom of the investigation kit, but I got everyone's prints and we ruled out all of them except for four. One set of them turned out to be the landlady and another set of them came from the woman in the freezer. That leaves two that we don't know who they came from."

"So it's possible we are looking for two people?"

"Either two suspects or a suspect and another victim. It looks like there was a struggle in the bedroom and we found a set of them gloves women wear to dye their hair. They were all torn up, so I imagine someone wore them who got involved in the struggle. They were little too. Couldn't hardly fit anyone with very big hands. Doesn't seem like anyone that little would be powerful enough to kill a big woman like that heifer in the freezer. Doesn't make any sense. Do you think that woman in the freezer might be Mrs. St. Claire? Maybe she went looking for her husband and found this little floozy and the floozy killed her. But wait, she was frozen solid. She wouldn't have had time to freeze if she'd just gotten killed by the floozy." Al's shoulders sagged. He'd been doing so well.

"That's okay Al. You're really doing some great thinking. We do know there was a woman in the apartment because she called the police." He picked up the transcript of Verbena's call.

"This woman was in a panic. She said she'd found two heads and then there was something she didn't finish saying because someone interrupted her. I'd assume she searched the apartment and found the body in the freezer. We should know by tonight if the body belongs to Arlene St. Claire. Bobby went over to her house to get fingerprints from there, and Al, you'll have them soon to match up with your frozen lady prints. And just for a starter, I think we need to find Charlie Callahan and bring him in for questioning. He may or may not be our man, but he was probably the last person to see Nate alive, so he is a suspect. Send out an all-points bulletin. Here is his last known description, but he's also disappeared, so we may have our hands full looking for him. Gary, write a press release. Include an announcement on Nathan St. Claire's death and ask for information on Callahan. Let's all get busy. Meeting over." He straightened up in his chair and grabbed his telephone.

"Please leave a message for Bobby to call me right away as soon as he gets back. I need all the information he has on Charlie Callahan." After ending his call he settled back for a rare moment of contemplation. The squad room buzzed with activity. His men were intent on a common goal, saving the public from evil, sinister specific evil, and he was the Captain who would guide them through the fog. This was what he was born to do. Life was good.

Meanwhile a little face watched unobserved as Verbena tried to put together a meal out of what she had found in Charlie's pockets. Beef jerky–the meat requirement was met–a mashed pack of crackers, and two breath mints. Watching Charlie anxiously, she inhaled the food. He was asleep in front of the only doorway to the outside. She'd checked the small rectangular openings that served as windows about thirty minutes ago and they were too small for a grown woman to wiggle through and escape. She was stuck here for now.

Mickey eased into her panicked mind. He felt her overwhelming fatigue; a tiredness so consuming he almost didn't feel her fear. Worse than the gnawing hunger, he realized that Verbena was afraid, very afraid that if she slept, she would never wake up. She twitched every time the man she watched, the one lying in front of the doorway, moved.

If only I could reach the axe, he heard her think. He winced as he followed her thoughts, then he transferred his attention to the man dressed in the West Alabama Regional uniform. He saw this man almost every night. Something was wrong. Every time he tried to invade the man's thoughts, he was repulsed. A surface like a giant sheet of ice enclosed this man, a cold barrier, pulsating with energy foreign to him.

Very carefully, Mickey crawled in through the small window. He knew no one would see him. No one ever saw him unless he wanted to be seen. He crossed to stand directly in front of the exhausted woman and looked at her closely. He liked what he saw and felt from her. Lightly etched laugh lines surrounded her bright-blue eyes. Her body looked natural, not skinny like some women he'd seen, but nicely rounded; a comfortable looking sort, with a soft lap and arms. He wanted to help this woman. She was so afraid. Reaching down inside of her mind, he sensed that she was a good woman. She would be part of his plan for protecting his Princess, and the time for beginning the "Plan" drew near, perhaps had even started. He opened his arms and wrapped them around her.

Verbena stiffened, motionless. Suddenly, she felt an unexplained warmth soothing all of the frightened, aching, lonely space inside of her. She returned Charlie's pants to the hearth and refolded them exactly the way that she had found them.

You can sleep now. I'll wake you if he gets up. Was that strange little voice in her head?

I'm really spent. Now I'm hearing voices. Smiling for some reason, she moved to the area of the cabin most distant from Charlie, curled up, and drifted into a peaceful rest.

Satisfied that she slept, Mickey examined the pile of possessions Charlie had brought in from the car. *Clothes, shaving cream, a tub? A book?* He could read a little bit. It was easy to learn when he could draw on the experiences of others. *Tax-i-derm-y.* He didn't know that word. He'd have to have Horse research it. Next, he pulled open a bedspread covering two cylindrically shaped objects and horrified, he stepped backwards. His fingers burned from the wrongness he'd just touched.

He'd seen dead persons before, but never like this. They fascinated him and he liked sitting by someone's bedside while they eased into the next world. Mostly when people die their remains seemed peaceful; and the spirit that ascended felt regretful, sad but prepared, floating gently onward to the unknown realm with a touch of anticipation for what was to be. That wasn't the case with the last remnants of the people he'd just found.

The screech of pain in the man-head's glassy eyes tore at his emotions. The stuff on the woman's face did not disguise the confusion she had felt in her last moments, and still felt somewhere in the oblivion; lost, wandering, and alone. No wonder the woman sleeping in the corner trembled in terror. Whatever happened to these people was a horrible distorted obscenity, and he understood now why he couldn't touch the heart of the creature stretched in front of the cabin door. A lump of malignant sewage, impenetrable and unrecognizable, had infected the being's rational mind, destroying the parts of it that were normally human. Whatever it was once, it was no more. He needed to get the woman out of there fast or she, too, faced extinction.

Concentrating, he located the boys. They needed to prepare a place where the sleeping woman could hide. Something inside his head told him she was part of the "Plan," and they all worked to protect and accomplish the "Plan." None of them questioned anything that had to do with it. First they'd make a place for her and keep her safe, and then he'd get her out. He couldn't go anywhere as long as the bad one was with her. Time was crucial. Right now he'd make things as safe as possible.

The axe in the corner had to go. Cheerfully, it propelled itself across the cabin, over Charlie's sleeping body, and into the river nearby. Mickey scanned the cabin. It seemed to be the only real weapon, so he relaxed. His face tense in concentration, he sat on the hearth, head propped on his hands, elbows on his knees, thinking out the next moves for himself and the Clan. Their future depended on the events of the next few hours, and he needed to choose carefully.

Chapter Twenty-Four

The Plan Begins

Barnes twitched like the Beaver from which he derived his nickname. Thirty minutes ago Lion had found him in the bathroom near Level Six and handed him a list of things that must be finished and in the cave by tonight. Adjusting his glasses, he read it once more. In a space of less than three hours he must produce the following items:

A sleeping platform for a woman
A table platform
Boxes suitable for clothes
Clothing for a small woman
Blankets and a pillow
A bathroom bucket
Toilet paper
Toothbrush, toothpaste, brush and shampoo
Towel, soap and rag

The platforms, at least, were ready. A few weeks ago he'd made some basic furniture and stashed it under the bushes, ready for use when required. Lion had told them months ago that when the "Plan" began they'd have someone staying in the cave. He'd already pilfered toilet paper, toothpaste, soap, and toiletries from the boy's bathroom. They were crude, but would do. Into the bag with the toiletries, he stuffed a blanket and a pillow stolen from the community linen closet. He'd never found a lock he couldn't pick. Closets were his favorite hiding places. The clothes were the problem.

He didn't know what grown women wore underneath their clothes. What if he got stuff and it didn't fit? It wasn't likely he'd have much choice anyway. Grimacing in frustration, he approached the cottages where the permanent hospital staff lived and looked for a clothesline that someone had left full of drying clothes while they worked their shift. Finally, he found one with women's garments blowing in the breeze.

Hmmm. The first set of clothes looked too big, but they were plenty informative. A blue dress the size of a tent billowed beside an item with two large cups held together by straps. Next to it hung a huge pair of cotton panties. Face flaming with embarrassment, Beaver realized he needed a smaller version of those. Fortunately, he found smaller clothes further down the line and he quickly pulled all of those items off and threw them into the bag before running as fast as possible back toward the main buildings. He hoped he had everything he needed, because he wasn't going to look at any of those items again. Two hours ahead of schedule, he hurried toward the cave to get everything set up.

Lion handed similar notes to the rest of his little band. He tingled with excitement and his hand shook as he penned furiously. Although he couldn't explain, the voice in his head told him what was going to happen, and so far it had always been right. Everything it predicted would begin, and the new Era was at hand. Soon, he and the boys would be happy and safe forever, if he just followed his instructions exactly. He wasn't sure just how he knew this, but he did.

He trembled with anticipation as he directed Horse to research the word "Taxidermy," and next he asked Fox to follow a man, dressed in a Ward Security Uniform, that he would see leaving the old slave cabin in a few hours. Wrinkling his forehead, he added a warning for Fox; he must not be seen, and he must be very quiet and very careful. He knew that Rat would have food for the visitor. He never had to tell Rat to do anything; Rat somehow just knew. Everyone was to meet at the cave at eight, ready for action, and ready for the New Age to begin. He countered all questions with a regal sweep of his hand and hurried away, whistling as he left.

Fox crouched behind a bush and focused his attention on the door to the little cabin. He remained alert, waiting for any sign that the man he was waiting to follow had resumed motion. The building remained quiet, and so did he, more silent than the tiny mouse that scurried across the wooded path right in front of his hiding place. He was good at following people and he knew this would be his moment of glory, his contribution to their future. He was ready and keyed for his task. They were all ready to protect a Princess they had yet to meet, and to start a new life they could not imagine, and now that it was drawing closer to the time, he could hardly control his excitement. Like the mouse, he trembled, but also like the mouse, he made no noise. His small shape blended in with the shadows beneath the trees and rendered him almost invisible.

Inside the cabin, Mickey still sat on the hearth, watching Charlie snore. His mind also turned to his Princess. He and Molly hadn't seen each other for a week. He could feel her sadness; he felt it whenever he followed her mind, but he understood that she wasn't upset with him. She had other tasks to accomplish that didn't involve him and he must stay away for her safety. It saddened him, but he obeyed the directives that she didn't even know that she had sent. There were many things that not even he understood, and he often felt a vague uneasiness as events occurred that he never would've predicted, but he continued to follow the prime directive--to protect and never harm.

Every creature's existence, even the abomination a few feet away, was a part of the weave of the fabric of existence and affected the future in some essential way. The removal or tampering with any part of a being's nature changed the future in an irreconcilable manner. Every being acted according to its basic nature, and could only be managed by removing temptation, not through control. The way of helping lay in enabling happiness, not creating it. Enabling was his forte, and protection of those that he loved, his goal.

He loved Molly. He felt bound to her in ways he didn't understand. It was if they were cut from one bolt of cloth and would always be joined. She was his Princess and his mission was to protect her, if he could. The first step in doing that was taking care of the woman who slept next to the cabin wall.

Fitfully, Ghost moaned softly in her sleep, curling closer to the trunk of a tree near the river, burrowing under its pine straw. The dreams haunted her again, and she understood little of the pictures that flashed through her canine brain. While asleep, her mind wandered, different, not a dog but a woman, and she moaned. Her body tore apart as her baby struggled to be born–but her baby was already born. Why did she still hurt? Terribly afraid, she twisted, trying to escape the tightening bands of pain that still racked her womb. *Oh, merciful God, please let this be over! Oh, God!* She was birthing a second baby, this time, a boy! She trembled with relief as some of the deep ache eased, and she leaned forward to examine this second child. She groped for the blanket to wrap it next to her first baby, her little girl.

Delight changed to horror as she examined the new infant. This child looked wrong, all rosy, with a head covered with bright red hair, the true mark of the devil on him. She must hide him or J.D. would kill him. He would know this wasn't his child. God cursed her for her sin just when she thought she might be lucky. The little girl was dark-haired with warm hazel eyes, but she knew this boy child would never pass her husband's careful scrutiny.

"I have ways of disposing of anything that comes from you that is not mine." She remembered his sneering, cold, voice as he said it. As a final act of revenge, he'd locked her in the cabin where her sin had been committed, daring her lover to come and take her, daring anyone else to want her in her ugly, swollen, state. Every evening when he set food and water inside the door, she was still there. He would take her home again only if he decided that the newborn babies were his and not the ill begotten offspring of her long-gone lover. One child would pass as his; one child would not.

Suddenly she heard footsteps. Twisting, she tried to see who was there. It was too dark–too dark. It was a man, but which man? Against all hope, she willed it to be her Charlie, but she knew it wouldn't be him. He was far away, or he would have already rescued her. She tried to hide the redheaded baby, but it was too late, J.D. was in the door.

"You spawned at last, did you?" Squatting, he opened the blanket to examine the newborns. "Two! My, aren't you fertile?"

She tried to see what he was doing, but his body blocked her view of the blanket. All she could see was his face, half-turned toward her, its features hard as he examined the children. One child made a soft mewing sound and she saw his face soften, but then it contorted with rage. Which of her babies did he have in his hands? Which one? It was the boy.

Jerking, Ghost forced herself awake, unwilling to see the end of this re-occurring nightmare. It had proceeded further this time and she knew that someday she'd see the end, and she wouldn't like it. Where was her little boy? She knew he was missing. Where was the little boy?

Her thought patterns resumed the slower cadence of the animal that was her hostess, and all that remained of her dreaming was a dull ache in the back of her canine skull. Most of the time she could push away the human thoughts, while awake. When they emerged, they disturbed and confused her. Whimpering softly, she curled deeper into the bed of loose leaves that provided warmth and protection from the cool night air. Having quelled the frightening images, she now felt hunger pangs, and a vague need to be somewhere that she knew she couldn't go.

She wanted her girl, but she couldn't go to her any more. She was sure that "they" would kill her if she went near the child that she loved, but she still wanted her Molly. She couldn't remember just who "they" were. "They" were human and so she must stay away from all humans until "they" stopped looking for her. It was hard.

She no longer hunted, and she needed food. Images of the kitchen dumpster just past the slave cabin flooded her mind, and she found herself moving down the dark trail, her eyes red embers against the white blur of her fur. Darkness was her friend, but she must hurry. Even the darkest hours would not last forever.

Strangely enough, Mickey thought about the white dog as he continued his vigil on the hearth in the slave cabin. His agile mind explored different scenarios in which the dog played a principal role, but nothing seemed right. Nothing about the dog was predictable. Like Charlie, he couldn't see into its mind, and this puzzled him. Unlike Charlie, the feelings she invoked in him were good, all warmth, love, and rightness–a complete opposite to the wrongness he felt whenever he attempted to probe Charlie. Why did the two of them affect him this way? What role did they play in the "Plan?" If he solved the mystery, he would have to find a way into at least one of them.

Before returning to Charlie, he monitored the progress of his clan members and saw they were ready for Verbena now. He couldn't take a chance that Charlie would wake up while he and Verbena stepped over his outstretched form; so he resumed his current mission, to obtain control of the man's resting mind. Maybe if he got closer, he could peel away some of the protective barrier that had been shutting him out so effectively.

Moving quietly, he approached the sleeping man and examined him closely. In the pale light, Charlie's face flushed rosy with sleep, and cruel lines could be seen around his mouth. The lines looked new to Mickey, shallow, and not well etched. Much older lines jagged from the corner of each closed eye, and they reflected hours of laughter, better times than the present. Mickey reached out to touch him.

Ouch! His hand burned. A barrier so cold and so hard that it seared anything it touched surrounded Charlie, scorching like dry ice, adhering to fingers and continuing to burn. Nothing could penetrate it. Mickey would just have to take a chance and hope that he did not wake this slumbering creature. If only he could get the door open a little. Easing over the man, he pushed it, and it opened slightly. Charlie moved, but did not wake. When Mickey looked outside, he saw red eyes glowing in the darkness.

Ghost heard a noise as she moved down the dark path and she stopped, looking into the green eyes of a little boy who peered out of the old cabin. She knew this little boy. She'd seen him with the group on the night that the boys fed her, in the cave, a long time ago now, it seemed. She felt a rush of caring for this boy, and a recognition that went far beyond the brief encounter that she remembered; but then he faded from her vision like a shred of mist that had never existed. Her attention was riveted to the man at his feet.

She realized that she was looking at the man from the guard shack, and she knew that her human side was beginning to win out over the dog. Overcome by a rush of feeling for him, a series of images flashed through her evolving brain, and for once she allowed them.

Almost dreaming, she saw the girl, and a younger version of the man in front of her, playing next to the river in a meadow full of flowers. He pulled the petals from a daisy and sang.

"I love you, I love you not!" The young woman laughed and snatched the flower from him, pulling the last petal, and answering him. "You love me," she giggled, and she pushed him to the ground. Next, she saw the man's face darken and the girl began to cry. "You'll find work," she told him. "You know I can't live with him any more. I have to come with you. He'll kill me. Please take me with you. Please. You have to take me with you." She wrapped her body around his waist. He untangled her arms and took her face in his hands.

"Eliza, if I could, I would. I'm no one. I've never done anything right. You'd starve with me. You're so beautiful and he's right, I'm nothing. He can take care of you and I can't. You can't come with me and I have to go alone. Let me go." He pushed her away roughly, and she fell, then she reached for him and wrapped her arms around his feet, clinging, and begging.

Ghost moved toward the cabin door, drawn closer, attracted by her strong emotion. Her memories exceeded her need for caution. Suddenly, she realized that this was the man from the ward. Why hadn't she recognized him before? How could she ever have attacked him? She remembered that he'd yelled at her and frightened Molly. Why was that? Didn't he know? He really didn't know. Confused, she stood in front of the door. Deep in her throat she formed a soft, guttural, whine.

At the soft sound Charlie's eyes popped open, and his gaze locked with that of the conflicted dog. He lunged toward Ghost, never seeing the small boy who jumped back into the cabin quickly, moving to the corner where Verbena was also awake.

Mickey waved to the frightened woman and motioned for her to follow him. She reacted far too slowly. He reached and grabbed her hand. She heard Charlie shouting from the outside and nervously, her eyes tried to locate him.

"You fucking dog! How the hell did you get back here? I'm gonna make a shit-burger out of you!" He looked for his axe, but it was gone. Ghost cringed, then shrank back, feeling a wave of malignant hatred wash over her, its icy tendrils shriveling her love and desire for Charlie, killing it as if it had never existed. Whatever the man had been, Ghost smelled monster now, and one not to be taken lightly. She bristled and prepared to defend herself, summoning the power that still dwelled within her. Unaware of the danger, Charlie moved toward what he perceived to be a defenseless animal, stepping out onto the path and away from the cabin door.

Mickey yanked Verbena's hand, pulling her, and then desperately inserted a command into her sluggish mind. Her eyes got big as she heard a voice inside of her head scream at her. *Now! We have to run. Now! Now! Follow me!* She stumbled behind him, tripping over the doorstep, but moving at last.

The depth of malice radiating from her former sweetheart transformed the spirit that inhabited the dog. Ghost reacted in kind, looming tall, now standing at a height rivaling the pine trees that surrounded her, white fur glistening hot in the moonlight, teeth elongating into a deadly leer, saliva dripping and running down her shining fur.

Charlie retreated. This was more than he expected. Way more than he expected! He looked again for his axe, but it was nowhere to be found. Then he saw it. As if propelled by invisible hands, it flew out of the forest still dripping cold water from the river, and it launched itself at him, coming to rest upright in the ground by his feet. He fled into the cabin and slammed the door shut behind him.

Trembling, Verbena followed Mickey through the woods toward the river. She couldn't believe her good luck. She was out of the cabin and had help, although she had no idea where she was going. After a few minutes she stopped looking nervously behind her and concentrated on not stepping in any of the hundreds of chipmunk holes between her and the dark unknown. Nearby, she could hear the river, and the river was flowing. Whatever the future held for her, she survived.

Chapter Twenty-Five

Parlez, Parlez-Vous

J.D. slammed the papers down on his immaculate coffee table. How dare any court tell him that he couldn't bring his daughter home! To his great surprise, he had made it out of the hospital alive, only to find when he arrived at Anna Johnson's door that instead of Tessie, packed and ready to go, a burly policeman had waited to hand him a restraining order. He was forbidden to approach any closer than five hundred feet to either "the minor child, Elizabeth Ruth Parsons, or Miss Anna Johnson, until an investigation of the events occurring at 1256 Sycamore Street was complete." Using every ounce of willpower that he possessed, J.D. had taken the papers from the policeman, thanked him for his time, and climbed back into the Caddie, but now he was home. He clenched his fist, and in a rare outburst of pent-up rage, he slammed it into the back of the sofa. With a loud crack, the top separated from the seat

Oh, Lord of Hosts, that triest the righteous, and seest the reins and the heart, let me see thy vengeance on them: for unto thee have I opened my cause. Beyond irritated, he surveyed the damage resulting from his moment of anger. *Cursed be the day wherein I was born: let not the day wherein my mother bore me be blessed. God! What would you have me do?* Now he would have to have this piece of junk hauled away. His gaunt frame radiating fury, he sat down on his mangled furniture and cradled his head in his hands.

His face still ached from the one hundred thirty-two stitches it required to repair the damage inflicted by the angry dog, and his new scar was double the size of the one he'd received in the accident several years before. Every minute in the hospital had seemed like hours, and he never knew which dose of medicine might prove lethal or what piece of electrical equipment might become his executioner instead of nurturing him back to health. He wasn't sure whether the final blow would come from hospital personnel, or from Eliza, or whether it would be intentional, or accidental: he just knew that if he didn't get out of there soon, he wouldn't survive. Everyone was an enemy, and with all of the bandages, he couldn't see or talk. Also, he found that he couldn't sleep, but he could hear, and what he heard was prime lawsuit material! Scrambling to his feet, he fumbled through the nearby coffee table drawer looking for paper and a pen. He would teach them to leave him and what was his alone!

Vengeance is the Lord's, and those who follow him! Seated on his wrecked sofa and with an Old Testament visage worthy of some ancient prophet, John Duke Parsons began scribbling notes, humiliating snippets of conversation overheard because somehow the staff seemed to assume that if he couldn't see, he couldn't hear. Some were humiliating, many were terrifying, but attuned to hear the slightest sound; he heard them all.

"Dat man done need ta go ahead 'n die." He heard a nurse's aide tell that to her co-worker as they shifted his limp weight to one side when they changed his bed. And later that night he felt a cold blade on his throat, then heard a whisper, loud and angry.

"Not in my hospital, you morons! You brainless fools! How in the hell would I explain a slit throat? Someone slipped when they were removing his bandages? You two are so stupid you need directions on the toilet seat to take a shit. Get out of my sight and start figuring how to do this thing properly or I'll have both of you arrested for being a waste of human skin. Now!"

After that, he never slept. Not for days. Now, tired and defeated, he couldn't form a plan to defeat his enemies who were, in his mind, most of this evil, God-forsaken town. It was too bad he couldn't summon a flood, or a tornado, or some force of nature, to just sweep them all away. His life had been damned difficult lately and there was no justice for the righteous. There wasn't any way to tie any of this to his lawsuit, either. Everyone already knew he was being persecuted and no one cared.

He knew whose fault it was, too. That evil, dark, child he had locked away in a place where she could no longer spread lies and poison the minds of others against him, or defy him openly with her disrespectful behavior. If he could make sure Molly never said another word, he could mend his fences. His fingers trembling, he fumbled in his pocket for the letter mailed to him from West Alabama Regional Children's Psychiatric Hospital.

"We want you and your younger child to visit, so that we can do an evaluation of family dynamics with all members present."

They would have to let Tessie go with him for that. Smiling for the first time, he felt a glimmer of hope. He'd call them right now, set up an appointment for as soon as possible. As soon as he had both of his children in his control, he would destroy Molly, then leave and find a new town and start over, in a place that never knew that his evil child had ever existed.

"The wages of sin is death," he quoted grimly as he dialed the number listed at the top of the page he clasped tightly in his hands. *I'll show that snotty bitch and this entire town full of mindless drones! They can't take my children! I'll be avenged.* The telephone rang cheerfully. At last he had a plan.

Rat stood quietly in the entrance of the cavern room as Verbena surveyed the Clan for the first time. She couldn't believe her eyes. *What beautiful boys! Who would let such children be out after dark in the woods? Their mothers must be very worried about them!* They stood before her–almost at attention–as if they needed her approval before they were allowed to move or sit. Her eyes wandered around the little room at the end of the dark tunnel. It was comfortable and snug, lit by candles and warm compared to the outside where the wind howled as it threatened rain.

An orange crate made sort of a table, and old desks and children's wooden chairs surrounded it. Someone had prepared a meal of cheese, peanut butter, and loaf bread, and as she counted the sandwiches, she realized they'd made one for her, too. How did they know she would be coming? There was a jelly jar tumbler of apple juice for her, too, and one of the chairs was larger than the rest, a tattered rattan pulled out of someone's front yard. Solemnly, a chubby little fellow stepped out from the group.

"Ma'am. I hope these fit you." He blushed bright red as she dropped the underwear he had so discretely tucked far underneath the print housedress. Suddenly aware of her torn and dirty pants suit, she reached to take the clean clothes.

"Why, I think they're just fine," she spoke quickly, hoping to minimize his embarrassment. Luckily, they were a size fourteen, and would be a little large, but would fit on her round little figure.

"Thank you very much. It was so nice of you to get clothes for me." Beaver glowed with pride. Verbena now had a willing admirer.

"How did you know I was coming?" The boys looked from one to another, trying to decide how they could explain the unexplainable to the waiting woman. Beaver formed words, but they fought him as he tried to force them from his mouth.

The "Plan." You're part of the "Plan." Stammering, he resumed his place with the other boys. His job was done, and done well, but he couldn't explain why he did it.

An older child stepped forward and with a courtly gesture indicated that she should take a seat in the larger chair. He was blonde, with clear blue eyes; a very attractive child. Verbena smiled at him as she settled into the soft, straw, cradle-like lawn furniture. Oddly, she felt at home. She closed her eyes for a second and allowed relief to wash through her tired body. It had been more than two days since she'd been able to really relax, and she felt every second of it keenly. No one would find her here. She felt safe at last. It no longer mattered how she got there, or how they knew to expect her. Her apple juice and sandwich remained untouched as exhaustion caught up with her.

As soon as she seemed comfortable, the entire crew resumed action. Each of them seemed to have a job to do, and they worked like a team. A very tall boy resumed hammering on something in the back of the room, and the pudgy little guy disappeared to somewhere else in the cave. She realized that she didn't see the child who brought her here at all. Where'd he go?

"Ma'am?" A very small child stood guard beside her. He was such a little boy, and so sweet looking. He had a little face with dark eyebrows and hair, and very alert deep-brown eyes. She smiled at him, and reached out to put her arm around him.

"Yes?"

"I don't want to be rude, but can you make Irish stew?" What a strange question, she mused silently. All sorts of questions reoccurred to her. Instead of answering, she had questions for him.

"Where is your mother, honey? What're you kids doing out here in a cave in the middle of nowhere?" Freddy looked terribly uncomfortable.

"I don't know," he answered. As he struggled to find a way to answer his goddess, a big kid came to his rescue.

"We don't have mothers anymore. We're all crazy or that real stupid kind of kids and we're in the hospital…you know, the Looney Hospital?"

Her mouth dropped open in amazement. *That* was where she was? The State Hospital for disturbed children? And how could these kids be loose like this? There was nothing wrong with them either. She'd never seen adults work this intelligently together. These were beautiful kids. What an outrage!

"There is nothing wrong with any of you. How can you be out here after dark without getting in trouble? Don't they miss you?" Suddenly the entire group gathered around her. When the handsome blonde child spoke for them all, she noticed that they deferred to him.

"Ma'am, they don't notice that we're gone. There're so many children. We've been chosen to be the Clan and we're blood brothers forever. We aren't sure why, but you're part of the "Plan." We've been chosen to take care of you."

Take care of me? She thought. *Poor little ones*, they needed someone to look after them. She examined each eager face and found herself soaking up the radiance shining from their animated features. *Such beautiful kids*, she thought again.

"If you're going to take care of me, then we all need to know each other's names," she smiled encouragingly. "I'm Verbena."

"Oh, that's such a pretty name!" the littlest one grinned.

"You're right! I'm sorry. I'm so rude!" Now the leader blushed and he hurried to remedy the problem. "I'm Lionel, but everyone calls me Lion," he informed her seriously. He motioned to each child as he introduced him. "This is Harry, known as Horse," he told her as he pointed to the big child. "Next to him is Barnes, our Beaver, who fixes everything for us; and Freddy, the Fox, who's going to take care of all our animals whenever we get a farm." Both the chubby boy and the little one beamed with pride.

"Where's the little boy who brought me here?" she asked.

"Ahhh, Mickey? Rat?" Suddenly Li looked uncomfortable. "I'm not really sure. He comes and goes. Sometimes he's just here."

"He never tells you where he goes?" This confused her; all of them seemed to keep up with each other so well. "He doesn't tell you where he is going?"

"He can't talk."

"How do you communicate with him?" She remembered now that he never really talked to her, but she heard him anyway.

"I don't know. We just know." Freddy piped up again. His question had never been answered.

"Ma'am...uh, Verbena. Can you cook Irish stew?"

"Do you have meat and potatoes?"

She looked around to see where they cooked their meals. How was that possible in a cave? The little one grabbed her sleeve and tugged.

"Come on! I'll show you!" She followed as he led her through the cave to the far entrance. There was a cooking fire lit and ready just outside the dark hole that led inside, and by it sat a pitiful little pile of carrots and potatoes, and some scraps of dried beef. How could she make a meal for the four sets of hungry eyes with this? Somehow, she would.

"Can you get me some cream?" she asked. "And some onions?"

"Rat'll get them," Horse stated solemnly. "He'll be here tomorrow. Let's go eat our sandwiches tonight, and he'll bring the other food tomorrow."

Suddenly, Verbena felt too comfortable in the soft wicker chair to ask questions. She heard the river trickling merrily through the trees. Tomorrow, first thing, no matter how cold it was, she'd find a sandy spot and bathe, and then she'd put on the clean clothes the kids had found for her. Little Fox slipped his hand into hers and she felt needed and loved and protected for the first time in years, if ever. No matter what else happened, she'd never let anyone hurt any of these sweet boys. They felt like hers now, and she wouldn't let them down. Whatever the "Plan" was, she thought she liked it.

Chapter Twenty-Six

Lull In The Storm

Molly stared ahead, avoiding eye contact with the young woman who alternated between questioning her and taking notes. She cradled the pad in her lap, trying to make the note taking less obvious, but Molly knew that her every movement was being recorded. She was tired of being examined by strangers, very tired of feeling like one of the fireflies she and Tessie used to chase and capture on summer nights and imprison in a jar, helpless and unable to move any direction without being watched. She could barely resist the urge to scream, but she had to be good.

"You're showing progress with your treatment, Molly." The woman oozed encouragement. "If you continue, we'll schedule a visit with you and your dad."

Something was missing in the statement. *Her dad? What about Tessie?* She had to see her sister. It'd been so long, and she missed her so much. She knew Tessie was lost without her. They needed each other.

"Will my sister be with him?" She tried not to seem too eager. It was better not give them anything that they could use against her, but she couldn't help it. The ache showed in her eyes, and the therapist saw it plainly.

"You really want to see her, don't you honey?" Molly couldn't help it. Tears slid down her cheeks, but she didn't cry.

"Yes, Ma'am." She continued facing forward and allowed the tears to puddle in her lap, soaking into the red sweater that barely covered the top of the too short, frayed, jeans she had pulled out of the "pick through box" in the ward. She hoped this didn't mess up her chances, but she was so lonesome. It'd been months since she'd seen Tessie, and weeks since she'd seen RatBoy or Ghost, endless blocks of time spent trying to be good so that she could recover her life.

She couldn't remember the last time she'd laughed, slept without nightmares or even had a hamburger with fries. She dreamed about chocolate milkshakes, thick and frothy, heavy with ice cream, and a soft bed with a pink pinwheel quilt primly tucked in on the sides. In this daydream the bed had soft lacy pillows that matched the bright bed covering, just like the ones she had seen at Verbena's house the time they had stayed with her. She never even saw her mother anymore, not even in her dreams. Everyone had deserted her and she was lost; lost in plain sight.

She felt a touch on her shoulder. The young woman, Carrie, had knelt so that they were at eye level, and she centered herself directly in front of Molly so that the child had no choice. She would either look her in the eyes or she would purposefully look away.

"You really miss your sister, don't you, Molly?" Unable to speak, Molly just nodded. "She'll be at the visit, too, honey. I've already stated in the report that it's important for your treatment that she be present. Now cheer up, Sweetie. We'll get you well."

Molly couldn't help herself. The therapist had dissolved her defenses and seen right into her heart. Whimpering like a stray kitten, she wrapped her arms around the kneeling woman and held onto her tightly. Carrie patted the child's back gently, then picked her up and carried her to the nearby rocker.

For the next few minutes she rocked her; the only sound in the room was the sound of the chair creaking, moving back and forth in cadence, the skinny kid pressed as close to the young intern as possible, no words spoken. The doorway opened a little, allowing a breeze into the non-air-conditioned room.

Molly faced the door, and suddenly she pulled away from Carrie. Her eyes were half-open and she saw a flash of color in the doorway, a quick blur there, and then gone. Her mind pictured a green silk kimono. "Mommy," she mumbled, half out loud. "Mommy still loves me."

"What?" Carrie couldn't make out what the child had just said. "What?"

"Nothing." Molly wasn't about to give them a chance to lock her up for good. An hour later Carrie penned her notes for Molly's medical records.

There has been a major breakthrough today. The child shows vast improvement. The family visit is crucial, with the sister present. There is a strong attachment between the siblings. Please expedite.

Back in the ward, Molly straightened the blanket on her cot tucking the corners in hospital style, fluffed the hand-me-down pillow, and stood back to survey the results. Not bad. Reaching under the mattress, she pulled out the little bear she'd found in the cabin so many weeks ago. One of its button eyes hung on by a thread, and its fur was missing in patches, but it had a wide smile embroidered above its little red tongue. She was saving this bear for her Tessie, and she knew her sis would love it, just like she did. Somehow, she would create a world where no one would ever separate them again. She *had* to take care of Tessie. Mommy wanted her to. Hugging the toy beneath her, she curled up on the cot and coasted into a sound sleep. Life was good. Mommy still loved her.

Not far away, she had friends she didn't know. After Verbena ladled fragrant-smelling stew into wooden bowls, the boys passed the thick soup around the circle surrounding the little campfire, giving the first taste to little Freddy, who tasted it and then almost inhaled his serving. With a grin, Harry took the next bowl, then Barnes, and finally Li. Scooping up a final bowl, she turned to hand it to Mickey, but he was gone.

"To the Princess who isn't here." Li raised his cup of hot chocolate in tribute, and the other boys answered.

"To the Princess."

In a little voice Freddy added, "to Verbena, too!"

The other boys laughed, but echoed, "to Verbena!"

"Who is this Princess?" Verbena asked, genuinely curious. The three younger boys all looked toward Li, their leader.

"She's the one that Mickey wants us to protect. She's part of the "Plan," and will be part of our family when the time is right. We watch out for her and try to keep her safe as best we can."

"Where is she? Is she here?" Verbena asked.

"She's here, but we don't see her very much. I've seen her in the school; Mickey showed her to me. She's pretty, and Mickey loves her. He says she's very good and has been hurt, but if she's okay, we will be too, and the "Plan" will happen. He says she has a powerful protector who'll protect us, too, if we take care of her. But he also says that very evil forces are trying to kill her and we must not let it happen."

"So what's she like? Can you show her to me?"

Li closed his eyes and tried to send Verbena a picture, but she didn't respond. It was so different with Mickey. Rat could always get his pictures. Verbena still waited for his answer.

"She's just a girl here, kinda skinny, and she's got straight brown hair and dark eyes, and usually wears red. Mickey really likes her a lot and he spent a lot of time with her, mostly in that old slave cabin, until lately."

Verbena shuddered at the mention of the cabin. It made more sense that Mickey would find her there if he'd visited it often with the girl. It still didn't explain how he was able to talk to her without using spoken words, but somehow that no longer disturbed her. It was getting late and she was sleepy. Little Fox curled up in her lap and dozed like a sleepy kitten. Harry reached for him to take him back with the rest of them when they faded into the night to make their way back to the wards, so that they would be in their cots at morning's first light.

"Thank you, Verbena," she heard first one, then all of the boys except the sleeping Freddy, tell her as they left.

She was alone, but for some reason she didn't feel afraid. After watching her protectors fade into the darkness, she moved back into the cave, carefully removed the housedress Barnes had procured for her, and wrapped up in the scratchy woolen blanket, stolen from the ward closet. She was fine and life was looking up. Soon she'd clear her name, and until then she had friends, sweet boys who needed her to cook and take care of them.

One by one, she pictured each little face. The only one she couldn't see was Mickey, and she felt the greatest gratitude toward him, the one who'd saved her life. As she tried to remember his features, she realized she might never have actually seen him that well. He came and went quickly, entering the group like a wisp of smoke, then gone just as quickly. All of a sudden, she felt his presence in her mind, a little voice that comforted and reassured her.

"You'll be fine. I'll take care of you. You're her friend."

How am I her friend? She wondered dully, coasting into a sound sleep and not moving until the first rays of sunlight reached the opening to the cave.

Chapter Twenty-Seven

Make-Overs

No matter how intensely he racked his brain, he couldn't figure a way out of this current mess. After hiding in the cabin for two days, he decided that his axe was no longer dangerous, so he retrieved it. On the third day he returned to work, only to find an old picture of him posted on the employee bulletin board with instructions to please call the Sicily Police Department if he was seen anywhere on the grounds. Not waiting to find out if he'd been fired, he returned to the parking lot to find that his car was gone. Someone must have recognized it, he guessed, by its license plates, stolen from the Beaufort Falls Police car formerly belonging to Nate St. Claire. It seemed a good idea to change the license plates when he left Beaufort Falls, but now he was in a hell of a mess.

There was no way to leave this remote place without hitchhiking, and since he was afraid to do that right now, he hid his face and returned to the cabin. The only good news was that there didn't seem to be any sort of a concentrated search for him at the moment, so he decided to just sit quietly for now. Also, there was Verbena to worry about. She knew far too much. He needed to find out whether she was still around or whether she'd prattled her story to the authorities. If she had, he was a goner, but remembering the horrified look in her eyes when he lied to her about her supposedly criminal status with the Sicily Police Department, he was willing to bet his life that she wouldn't say a word to anyone. He was safest just staying right where he was, hidden quietly in plain sight.

His appearance was another real problem. Should he grow his beard back now so that he didn't look like Charlie, or did that make him look far too much like his old identity, Nate? Would hair be an option at this point? There was no chance of getting a wig. He had no money, and little in the way of provisions. Wincing, he examined his remaining stock of edibles. Three cans of beans, part of a slightly moldy loaf of Wonder Bread, and a jar of peanut butter were all that remained of his carefully hoarded stockpile of canned goods.

At least he still had beer left. He was amazed how quickly he'd developed a taste for warm beer once he moved into this godforsaken, primitive corner of the woods. One thing he knew. There was no way he could leave this cabin, even if he starved, until he looked different, and he couldn't look like Charlie, or Nate, or the picture on the bulletin board. That didn't leave him a lot of options.

"Old Man, I don't know what I need to look like now." He gave his friend an affectionate pat on his elaborately coifed, shrink-wrapped locks. No matter what happened, his old buddy Nate was there for him. Stepping back, he decided he needed inspiration and popped the cap on one of his precious remaining cans of Pabst.

Swigging manfully, he swallowed, then resumed his nervous pacing, coming to a stop directly in front of his two bodiless pals. He felt the familiar twinge of regret as he examined Nate.

"It's a shame I let you go and get so dark, Old Man." Shrugging, he turned to Arlene and scanned her frozen features critically. She looked a little bit yellow to him, not a good thing. It was time to apply a little more makeup and make sure she retained her lily-white hue.

"Looks like you can use a little touch up, Old Lady. It wouldn't do to have you look frowsy for the Dude here." There was some makeup here somewhere, he remembered, bought a few weeks after he gave the original assortment to Verbena. Ransacking the bag below the couple, after a moment he pulled out a small bottle of *"Scandinavian Queen. The Foundation used by Royalty Worldwide"*.

"Use sparingly, applying small dot to each cheek and to the forehead area," he read aloud. Removing the shrink-wrap protecting Arlene, he set her on the hearth. After applying a liberal amount to her face, curiosity got the best of him. He squeezed a little bit onto his finger, smelled it, and rubbed it onto his own face.

Hmmm. Not bad. It felt a little heavy, but didn't itch. He wondered, if he put enough of that on, could he pass himself off as a woman? He had some other stuff he'd bought when he'd bought the foundation. Reaching back into the bag, he pulled out mascara, eyeliner, some red stuff called rouge, and a bright red lipstick. Grinning, he applied it to his cheeks and chin. He peered into the handheld mirror he used for shaving, and grimaced. *A little too much.* Well, it would take some practice, but he thought he could probably pull it off.

What about his head? *A scarf. That would work.* He had a sheet he could cut into squares. *Women's clothes?* He knew where there was a clothesline nearby. Floleeta was about his size and she lived here in employee housing. She was one hunk of a woman, and a couple of her man-sized uniforms would never be missed.

"Why, don't you think I'm gonna be one fine looking lady, Mrs. St. Claire?" He'd have to take her to the nearest community bathroom to re-shrink her, since the cabin was without electricity. Thank God he remembered the hair dryer and the plastic when he left the apartment. He felt better now that he had a plan.

Putting all of his supplies away, he washed his face using the bucket of water he'd brought from the river nearby. He tucked Arlene, the plastic, and the hairdryer into a bag and then, avoiding the main path, he set off through the woods to the clothesline, which was quickly becoming the neighborhood's high fashion boutique. Soon he would have it all under control again. He would survive.

Thirty miles away, in nearby Beaufort Falls, Spike and Virgil were not nearly as happy.

"I did it just like you said, Spike! I dug a twelve-foot-deep pit and I lined it with the knives, just like that big adventure movie we saw. Then I covered it with the finest ply board I could buy and I scattered leaves all over it. It should have worked!" Virgil was exhausted. It had taken him hours this morning just to wash away all the mud from his all-night work project.

"Did you use thin ply board? Real thin stuff?"

"Well, yeah, but nothing cheap! Only the best! Good quality!" Sighing, Spike brushed the leaves aside, and using his flashlight examined the fine print on one end of the new boarding.

"Rated up to 600 pounds? You fucking moron!" He watched as J.D. disappeared safely into the distance, clothed in his suit and with his Bible tucked primly under one arm. Totally disgusted, Spike turned and strode off in the opposite direction. "I'm gonna hafta get me a new partner," he mumbled, shaking his head.

Chapter Twenty-Eight

Homeless Waifs

Anna wiped away tears for the third time that morning. First, there was the court session scheduled. Pending the results of the evaluation done by the family counselor who would examine the dynamics between J.D. Parsons and his two children, a determination of the best placement for Tessie and her sister Molly would be made. It was only due to her long-standing influence in the department that she was allowed to accompany Parsons, and it was in spite of his angry protests. She'd spent the entire previous week convincing her supervisor to ignore him.

After fifteen years of service, she received her first disciplinary action; a warning that she was becoming far too personally involved with her little charge. It might be in Tessie's best interests and her own, her supervisor told her, for Tessie to be placed in the young children's home to wait for a more permanent solution. There was no question that J.D. wanted the child back, and the charges Anna had made as to his mistreatment of the child were sketchy and improbable.

"Miss Anna! Miss Anna!" The blonde head full of curls rounded the corner and Tessie's sweet little face radiated excitement. "Look what Molly sent me! Look!" A ragged, one-eyed teddy bear trailed in the dirt behind her. It must've come out of the box the department gave her to give to Tessie. Distracted by her thoughts, she'd given it to Tessie without even looking inside.

"Let me see that." She reached for it, but Tessie clutched it protectively.

"I'll give it back. Let me see it, honey."

Reluctantly, Tessie handed it to her idol. It was brown, and had been fuzzy. Through years of use, patches of the fur had worn away, leaving it threadbare; only a jaunty smile revealed the expensive toy it had once been. "See. Molly sent it to me!" Sure enough, it had a note pinned to its front.

FOR TESSIE PARSONS
I LOVE YOU. I WILL SEE YOU SOON.
☺
MOLLY

She handed the toy back to the excited little girl, and ducking her head, hurried out of the room. Damn! She was going to be no good at all if she kept erupting into tears at each small provocation. Choking back her strong reaction, she groped through her desk drawer looking for a tissue.

"Miss Anna?" Tessie stood in the doorway, sunlight pouring through the glass patio doors and framing her golden curls like a halo. "Miss Anna? Am I ever gonna see Molly again?"

"Soon, Honey. You'll see her, soon." The meeting was scheduled for a Wednesday evening a month from today, and it was to consist of herself, J.D., Tessie, Molly and the mental health worker who had insisted that Tessie be present. Her supervisor denied her request to be present during the actual session, but at least she was allowed to accompany them and to remain in the waiting room while the evaluation of "the family group" took place. In her opinion, it wasn't enough to protect Tessie, but it was the best she could do.

Against her will, she pictured the other child in the picture, the strange dark child. She could feel the child's glare even from here, black eyebrows in a straight line, the child's arm thrown protectively around her little angel. The state facility was sadly inadequate to help anyone; especially its little children, and she felt great remorse whenever she was forced to send a child to it for care. Treatment was almost nonexistent, and life in a ward shared with up to twenty other children had to be difficult. No privacy, no personal attention, nothing that she knew was essential to young children was provided there, but it could not be helped. Where else could she send a child who was dangerous to herself and to others? At least she was no longer a danger to Tessie.

She had a hard time picturing Molly ever being a danger to Tessie, though. She remembered the struggle Molly made to remain with her sister, the way she would routinely stand between J.D. and Tessie, the way she would hurry to help her sister whenever the child was given something difficult for a kid her age to handle. The way she screamed Tessie's name when they removed her, kicking and struggling, while they took her away. Everything she saw indicated that Molly adored her little sister and went to great lengths to take care of her.

Even when her personal feelings were involved, the objectivity she acquired during her years of being protective services for the county forced her to admit that Molly was fiercely protective of Tessie and the closest thing to a mother the little girl may have ever experienced. Too often she crept into Tessie's room late at night to give her a last warm hug, only to find her pillow wet from tears, and she had to admit that the child most likely missed her sister, not her dad. Often she appeared about to ask questions, only to turn away with her thoughts unexpressed. Was Tessie afraid to talk to her? She had to find out.

"Tessie? Can you come here a minute?" Thumb in her mouth and clutching the little bear tightly, the child approached Anna slowly, standing in front of her anxiously. Was she always this afraid of adults? Funny. Anna had never really noticed it until this minute.

"Honey, have you missed your sister a lot?" Tessie took her thumb out of her mouth and examined it carefully. It was a fine stubby finger, callused from much sucking on it. She said nothing.

"It's okay to talk to me. I'm not mad. Do you miss Molly a lot?" Tessie shifted from one chubby leg to the other.

"Sometimes." Tessie wrapped both arms around Anna's legs. "I'm sorry." She began to cry softly. "I'm sorry. She's not dead? She's really alive? I'm really going to see her? I didn't know she was really alive. Daddy said he'd make her go away forever. He said he'd make her be a devil in Hell. He said she'd be mashing teeth and whaling." Tessie let go of Anna's legs and sank down onto the floor, sobbing now.

"You thought Molly might be dead? You thought you might never see her again?" With horror, Anna thought of the Bible verse that J.D. must have quoted. What an awful thing to tell a little child about someone she loved. How long had Tessie held this fear inside and pretended to be happy? It was time to get to the bottom of whatever had been going on between J.D. and his children. Who knew what both children went through living with that man? Tessie couldn't answer. Anna scooped her up and held her closely.

"You poor baby. Of course you thought she might be dead. She's not, Tessie. She's fine." She hugged the little girl and rocked her, trying to help her regain control of her emotions.

After a minute, Tessie's agonized sobs lessened, and finally she lay quietly in Anna's arms, eyes closed and her well-used thumb in her mouth. Anna thought about putting her to bed, but it might be better to ask her about Molly now, while the subject seemed open.

"Tessie, what's your sister like?" Tessie's eyes popped open and suddenly she had words, many words for Anna, words rolling out on top of words, barely decipherable.

"Molly's good. She takes care of me. She won't let me get into trouble. She gets me things, makes me pretty so that Daddy likes me. She keeps the scary things away at night. She makes people be nice to me. She won't let them hurt me."

"Who, Tessie? Who wants to hurt you?" Tessie wouldn't respond to this. She snuggled into Anna's arms and refused to say another word. The look in her eyes tore at Anna's heart, but she knew the conversation was over. She may have misjudged the older child. "Tessie, would you like to live with me?" Anna's voice cracked slightly. This was a very important question. Tessie pulled away and looked at her sadly.

"No, Miss Anna. I can't."

"Why not, Honey?" Anna was surprised at her answer. "Why not?"

"I live with Molly. I only live with Molly. I want Molly." Tessie began to sniff, ready to cry again. "I'm sorry. I want Molly. I want Molly. I want Molly." This quickly became a scream and suddenly Tessie was flailing, kicking and fighting, trying to get out of Anna's arms. The social worker tried to comfort the child, but to no avail. She carried the struggling little girl to her bed.

"Quiet, Honey, it'll be all right. I'll fix it."

It took an hour for Tessie to calm and finally sleep in the big bed. Anna curled up next to her, but her mind raced ahead.

She realized that there was no future with this child without her sister, too. Maybe it was time to learn all that she could about the strange older child. It looked like she'd need to prepare for two children, not one. Sighing, she headed for her home office and began reading all of the records on the Parsons girls one more time.

Verbena took a nail out of her mouth and reached for the hammer. Beaver did incredible things for the extra room in the cave, but he had school, and her boys needed help. She knew that soon after 3 PM he'd arrive with more lumber to build more storage area, or other supplies to improve the place. The tall shelves had supplies neatly stacked, each one labeled as to its content--blankets, sheets and pillows, all meticulously stolen from the general closets at the hospital one at the time, so as not to attract attention. What a hardworking, chubby faced little boy he was.

It hurt her to think of the hours the little boy must have spent on the wooden platforms that passed as beds. Each sleeping platform was created from a crate that advertised a different staple--Bearcat Baked Beans, Sweet Sally Sweet Potatoes, County Farm bushel-packed collards. A festive bright red and green cloth, obviously a stolen Christmas tablecloth, separated the two rooms affording privacy to the sleeping quarters. Next to her platform he'd placed a cardboard box covered by a frayed kitchen dry towel and then placed a bouquet of blossoms in the middle of the improvised "bedside table."

Each boy was precious in his own way. Little Freddy had brought her the flowers yesterday, bluebells in a Dixie cup. She had no idea where he'd found them so early in the spring. April showers were just beginning to bring the flowers, and it was still cold outside. The trees were only beginning to show buds which eventually would become leaves, and the main color was still monotone gray from trailing Spanish moss; the same, no matter what the season. She was beginning to understand the order that the boys imposed on the chaotic environment in which they were placed, and her respect for them deepened daily.

Every night Mickey arrived around five with a bag of food, and she prepared the supper meal. There was always enough for her to eat leftovers the next day for lunch. She gave him a list and he turned up with spices, oregano, fresh garlic, and mint for tea. Gradually, she accumulated an iron cooking pot and fry pan, both rusty when brought to her, but she scoured them at the river with sand from the small beach not far from the cave. First thing each morning, Horse appeared to take her five-gallon plastic container to the nearest bathroom for pure water, which she used for cooking, washing dishes and making the tea.

She made sure he had something for breakfast before he hurried off to class. She knew that he must miss the mess hall while filling the jug, and he was far too big a boy to miss a meal. He stood, shoulders hunched, eating his homemade biscuit or his sandwich made from leftovers from the night before, and he always thanked her, embarrassed that she had spent time making food for him. She couldn't find the words to tell him how much she enjoyed it. Fussing over him and the other boys was satisfying to her, deeply fulfilling, and she spent her mornings cleaning and her afternoons waiting for the minute when they all appeared, chatting eagerly about the events of their day. She felt comfortable now hugging the younger ones, and she was waiting for Mickey to come up with a needle and thread so that she could mend Li's jacket and put a pocket on his jeans.

Only Mickey never seemed to need anything. He came and went as silently as ever, often guessing her needs before they were expressed. Like the others, she became used to his nonverbal communication, no longer questioning why or how. He just was, and that was enough.

Tonight was a special night! One week ago tonight she had become a part of their lives, and this morning Mickey appeared with a turkey ready for her to cook. Earlier she had built a spit for it, and all afternoon she slow roasted it, basting it with the dripping juices caught in her metal pot, strategically set close under the fowl and out of the flames. From cornmeal obtained several days ago, she'd made cornbread dressing, and she had an acorn squash for each of the boys, baking them on rocks set in the low coals of the wood fire.

As much as she disliked canned foods, she was glad that she had a backup of green beans and old-fashioned succotash, not her favorites, but the boys seemed to like them. Soon the drippings would be gravy if Mickey showed up with his usual gallon of milk, fresh from the hospital walk-in, its glass bottle sweating on the sides from its few minutes out of the refrigerator. Her boys could really drink milk! She smiled when she thought about "her" boys. Speaking of "her" boys, she heard noises outside. Giving the object she was constructing one last tap with her hammer, she headed for the campfire outside.

They were clustered around the cooking bird like a Norman Rockwell painting, little Freddy extending a finger to taste the oil dropping from the bird, trying to catch it before it reached its waiting pan. She grabbed his hand before he could burn himself. Every face radiated excitement: noses twitching from the odor of the thick fragrant vapors, saliva almost dripping from four half-opened mouths. Four sets of eyes beseeched her, unspoken pleading, starving angels waiting to be fed. She felt a tug behind her and Mickey stood silently, holding her jug of milk and two bright red cans, which he pushed proudly into her arms.

"Cranberry sauce! You have cranberry sauce!" A treat like this was almost unheard of at the hospital. To have intercepted it before the kitchen help stole it was a feat indeed.

Verbena had only been there a week, but she had already figured out the realities of feeding the poor and the mentally ill. What no one else wanted, plus peanut butter; those were the staples of life for them. Her boys saw little of any sort of treats and probably had never tasted cranberry sauce at all. Grinning, she held the cans skyward and began a merry Irish jig.

"Supper in thirty minutes! Come see what I did today! Come on! The food will still be here when you get back!"

Almost dragging Beaver and Freddy, she forced them into the cave to the place where she had been working. Barnes gasped. The planks he had dragged into the cave, planning to build more shelving, were now a large picnic table, complete with plank seating on the sides.

"Now we can all sit and eat together!" Verbena beamed. While Beaver inspected the underneath, Horse sat tentatively in the middle of one side of the bench. When it didn't give under his weight, everyone else found a spot. Suddenly, Freddie scrambled up on the table and threw his arms around Verbena's neck.

"It's pretty, Verbena! It's so pretty!" It was pretty. The old planking Barnes found stacked by the trash once had once been cedar lawn furniture, and it had a cheerful red gleam that matched the room divider perfectly. She was pleased. So pleased; maybe nothing else in her life had ever pleased her so well. She belonged here with these children. If only she could stay hidden and not be torn away from them, her life would be better than any time within her memory.

"Uh, Verbena...when do we eat?" Li struggled to appear polite, but the rich aroma of cooking turkey brought tears to his eyes. Verbena grinned. Time to get back to the prime directive. Food first, credits later.

"Okay, Li, I have a job for you." She handed him the can opener and the cans of cranberry sauce and she went back to rescue the drippings and make gravy. Soon the dressing was ready and the gravy thick, and two hours later they cleared the new table and the group watched Horse and Barnes battle each other in a game of checkers. The round little boy snickered evilly, and the rest of them laughed as he gleefully captured one after another of Harry's players.

When they left later, Verbena curled up in her bed and thought about the change in her life after just one week. She almost felt it physically as her biological clock stopped ticking. She'd found her children, and now she just had to figure out how to keep them.

Chapter Twenty-Nine

The End Is Near

Not far from the cave, Ghost limped toward the luminescent glow of the moon, reflecting off the water in the quickly moving river. It would soon be spring and flowers would bloom, and trees would grace the sky with new branches. Everywhere, the world was pregnant with the anticipation of new life, but the starving dog knew that she would not be there. Every bone in her body ached, and her beautiful white fur now hung off her bones in ragged patches. Her eyes, so blue only a month ago, were now a dull white.

She was a dog, but she also was the woman. She was dying, but a part of her experienced surges of great power. Her head hurt, too, and the thoughts that raced through her mind unnerved her. She had no frame of reference to associate them with her current physical state.

Depleted, she worked her way deep into the dry grass near the path, planning to hollow out a warm spot and rest. She curled into it, whimpering, but could not get comfortable. It was a struggle to move, but she was restless and soon forced her tired legs to carry her back down the little path. Somewhere here, there was a cave. She vaguely remembered it from what seemed a lifetime ago. Someone gave her food in that cave, and she associated it with kindness and comfort.

The last time she had eaten had been so long ago that she no longer felt hungry. She knew she needed to hide, but she couldn't remember why, so she avoided the dumpster that had furnished such good meals to her and her pup so many weeks ago.

She heard a faint rustling near her feet. Instinctively, she lunged at it, tasting sweet fur in her mouth and inhaling the pungent gamy fragrance of live field mouse. She almost swallowed, but caught herself just in time and spat it out, reluctantly. It scurried away, and the woman in her resumed control.

"I am human," she thought, as she stumbled along the trail. Death didn't scare her. She'd experienced death and was grateful to have been given a small taste of life once more. She had only one wish before it claimed her this time, and that was to see her children again, and to find the lost one, the lost little boy.

Squinting, she made out the back of the cave, a small indention in the side of a dark cliff almost parallel to the gushing river. Here she could sleep peacefully. She felt a benign magic here reaching out to her, soothing her, a comforting flow of some positive force. She felt safe here; she could feel it had been the refuge of other fugitives in the past, and it would suit her purposes nicely. Sighing, she settled in to sleep, hoping it wouldn't be her last. She still had much to accomplish.

The dream began quietly, murky pictures and shapes, stars and a big open sky, but soon became *the* dream. Ghost twitched as Eliza filled her dense canine mind with human words and images. She hurt, and was frightened, and something precious was being taken away from her. She saw the foot; the shining aura of its spotless leather, and the smell of the polish nauseated her. She would have vomited if she had eaten anything.

She had a human arm and she reached for the man's leg, but he pinned her arm solidly onto the rough floor with his foot, stepping on it viciously, grinding it into the rough flooring beneath. It hurt, but the pain didn't stop her. She tried to pull herself up but could only make it as far as her knees.

"No! Please, no! Give him back to me. He's mine. He's not yours, he's mine!" From a fog of fatigue and pain, she heard his cold voice, almost a snicker.

"Yes. That *is* the problem, isn't it, you faithless whore? This pathetic little whelp is not mine. You had two! You faithless whoring bitch! You had one for each of us, didn't you? One of mine, and one of his. God will punish you for eternity, you foul scum! You, and the garbage you allowed into your body, will remember the man you disgraced."

"My babies. Please, please give me my babies! I'll be good. I'll do anything you want me to do. Give them to me!"

"Oh you'll get one of them, you slut. And you'll take care of my daughter and educate her in the way I direct you; this girl child and any other children you bear that I know are mine, and mine alone. And you'll return home with me and be faithful to me, and mine. Every day of your life you'll hear the screams of the child you'll never see again. I took you out of the hovel where you learned evil, and I'll be responsible for the re-education of your immortal soul. Say goodbye to this pup of Satan's. Look at it for the last time. Look at it and remember! Always remember what happens if you betray me!"

Holding the little boy by one foot, he swung the infant around so she could see his little face. It gasped in surprise and hurt, its new eyes still unfocused, and its lungs drew air for a gusty cry.

"Kill me, but don't take him away! Please! I'll be good. I'll never let him get in your way. I'll take care of them both. You'll never see him at all. Please let me have him. I'm the one who sinned. He is innocent." Finally running out of words and weak from the loss of blood, she'd still managed to wrap her arms around J.D.'s legs and she'd reached hopelessly for the screaming infant.

He shook his leg to shake her free, and when that didn't work, he kicked her soundly, his shoe bouncing off her tear-streaked cheek. Cowed at last, she'd curled up into a tight ball, sobbing quietly, and had listened as his steps took him out of the cabin and down the dark wooded path; her boy child, like a snared rabbit, struggling and screaming piteously, dangling from one well-cared-for hand.

"Someday I'll kill him. I'll kill him! I'll hurt him and then I will kill him." Her mumbled words comforted her, and after a few minutes she quieted and reached for the other baby, warmly wrapped in a soft blanket a few feet away. "Little mouse, I will take good care of you. He won't dare kill your brother. We'll find your little womb-mate again someday. I'll play his game and I'll take care of you, and when it is time, we'll go and find your brother. Eat now, little dark one." Following instinct centuries old, she placed the baby's mouth on her nipple and the tiny child pulled hungrily. The next morning J.D. returned and took them home.

Ghost jerked awake, not able to sleep again that night. She finally had dreamed to the end, and soon she would fulfill her promise. As the strength in her body ebbed, she felt her spiritual power growing, pulsating within her, waiting to be unleashed. Relaxing, she whimpered, resting, mind wandering idly, wondering how it all would end.

Chapter Thirty

Court In Beaufort Falls

Grimacing, J.D. took another swig from the dark bottle. He hadn't tasted his pal Ancient Age for almost three years, but today he needed its numbing solace. Scowling, he remembered his finest moment and his most humiliating defeat.

The case of J.D. Parsons versus the Beaufort Falls Medical Center lasted three days, and was big news in the small town and in nearby Sicily. Paper after paper sent reporters to sketch the participants. J.D. could barely restrain himself as he watched the artists painstakingly rendering his features to paper; then even more carefully sketching the man by his side, his Sicily lawyer, who ran rings around the staid, less colorful, legal group representing the defense.

John Wilkes Magillacutty was a sight for sore eyes. Immaculately garbed in a sparkling-white, three-piece suit, he accented the "Good Guy" effect with a massive ten-gallon hat and impressive high-heeled alligator hide boots. Texas photographed well in most small southern towns, and he needed to win this case.

After much consultation, he and J.D. reduced the requested damages to one- hundred-thousand dollars. If the lawyer won, half of that would be his, but only if he won. In contrast, J.D.

wore black. The simple man of God look went over big too, and as long as Johnny Cash stayed popular in this area of the country, Magillacutty knew how to work a jury. He and J.D. spent a month practicing just how to act in front of this jury.

It surprised J.D. that the lawyer he'd dumped so precipitately when he got his caddie from the city would even take his case. He was more than willing to take direction, just to keep this impressive genius on his side. Each time John Wilkes swaggered, J.D. became more humble and godly, until the jurors barely even heard the counsel for the defense at all.

Beaufort's lawyers were a dull bunch; plump with full briefcases from which they read one lengthy medical diagnosis after another, until bored beyond all comprehension, the jury slumped onto the wooden bench in a long group nap. Before it was over, almost everyone who had ever worked at the medical center had testified for the defense.

"Yes, I'm familiar with the man seated in the front row." Nurse after nurse after nurse verified the time he had spent in the hospital. "No, I never saw him mistreated or neglected."

Only the guilty manner in which each looked toward the stern face of their boss who sat on the other side of the courtroom gave them away. A. E. Beaufort, III, stared impassively ahead, not responding to any of the anxious glances in his direction. John Wilkes stayed as subtle as a sledgehammer in his cross-examination.

"You haven't been directed in your testimony in any way?" Sarcasm dripped from each word as he sneered openly at the patrician features of the hospital administrator who was seated across the courtroom from him. The final straw for the defense came when the poor black nurse's aide, who had tried to fit J.D.'s living body into the body bag, was forced onto the stand. John Wilkes began gently.

"We all realize you were only doing your job. You did nothing wrong. Can you tell me what happened?" John Wilkes spoke softly to the nervous lady. She could barely choke out the words and never took her eyes off A. E. Beaufort. She was visibly uncomfortable, sweat running down her new Sunday-meeting dress and staining its front, and her eyes were huge in her wrinkled face. Often, she wiped her neck with a huge handkerchief that she held in one swollen, work-reddened, hand.

"I puts the bodies in tha bags when they is dead 'n I wheels 'em down to the morgue. They tole me to sack 'im up 'n I did, but he jumps out 'n when I goes to stuff 'im in, he falls on tha floor. Ain't that what's happened, Mister Beaufort?"

The jurors were all awake now. Beaufort shifted in his chair and expressed his disgust by examining something far from the scene in front of him, some occurrence out in the hall. The woman didn't take the hint and continued her undisguised appeal for help, attempting to make eye contact with the embarrassed dignitary. Hiding a gleeful grin, John Wilkes continued his examination.

"And this body was dead?"

"No Sirh, it wa'n't dead. When he hit the groun', Mr. J.D., he commenced to thrashing aroun' 'n makin' noises..."

"And you helped him back onto the bed?" The woman looked desperately to Beaufort for help.

"Ah, no Sirh."

"You didn't help the poor man back into his hospital bed? The man who was cruelly misdiagnosed as dead and that you almost took to the morgue?" John Wilkes' voice increased in volume as he turned to the jury for sympathy. They were hanging on his every word, waiting to hear what other indignities poor J.D. suffered.

"And what did you do, may I ask? What assistance did you render the poor helpless man at your feet, rolling and thrashing around, begging for the aid of some qualified member of the Beaufort Falls Medical Center staff to alleviate his pain, maybe even save his life at this very crucial moment?"

"I done run, Mister. I ain't never seen no dead body ack that way 'n I ain't never bagged no haints." Tears flowed copiously down her dark face. Reaching the limit of what she was able to endure, she half-rose, then stood and let herself out of the gated wooden cubicle, leaving her hankie behind."

"Ma'am, you aren't allowed to leave the box yet!" The bailiff tried to retrieve her, in vain. She fled down the hall and out of the courthouse before he had the presence of mind to follow her. All eyes turned to John Wilkes, frozen in mid flourish. Turning so that the reporters could photograph his best side, his face was a classic study of exasperation and patience. Flashbulbs popped illegally on every side. A few remembered to photograph J.D., who was doing his best to look ill and pathetic in the nearby front row.

"Would you like for me to have her returned to the stand?" Even the judge was a bit puzzled as to the proper procedure to follow when a witness made a successful getaway. Voice dripping patience, John Wilkes answered.

"No, your Honor, I think we have gotten all the answers we need from that witness." A. E. Beaufort didn't return after the lunch break and wasn't seen in the courtroom again.

When J.D. took the stand, he was very careful to let his lawyer lead him. He'd developed a wealth of respect for the man's instincts during the month they'd practiced his testimony, and at John Wilkes' insistence, he'd gotten "humble" down perfectly. He believed his part; a poor man of God who'd entrusted his life to the facility several times, and each time he found himself nearer death's door after several days in the hospital than when he'd been admitted. No, he didn't know if anyone at the Center had a grudge against him. They were just negligent and careless, and the pain he suffered due to their ineptitude was agonizing.

"Yes. I lost days of work, due to the time spent in the hospital, when I should have been earning money to support my children. I have two. One is a special needs child, currently undergoing treatment."

"Isn't the other in the custody of the State due to your mistreatment of her?" The lawyer representing Beaufort Falls looked toward the jury, hoping for a shocked reaction.

All eyes returned to John Duke Parsons, waiting for his reaction. There was none. He remained quietly composed, staring at his hands, which were meekly folded in his lap. Glistening with wronged innocence, he lifted his eyes to meet their questioning stares. *Lord God of Hosts, please help me.* He and John Wilkes must have practiced for this moment a thousand times. None of the intense anger consuming him showed on his face.

"Tessie, my littlest angel, was removed from my care due to the danger presented to her by her sister, who's unstable and violent, and the authorities haven't yet finished the studies needed to place her back in my custody. I'm counting the days until she is back home again."

Fortunately, no one watched John Wilkes right then. As it became apparent that the lawyers hadn't done their homework and weren't going to counter with the fact that Tessie wasn't removed until after Molly had been gone several months, he expelled a long sigh of relief. He was right in his assessment of the Beaufort Falls team. They were civil lawyers, not used to dealing with a jury. They had no clue what to research or how to manage people. J.D. exceeded his expectations as a credible witness. The jury bought his story; hook, line and sinker.

Sure enough, the counsel for the defense ignored the sympathetic looks J.D. received from the jurors and waded right into quicksand.

"Isn't it true that you're a violent man, given to outbursts of rage and very demanding of your children?"

"Objection, your Honor!" John Wilkes quickly attempted to sidetrack that line of questioning. "This has no bearing at all on the case at hand!" Before the judge could uphold the objection, J.D. answered. For the first time in his life he was getting the recognition he deserved.

"I don't mind answering the question." John Wilkes held his breath as J.D. continued. "I'm a stern man of God. I'm just, but I believe in discipline. My children have rules and are required to act in a Godly fashion, to perform chores to help run the household, to be mannerly and polite to all. If this makes me an unfit father, then I think more parents should be unfit like me. I admit that I've been on edge lately, but my health has been poor, mainly due to the blundering treatment of the medical facility in question today. I've been careful to moderate my responses where my sweet little girls are concerned. All I want in the world is to have my little children back home with me, and to have my sadly destroyed health back, so that they have at least one parent left to care for them until they reach maturity and can care for themselves."

The defense couldn't have made a bigger mistake if they'd planned it. The jury belonged to J.D. now, and the rest of the trial was merely a formality. Beaufort and most of his defense team weren't even present for their final arguments on the last day.

After the defense finished, John Wilkes reexamined several members of J.D.'s church who testified that when they had visited him in the hospital the last several times he was hospitalized, not one nurse had visited the room during the four hours or so that they were present. With that information fresh in their minds, Magillicutty concluded, and the judge sent the jury out to make their verdict. The outcome wasn't really in doubt, but the amount of the award could vary dramatically, so J.D. and his lawyer paced nervously, awaiting the decision of his peers. After a record sequester of only one hour, the jury filed back in, satisfied looks on every face.

"The jury finds in favor of the plaintiff, John Duke Parsons, for the amount of seventy-five-thousand dollars and forty-nine cents, to be collected from the Beaufort Falls Medical Center, at a time agreeable to both parties. The above amount is to cover injury, suffering, court and legal costs incurred due to the negligence of the named organization." The judge read the short document impassively; then called both lawyers to the bench to give instructions for collection of the award.

Although God was on his side, he hadn't really anticipated that victory could be this easy. On his right, he watched the lawyers from the facility that caused him so much suffering, waiting for some indication that they were vexed or some sign that they felt punished for their grievous sins, but the three men were laughing and joking with each other. They didn't seem in the least concerned that they had lost the most important lawsuit ever to be tried in the local courts. Something was wrong, very wrong, and all sorts of alarm bells reverberated through his head. Easing to the end of the front row bench, he strained to hear what the lawyers and judge were saying.

"Your Honor, I am afraid that I have an announcement to make, and it may make a difference in the disposition of this case." A man he had not seen in the courtroom previously was trying to get the judge's attention

"The bench recognizes Mr. Ernest Arnold. You may proceed." This couldn't be good news. Fixated on the stranger in the same way he regarded any other legion of the devil, J.D. sat motionless waiting for calamity to strike. And it did.

"Your Honor, it is with regret that I must inform you that the Beaufort Falls Medical Center no longer exists. As of one o'clock this afternoon, it was bought and absorbed by a group of concerned citizens in Sicily, and it is no longer responsible for any actions pending against it." Moving forward, the man handed the judge a fistful of legal looking documents, and his Honor reached for his reading glasses, put them on and then skimmed the paperwork quickly.

"Hmmm. These look to be in order." Minutes passed. "Ahhh. Here it is." Squinting, he read the next-to-the-last paragraph on the next-to-the-last page out loud.

"Ashley Eugene Beaufort Memorial Hospital and Research Center will absorb no debts, judgments, liabilities, or outstanding judgments from the company previously known as Beaufort Falls Medical Center. All assets become property of Ashley Eugene Beaufort Memorial Hospital and Research Center."

J.D.'s attorney recovered quickly.

"If it's permissible, may I see those documents, please?" The judge handed them to him with the paragraph still visible, but the lawyer shuffled the papers, turning his attention to paragraphs from the first page. J.D. could no longer hear any of the words that were being exchanged, but he couldn't mistake the panic in John Wilkes' eyes as he found the passages he feared.

"You may, of course, pursue collection with the original defendant, if it still exists, or the receiver of the moneys resulting from the sale." With these last few words, the judge recovered the papers, handed them to the defending lawyer, and then reached for his gavel to dismiss the case.

"Court adjourned." His job was finished.

Methodically, Mr. Arnold replaced the papers in his briefcase and was turning to leave when he felt a hand on his elbow.

"You'll send us a certified copy of all documents you have regarding the sale of Beaufort Falls Medical Center by 5 PM this evening?" No longer radiating confidence, this was more of a request than an order from a man who fifteen minutes before had been the star of the show. J.D. wondered, was it just his imagination or had John Wilkes just shrunk two inches?

"Of course, of course." Mr. Arnold was busy receiving pats on the back from three cheerful-looking defendants who did not look like they just lost an expensive lawsuit. John Wilkes didn't even return to J.D. Instead, he moved toward the door, forcing J.D. to run to catch up with him before he evaporated into the crowd.

"What's wrong?" There was nothing humble or godly about J.D. now. Bristling, he gripped his lawyer's right arm and refused to let go when the man kept moving.

"I don't know yet. I have to study the papers. I'll call you as soon as I know," Magillacutty mumbled in an octave that J.D. had never heard from his golden throat.

"When will we get the money?" J.D. refused to lose the victory he'd fought so hard to win. "Someone will have to pay us. Right?" John Wilkes avoided eye contact.

"Let me read the papers. I'll let you know as soon as I know. Let me go for now and I'll talk to you tomorrow." He shook out of J.D.'s grasp and left the courthouse quickly, leaving his client standing rooted to the floor, the last person to leave the rapidly emptying courtroom.

Shaking his head sadly, J.D. returned to reality, and turning the now-empty whiskey bottle bottom-up, he tossed it into the rapidly growing stack of bottles next to his front door. Somehow, even in this condition, he was too anal to leave them where he'd finished them. Old habits die hard. He finally had his answer. After six days of calling Sicily long distance just to be told that John Wilkes Magillacutty was not in his office, he finally gave up. He'd been far too drunk to drive to Sicily, so he just waited, and here was his answer. He'd almost been too drunk to sign for it an hour ago when the postman had knocked on his door, and now he just wished the postman had never come. Two hours ago, he'd had a future.

"For the thing I greatly feared has come upon me, and that of which I was greatly afraid is come unto me." Not even these words from Job comforted him. A few minutes ago, he'd been a rich man. Now it appeared that he had lost even the meager possessions he had worked his lifetime to accumulate. Numb and barely able to comprehend them, he read the unbelievable words once more.

"It appears that the money is not collectible. The money paid for the Beaufort Falls Medical Center is placed in a irrevocable trust for the betterment of Beaufort Falls, in memory of the late Ashley Eugene Beaufort, and its only obligation is a yearly income payable to his grandson, Ashley Eugene Beaufort, III, and his heirs, for so long as the new facility, the Ashley Eugene Beaufort Memorial Hospital and Research Facility in Sicily,

Alabama, exists. There is no way around it. None of the money is touchable. It's a totally new facility and in no way responsible for the debts of the old, and no individual can be held responsible for any debts incurred by the facility, so the income going to Beaufort can't be touched either." But then the situation became grimmer.

"As discussed at the onset of our business relationship, I will receive no fees for my personal investment of time; however, legal fees and court fees incurred must be paid, along with the moneys expended to my research and law clerks, all of whom are awaiting payment. Please remit $13,457.43 to my office by Thursday, March 21st, or I will be forced to file the documents placed in my name as collateral so that your house will be sold to ensure prompt payment. "

His face contorted with rage, J.D. crushed the fragile stationery in his clenched fist, but he knew it wouldn't save his house. The lawyer wasn't to blame. It was just the nature of the beast, he reflected. John Wilkes Magillacutty was just holding his hand out for his thirty pieces of silver; he wasn't the original betrayer.

It all started with that whore Eliza. It was the bitch and her babies. It was a shame he didn't get rid of both of those babies, the boy and the dark girl. Maybe neither of them was his. The only good thing the bitch ever produced was his Tessie, and he was going to get her back, and soon!

How could he have missed the mark of Satan on Molly? Was it because it was so obvious on the boy baby? What a fool he was ever to have thought Molly was his seed. What a fool. Eight years of carefully instructing the spawn of the devil in the ways of the Lord? It was sacrilege, but he would soon set things right. Quoting the book of Job once more, he remembered a more appropriate passage.

"Remember, I pray thee, who ever perished who was innocent? Where were the righteous cut off? Even as I have seen, they that plow iniquity and sow wickedness reap the same. By the blast of God they shall perish, and by the breath of his nostrils are they consumed." The anger sobered him and quivering with fury, he strode into his kitchen and yanked open the cutlery drawer. Reaching inside, he removed his whetstone, then a seven-inch long paring knife.

"The wages of sin is death." This had a very nice cadence to it. *"The wages of sin is death. The wages of sin is death."* With each stroke of metal against stone he repeated his new mantra. As soon as he got Tessie back, his enemies would die. He had nothing more to lose.

Chapter Thirty-One

Female Things

Charlie shifted his feet nervously. Applying for work was nothing new. Applying to work at his place of former employment while dressed as a woman *was* new, and his greatest fear was that some woman would walk by and recognize her dress. He cleared his throat, resisting the urge to practice his falsetto. The floor supervisor approached him. Demurely, Charlie lowered his eyes.

The man examined him closely and Charlie wondered if his makeup was running. No matter how hard he tried, he just couldn't get it to hide his five o'clock shadow for long. It would have to do. Without a car there was nowhere else he could work, and without money, he had no easy way to get a car. Not to mention he was starving, and only one step above robbing the dumpster. If only he could get them to hire him and pay him cash, he'd only have to work a week or two before he could make his getaway. To hell with the car. Right now, with a few bucks, he'd take the bus to anywhere else but here.

Dressing took him hours, but he had little else to do. The stiff, stretchy, white hose he found hanging on the line were murder to pull over his rear, but they felt good on his legs, tingling and snappy, and they were thick enough to hide his leg hairs. The dress was navy blue polyester, very appropriate, he thought, for a woman of his mature age, and it never needed ironing

"Next." The man turned and Charlie followed him into the dimly lit office on the bottom floor of the Administration Building. He thought he saw approval in the supervisor's dark eyes.

"Why do you want to work for the West Alabama Regional Children's Psychiatric Hospital?"

"I'm living with my sister Elsie and I need some money to help her with the bills. Her husband died and I came up from Florida to help out with the house and the kids, but she don't have enough money to take care of us all. I ain't never worked before, but I can peel potatoes and wash dishes right good. I'll take anything you pay me, but I need a job real bad." It wasn't so hard pretending to be female. He could see that the man believed him.

"When could you start?" It was going to happen. Charlie felt three tons lighter. It didn't even matter that his crotch was sore where the panty hose fit a little too tight.

"Today, if you want. When would I get paid?" The super looked closely at Charlie one more time. She sure was big, but those North Florida swamp women were known for being on the brawny side. Well, at least he wouldn't lose this one to the cook. He'd sooner mate with the yard rats than this heifer.

"Checks go out on Fridays." Charlie panicked. There was no way he could ever cash a check.

"Can I have mine in real money? I do'n have no bank account and I do'n think anyone will open one for me until I get some money. I'll work for cheaper if that's a problem." The manager sighed. Always there was some problem. He sure could use some help right now. The former scrub-lady had quit two days ago, and the rest of the staff would, too, if someone didn't get in there and clean up, right now.

"Well, I guess we can find cash for you if you're a good worker. Let me get you a uniform and you can start right away. You're about a size twenty-two? Charlie just nodded. He would have to take a look on the tag in the dress he was wearing. He had no idea what size it was, just that he was lucky and it fit.

"Sign these. You can write, can't you?"

"A little." Charlie didn't want to have to do too much writing.

"Well, it isn't rocket science. Just put your name in all the spaces and write your address and I'll fill in the rest." Gratefully, Charlie scrawled Charlene Baker in each space, added the address of a pathetic hovel he had seen down the road, and shoved the papers back to his new employer.

"Thank you, Mister! Tell me where I can change my clothes and I'll get started right now." The director motioned him toward the ward bathroom and then pointed down the hall to the large kitchen area, where the meals for the institution were all prepared.

"Down there, when you are through. Just tell Lenny I sent you. He'll get you a uniform and tell you what to do." Charlie hurried toward the kitchen before the man could change his mind. Fifteen minutes later, he emerged from one of the hall bathrooms, once again in a West Alabama uniform, only this time it was a skirt. Lenny hardly looked at him when he reported for duty.

"Back there. Wash some dishes. Call me if you need help finding anything. Wait a sec. Here's a timecard. Go punch this in the machine over by the door." Charlie realized the cook had never even asked his name. This was great! It was going to work. No one would ever think of looking for him here, especially not as Charlene.

Humming cheerfully, he carried his first huge stack of dishes to the triple-sized industrial sink. The warm water felt good on his hands and he could smell the wonderful aroma of food cooking. It looked like it was going to be hot dog night and he could smell the buns cooking. One more thing he had to know. Wiping his hands carefully, he left his place in front of the sink and went to find his boss.

"Lenny," he asked plaintively, "do I get meals?"

"Yeah. Yeah." Lenny had a thousand things to do and no time to answer foolish questions. "Yeah. All you can eat." Charlie grinned. Things really were looking up.

He didn't see the green eyes watching him from the cooler or the little form that slipped past him into the night, carrying a backpack full of ham, cheese, and cans of corn for another meal in the making. Charlie confused him, but he found that the people around him frequently weren't what they seemed to be. He knew this was the man he had left in the old slave cabin, but he didn't understand why he was wearing women's clothes.

He could feel the man's basic emotions and he felt relief, a strange gaiety, and something that wasn't right. He could feel that the man was hungry and would soon eat, but there was nervous tension as well. Mickey pulled back from its cold wrongness. Everything about this man was terribly different, and he needed to know why.

He stopped in the clearing and focused on Charlie, watching him through the open window as he scraped and cleaned the plates. The man who had introduced himself to the director as "Charlene" sang softly–what song was it? It was something about a hound dog. Reaching hard, he tried to gain entrance into Charlie's thoughts again, and he found less resistance than before. The man was wondering if he should get his fingernails done. More puzzled than ever, Mickey moved into the darkness and began his nightly walk to the cave.

A few miles away, Verbena also handled plates, but she was arranging them on the new picnic table while waiting for her nightly groceries. Horse had turned up with an entire set of dishes, pretty china with pink and blue flowers, and bashfully bestowed them upon her that morning. She'd spent more than an hour washing them in the river and then admiring their delicate patterns in the pale spring sunshine. Every day was filled with a new joy for her. She set the flowers that Freddy found and picked for her every afternoon in the center of her new table, and placed the silverware that Beaver had carved from wood for each of them at each place. These were her treasures, she thought; then she changed her statement. The boys were her treasures, not the things that they made. She couldn't remember ever being so loved or so needed before in her entire life.

"Mickey?" She thought she heard a noise, but it came from the back of the cave, not the front. She heard it again. "Mickey?" Once again there was no response. "Mickey, is that you?" Only the echo of her own voice rang in the pristine silence. No one was there, or at least no one who wanted his presence known. Panic enveloped her.

What if it was Charlie? What if he found her here? She looked for a place to run, then decided to investigate first. What if it was just one of the boys home early? Reaching for the butcher knife, she walked to the front of the cave and it was empty. Holding the knife close by her side, she reentered her home, and scanned carefully, exiting this time from the back. Then she heard the noise again, a faint whine, that of an animal in pain.

The back of the cave was made of a sheer wall of rock, facing the river, and their little niche was just one of dozens of small holes in its surface. Worried now, she examined the nearby recesses. A hurt animal could harm her or her boys if it was hungry enough. Following the contours, she saw a patch of dirty white, and then she moved back to look at the creature inhabiting the crevice in the rock.

A wolf-like dog stared back at her, its blue eyes glazed and barely able to focus, its bones jutting painfully from its gaunt body. The sun caught the animal, forming bright rainbows in its fur, and for a fraction of a second she saw a woman, an emaciated woman, dressed in a green silk wrap, but the illusion faded as quickly as it came. A wave of sadness washed through her.

She didn't understand exactly why, but she felt compelled to help this creature. A strong maternal bond perhaps, or the joining of two like souls who knew nothing but the cruelty of life and the agony of loneliness; some strong, barely understood need to bond with the pitiful animal erased all fear, and she put her knife down on a nearby rock.

"Poor little mother." Why did she say that? Coming closer, she could see that the creature was, indeed, a female and probably had whelped a pup not that long ago. The ribs protruding from her sides indicated that things hadn't gone well for her. She reached forward and touched its nose. It was warm and very dry to the touch. Ghost pulled back sharply, then the slightest tip of pink tongue emerged, touching Verbena's hand gently.

"You poor, dear. I bet I've got some scraps for you. I'll be right back." Soon she realized that the animal was in no condition for food, though; first it needed a warm blanket and some water. It looked seriously dehydrated and very weak. Verbena pulled the blanket off of her bed and grabbed her spoon and filled a pretty china cup with water.

Ghost was half out of the hole by the time she got back. She carefully spooned water into the animal's mouth and Ghost lapped it gratefully. Although the dog was knee high to her, Verbena scooped her into the blanket and carried her into the cave like a baby. The Clan had a new member, if she could save it. A dog was a good thing to have around, Verbena rationalized, a very good thing.

The boys were delighted to see the dog when they arrived at the cave later and Li eagerly gave his approval to the new addition. Only one member of the group recognized the pathetic heap of bones as the proud fierce animal that had entered the cave earlier and shared their meal in what seemed like a century ago.

For the second time that night, Mickey was confused. The creature wasn't a dog, he could feel that, but once again he encountered a barrier that wouldn't yield to his soft psychic probe. This time the force he sensed wasn't cold, but fiery hot, seething and powerful, and it hurt his head when he tried to penetrate it. Obviously, more than one sort of creature was afoot that he did not understand.

While the others clustered around Ghost, he vanished quietly. He had an awful lot to think about, and it was time to try to understand the next step. Change was inevitable and the time of awakening near. He had no inkling of what to expect next.

Chapter Thirty-Two

Girls Will Be Girls

"Honey, you do that like you ain't never put lipstick on before. Where you been, all your life, in a barn? Gimme here." Charlie held very still as the tiny woman stretched to apply Pink Passion lip color to his pursed lips. He thought about kneeling so that she wouldn't have to stand on her tiptoes, but reconsidered. It would get big dirty spots on his white hose, and besides, her outstretched arms gloriously accentuated the view of her breasts straining against the white material of her uniform. It was all he could do to concentrate on the mirror and not look down.

"I'm a girl. I'm a girl. I'm a girl."

The mantra he recited silently wasn't working, and he was afraid she'd feel something extra pressing against the front of his white dress if she leaned any closer to him. The scent she wore drove him insane. All in all, the women's bathroom was a joy he'd never anticipated when he became Charlene, and it never ceased to amaze him the number of things women did in there. It was like a club, and he was thrilled to belong. He was even tall enough to see over the top of the stalls as long as no one caught him doing it. Since most of the women wore their regular clothes and changed to their uniforms once they got there, it was worth looking.

The girls were so nice to him, too. As soon as they heard that he was working to help his poor sister recover from the tragic accident that cost her a husband and the use of her legs, they all wanted to help. Generously, they volunteered tips as to how he could accentuate his height and where to find the best deals on clothes and makeup for someone his size. Sissy even had a diet she thought would work for him if he wanted to "slim down." He loved being the center of their attention and tried as hard as he could to forget just how desirable they all were, so that he could be a proper lady.

When the lipstick was on straight, he followed Karen back to the kitchen to finish the shift. They had fifteen minutes left and she was going to give him a ride into town to the drug store so he could buy a few little necessities, some deodorant and a little eyeliner, both long exhausted. This was so exciting! It was his first time off the West Alabama hospital grounds in weeks.

If he had a few more dollars, he'd just take the ride into town and then catch a bus, but if he did that, he'd lose everything he owned. He couldn't imagine living without his friends, Nate and Arlene, and he couldn't figure how he would transport them safely on public transportation. Besides, he was getting along great at work. His enthusiasm was contagious. After a week of not eating and contemplating the electric chair, working was good! Lenny was proud of the way he took right to scraping the plates and disinfecting in exactly the approved manner; he was a real scrubwoman prodigy! Now he even had a ride to town.

Two hours later, he laughed and giggled with Karen as she drove her old car back toward the hospital grounds to take him home. He smelled like the Tasty Burger and had his precious bag of cosmetics stashed under the seat.

"Where is it you live? I can't wait to meet your sister and those precious little kids of hers. I might even have some clothes from my little Rose that would fit her baby. If it's not too much trouble, I'd love to stick my head in and say 'hi.' She sounds like such a brave woman. I'd love to help."

"Oh shit." Quickly, he glanced up to see if Karen had heard him, but she was busy with her own thoughts. Why hadn't he anticipated this? He was so screwed. What could he do? It was time to think and think fast before they got any closer. He'd planned to have her let him off at the entrance to the hospital.

"I don't want to put you to any trouble and I know that she wouldn't either. She's still really shy about her condition." Charlie saw the entrance driveway looming ahead. "You can just let me off here."

"Oh no! I couldn't leave you so far away! Walking alone in the darkness here on these grounds? I'll drive you right to your door. Are you sure she would mind a quick visit from a friend? I'd really like to meet her. I won't stay long." Charlie started to sweat under his makeup. In good light, he knew his beard would begin to show. He had to get out of there soon. Why did he agree to get stuck in someone's car with no graceful exit? He was a fool, a total idiot. He deserved to get caught! What could he say to get rid of her without causing suspicion?

"Uh, one of the kids may have the flu. Flossy was looking pretty sick earlier today. I didn't want to say anything in case they wouldn't let me wash the dishes, but it would really be good if you didn't come in."

"Isn't this your house right here?" Horrified, Charlie saw that she'd stopped right opposite the hovel he'd listed as his address on the application. How did she know that address? Then he realized she'd just put two and two together from the information he'd given them all. This was the only house on the road right down from the hospital. In fact, this was the only residence for at least a mile. What fucking bad luck!

"Thanks for the ride!" He hopped out quickly before she could decide to follow. It was with great relief that he watched her pull away, but just in case she watched him from her rear view mirror, he walked toward the house. As she disappeared into the darkness, his relief turned into irritation. Now he had a thirty-minute walk back to his cabin. All of this was unnecessary grief; just so some self-righteous biddy could think she was doing a good deed. Kicking pebbles, he moved up the driveway next to the house. Maybe he could find a path behind it that would cut some time off his trip.

What a strange place he'd listed as his home. It was actually a shanty; its weather-stained planks met at odd angles and the entire structure looked as if it could be blown away by the smallest storm. A sagging front porch barely attached itself to the main frame, and, as might be expected, on it sat an old washing machine next to a ragged front porch swing. The entire house was barely larger than a shed, and only the smoke escaping from the chimney on its roof indicated that people actually lived there.

The yard was equally squalid. An old Ford leaned to the right, resting on two flat tires, next to a woodpile and a chicken coop, where a couple of scrawny chickens awaited their fate as a future Sunday dinner.

"I can't believe I listed this place as the place I live." Disgusted, he gave the back of the old car a kick. Still, he was here and he was curious. He might as well learn all he could about it. Karen was certain to ask more questions and he would need answers. He guessed he could just claim he was lost and needed directions if anyone caught him wandering around. That would work.

Someone had covered the windows with bright-red, feed-sack curtains. At some time in their meager existence, the chickens had actually eaten commercial chickenfeed, obviously *Birdie-Bye, Cream of the Crop, Corn Mash*, as the lettering on the burlap read. As he came closer to the house, Charlie heard children's voices, and since one curtain was slightly open, he couldn't resist the urge to peek inside.

He looked into a living room where four laughing little girls entertained one painfully-thin, mocha-colored old man. Along one wall a fire blazed in an open fireplace, and just barely visible, he could see the kitchen where a huge black woman cooked over a wood stove. Charlie inhaled deeply. Whatever she was cooking smelled heavenly.

A high-pitched giggle interrupted his dream of food. The old guy sat on a battered couch surrounded by the wire-haired children, dressed in pajamas, and he appeared to be finishing a bedtime story, a good one if the looks on the faces of the little ones could be trusted. Straining to hear, Charlie leaned closer to the cracked window.

"Paw Paw, tell us another un! Please! Please! Oh, please!"

"Ain't no time for no mo' stories. Gladys, ain't you got that bacon fried by now? Cornbread 'n collards ain't never took so long befo. You knows I has to git ta work." Something about his face looked familiar. Charlie knew that face from somewhere.

"Homer, hep me git this wood in the stove. I's gonna need mo' if'n I get this cooked in time fo' ya ta eat."

In the light reflected from the fireplace, Charlie got his first good look at the man—creamy-dark skin stretched over a small skull, coarse, fuzzy-white hair, and the long, finely etched nose not typical of his race--*Homer. She called him Homer!*

Suddenly Charlie remembered the old man who'd had the audacity to tell him how to do his job when he started as a security guard not long ago. *Damn uppity, janitor! So this is* his *house?*

"Paw Paw, lemme help." The littlest child ran up behind the old man and threw her arms around his legs. Homer kneeled and hugged her close. Tears slid down the wrinkled corners of his sad old eyes. The doctor had given him grim news this afternoon and he hadn't been able to shake his aching sadness all evening long.

"I do'n know what I'm gonna do 'bout dis. These younguns here needs me. I ain't gonna be around ta hep 'em. Oh, Lawd, how comes ya ta want me in Glory now when they caint do wifout me? I ain't smoked nary a cigarette for years 'n I gets the coughin' curse now? Wha'll they do wifout me? Wha'll they do? They is like bright stars sprinkled on yo' night sky and yo' has to have me leave um now?" he mumbled quietly to himself, as the tiny girl turned to listen to her mother calling from the kitchen.

Since her husband had disappeared two years ago, Gladys needed the little bit her father earned working night shift at the hospital to supplement what she could eke out cleaning and caring for white folks' kids in Sicily. If they hadn't already owned the house, they would have lost it. It was all she and Homer together could do to earn the taxes each year. Working nights while she worked days allowed him to be able to take care of this littlest one, barely five and still too young for kindergarten, while she and the rest of the family were gone working and going to school during the day. Leaning away from the baby, he coughed, each hacking rasp shaking his entire body.

"Ya okay, Paw Paw?" The child returned to help him, worried about the violence of each convulsive shudder.

"I'se fine, honeychile. Now run back 'n hep Edna plait Nina's hair. You be my pretty, little, diamond-girl, Imaline, the queen of my heart."

"I loves ya. I loves ya, so much." Before returning to hover near her sister, she planted a kiss on the tip of the white-haired old man's nose.

Charlie examined the sad face, a portrait of futility, as light from the fire flickered across it. What a noble profile. He could see it sitting on his shelf next to Nate and Arlene. That white hair could be fluffed out nicely. He continued watching, as Homer helped his daughter move the huge tree trunk into the stove.

"This ain't never gonna burn lessen we brings some twigs out frum the woodpile. I be back in jist a flick of a coon's tail." He summoned the energy to walk briskly toward the backyard stack of wood. It would be better if Gladys and the kids didn't know he was sick. She would never let him keep working. He needed to stop at the outhouse, too. Suddenly, he had to piss like a racehorse.

A strange sight met his eyes as he rounded the corner. A huge, very white rear shimmered in the moonlight. As he watched, it pulled away from his window with a jerk and the person peeking in turned to face him. Shock turned to incredulous surprise as the face came into focus. He was more perplexed at his recognition of its owner than angry that the man was looking in his window.

"What the hell you do'in dressed up lak a woman 'n sneakin' roun' my window, boy? Ya ain't no girl 'n yo sho ain't pretty in that getup."

Charlie said nothing. He reached for the axe sitting conveniently nearby. A heartbeat later, he disappeared into the woods, cradling a new trophy, holding it away from his white uniform. Homer would never cough again.

A mile away, Verbena tried one last time to coax Ghost over to Mickey. Neither liked it. Whenever she talked to Mickey, Ghost growled, baring savage teeth and bristling white fur. Mickey didn't seem to like the dog, either. She would turn her back and he would be gone, vanishing like a wisp of breeze. She didn't understand it at all. Around everyone else, the dog was a model guardian; only Mickey seemed to disturb it, and only when she talked to Mickey. It ignored him otherwise, almost walking through him as if he were not there at all. It was a mystery she wanted to solve, because the only time Mickey came around now was to bring the food. She missed him and it was the dog's fault. She wished she could figure out why.

Chapter Thirty-Three

Almost Encounters

"*N ow the day is over
Night is drawing nigh.
Shadows of the evening
Steal across the sky.*"

The sweet voices of the children lingered even as the last notes of the song faded into the dusk. Anna Johnson couldn't believe the sadness reflected in the faces of her little group. These kids were tired, already battered by life at the tender ages of nine through twelve, and there was none of the rambunctious play she associated with childhood. They behaved more like the residents of an old people's home, serious and quiet, speaking only when spoken to, frequently distracted by inner thoughts and staring blankly ahead.

Over the years her job had rendered her immune to most misery, but the contrast between these children and even the most abused ones she had placed in foster homes tore at her heart. The difference between them and the little wonder who now made her life worth living was like the difference between the warmth of summer and the damp cold of an Alabama winter day. Their sagging little shoulders and barely-discernible whispers strengthened her resolve to protect her dancing angel from a fate like this, and to make sure that her life was full of laughter, a family, and fun.

In fact, Tessie's happiness was the entire reason she was here. She missed her sister. Now that she felt comfortable with Anna, her last words every night were a little prayer, always the same.

"Oh, God, please teach me how to be good, and please take care of Miss Anna, and please take care of Molly, and let her get well and come home. Please, let her come home tomorrow." Anna would hurry from the room so that the little girl wouldn't see the tears in her eyes. She'd fix things for her if she could. She'd made a solemn promise to herself that if Molly made Tessie happy, then Molly would also have a home; however, getting custody of Molly would even be more difficult than retaining custody of Tessie. It was almost impossible to obtain information about Molly as long as J.D. blocked her at every turn. The department forbade her to have any contact with Molly, or to allow Tessie to see her sister, until after the custody hearing was over.

"Any intervention at all could tip the balance and give Mr. Parsons material he could use in a lawsuit, Anna. I'm sure you understand how delicate our position is right now."

Anna didn't agree with her supervisor, but she didn't argue. Since petitioning for permanent custody of Tessie, she knew that even after thirteen years of taking care of the rejected little ones of Beaufort County, her job was still very much on the line. If she pulled the miracle off and did get custody of the two girls, she would most likely just sell her pretty house and move somewhere else, like Atlanta; somewhere the people weren't all so provincial. With her experience she could get a job anywhere, just so long as there were no black marks on her record.

Keeping this in mind, she accumulated information on Molly very carefully, examining her school records while on official business, picking up little bits and pieces of information that surprised her and did not fit the mold of the sullen child she encountered after the fire-starting incident.

"Mental aptitude considerably above normal."

"Consistent A or B student"

"Conduct satisfactory"

Continuing, she read comments from several of Molly's teachers. "A quiet child, but a real bear if other children or animals are threatened." This teacher recorded an incident in which Molly backed down a school bully who threw rocks at a stray cat. Another teacher noted.

"Molly's a brave child who's mature beyond her years. She loves to sing."

Loves to sing. Anna smiled as she scanned the little faces in front of her. Yes, there she was. She sat on the very back row behind the big kid with the faded Braves hat, very securely tucked in behind the boy. It bothered Anna that the child was so clearly afraid of her.

It was a stroke of luck that the request for a volunteer to work with patients of Molly's age group at West Regional appeared on the department bulletin board the day after she examined the kid's school records. She seized the phone and volunteered, and then her next call was to a friend of hers, a friend who previously could not help her. Weeks ago, she'd found out that Carrie was counseling with Molly and had called her, begging for information, but Carrie was an intern and even more afraid of losing her coveted position than Anna.

"I can't, Anna. I really can't. I'm lucky I got them to leave me with this kid. Usually they shuffle us around so that we can view different disorders, but I've been lucky here. She's pretty normal. I don't even know why she's here and she needs a friend more than a counselor. Sometimes when I look into her eyes I can almost see her soul. She has no one. I can't hurt her by getting taken off her case. Besides, they watch us carefully. I could get dumped. Sorry."

She didn't mind pulling strings, though, and making sure that Molly was assigned to Anna's singing group. Doing that was risk-free. The floor manager was on the cutting edge of treatment protocols and insisted that each child be assigned a free-time activity that required mandatory attendance. No one was going to say West Alabama was behind the times. The current trend was to send those kids out to be socialized! If there'd been any normal kids at all, he would have mainstreamed them, but that was impossible in an actual mental hospital. Mainstreaming was in!

Anna grinned. Yes, mainstreaming was good. Speaking of that, she once again tried to make eye contact with Molly, but the kid squirmed back behind the hefty boy in front, completely blocking Anna's view of her.

Molly was terrified. Nothing she did would ever work out right. Why was this woman here now when she was trying so hard to be good, not to make any mistakes, not to do anything that would cancel Tessie's visit on the twenty-fourth. She remembered the woman. She was the woman who took Tessie. Why was she looking at her, staring at her? She wanted to run, but there was nowhere to go. It was better just to sing and hope Anna didn't recognize her, but the words caught in her throat as she tried to sing the familiar invocation.

A part of her wanted to ask the woman about Tessie, but she was afraid; afraid that she would say something wrong. Everything she did had to be perfect right now, beyond perfection. She no longer saw RatBoy or Ghost, and they faded into her memory like the little house on Sycamore

Street, the lifetime in which had she belonged somewhere, meant something to someone, and was able to control her life in small, but precious, ways. Now she showered, ate, and moved in concert with a hundred other children, never by herself, but always alone.

"Let's go through that one more time. Concentrate on staying together, children. You're sounding very good!"

What a phony! A spark of anger surfaced. *Acting like she cares about any of us! What do we matter to her?* Still, a part of her hoped that Tessie was still with Anna and not their dad.

She had been good to them when she was seeing him, and she really did seem to care about Tessie. There was no mistaking the light that would shine in her eyes when she looked at her. Miss Carrie told her that the social worker lady was taking care of Tessie, and that Tessie was happy, and Molly hoped that was true. People lied to her so often. She wished she could just ask the woman. She wished she weren't so afraid.

"Now the day is over." If only it was over. She could feel Tessie's little arms around her and smell the sweet fragrance of her curls pressed into her face. Tears began sliding down the contours of her rigid face, and she barely forced hoarse mumbling through her clenched teeth.

"Night is growing nigh." Her shoulders began to tremble slightly as she concentrated on not losing control. It always seemed dark to her lately as she groped her way through the shadows that followed her, no matter how hard she tried to lose them. She wouldn't cry here. She mustn't cry, no matter how it hurt.

The woman must never know what she thought or felt. No one must know. The knot at the base of her stomach tightened and she felt nauseous. Not here. Not now. Not ever.

"I hate them!" She burned with the anger that was her friend. It allowed her to carry on, to function, to be perfect. Lately it was her only friend.

"Shadows of the evening
Steal across the sky."

That was better. She was in control now. She would be perfect. She would see Tessie. Nothing would get in the way of that. Nothing. The session was over for the day and once again she'd made it through without an error. As they filed out, the woman moved toward her and tried once again to force eye contact. She averted her eyes and kept moving. Relieved, she hurried down the hall, safely out of Anna's reach. It was over for another day.

In the cabin, not far away, Charlie hummed as he finished fluffing Homer's bright white hair. It was worth the washing and washing and washing to get it sparkly clean after its week in the preserving chemicals, which had left it a disturbing yellow color, not right, in his estimation. Who ever heard of a blonde Negro? All in all, he was pleased with his work. This head preserved the quickest of any of them and he had such a nice perky little bowtie at the bottom of the shrink-wrap, too. He'd kept a little bit of the neck with this one and it was an attractive addition.

Karen really had taken a fancy to Charlene and he cheerfully accompanied her to church and raided the clothes closet there for wearable garments and such. He now had three new dresses, as well as the odds and ends he needed to spruce up Nate and Arlene. This was just way too easy. No matter where they looked for Charlie, they never seemed to look at Charlene twice. Charlene was not Charlie. And Charlie was not Charlene.

They were looking everywhere for Charlie. He enjoyed watching the daily updates as he was rumored having been seen almost everywhere. The discovery of a headless Ward Captain not far from the grounds had far more effect on the hospital staff than the national news about the capture and sentencing of the Son of Sam. He was famous! It was the topic on everyone's tongue and Charlie loved it! Life was good.

And in another part of the universe, so close and yet so far away, Virgil closed the case and turned to face Spike.

"I don't know how ta use any of those things, Spike. I don't know how to shoot no mortar. Where'd ya get all this stuff anyway? We got any of that money left? Any at all? I love you like a brother, but you're starting to scare me. Let's just quit this job and get out of here." His words fell on nothingness. Spike was gone.

J.D. twitched, hooking one long arm under a twisted top sheet. Its clammy material contributed to the chill that shook his body. The night sweats were taking a toll. During the last week he'd lost ten pounds; weight he couldn't afford to shed. His repeated hospitalizations had left him with a series of medical problems and the nightmares, which had begun the night after his Notification of Seizure, were tearing him apart mentally and emotionally, just as savagely as vicious dog did every night in the dream.

A low scream began in his mind, surfacing from his lips with great difficulty. Sharp fangs dripped blood, his blood, and he could feel the tearing hot pain of each tooth as it sank into his side. Even as the creature ripped him apart, he could see its cold eyes, cold icy blue, totally lacking in emotion. Just the slightest hint of a satisfied smile would be visible from the animal's leering jaws, and as the dream would end, he'd always hear a growling howl that tapered into a chilling laugh.

It was her laugh. Eliza would win. She would eat his soul as she ate his battered body. A sharp intake of life-giving air woke him, and he pulled himself out of the damp sheets, realizing that they were wet from the tears running down his cheeks. His life was over. No house, no car, no children. She would win. In three weeks, everything he'd worked to accomplish would be gone and she would be victorious. Right now, he couldn't even work effectively. He moved through his duties at the garage like a zombie, dropping tools, putting things up in the wrong places in his toolbox. He couldn't sleep. He couldn't work. Life as he had known it was over.

Oh, God, protect me from the denizens of the devil who pursue me. His pleading fell on deaf ears. For some reason even his God had forsaken him and he didn't understand at all. Only the demons nipped at his heels. He could see them. He saw them following him to work, to church–everywhere. They were two evil imps, a round one and a small one, omnipotently present, following him a few feet back as he walked to work. They would sit, drinking coffee in the restaurant across from the garage where he tried to work, even waiting for him at the end of church services on Sunday. He knew he had to be hallucinating; it must be an after effect of the spider bites. If he turned and waved his fists at them, they just stared at him, blankly.

"Vengeance is mine, sayeth the Lord." His voice rasping, he forced the words of a hymn that more often than not brought comfort to his tortured soul.
"Faith of our fathers! Living still,
In spite of dungeon, fire and sword:
O how our hearts beat high with joy,

When'ere we hear that glorious word."
His voice became clearer as he reached his favorite verse.
"Our fathers, chained in prisons dark,
Were still in heart and conscience free:
How sweet would be their children's fate,
If they, like them, could die for thee."
Molly was not his child. She was a foul product of Satan, an abomination, and as soon as he removed her stench from the earth, his life would be restored. This was his test and he would be a faithful soldier for his King. He was his Lord's instrument and he would emerge victorious from his trials. Comforted, he shed the sweat-soaked nightclothes, showered, and dressed for work. Every day now was a test of his courage, and he wouldn't fail.

Chapter Thirty-Four

Hidden In Plain Sight

"This case is a pisser." Seated on an old stump, well within the crime scene tape, Sheriff Joe Henry scratched his nose. No matter how many times he'd painstakingly surveyed each object within eyesight, he was no closer to the solution of this gruesome puzzle than he had been a week ago. He wished he could bring the axe back and put it in place, but the fancy new crime lab in Montgomery needed to examine it and it would be back in time for the trial, if he ever arrested anybody. Everything was wrong.

He squinted at the paint marks that outlined the blood spray. It took one hell of a heft of an axe to create a spray trail so far from the location of the body, and to remove a head from the neck with one blow delivered sideways, while both perpetrator and victim were standing.

One clean blow. That was what the little girl who witnessed the murder kept saying. *But from a woman? Not possible. Women just didn't heft axes that accurately. Not even big women. They had to be looking for a man.*

Poor little girl. She seemed like such a sweet little pixie. She followed him everywhere. The sharp, snap of a twig let him know his shadow stood quietly behind him now. Imaline, that was her name. Seemed like her momma called her Ima, though.

"Ima, that you back there?"

"Yessah."

She was shiny-dark and had huge white eyes with very black centers. Good thing she was so young. She didn't seem all that traumatized by her experience, just confused. She told the same story to everyone who asked her.

"Tell me one more time, honey. You followed your granddaddy outside?" She nodded her head slowly. "And what happened?" he continued.

"Dah white nurse thing hit 'um wif tha axe."

"What did this 'nurse' look like?"

"She's big as a house, all white 'n shinin' like, 'n she had light shinin' out her head, and red, red lips." Time to take a different direction with his questioning.

"What makes you think this was a nurse?"

"She gotta white nurse dress on."

"You're sure about that?" The kid never varied.

"She be like that woman what gived me shots. Only real big!"

"Then what happened?" He leaned toward her from his perch on the stump.

"She take these long red fingers and picks up my Paw Paw's head and she floats up to the sky."

Joe pretty much figured that whoever did this to the kid's grandpa disappeared into the woods, which were slightly uphill from the house. He knew his witness was worth nothing in court, so he'd better find some physical evidence to pin on whomever they arrested. The chief suspect was still the creepy preacher who'd disappeared from Beaufort Falls right at the same time Nathan St. Claire went missing. But the preacher was a man. He had to try one more time.

"Are you sure it was a woman nurse you saw? Could it have been a man in a white coat?" Maybe the crazy sucker had some kind of a ritual concocted where he wore a lab coat or something white. It really was a mystery the way the man had just dropped out of sight, not seen or heard of by anyone for almost a month. Lips pursed tightly, the little girl stared resolutely downward and nodded, stubbornly.

"No sah. It be a big, big, big nursey woman." Two tears slid down her cheeks. "Mister Sheriff. Paw Paw ain't never comin' back, is he?"

Damn! He didn't want to upset her. He'd become very fond of the tike during the last few weeks. He reached forward and put a huge hand on the top of her tightly braided pigtails.

"Hon, your Paw Paw is looking down from Heaven and he's very proud of you girls and your momma. He's happy, and even though he wishes he could be with you, he's eating at the good Lord's table." She jerked away from him and ran inside the weathered shanty, slamming its rickety front door hard enough to shake a shingle off the leaning roof. *Damn it!* He gave the stump a good kick. Well, he had one more lead.

Someone at the hospital had called him and reported leaving one of the kitchen workers here at almost the time of the killing. Maybe he had another witness. If the worker were male, he'd actually have a suspect, but this was the kitchen scrubwoman, who for some reason had told another worker that she lived in the pathetic shack that had been the victim's home.

He pulled his scratch pad out of a uniform pocket. Mrs. Karen Thorogood, that was her name. She was supposed to be on duty tonight so he guessed he'd just stop by the hospital on his way back. Maybe the mystery witness would be there, too, and he could check out her story. Not much of a lead, but he was tired of staring at that old wreck of a car and watching the rust form. Groaning, he stretched his full six-foot-four body, climbed into his squad car, and disappeared down the dusty road.

Karen and Charlene were just finishing cleaning the big iced tea vat when the sheriff pulled up to the back entrance of the kitchen. Tea was cheaper than milk, so the little inmates drank a lot of the cool, southern-brewed liquid, summer and winter, and it didn't matter whether it was hot or cold outside. This huge tin container had to be scrubbed every evening or the bacteria that grew in it would make everyone who drank the tea sick. Charlie almost dropped the thing on his foot when he saw the squad car pull up.

"What's wrong with you, honey? You not feeling so good tonight?" Earlier that evening Charlene confided in Karen that her periods were real gushers lately, and she might need to be excused at any time. Charlie had noticed that nothing bonded the women quite like childbirth or bad periods, and he knew he had no hope of coming up with a kid. As Joe strode toward them, he could feel one hell of a case of cramps coming on, but he didn't move fast enough. Before he could clutch his middle and make his exit, Sheriff Henry stood directly in front of the two of them.

All Charlie had time to do in the form of remedial action was to straighten his blonde wig. He hoped that his makeup covered the sudden paling of his face. He could feel the blood draining all the way down to his toes.

"You ladies know where I can find Karen Thorogood?"

Oh, please God, don't let me have to say anything. It'd been a long time since Charlie had said a prayer and he was surprised at how easily the words rolled through his head. He'd play it cool. He'd let Karen do all the talking.

"That's me, sheriff." Sheriff Joe was a familiar face to almost everyone in Sicily. The local news questioned him every night as to the progress being made on finding the head-lopping murderer, as they were calling the man who'd killed and beheaded at least three people so far. Charlie slunk behind Karen and tried to look smaller.

"We got a report at the station that you might have some information that would help us find our killer, Mrs. Thorogood. Is there a place where we can talk?" Karen looked at Charlie nervously. She hadn't exactly told Charlene yet that she had talked to the police about letting her out at the house where the murder occurred, and Charlene didn't look any too happy at having the sheriff talking to her. She wondered if maybe she'd made a mistake. Charlene was far too big a woman to become an enemy, plus Lenny would ream her out good if the iced tea wasn't ready in fifteen minutes, when supper started.

"Uh, now's a real bad time." She ducked her head and tried to continue toward the prep station with the inner filter of the tea vat. She heard Lenny's yell from inside the kitchen.

"Come on, Karen. Bring that vat," but Joe wasn't going to be put off so easily. He didn't drive all the way out here from town just to be brushed aside.

"Ma'am, I'm afraid you are required by law to talk to me. We can do it here or we can do it downtown. Which is it going to be?"

Charlie wanted to leave, but if he did, he'd have no idea what Karen told Sheriff Henry. No matter how much he wanted to run, it made more sense to stay. In fact, Karen looked as guilty as hell. He might have to say something just to keep the sheriff from arresting her. He sure didn't want her saying anything other than whatever she'd already spilled. He hoped his wig stayed put, his makeup looked good, and his

hose were straight. It was hard being a woman. And his voice–
he didn't have time to worry about whether it stayed in a high
octave, but he'd had lots of practice talking in a falsetto lately.

"Ah, sheriff?" Joe looked around. That was one big woman
standing next to the large metal container that held tea. Pudgy
was not the word for her. She looked like his Aunt Beulah on
steroids. Beulah had always scared him, even without her
wooden spoon.

"It ain't Karen's fault she was at that house. I lied to 'um. I
was afraid they wouldn't hire me if they knew I didn't have no
transportation and I live in town. I needed this job something
desperate. I told her to let me off there and I walked back to
town."

"You walked eight miles to town?" Joe couldn't believe
that.

"No sir. Not all the way. I walked about three miles to
James Crossing and from there I caught a bus." He was
mighty grateful he knew the schedule and had actually taken
that bus a few times. In fact, if he didn't have so much to carry
he would've taken the bus out of here already. As it was, he'd
wait, if he could, until he could bring everyone. He didn't
want his little family falling into uncaring hands. There was no
way he could make that journey carrying his washtub and
chemicals and all of Arlene's hair stuff. His little circle of
friends deserved better than that. He'd wait until he could buy
or steal a car.

Joe looked down at the woman's big feet. They were
comfortably shod in large white tennis shoes. Yes, she might
be able to walk that distance in those.

"So you were at the victim's house at approximately dark
last Tuesday? Did you see or hear anything out of the
ordinary?"

"Nothing, Sir. Just as soon as Karen got out of sight, I followed behind her on foot. I never went near the house. I had a long walk ahead, and I wanted to finish as much as I could before it got too dark." Charlene turned to Karen. "I'm sorry I lied to you. I know it was bad of me."

Karen was so relieved she didn't care at all. She knew that Charlene hadn't told her the truth and she'd spent hours trying to figure out why the woman would lie about something as simple as where she lived. She wondered if she even had a needy sister now. She had been looking forward to helping the poor dear, but at least she was off the hook with the sheriff.

"It's okay, Charlene. We can get this straightened out later. Right now we've got to get the tea on the table. Can we finish our work now, Sheriff Henry?"

Joe scanned the two of them, a perplexed look on his face. There was something awfully funny about that big woman, but they were women and he was definitely looking for a man.

"I guess I know where to find you two if I need you. Don't leave town, either of you." But he was talking to their backs. Inside, he could see Lenny gesturing angrily, so he figured the interview was over. Another night wasted. He couldn't help but be amazed at the size of that scrubwoman, though.

A few minutes later, Karen listened through the bathroom stall door to her friend, as Charlie heaved into the porcelain bowl.

"Those must be some horrible cramps you got, hon. I don't believe I ever had any bad enough to make me throw up. Can I get you anything?" Charlie didn't answer her. He didn't know how he would touch up his makeup well enough to hide his rapidly emerging five o'clock shadow if this busybody didn't go away. Maybe he really was turning into some pussy woman. He had to hang in here for at least one more payday. Why did that meddling old man have to recognize him? He'd have to have a good talk with Homer when he got home tonight.

He didn't see the bright green eyes that watched him through the hole in the bathroom wall. RatBoy didn't think it was a wrong thing to do. He knew Charlie was a man, so it wasn't like he was peeking on a lady. He was getting better at deciphering the thoughts that went through Charlie's head.

He felt his illness and he felt his fear. He knew that the man had hurt Homer and he could feel the icy coldness in his mind. Studying Charlie tired him, but he had no choice. There was still a lot to learn about him if he was going to be able to keep his little clan safe. He could feel, evil or not, that the man was part of the "Plan," and he had to know what was ahead. The time was approaching when every move would be crucial, and any mistake could mean the end of everything. It was his job to watch them all. He was the Watcher and he wasn't finished yet, this long night.

Chapter Thirty-Five

Plans

J.D. surveyed the petition with horror. The uptight bitch wanted Tessie, so that was what it was all about? The fussy old maid wanted a baby and she was going to take his? She had actually coerced the system to write the document before him, a piece of paper so dripping in treachery and deceit as to almost singe his fingers. And, to think, he'd even considered making her his wife! He'd rather lie down with a viper, a snake, than to foul himself with her flesh. She could have had both of them and a life that was paradise, taking care of his little house, cooking, never having to work outside of the home again. Well, she wouldn't keep Tessie. He had a plan of his own.

Reaching under the sofa, he pulled out the leather-bound case and went through its contents. Passports. John Duke Parsons and Elizabeth Ruth Parsons–two tickets to London, England. Soon, he and his little one would be merging into English crowds, starting a new life. It surprised him that he was able to obtain all of this right now, with so much of his life legally entangled, but no one seemed to be thinking about him at all. It was almost as if he were a nonentity, a cardboard cutout that was supposed to bend and be blown in whatever direction the forces of evil decided to push. Well, he had news for them. He would determine his own life, and with the assistance of the Lord, he and Tessie would leave all the local yokels sitting in the dust.

It was so simple. Before anyone could freeze his bank account, he had pulled out the three thousand dollars in his savings account and sent for the passports. They might have Tessie, but he had her birth certificate. Sixty dollars each to a courier from Miami, and they were ready to travel. He had a cousin in Atlanta who would buy the Caddie, no questions asked, adding to his little nest egg, and he and Tessie would leave for New York City, and then on to London, before anyone would know they were gone. All he needed was Tessie to make his plan a working reality.

Molly? Making his plan a reality brought her to mind. She was the key. The family visit was the only time he and Tessie would be together. He'd tried everything. Family and Children's Services wouldn't even allow him to take Tessie to church. No matter how much he threatened or begged, they merely reassured him that a decision would be made "in the best interests of the child," based on the evaluation to be made later that month. Tessie was "in an appropriate fostering situation," and would remain in it, for now. As if he didn't know she was with that bitch, Anna.

For the first time, he noticed that Molly's name was also on the petition. What on earth did she want with that little worm? He had plans for Molly, and none of them included leaving her to be raised, in luxury, by the godless system. Molly was evil, a heretic, a creature with no soul, an aberration of the devil sent to test him, and he wouldn't be found wanting. As a soldier of Christ, his quest was to eliminate creatures such as her; to put them to the sword as in days of old. It was his duty to be sure that she wasn't left to harm anyone else, and he'd do what was required of him. She mustn't be left behind. The evil whore who was her mother wouldn't win this round. They would roast in Hell together before his visit was through.

Shivering, he reached for the fiery liquid which kept him going during these troubled times. His nightmares were worse, and he struggled to get through every day. He suspected he would soon be let go at work. It didn't matter. None of it mattered any more. None of the dimwitted inhabitants of this town, or their pathetic vehicles, mattered. Only God mattered; Jesus, God, and Tessie. Jesus, God, Tessie, and Early Times. He took one more swig of lunch, and then reverently returned the bottle to its brown paper bag. God would allow him his little sins. The glorious future awaited him and his little angel.

Standing tall, he marched out of the little house on Sycamore Street, slamming the door as he left. Piss on the house—he was a soldier of God!

"Onward Christian so-ol-diers

March-ing as to war.

With the cross of Jeee-sus

Going on before!"

The notes of the old song echoed off the walls of the houses that he passed as he walked the few blocks back to the garage. People looked at him strangely, but he ignored them. Everything would be fine. His Jesus would protect him. He was a sword-bearing warrior, in the battle for good. Nothing could harm him, and he would set everything right again.

Chapter Thirty-Six

Dreams

L ater that night Molly stirred restlessly. By force of reflex, she reached for a comforting handful of fur, then winced as even in her sleep she remembered that her protector was missing, no longer pressed reassuringly close to her, a form almost as long as the little girl. She dreamed about Ghost, though, and in her dream the Ghost-Dog merged with her faded memories of her mommy. It always began at the little house on Sycamore Street.

Moaning, Molly began the process of waking up in the narrow cot. Even after the months of making this strange place her home, the fluorescent lights still burned into her eyes and disturbed her rest. She couldn't sleep deeply here. She pulled her blanket higher to hide her eyes, and her exposed feet became blocks of ice. Whimpering a little, she coasted back into the dream.

This time it was Ghost who snuggled with Tessie, and her. Tessie was no longer a toddler but a little girl, and Ghost talked to them in funny little yelps. They understood her, and laughed with her. Each child had arms tightly wrapped around the dog and she licked Tessie, trying to clean her ears. Molly giggled and held onto her sister, trying to keep her still.

"Silly! Be still! Mommy can't clean your ears if you squirm like that." Ghost felt like her mommy. She felt good and loving like her mommy, who'd never come back. Awake now, she tucked the blanket around her cold feet. She could feel the tears starting. Now she was away from all of them; her mommy, Tessie, Ghost, even her friend RatBoy, all taken from her. Now she was so very alone.

Another creature stirred restlessly in the night. Ghost slept with her body guarding the entrance of the cave, but she couldn't pull the reason she must be on guard from the dark recesses of her fractured mind. Her sensitive ears caught a slight rustle. A mouse scurried across the leafy pathway just outside the door. She jerked awake, becoming alert instantly. Concerned, she circled the perimeter of her beat, sniffed each empty bunk, and placed a cold nose on the arm of the woman who had saved her life, the only inhabitant of the cave at this late hour.

All was well. It would be safe to leave her for a little while and melt into the darkness, like a thousand ancestors before her. Trotting out of the front of the cave, she stopped briefly in the pathway to lock eyes with a frightened chipmunk. It was safe. Thanks to Verbena, she would never have to hunt for her food again. After a few seconds of frozen terror, the little animal scurried off into the night.

It was a typical Alabama spring pre-morning, chilled humidity promising new life in the weeks ahead. The cold rains would come and wash the remaining dead leaves from the trees, allowing buds to open on the nearly naked limbs. This had already happened on the early blooming varieties, leaving a lot of the nighttime Heavens exposed. The moon was small and bluish-white, so different from the full-yellow moon of summer, and the stars were small spears of bright white light in the black sky. Nothing was complete yet, and anticipation lent a sharp bite to the breeze that ruffled the soft fur on the dog's back. She stretched, ambled toward the open field a few hundred yards ahead, and then gathered her muscles under her and ran, exalting in the strength flowing through her. Cresting a small hill she stopped, turned twice to form a warm indention in the dead underbrush, and sat.

She could feel the powerful force growing inside of her. It grew stronger every day, but she had no clue as to its purpose, and few memories existed before the day Verbena found her in the crevice behind the cave. She barely remembered her puppy, or the human children who owned her soul as well, and she was happy this way. The heat was still there, and one day it would return to burn and consume her, but she was safe right now.

Clearing her vocal passage, she raised her white throat and sang cadence to the moon, and in the distance she heard the answering howls of her canine brothers and sisters. No longer hungry, it was easy for her to indulge her primal nature. If only she could remain this way forever, free of conflict and in tune with the world around her, but deep inside she knew that it couldn't last. Somewhere within the dog a woman waited, resting and gaining strength for the battle ahead.

Others slept during the chilly hours of the morning, and others dreamed as well. Not far from the hill where Ghost sang in the night, her long-lost love dreamed also, of a day they had spent together. Nine years ago, and in the very same spot where he lay this night, he had held her in his arms for the last time. She had clung to him, hopelessly entwined, as if she could attach herself to him permanently and by entwining her body closely enough with his, she could stay with him, forever. It seemed she had, he thought, as he slept. She had stolen his heart and his soul and he never would get either of them back. Nothing in his life worked after he told her that he couldn't see her again. In this very cabin, she'd stolen the part of him that was the most human, and he couldn't bring it back. Nothing had mattered to him since that day.

Sunlight had streamed in through the small opening they had left uncovered from the cabin window, making kaleidoscope patterns on the floor, but he had felt anything but happy as he lay on the old blanket with his arms wrapped around Eliza, holding her close to his heart.

"I can't see you again. This is the last time we meet." He tried to dry the tears that soaked his cheeks as he pressed her closer to him.

"I don't care. I don't want to live without you. I want to be your wife and bear your children."

"You can't. You have a husband and he'll never let you go. He'd kill us both first." Tenderly, he had removed each article of her clothing and put them on the hearth, pulling her down onto the blanket with him so that he could look at the curves of her young body before merging with her one last time. "You are so beautiful." He knew he should leave. What he and she were about to do was wrong in the eyes of God and man, but he wanted her so, he loved and desired her. In other circumstances, he would marry her, and they would have children together. But this would be the last time they made love, and they both knew it. She continued sobbing as he entered her, and she would not let him go when their passion exhausted itself. Finally he'd pushed her away, found his clothes, put them on, and left without another word. He had no more words left to speak.

Charlie Callahan woke with a jerk and reached for the six-pack of beer he'd begun before coasting into slumber. It was no use. His night was over. Grabbing his flashlight, he went to check on his friends, the heads.

"Well, Homer, we all had the one we loved and lost, didn't we, Old Man? She was a beauty and it ain't like I'll ever get to see her again now. Eliza is dead, just like you folks now, dust in the graveyard, fodder for the worms." Pulling his new head down from the shelf, he tugged at its wooly white Afro, pulling and fluffing it so that it stood out from the wizened little face like a halo. He loved talking to Homer. His exotic visage always appeared wise to Charlie. In his mind, Homer was a tribal chieftain who could magically influence the universe for him in many positive ways.

"Nothing's been right since I left her, Old Man. I should have stayed and faced that asshole of a husband of hers. I never even met him. I never came to her funeral. I never heard she was dead until a year after she'd died. She was the best part of me. Everything else I've ever tried to do since I left her in this cabin went to shit. And my life's full of it too. Shit. I've had one big fuck-up after another, like that woman who's going to get me caught. She has to be on the grounds here somewhere. I know she hasn't squealed to the authorities yet, so I bet she's right here, hiding in plain sight just like I am. I did one thing right. I sure scared the piss out of her. I guess I'll have to take care of her when the time comes."

One more beer would calm him down for the night. Placing Homer back on the shelf, he settled into his blankets and soon snored peacefully, warm with his memories of Eliza's arms around him.

J.D. dreamed too, but not peacefully. He twitched with poorly repressed anger as he relived his past. He remembered peering in through the window of the cabin on the hospital grounds, watching a man's pink rear end moving up and down on top of his wife, her blonde hair spread out on the dark blanket like the angel that she was not.

It had been a slow day at the service station, so he'd left early, around noon, singing his hymns and thinking about the list of things yet to do on the little house that he and his young wife had just moved into on Sycamore Street. The fixer-upper needed a lot of work, but he loved the feel of the hammer in his hands and the smell of fresh lumber, neatly cut with his saw.

As he turned the corner, walking quickly and inhaling the fresh spring air, he saw Eliza lock the door and hurry up the street in the opposite direction. Something about the way she turned the key in the lock, the distracted way she moved, led him to believe she wasn't headed to the little store on the corner for a few groceries for their supper. Curious, he followed her.

She boarded the bus on the corner. Running, he beat the bus to the next stop. He pulled his faded jeans jacket over his shoulders and pulled his hat down over his face. At worst, she would see him and want to know why he was on the bus. What did he have to lose? She stared vacantly out the window and never saw him board, unresponsive to anything in her immediate surroundings. He walked right past her to the back of the bus, and she never saw him at all. He wondered what on earth could have her so firmly entombed in her own mind that she didn't even recognize her own husband?

After a forty-five-minute ride, she pulled the cord at the West Alabama Regional Children's Hospital. Surprised at the destination, he got ready to follow her.

Who could she be visiting there? He was consumed with curiosity now. Did she have a secret that she'd never told him?

Maybe she had a sister or brother there? He'd rescued her from a family of drunken imbeciles. That was entirely possible. He let the bus move one more block and then he ran, catching up with her just as she disappeared down a wooded trail. She walked quickly and he followed her, just out of her sight. This certainly wasn't the main entrance to the waiting room areas where she would meet an inmate. Finally, she entered a cabin and put her scarf over its only window, leaving a small area open to let in fresh air.

He watched her meet a man whose face he could not see. She enveloped the man in her arms and he watched, fascinated, transfixed like a man watching a snake eat a young animal, as they entwined and mated on the ground like dogs. Inwardly howling, he ran away from the dark cabin, ran back to the bus stop, raced home to decide what he should do next. Would God allow him to remove this scum from the earth?

When Eliza arrived home later in the day, he was waiting for her. He beat her, not for the first time, but this time he left bruises and bumps in places where they could be seen, crowning it all with a liver-colored shiner to her right eye. He beat her and then he claimed what was his right by law, until every part of her body that had once been full of love and tenderness now bled from his rough use.

"Call your lover!" he demanded, but all she would say was that it was over between them, and her lover would never be back.

"Call him!" he continued to demand, but she cowered in the corner and wouldn't speak, no matter how much he hurt her. When she lay limp and unresponsive, he pulled her out to his old truck and took her back to the cabin. During the day he locked her in the tool shed while he worked, using a padlock, and every night for a month they waited together at the cabin, waiting for Charlie to return, waiting with J.D.'s hunting rifle loaded, as he hoped for easy prey.

They were never bothered at the cabin. It was as if it was a remnant of another age and no one but them knew of its existence. Finally, J.D. became convinced that Eliza would be his, and his alone, but he never let down his guard or trusted her more than a few feet away from the little house on Sycamore Street.

The wages of love and sin are relentless, and nine months later the cabin served another purpose. While Eliza was his now, and docile enough, he couldn't be sure about the baby she carried. Few people knew she was with child, and he preferred it that way.

"My wife stays at home where she belongs. When the baby is ready to be born, she'll go and stay with her sister." Very concerned about her rapid weight loss, the dark circles under her eyes, and her silent manner when at church, their pastor had asked if she was receiving any medical care at all. J.D. had said nothing. He'd shrugged his shoulders and strode off, leaving her to follow him silently. No more was said, to his face.

Nothing was collected for this first child, nothing at all. When her family brought her a few little baby clothes, some of them remnants of her own birth, he lit a fire with them in the tool shed, destroying everything except a little bear she had hidden under the porch steps. His anger burning impotently inside him, he waited to see what his willful whore of a wife birthed, certain that he would know if it was his and forming a plan for what he would do if it was not. *The will of the Lord will be made manifest when the trial is upon me. I will wait for His will to be done.*

Before he could reach the conclusion of his horrible dream he awoke, feeling more resolved than ever to finish the nightmare Eliza had begun so long ago. He read his Bible and waited. Seasons pass slowly in Beaufort Falls, but they do pass. Nothing and no one sleeps forever, not even the dead, and life continues along the same lines until a storm cleanses the air. Nothing is what it seems, in Beaufort Falls.

Chapter Thirty-Seven

The Halls Of Prosperity

A. E. Beaufort, III, had more money than he knew how to spend. The former administrator of the Beaufort Falls Medical Center, now defunct and in the hands of the concerned citizens of Sicily, made a nice fee off the "sale" of the hospital. From the principal of the money from the sale, he received a steady income of fifty thousand dollars a year. His family money was put up in lovely bonds and investments in excess of a million dollars, the remainder of the fortune that built the hospital and most of the town. It was untouchable, but the interest from it alone provided more than a comfortable subsistence and he longed to spend it in a way that let people know he had arrived.

He purchased a Jaguar. No one in town could tune its sixteen-valve engine and it sat shining in his garage, awaiting a mechanic from Birmingham. He bought a few snazzy English tailor-made suits and made a trip to London to have them fitted. No one seemed impressed. In fact, he suspected that a few of his colleagues might actually be laughing at him behind his back. He couldn't swear to it, but he'd caught grins on their faces while he discussed the most serious of topics. But today he saw something that he really wanted, something possibly out of his grasp, and he burned with the desire to own it.

He considered his opinion valuable and, with so much time on his hands, he joined every committee having anything to do with hospital administration in the state of Alabama, traveling frequently. Today he attended a meeting of the Sicily Facilities Improvement Committee, held at the West Alabama Regional Children's Hospital in an antebellum mansion located on the grounds of the hospital; the residence of its administrators since before the War Between the States. Unlike the rest of the buildings, which were quickly falling into a state of disrepair, this old home had been kept up nicely with state funds, and it combined graceful columns along the front with every facet of the old southern architecture.

Exquisitely designed, it boasted a ballroom on the bottom floor and a wraparound porch on its front and back. Its outdoor kitchen and slave quarters were located discretely away from the main grounds of the hospital itself, in a lovely strand of woods near the quickly running river. Everything about it was perfect. Its low-hanging oaks trailed strands of romantic Spanish moss and the heady fragrance of mimosa trees perfumed the air during long summer months.

It wasn't summer yet but Pryor Akins, the administrator in residence, didn't mind taking A. E. on a tour of the house and grounds and pointing out each fragrant tree. Pryor was right proud of his home, and he didn't mind showing it off to the man who had everything. A. E. wanted it. He lusted for it mightily. He could hardly concentrate on the direction that the conversation took during the meeting in the home's lovely library, complete with its built-in shelves and ladders that provided access to mysterious top regions. He pictured himself suitably clothed in a smoking jacket, reading periodicals alone in front of its huge fireplace. He had to have this house. He would pay anything for it.

"A. E., have you heard of the new idea they are trying out in Birmingham this fall? A. E.?" Pryor tried to get his attention.

"Ah--what, Pryor?" Reluctantly, he pulled his gaze away from the carving of the ornate border along the lower edge of the nearest bookshelf.

"The group homes. Some wild dreamer is actually taking the urchins out of the dorms and paying people to live in little homes and to pretend to be parents to them. What do you think of that?"

Wasting precious space and money on the mentally defective? "Really?" A. E. thought it best to test the waters and see what some of the rest of them thought about this idea before committing.

"Sounds like it's a good idea if they can find people who'll do it," the head of the Home for Mentally Challenged Adults in Montgomery volunteered, cautiously. "Wonder how much you'd have to pay someone to live with our patients?"

Pryor wondered too. He could picture the grounds of West Regional being reworked into small houses with his brother-in-law supervising the construction. "It might work. Maybe we ought to give it a try? Mattie, put that down as an idea for further research and development." His secretary, already taking the minutes of the meeting, scribbled furiously.

Beaufort's wandering mind had already transferred to other things. Staring dreamily into space, he imagined that he was hosting his first big party in the ballroom. Everyone was there, the governor, the mayor of Montgomery–the rest of the meeting was a blur to him. He would see whom he knew on the management committee for the property and he'd make them an offer tomorrow–an offer they couldn't refuse. They certainly didn't need the property to run the hospital and Pryor could live elsewhere. No one had provided *him* with a home when he was running the medical center. What a tremendous waste of money!

He smiled and shook Pryor's hand as he left, thanking him fervently for the tour of the property and expressing his intense admiration for it. He would be seeing him again soon, he assured him. Pryor was a little surprised that this wealthy and influential man suddenly had taken such a liking to him, but it was a step up in the political chain around here and he could see the other administrators looking at him, enviously. That was envy he saw in their grins?

"We'll have lunch here soon," he promised A. E.

"Very soon."

Thirty minutes later, A.E. was on the phone with the governor. As soon as a few legal strings could be pulled, Pryor was going to need a new home and the 'lord of the manor' was planning his housewarming party.

Not far away in the drafty hall of Section Ten, Female Dorm, Molly unwrapped a little package pressed into her waiting hands by the "Singing Lady," as most of the children called Anna. Molly was beginning to look forward to her visits. Grudgingly, she admitted that the woman took good care of Tessie, and lately seemed to like her, too. Now, her one high point of each week happened each Tuesday, when Anna showed up to lead them in songs. Each time, she brought Molly something from Tessie.

The first time it happened Molly had been terrified and waited for hours before opening the little package. The woman caught her by a handful of sweater before she could slip away.

"Take this," she whispered loudly, looking in both directions before slipping an envelope in Molly's back jeans pocket. "Shhh! Don't tell anyone!" Then she moved away, greeting other children and hugging a few who were now very fond of her. Molly ran from the doorway, not stopping until she was out of breath, and halted in the little meadow that was not far from the slave cabin, where she once played with RatBoy and met Ghost. She dropped it onto the ground, waiting for it to explode like a bomb, and when it didn't, she carefully opened the envelope and looked inside.

Dear Molly
Miss Anna loves me. She loves you too. She says
you will live with us. She is nice.
I love you.
Tessie

Under the signature there was a lipstick smudge kiss, obviously sent by her little sister playing dress up. She could hear her happy laughter, and she put the letter under her sweater, next to her heart.

Now she waited by the door every week to get her note. Sometimes there would be other little gifts, all obviously chosen especially for her by her sister. A red barrette because Tessie knew she loved red. *Bit O Honey* candies, her favorites! Most important to her, Tessie had held all these items, and she could feel the love in them. She saved the candy, not eating a single piece. Anna seemed to know she might do this, because the next week she brought *Bit O Honey* candies for the entire group, so Molly was able to eat a few and enjoy them. She smiled at her often, and now Molly could smile back. The improvement was noted on her chart and her schoolwork had gotten better.

For the first time since she gave up Ghost and RatBoy, she had a reason to exist. The anticipated visit seemed closer each week. She gathered her dark hair into the red barrette and sang as she walked from dorm to classroom now, and Mickey smiled as he watched her from the side of the little trail. He'd do nothing to upset the balance she had recently established for herself, no matter how much he wanted to be around her. He felt the improvement in her mind, and that was enough. His Princess was learning to cope with her life, and he was happy for her. He felt her think of him often, and that was enough.

Her life is so hard, so hard, so much harder than mine. It was odd; he never thought about his existence at all. He came and went like the breeze, no place that was his own, no home, no cot in the dorm, no place in a schoolroom. When he wanted to be somewhere, he was there. When he wanted to know something, he reached into someone's head and found what he needed to know. Smiling, he turned away from Molly and began checking out the rest of his clan.

They were clustered around Verbena in the cave as she told them a story about the day of the big fire in Beaufort County. She'd been driving along the main road that was lined with the majestic water oaks that were consumed in the flames several hours later. Out of the billowing smoke, two little girls she knew and loved dearly came running right between the trees and almost in front of her car. She screeched to a halt and scooped them up, pulling the younger one into the front seat while the older child scrambled in beside her.

"Where is J.D.?" she asked, but neither answered. They were in shock, their eyes dazed and almost lifeless, both looking straight ahead. She had rather fancied their father, the Reverend John Duke Parsons, at one time, she explained.

Suddenly the older child looked at her and said the strangest thing.

"Get the hell out of here if you want to live, bi...uh, creep!" Verbena didn't want to use that sort of word around her boys. She had no idea where that child had learned that language, she told them. She had never heard her use it before or after that day, but a cold chill crept up her spine that even the heat of the flames now approaching the road couldn't warm. She could see that the boys loved her story and even the dog, Ghost, seemed transfixed by her words.

"I flew outa there!" she continued, waving her hands to emphasize the speed with which she raced her car through the flames back to Beaufort Falls. "I never saw a fire move so fast!"

Somehow, J.D. survived without a scratch, but it was several days before he came to pick up his girls. She'd never asked him why he hadn't come to get his children, or where he'd been during the time that he'd been missing.

"That man never cared what I did for him," she told the listening children, plaintively. "He never cared at all." She wiped a little tear away from the corner of her eye. That was too much for little Fox, who adored the beautiful woman who laughed and cuddled him, and cooked, and took care of them all.

"He's an evil, evil, mean, man! When I grow up, I'll shoot him for you! I love you, Beeny, I love you!" Leaping over Horse, he threw his arms around her and wiggled into her lap. The warm little arms around her reminded her once again what was really important to her. These children were important. They deserved a chance at a normal life. They needed her. Suddenly, she didn't need a man to make her happy, and her whole world narrowed to her life in the cave.

"Okay! Enough. Enough!" Laughing, she hugged the little boy and set him down. A glance at her watch snapped her back to the reality of the dual existence her little boys lived. "You have to go, guys. Right now! Hurry, before you miss bed check! Run!" They disappeared into the darkness and she looked for Ghost, but Ghost was gone.

Quietly nearby, another clan member relived her not-so-distant past. Memories that were a part of her, and not a part of her, tortured poor Ghost; memories belonging to something that moved within its own realm of existence and threatened to split the fragile, organic brain that now housed it. The poor dog tried to bury her head in a hole. She writhed in pain, as something inside tried to break free from the bonds of mortality and threatened to crush the bone and cranial matter that held it in. Finally, she lay still, stretched out in the darkness, mercifully unconscious. The power was growing. Someday, it would be avenged. Soon.

Chapter Thirty-Eight

Busted

Charlie straightened his hose. He wondered how long he could keep pretending to be female. It was just too easy. He weighed two hundred and thirty pounds, had hands the size of small melons, a husky voice, and frequently sported a five o'clock shadow, but still no one questioned the charade.

He was bored. He wanted to leave, but where could he go? Where else on the face of the earth would he find people this stupid? Besides, he had to be at work at four and Lenny and Karen depended on him.

He knew how to make the tea, and he was the only one who could reach the topmost shelves. After they reorganized the kitchen to suit him, it would be downright uncivil to leave them now, but if Lenny pinched his butt one more time, he was going to cold-cock the horny bastard, and that would be the end of his job.

He tried to save for a car, but it seemed that all of his money went toward being an attractive woman. He liked being able to enjoy the attributes of both sexes. Half turning, he examined himself in the new full-length mirror that Charlie the man mounted to the cabin wall for his alter ego, Charlene the woman. The new blonde wig looked smashing, simply smashing! He got tired of having his head wrapped in a scarf and the first wig he purchased was such a shabby thing. The sympathy he got from Karen over his "bad hair cut" wore thin after about a month. He felt like a regular housemaid wrapped up in a kerchief all the time.

The first time he had his nails done, he liked the heady sensation of feeling pretty. Now attractive fingernails were a part of his budget. He was glad that women used stalls instead of urinals, and he figured that unless he had an accident and ended up in a hospital, his secret was safe. He needed to keep all of his secrets safe. Even when he went back to being a man, he thought that he just might want to look into one of the service professions. With a little training, he might make one hell of a fine hairdresser.

Several hours later, he finished the last of the little plates and disappeared into the pantry for a smoke. Squatting, he settled his bulk onto an industrial-sized can of peas and he took the pressure off his long-suffering feet. Women just didn't have comfortable shoes, not even when they were tennis shoes.

Women. Against his will, his mind drifted back to the last time that brassy redheaded bitch had fondled every nerve-filled spot on his then-so-male body. Damn, he missed sex. Relaxing, he let himself remember.

He could feel her long red fingernails tracing a delicate line down his throat, then her fingers caressing the hair on his chest. She always took her time. All he ever wanted to do was to rip that candy-pink, tight little uniform off of her, but she had been infuriatingly slow, grinning at him and daring him to make her move more quickly. Red and pink, those were her colors, and he just couldn't help himself–red and pink–they got him hot, instantly. Red–there had to be something red in the pantry. Tenderly, he stroked the side of a large can of stewed tomatoes, but somehow they just didn't do it for him. He needed something softer. The walk-in–there were tomatoes in the walk-in, real tomatoes. Hefting himself off the can of vegetables, he let himself into the giant refrigerator.

Hmmm…tomatoes. After moving several crates he found the one he needed. Two nice smooth, round, south Alabama cherry-red sweetie tomatoes hung au natural from a piece of genuine tomato bush, but they needed a frame. Burlap bags, which one would do? Not the bag of onions or the one of lettuce, too lumpy. A flour sack? No, not flour. Hidden under the produce, in the very back of the walk-in, he found a bushel sack full of multicolored marshmallows.

Why did they have a huge bag of marshmallows in the fridge? Oh hell, who cared? He guessed they must be left over from the goodies the church folks brought out last Halloween for the retards. Nice church people. The treat came in a laxative-pink bag as purdy as could be, and it was so soft. He patted the bag lovingly, and moved it out onto the main walkway floor. Being very careful not to break the stem, he fastened the tomatoes to the burlap bushel sack-front. Grinning, he stepped back to admire his work. Not that classy a broad, but he couldn't be picky.

"You'd be a finer looking lady if you had a head." Closing his eyes, he pictured Verbena's features on top of his creation, and touching himself he smiled, as he found he was ready for action. Did he dare do this? Strange. He was standing in a refrigerator and he didn't even feel cold. Three crates should get Flobaby up to about the right height. Every ounce of his being longed to shoot his juices into something with as much friction and force as possible, but it wouldn't do to make a mess. What if he made just the right sized hole in the bag?

For a brief instant he wondered if the door could be locked from the inside, but it was only briefly. Pulling his skirt up he tucked it into the waistband, lowered his panties and gingerly pushed into the artificial woman. Soft bouncy balls of sugar supported him on every side.

The resulting sensation after his time of forced celibacy sent tingles from his toes all the way to his pretty new wig. A shit-eating grin on his face, he closed his eyes tightly and started pumping, leaning into his new found lover who obligingly sprang back into shape each time he moved away. This was absolutely the best he'd felt in two months. Slack-jawed, he couldn't help but moan.

He never saw the door open, but he heard Karen scream. Lenny was right behind her. He drooped like a limp worm as he turned to face them. Neither interfered at all as he charged out of the cooler and disappeared into the deepening shadows of the early evening, with his bare ass shining in the mild spring breeze, and smashed tomatoes all over the front of his white uniform top.

Chapter Thirty-Nine

Loneliness

Molly looked away. The teacher looked at her strangely. What did she do? Was her sweater buttoned straight? Did she have some little remnant of breakfast clinging to her mouth?

"Molly, we're waiting. Did you bring your report?" *Oh yes, the report. What I want to be when I grow up. It was so funny. The grownups in this place didn't realize that none of us retards are going to grow up. All anyone here wants to do when they grow up is to leave. Go. Run. Go away from here.* She reached for the scrap of paper she penned yesterday while sitting under the trees near the ball field. Time to play their game. Time to pretend she was normal. *If you tried hard enough, it could almost make it so. Except that hours and hours of waiting didn't make Ghost appear. Not even a flash of white between the trees. Okay. Show time.*

"What I want to be when I grow up. I think I want to be a teacher." She had given the subject a lot of thought before she chose her profession. Everything was for appearances. If she made one misstep she would never be allowed to see Tessie and the visit was only days away now. Nothing could go wrong.

"Teachers are able to help people. They learn things kids need to know and are able to make children's lives interesting." Ah. Mrs. Roberts had a smile on her evil face. She was on the right track.

Looking around her, she noted that Kenny was about to fall off his chair again. Not now. She had to impress this old lady and get a good report sent in for her schoolwork. If he fell off the chair, he would start screaming, and then no one would even hear the rest of her report. She wouldn't get a good grade and then she wouldn't see Tessie. Better hurry.

"Teachers are loving people." This was a lie, but the old witch bought it. She could see Roberta Roberts get that little smile on her face that meant she believed and that was all that mattered.

"Yes, Molly, go on, please." *Oh yes. She bought it, hook, line and sinker. Good.*

"They give their lives to help children so that the children can be strong and smart. They make them smart, so they can survive, and even become famous someday. They are real hu-man-i-tar-i-tans." She hoped it didn't count against her that she stumbled over that word. It was so perfect. "I want to go to Teachers' College in Sicily and become a teacher just like my teacher, Mrs. Roberts. The End."

"Very well done, Molly!" A crash followed and Kenny took the plunge. Muttering cusswords under her breath, the saintly Mrs. Roberts strode over and picked the screaming child up by one ear.

"Shut up, Kenny." Most of the kids in the class agreed silently; at least the ones who listened at all.

"I want my mother." The snotty-nosed little runt wheezed as Mrs. Roberts deposited him in the corner. He would soon wind down over there with no one paying any attention to him.

We all want our mothers. Molly winced as her thoughts returned to Ghost, and then to her mommy, dressed, as always, in her soft green-silk kimono, just like Molly remembered her. Neither provided any comfort to her as she thought about this place she was forced to make her home; this place of huge empty halls and no heat, the noise of a hundred children, none touching each other in any way that wasn't harsh.

If only she could find Ghost and curl up near her soft white fur again. She would be okay if she could find Ghost, but she knew it would be dangerous, even after her visit with Tessie. Ghost was not wanted here. A security guard here would shoot her if she so much as showed a nose around a door or emerged out of a closet. The dog would be killed instantly.

Ouch. She felt a poke from behind her. Snickering softly, Debbie hid the ruler in her desk. Without her protector, Molly was a target for Debbie and her little gang. Debbie had never forgotten the few minutes of terror she'd experienced when she faced Ghost, and she punished Molly every day for making it happen. Molly Parsons. Debbie Perkins. The awful kid was seated right behind her in every class and at every event, except music. Debbie grinned, and the two kids, one on each side of Molly, grinned back. They knew Molly would never turn around and retaliate.

Pictures raced through Molly's mind as she struggled with her desire for revenge. If she did anything, she would get into trouble. After the visit, she'd take care of this little problem. She pictured Debbie's leering face changing expression as a long red mark extended from eyes to mouth, and the child picked herself up from the position the back of Molly's hand would send her. She pictured her turning tail and running in the other direction. It was very satisfying. *Later*. She would make the whole bunch of them pay, but not now. Still, it would help if she had just one friend. With Debbie as an enemy, not one other child in the place would even speak to her, and she never saw Mickey. She missed his dancing eyes and funny pantomimes. *Where was Mickey?* She'd like just to see him, even if nothing else. Just to see him for a minute.

Suddenly, he was there. He appeared in the doorway of the classroom, gestured toward Debbie, and made his silly monkey face. Responding to Molly's look of delight, he put both hands around his own neck and pretended to hang himself. Then, taking three jumping hops, he pretended to kick an imaginary opponent in the butt. She couldn't help it; she laughed out loud.

Mrs. Roberts turned to see whatever it was that had caught Molly's attention, but as far as she could see, Molly was laughing at vacant air. Well, this wasn't the first kid in this class to see things that did not exist, but she was sorry to see it happening to the one fairly normal kid that she taught. After all, this was the loony bin. What did she expect, taking a job in a place like this? Shrugging, she moved to her desk and called for the next report.

"Kenny, do you feel well enough now to read your homework assignment for us? I guess not." Cheerfully, she marked a big black "F" under his name. "Debbie? How about yours?" She caught Debbie totally absorbed in whispered conversation with the buddy next to her.

"Uh. My report?" Suddenly Debbie had that "deer in the headlights" look.

"Yes, your homework. You remembered to do your homework?"

"Could you call on me last, please, Mrs. Roberts? I can't find it. I know it's here somewhere." She began rifling through books and notebooks for a report everyone who paid attention knew didn't exist. Mrs. Roberts wasn't the only one who smiled as she marked a second big black "F" in her record book. Molly grinned from ear to ear. Her day was improving. She just might make it through another one without killing anyone. Sometimes life was grand. Mickey grinned too, from the hall. He needed to find a way to visit his Princess. She needed him.

Chapter Forty

Eliza Resurfaces

Ghost tilted her velvet head upward and sang into the howling wind. Gales always affected her in this way. The high-pitched whine of each gust made her restless. The sharp cracking of limbs above her only heightened the feeling that she was supposed to be something else, someone else. She felt exposed as the sharp edge of the air lifted her fur and cut into the tender flesh underneath. It pulled her out of the skin that had been comfortable into the dark recesses of the night. Lightly, she floated above the animal that was her home, away from it, and watched as its now-empty shell settled gently to the ground, to wait for her return.

Eliza was free again, free to wander, to find the object of her increasing anger and curiosity. Things became clear to her again. None of the cobwebs that obscured her memories while she was within Ghost remained; as Eliza she remembered her mission and wafted westward toward Beaufort Falls.

It'd been a long time since she'd traveled in that direction. The winds blew her quickly toward the evil that she felt compelled to confront. He lived still, she could feel it, and he shouldn't live. He should die. He had hurt her children. He had hurt her. He would die. She would kill him and feel his blood run warm down her throat. For a moment, she savored sensations that were familiar to her as Ghost, sensations of touch and warmth and taste. It was lonely being part of the night air, as cold and hard to reach as the crystal stars so high above her. She would miss the feel of the dog when it was time to leave it forever.

She saw the little house that had been so dear to her. She remembered sweeping the porch, shaking the rugs, polishing the little bits of furniture with lemon oil. She smelled its clean fragrance propelled by the strong wind that blew open the front door and beckoned her in. Another strong odor assailed her—the smell of cheap whiskey. It seemed odd that she still had senses. A part of her still clung to Ghost's earthy mortality, but the creature that she had become joined with the wind and had power far stronger than the sharp bite of a dog. She stood in the open doorway and looked at the gaunt caricature that had once been her husband.

"On Jordan's misty shores I stand. At Heaven's Pearly Gates." J.D. slurred the words to the old hymn, hunched over his shot glass. Just a drop or two of liquor remained in the fifth of Early Times. Morosely, he lifted the bottle and glared at the trace of golden-brown fluid at the bottom. *Some friend you turned out to be. Here I am starting a journey, and you ran out on me.*

For the hundredth time since he finished packing yesterday, he looked to be sure he had everything ready. Car keys, they were right on the edge of the table. Now where did he put those suitcases? For a second he panicked. What happened to his things? The scant two bags he packed contained everything he and Tessie would need for a new beginning in England, including the difficult-to-obtain passports and some other fake ID. As soon as they got there, his sweet little girl would become Beth, never again Tessie.

316

He renamed her Bethel, and he was Caleb. He was proud of the new biblical names he had chosen for the two of them.

The caddie had been sold. His cousin would take possession as soon as he and the one child he wanted to keep reached the Atlanta Airport and boarded the plane to New York. All he had in the world, after all of his years of hard work, were the few little things in the trunk of the car, and the plane tickets that meant a new beginning. His former lawyer now owned the little house on Sycamore Street. He couldn't believe that his big-city kin was dumb enough to give him money in advance for the car without a title, but that was history now. The Lord was protecting him and J.D. would make things right with his idiot cousin someday.

Nothing mattered but that he and Tessie…uh…Beth, get away. Well, one other thing mattered to him. It was time he removed the other horrible creature birthed by his evil wife. How could he have been foolish enough to believe the child was his? What insanity possessed him? They were twins. Of course, they had the same father, and there was no possible way he could have spawned the flaming redheaded monster. What made him bestow his time and energy on the ungrateful little whelp who laughed at him, mocked his every move, the twisted Satan-child sent to make a fool of him by the enemies of the Divine. Molly was no child. She was a demon, so different from his fair Tessie.

Perhaps it was only Tessie's birth that allowed him to see what a real child was like. This was his chance to get her back and to make things right, to restore the balance of goodness to what it would have been if Molly had never been born. This was his last chance to make things right with his God. He would survive and he and his child would live the way they were meant to, in the Promised Land. He had no doubt but what God would protect him and find him a place, in England.

Reeling from the whiskey, he lifted the chair cushion, removed and lovingly fondled a large sheep-shearing knife. Such a beautiful weapon, razor sharp, sharpened by him just yesterday, it gleamed in the flashes of intermittent sunlight pouring through the open doorway. Like the ancients, he must prepare himself for the battle yet to come. Reverently, he knelt before the chair, touched the shaft of the sharp blade to his lips, and began to recite scripture as if it were his prayer.

"If a man has a stubborn and rebellious child
who does not obey her father and does not listen to
him when he disciplines her, the father shall take
hold of her and take her to the elders at the gate of
his town. He shall say to the elders, 'This child is
stubborn and rebellious. She will not obey me. She
is a bastard and a whore.'

And all the men of the town shall stone her;
stone her until she is dead. You must purge the
evil from among you and all of the world will hear
of this and be afraid."

Yes, Molly must die, and it's my duty to kill her. For the briefest instant a soft shadow passed over his hardened features. *It's sad to sacrifice a child, but I have to remember she's no real child, but a pawn of the evil one. She's a demon and an imp from Hell, and as soon as she's dead she'll return to the eternal flames from whence she came. For the good of everyone who would ever come in contact with her, I must fulfill my obligation*

Feeling his thoughts, Eliza heard nothing after the word "dead." Anger seethed from within her, shimmering in waves of heat and color, trickling through the doorway, red flames barely visible to the eye, completely oblivious to drunken John Duke Parsons, who glanced at his watch as he fondled his weapon.

Lord save me, I've got one hour before I pick up Tessie! He realized he had to sober up or he'd miss his appointment. Tenderly, he set his implement of justice on the couch, staggered into the bathroom, stripped, and stepped into the shower. He turned the knobs, adjusting the water temperature to cold.

Eliza concentrated on the pewter dials, using her will to try to turn them, but nothing happened. The man should die. He should be boiled like a lobster; screaming and clutching his bare skin, bronzed pink in a haze of fire-hot water, wafting trails of steam and flesh into the quiet neighborhood air, but she was still too weak; still influenced by the mortality that lingered within her.

Frustrated, she followed the water pipes into the wall, looking to see where they might go. They led down into the basement to the huge gas hot-water heater. J.D. had planned on having a large family and had factored lots of hot water into his plans. If she could only produce one breath, a little burst of air; that would be all that she needed. Concentrating, she managed a tiny gust. The flame went out and gas began filling the basement, windows all tightly closed to prevent burglary.

Upstairs, J.D. dressed carefully. He felt better now. The cold shower restored his senses and sobered him. Habit returned. He donned his underwear, his crisp white shirt, and then pulled a black trouser sock over each foot. No one would ever know that he experienced moments of weakness. His black pants slid over lanky thighs and he slipped into his suit jacket. He spent an extra few seconds with his tie. It was discrete, a nice blue, and knotted perfectly. The first few molecules of gas eased up the stairs, into the kitchen of the little house.

Glancing at his watch, he realized that he must hurry if he were to make it on time. It would be just like that meddlesome bitch Anna to take Tessie and go without him if he was late. He couldn't have that happen. They had to be in his car.

He slid his feet into brightly polished black shoes and began closing windows. Even if it wasn't his home anymore, and he would never see it again, he couldn't leave it unlocked. He would leave it properly secured. Grabbing his knife and his keys, he bolted the wooden door for the last time, and without a backward glance, eased into the comfortable seat of the caddie and drove away. He never heard the explosion when Eliza's fury managed to ignite the spark that blew the little house into a hundred thousand pieces, each competing with the next in a race to reach the hard ground first.

About fifty yards away, Spike and Virgil saw the explosion. While it surprised the two of them, they were in too much of a hurry to follow J.D. to worry about what caused it. They had a contract to meet and a payment to earn, and it was long overdue. If they didn't get J.D. killed soon, A.E. was going to forget that he ever hired them. Today was the day. They had the mortar loaded in the jeep and J.D. was going to bite the big one, no matter where they had to do it.

"Spike, what if we get caught?" Virgil was a little apprehensive about running around sleepy Beaufort Falls with a full-sized mortar, stolen from the local armory, in the back of an open jeep.

"Never happen. We're too fast for the likes of this town." Still, he pulled into a driveway and hid behind some bushes as they waited for a woman and child to climb into the Cadillac with J.D.

"We can't get him now. He has people with him." Virgil was almost in tears. All he wanted was for all this to be over with so he could go back to putting groceries on the shelf at the Magic Pantry. Besides, using the big gun scared him. Even though they had practiced with ammunition taken at the same time as they stole the gun, it was hard to aim, and unpredictable in its range. The only thing he could guarantee was that it was going to blow up something. Gaping holes in the field where they practiced proved that, large gaping holes. He just hoped it wasn't them.

"Shut up, Virgil. They don't look all that happy. Maybe he's just giving 'um a ride somewhere."

They settled into a position about fifty yards behind J.D. and his passengers, and kept following. Today was the big day. If they didn't kill the man today, A.E. *would* make them give the money back. He was sure of that, and the money was already spent. A.E. was a fucking tightwad who expected results. Today was the day.

Mickey stretched forward to see the waning rays of the sun, fitting on his perch in the tree as if he were just another branch sprouting from its gray surface. Some days he almost felt that he knew the truth and had answers to the questions that plagued him. Why wasn't he growing like the other children? Why was it he never needed to eat, or to sleep? How was it that he could see their thoughts and could just be places when he thought about them? Why was he different? Unlike the other children, he just was; or when he wanted not to be, he wasn't. His brow wrinkled as he wondered. He sure was glad he didn't do this often, but this was one of those days. Just as he started to jump out of the tree, something underneath him caught his attention.

It was the white dog, but she looked dead. Only a slight movement of her ribcage indicated that she still lived. She was deeply asleep, her lips drawn back almost in a snarl and her legs were curled tightly beneath her. He moved away from her and settled down to watch.

Suddenly, she twitched and moaned, and her eyes opened with a jerk. Mickey blinked. For a second he thought he saw a flash of green slide into the limp body of the animal. Now Ghost was on her feet, dazed and confused. She shook her fur, stumbled, and after a moment ambled off down the wooded path. Something had happened right before his eyes, but Mickey couldn't figure it out. Immediately before the dog woke, he saw something human and felt a stab of agony as it formed itself into something else; then he felt sadness and relief, mixed. As those feelings faded, he felt nothing. Mickey had a peculiar sense that he might know that dog, but he couldn't remember from where. It was the same sort of feeling you get when a familiar phrase escapes your memory or you can't remember your old phone number or the first name of your oldest, dearest, no longer around, best friend. Curious, Mickey followed Ghost into the cave.

Sheriff Bobby Cox of Beaufort Falls scratched his head and tried to decide whether or not this fire should be a crime scene. It'd started with an explosion, but the fire department already had assured him that a gas leak had caused it and the resulting intense flames. His last call to this residence had been several months ago, but he'd heard that J.D. lost the house to that shyster lawyer Magillacutty, and that by itself made it a possible arson. Where was J.D.? It wasn't like him not to be close by. Usually he was annoyingly underfoot at a time like this.

"Bubba, see if you can find J.D. Parsons. Someone needs to tell him that his house is on fire. And when you find him, see if you can check out that car of his for flammable substances. Quietly. We don't need to put ourselves on his long list of potential lawsuit candidates. See if you can help him out by putting something in his trunk for him." Bubba hurried back to the radio to put out a discrete bulletin to "stop and assist one J.D. Parsons." It looked like it might become a hot time in the old town tonight.

"I'll bet fifty bucks J.D. burned that place down himself. He is one damn poor loser," Bobby mumbled to himself, as he headed back to the station to await any other impending disasters of the night.

Chapter Forty-One

The Family Is Dysfunctional

A. E. Beaufort spoke angrily to the realty agent on the other end of the line. "Of course I want to sign the papers at my new home. I want to inspect it one last time before I sign all that money over to you. Unless we meet on the site, the whole deal is off! One hour! One hour, or forget it!"

Beaufort got his way, always. Damn. This was going to make the whole thing so much harder. It was going to be very difficult explaining the sale to Pryor; he was a good man, and it really wasn't right. Ernie knew him personally, and even if the board offered Pryor more money it would never make up for the time and love the man had sunk into the beautiful antebellum home. No one else, certainly not that prick Beaufort, could ever make it prettier than the house and grounds were right now.

Dreading the hour ahead, he reached for his coat and moved toward the door. This wasn't going to be easy, but he supposed he had no choice. He just hadn't wanted to be the one to have to tell his old friend. Pryor wasn't going to take this news well, not well at all. He'd thought he'd had low points in his career before, but this took the prize.

Meanwhile, at the mansion, Pryor Akins was putting the finishing touches on the office he had created hastily on the bottom floor of the stately home. Recent rumors indicated that any part of the vast institution grounds not used as a working part of the hospital would be sold, and he would find himself looking for another place to live. This should do the trick. He couldn't wait to tell them in the board meeting on Monday that the counseling staff at the hospital loved using it for their sessions.

He anticipated calling several of his staff members in to talk to the Ways and Means Committee and to insist that the relaxed atmosphere in the new mansion office made their jobs easier. He expected the first counseling session to begin within the hour, and the whole future of his home might depend on how well it went.

He knew that the house contributed to a lot of his prestige within the mental health community. God knows his salary was pitifully small, and running the institution with its many problems was a major headache. He spent most of his paycheck and his time fixing the place up so that it was a proper home for himself and his wife. Even the thought of losing it and having to find somewhere else suitable to live in this forsaken part of Alabama kept him up at night.

For the third time, he rearranged the bouquet of lilies, daffodils and baby's breath he'd picked from the garden just for the occasion; and then he rearranged the furniture one last time around the large fireplace that took up one entire side of the office. With a sigh, he settled into one of the chairs to wait. He was only minutes away from knowing if his plan would work.

A few feet away, Carrie tried to quiet the butterflies fighting with her breakfast. Why was she chosen to be the first counselor to use the new deluxe office? She was nobody. All she knew for sure was that after more than a month of trying to set up this very important meeting, suddenly it was on the agenda immediately. Something wasn't right about this whole thing, but she was damned if she could figure out what. Why the urgency now?

She reached down to touch the serious, hazel-eyed waif with her. Her eyes were dark and tired today, and she showed every sign of spending the entire meeting quiet and withdrawn. Molly didn't respond when Carrie stroked her hair. She examined the child's little face carefully.

Dark rings centered under Molly's eyes, and her features weren't really those of a child. She was a miniature little old lady, right down to the ratty cardigan sweater and the boxy knit pants. She had an ancient look about her and should have had a thousand wrinkles. Poor kid. She felt the child's shoulder and it was as tight as the leaf spring on a 66 Chevy, carrying the weight of the cares of the world all wound up in one little body. She was rock-hard rigid, and afraid. The only cheerful note about her was the splash of bright red from the old sweater.

"Molly, try not to be afraid. I'm here with you. Do you want to go back and live with your dad and your sister?" After hours of talking with Molly, she still didn't have any idea what Molly wanted to have happen. The kid revealed nothing of what went on inside her little head. Carrie watched her begin the painful process of trying to phrase what she thought Carrie wanted to hear.

"I want to live with my sister. You're sure she's coming? She'll be here today?" *Okay. J.D. was conspicuously absent in the child's reply.* She needed to get to the bottom of this whole thing. They were at the mansion, only feet away from the door that opened to the site of the most important counseling meeting in her short career, and in Molly's future. She needed to know exactly what went on in that household when it was just J.D. Parsons and his two children. Her hand tightened on Molly's shoulder and she crouched down to be eye-level with the child.

"Molly, you know this is a very important meeting. Molly?" She forced Molly to look her in the eyes. They were such old eyes, so tired, so tortured. It was difficult staring into the recesses of the child's hurt soul. For an instant she saw raw longing there, deep pain, and then they glazed over protectively.

'Yes ma'am, I do."

"Did your father ever hurt you or Tessie? I have to know about it before we go in." Molly broke eye contact and tried to move away from Carrie, who'd heard a noise at the end of the hall and looked up to see J.D. and the pretty little blonde girl approaching. Her friend, Anna, was many feet behind, still opening the door. If she had any doubt as to the way J.D. and Molly felt about each other, it was answered in the exchange of looks that passed between them. J.D. saw no one but Molly, and his eyes blazed with hatred.

Quickly, she put her arms around the little girl to protect her, but what she felt astonished her. Molly pulled away from her, but not in fear. She struggled to move toward J.D., and Carrie had to hang onto her to keep her in place. She heard a soft feral growl come from the kid and almost let her go. The heat flowing from Molly's little body sizzled.

The child's features contorted into a grimace of fury that answered every question. Only years of abuse could cram that much hatred into a child's little heart. That man must never take either of the children back home with him, ever again.

The moment passed, and she watched as Molly looked at her sister.

"Tessie." Molly spoke softly, but the word contained all of the love the child hid so carefully from the world. The little blonde angel didn't wait to be asked, she ran toward her sister, laughing and throwing her arms around her. Carrie watched J.D.'s reaction as he carefully erased all trace of anger and irritation from his features. She was looking at another man now, a perfect father.

"I guess we'd better start the meeting," he suggested cheerfully. "It seems the kids are glad to see each other."

Yes, it's time to start the meeting, Carrie thought as she wordlessly escorted J.D. and the children the rest of the way down the long entrance hall. She had all of the answers she needed now. Like a good hostess, she opened the door to the office and showed her little group inside. They entered and stood looking at the cheerful fire, the flowers, and the hospitable face of Pryor Akins, who motioned them into chairs. Anna moved to come in also, but Carrie stepped into the hallway and shut the door.

"I can't let you be a part of the meeting. I'm sorry, you know that, but it's okay. I understand."

"I need to be there," Anna stumbled over her words trying to let her friend know that she should be on her guard. "You understand? You do? Are you sure?" It was so important for Carrie to know what a monster J.D. was. "He's an evil man," she spoke simply. "He twists things." Carrie knew that her friend was hurting and she wrapped her arms around her briefly.

"Wait here." She found a spot at the entrance to the hall where Anna could sit on a small bench and still be close by.

"Don't worry. I won't let him have those children."

"Good." Anna settled herself anxiously on the bench and hoped that her friend had the resources she would need for the job ahead of her. The next few hours would determine the future in ways none of them yet could comprehend. The time of reckoning was at hand.

Things were not going well on the other side of the grassy knoll, just five hundred yards away from the pristine southern mansion.

"Damn thing is harder than shit to set up and aim." Spike was sweating in the hot spring sun, and he hated sweating.

"Turn it a little more front-ways, Spike." Virgil tried to be helpful. "We gotta hit the walkway, not the house. Beaufort's buying that house, I heard. He'd really be pissed if we hit the house."

"Turn it yourself, Turdhead." Beaufort owed them more money when they finished their mission and he didn't want to hear anything about him buying a house. Besides, Spike was sick of struggling with the thing. It was old, it was heavy, and it wasn't all that accurate. They'd found that out while practicing with it.

"What if he still has that kid with him when he comes out?" Virgil worried too much. It was always something with him. Nothing worked out perfectly.

"Then you'll go down there and get the kid and then I'll blow him away. It'll be all right. It has to be all right. It's our last chance."

Sure enough, that shut Virgil up. Virgil hated that idea. In fact, that idea absolutely sucked. There were already too many people in that house and he didn't want to be a murderer. He really had a bad feeling about this plan—a very bad feeling.

Things were not going to be all right at all; he could just feel
it.

Chapter Forty-Two

Apocalypse Now

Charlie didn't know whether to be pleased or saddened. After all this time he'd spotted the bitch at last. There she was, about fifteen feet in front of him, digging up some kind of toadstools and putting them into a wicker basket. "I guess it's time to do the dirty deed," he mumbled to himself. No matter how much he knew he needed to close this chapter of his life for good, he could picture Verbena dressed in her pink uniform from the doughnut shop, and the thought of having to hurt her repulsed him.

Desperately, he looked around for some sort of a large tree limb that would make a good weapon, but nothing looked right. The flowers and new green shrubbery were light and fragile, nothing that would pack the kind of wallop he needed to make sure that Verbena went down and never got back up, preferably before she ever saw what hit her. *If she would only stay here long enough for me to run back to the cabin and get my axe*, he wished.

Quietly, he backed back down the path and ran a fast fifty-yard dash through the briars and underbrush back to his temporary home. Hefting the fireman's special onto his right shoulder he ran back, only to find Verbena moving quickly along the woodsy path in the other direction. The only course of action left was to follow her, so he did. He kept her just in sight until she disappeared into the side of a small hill.

A cave. No wonder I couldn't find her. Rubbing his eyes and moving the heavy axe to his other shoulder, he edged close to the entrance, but he couldn't see a thing, just a long dark tunnel into the side of the river bluff.

It's a slave cave. Everyone in these parts knew about the old slave caves. Like the cabins, the caves were part of the history learned by every Alabama schoolchild, and kids loved to explore them, to their parents' horror. Because they were carved in sandstone, cave-ins happened frequently, turning a cavern into an instant grave. Slaves, running from cruel owners, had hid in the caves for weeks, or months, until abolitionists could engineer an escape for them. They always had an entrance and an exit, so that the slave could make a fast retreat. If he wanted to trap his quarry, he'd better go plug the exit.

Very quietly, he eased around the briars and underbrush covering the side of the hill until he reached the back, where he found a blazing campfire and food cooking, a turkey sizzling on a spit and a large pan full of carrots and cabbage simmering on the fire. The toadstools he watched Verbena pick still sat in the basket, which was placed next to the trickling river. He scanned the scene for something he could use to block the back of the cave and spotted a large boulder, flat on the top but nicely rounded underneath; that would do nicely. It may have even been removed from the hill a hundred years before to form the exit.

Inside, Ghost turned her head and pointed her ears toward the back of the cave. She thought she heard something, but couldn't be sure with the happy chattering going on around her. Fox's party wasn't going to be a surprise party. In fact, he was having the most fun of anyone, helping Verbena mix up ingredients for his cake. Each of the boys also helped; Horse cracked pecans for it, Lion broke and separated eggs, Beaver measured out just the right amount of sticky honey. Soon it would be poured into the ancient black Dutch oven and be placed in the coals to 'bake." Fox was definitely having the most fun of all. Sifting flour was more fun than he ever imagined he could have cooking. He turned the handle of the castaway sifter vigorously, raising clouds of white dust, becoming far whiter than the bowl he attempted to fill.

Verbena looked from one to the other, happier than she'd ever been in her life. None of them heard the faint scraping as Charlie moved the boulder into position to block the exit; not even the vigilant dog, which was still trying to sort through vivid confused visions racing through her tired brain.

It sounded like a hundred lawn chairs being dragged across a gravel pit to Charlie, and suddenly he was terrified Verbena would hear and come running out of the front of the cave. After all this time, he didn't intend for her to escape again. After all, she was the only witness who could put his head in a noose. Panicked, he flew back to the front, only to come to a rest behind a tree right across from the entrance, relieved to find that nothing had changed.

"Nervous are we?" he queried himself. A little courage before making his move would take the edge off his anxiety, he decided, so he nested in the fallen leaves and reached for his old friend, Jim Beam. A couple of swigs would calm his nerves and give everything time to settle down in the cave. He wanted to catch the surprise on Verbena's face when he waltzed in. She sure wouldn't be expecting to see him again. The whiskey was a nice treat.

It was a good thing that he knew all the secret spots in the kitchen walk-in. He guessed he was an ex-employee now, but he still knew where to get his food and drink. Just another sip or two and maybe he'd be ready to pay his old girlfriend a quick visit. The clock was ticking...

J.D. pushed the two little girls in front of him, one hand firmly clamped over Molly's mouth, the other gripping Tessie's hand. He never imagined it would be this easy. When the dingbat counselor closed the door and moved into the hallway, he turned to the smiling Akins and gripped Molly's shoulder.

"Where's the bathroom?" he asked, catching Tessie's palm in his big one and giving Molly a firm push toward the door. She began to speak and he squeezed her shoulder harder, with enough pressure to crush her small bones. Akins, busy pointing down the hall, didn't see the agonized look on the child's face. Always the good host, he pointed several doors down and stepped aside so that they could pass. Carrie, on her way back from talking to Anna, saw the little group leaving.

"Stop them!" she screamed, but Akins stood frozen by the office door, confused. J.D. lifted the struggling Molly into his arms.

"Run, Tessie! Run to the car. I'll save Molly!" Thrilled that Molly was coming with them, Tessie flew toward the caddie, leaving her dad to back out of the door that shut in his face as she dashed out.

"There he is! Oh, get him, Spike! There he is. And the kid's already in the car! Shoot! Shoot!"

Spike leaned over the sight on the cannon and grimaced as he tugged on the firing pin. Suddenly Virgil saw Molly in J.D.'s arms. Lunging, he pushed his body into Spike and the gun moved slightly to the right–the wrong direction.

Horrified, they watched the western end of the beautiful white home disappear in a cloud of dust. Never before had they seen such destruction. The noise alone deafened them. To make matters worse, they watched as Beaufort himself, accompanied by a shocked realtor, pulled up in his snazzy new sports car. J.D. never paused to look. The caddie disappeared as Anna, Carrie and Akins emerged from the still-standing end of the smoking building.

"What do we do now, Spike?" Tears were pouring down Virgil's pudgy cheeks. "What do we do now? He ain't never gonna pay us now, even if we do assassinate that shit-head. What do we do now?"

A terrible sadness descended on Spike as he stood watching the scene below him. The women were striding toward the parking lot, following J.D.'s exiting vehicle. A. E. Beaufort got out of his little car, handed his jacket to the bewildered agent, and socked the already totally immobile West Alabama Administrator in the nose. Pryor Akins reeled from the blow, then collapsed onto the ground amid the ruins of his home, hugging his knees and moaning loud enough to be heard by the inept assassins.

The ironic tragedy of the entire progression of events inscribed nobility onto Spike's rough features in a way that no other series of events in his life could. Life was not just. Hard work does not result in a payoff. There comes a time when you just had to cut your losses and leave.

"What will we do?" Virgil's plaintive wail deserved an answer.

"Well," Spike hesitated, deep in thought, remembering the gaudy new posters that had just appeared in Beaufort Falls the previous day. "Well, I guess we'll just have to join the circus."

"Okay." Virgil brightened. He loved the elephants. He could picture himself training elephants, riding at the head of the circus parade high on a swaying back, sitting on the little red rug that looked so precariously fastened. *How did they get those things to stay on?*

Shoulders slumped; Spike started the short walk back to the jeep. Lost in excited anticipation, Virgil started after him, and then turned back to the scene of the crime.

"Hey Spike! You forgot the gun! Come help me with it. I can't get it alone."

"We don't need it." Spike kept walking, and after one last look in the weapon's direction, Virgil followed.

J.D. Parsons stared ahead in disbelief. How could anyone have found him so fast? Beaufort Falls Sheriff's Deputy Bubba Dumas stood by his squad car next to the parking lot exit, blocking his route to freedom. Cursing, he pulled the caddie into a parking place and pulled the two little girls out of the passenger side. For just a second, as he shifted his grip, he made eye contact with Molly.

"Father. Where're we going?" She tried to be calm and respectful and not wiggle, even though he was hurting her.

"You shut up. In a few minutes it'll all be over and you'll be knocking on the gates of Hell." Almost involuntarily, he reached under his suit jacket for his belt to be sure that he had his knife, and Molly froze when she saw it tucked casually next to his waist. He scooped Tessie up into his arms and half ran into the nearby woods, dragging Molly along. Pushing back the weeds, he searched for the path that had been so familiar to him during the nights he'd forced Eliza along it during the month of her terror and humiliation at his hands. Finally he found it, faint but still recognizable, and dragging Molly by the collar on her sweater, he ignored her choked gasps for air.

The path came to an intersection and he stopped, scanning his memory. A right led to the slave cabin, but he had another destination in mind. Intent on his mission, he turned left, heading toward the river and other memories even darker than the hours spent vainly waiting for prey that never arrived.

Molly was too afraid to even try to get away, as her little legs struggled to keep up. Her pants were cold against her thighs where she had wet herself, but she didn't care. Her shivering came from the realization that her father was going to kill her and there was little she could do about it. She wondered if it would hurt, and if she would see her mother again once it was all over.

Dear God, forgive me, she prayed silently, beginning a prayer she had learned early in her life and that she needed for courage right now. *Please forgive me my sins, and take care of me. Please send my mommy to get me. Please, don't let it hurt.*

All she could think about was the bright glint of the knife blade and she knew it was sharp. She'd sharpened it for her dad hundreds of times, honing it always to the outside so as not to nick the edge and ruin it. Tears began to run silently down her face and her shoulders began to shake with dry little sobs. She didn't want to die.

Charlie Callahan found his courage and leaving his bottle in the leaves, strode boldly into the little cave, his huge axe balanced against his left shoulder like some Alabama version of Paul Bunyan. The entrance curved several times, its last loop giving him no warning that Verbena was not alone. Suddenly, he found six sets of eyes on him; five human sets and one decidedly hostile, big white dog. One other pair he didn't see until Mickey slipped by him quietly, coming to stand next to the large dog. A soft growl originating in the back of the animal's throat stopped him cold, frozen in the entranceway, while Verbena and the children stared at him in mute disbelief.

The moment ended as Ghost tensed, poised to lunge, and Charlie lifted his axe into position, only to be distracted by a noise to his left. Little Fox dropped his flour and threw himself at Charlie, determined to protect his pet and his friend. Horrified, Verbena screamed.

"No, Freddie! Stop!"

Charlie backed up, stooping to grab the little boy.

"Get back, Ghost. Get back!" Ghost bristled and growled, but reluctantly obeyed Verbena.

Suddenly, Charlie was at a loss as to what course of action to pursue. He wanted Verbena, but he'd never harmed a kid in his life. Now he held an angry little squirming and kicking tike in one arm, and a heavy unsteady axe in the other. Between him and the person he wanted to kill bristled an angry dog and five more little children. Someone was going to get hurt, and at the moment it seemed likely it could be him.

Carefully, he put down the axe and sighed with relief as the furious dog backed up a couple of feet at Verbena's command. The last thing he wanted to do was to hack Verbena to pieces in front of what looked like a cub scout meeting. What shitty luck! It never occurred to him that Verbena might not be alone, much less surrounded by children.

What the hell were little kids doing out in the woods, in a cave, and what on earth was he going to do with the little tiger he had by the scruff of the neck? He'd sooner cut his own head off than to hurt a kid, and this kid was doing the best he could to reach him with a series of roundhouse punches that would have made a prize fighter proud. He was afraid to put him down. He might have to hurt him.

All of these emotions crossed his face as he stood holding the struggling child. He had no idea what to do next, but he knew that if he were to gain control of the quickly deteriorating situation, he would have to do it right away. Fortunately, Verbena solved the problem for him. All that she cared about was Freddy, and she had to get Charlie to let him go. Choking back fear, she spoke calmly to her little champion.

"Freddie, stop that. Charlie's a friend of mine. He's come to visit." She spoke quietly and with only a slight quiver showing her fear. "Charlie, please let the little boy go. He won't hurt you." Half embarrassed, Charlie set Freddie down, preferring to cradle the axe. To hell with the kids, he couldn't risk losing Verbena again. She was the only person alive who could put him on "death row," and although it pained him, she had to die.

"What are you children doing out here in the woods; don't you have homes? You need to go home, wherever it is. I have business with Verbena. Get out of here. Now!" He waved the axe and the reaction was immediate. Verbena reached for Freddy and pushed him toward Li, stepping in front of her little brood.

"Get them out of here Li. Get them out of here right now. Please. I'll meet you outside by the river when all this is over." No one could mistake the urgency in her voice, and without a word, the clan leader began moving his group backwards toward the exit.

As soon as he got them into the tunnel leading to the storage room and exit he felt better, but they weren't clear yet. He could still hear voices from the other cavern room as they left, but they faded as he put distance between them. Something was wrong, though. He should be able to see sunlight streaming through the back entrance, and all was dark. Freddy slipped past the others and raced toward the back, hoping to run out the exit and back around to the front to save his "Beeny."

"Li?" The little guy's voice was strained, confused. "Li. We can't get out. Someone moved the rock." Horrified, Li stopped and looked ahead. The boulder he used to put cooking utensils on while they cooked was now solidly in front of the only way out. They were trapped. Desperately, he surveyed the storeroom. Deep crevices lined the cave walls. Barnes had built planks into them to hold the supplies he so carefully collected for the "Plan," for their future.

"Li," Barnes' voice was choked with fear, but he managed to form words. "Li. We can get under the shelves." Even Harry managed to fit his long frame under one and was soon safely out of sight.

"Oh, God, protect us," Li prayed for himself and for his little clan. "Stay hidden," he instructed them. He didn't even want to think of Verbena's probable fate, trapped in the main room with the big man with the axe. "Cover your eyes and don't come out until I call you." Satisfied they were all out of view, he tucked himself into a corner to wait.

Not far from the cave, Molly begged, too.

"Please let me go, Father. I never hurt you. I never did anything wrong to you. Please!" She could hardly talk through the tight constriction that used to be her throat, and it didn't matter. Her father wasn't listening. He mumbled wildly, oblivious to her cries.

"From the bowels of the earth into the grave you'll go, with the other one, the other foul creature spawned by evil; you'll lie by him. You'll share the same grave. You'll lie with the other and the gates of Hell will open. You'll be swallowed up by the ravenous beast. God turned his face from..."

Scraping the path, Molly tried tripping over roots to slow them, but when J.D. reached down to pull her along; she saw his glazed eyes and she knew it was hopeless. Resigned to her fate, she scurried along, no longer resisting. He found the cave easily and he paused to settle Tessie onto a little pile of leaves right outside of it, never releasing his grip on his older daughter.

"Stay here or I'll take the strap to you," he threatened Tessie, who, after one look at her father's face, did as she was told. Molly squirmed, trying to get away, but J.D. shoved her into the entrance of the cave.

It was dark inside the tunnel and J.D. blinked, trying to adjust his eyes to the sudden absence of light. He moved along cautiously, pushing Molly in front of him single file, until suddenly he found himself in a large room. To his great surprise, he was not alone. Mouth open, he gaped incredulously at, of all people, Verbena, the dog that haunted his dreams, and the biggest man he'd ever seen holding an axe in his hands. Molly revived immediately.

"Ghost!" Her friend was there! She would live! It was too much for the dog. Growling, shrieking decibels higher than the human ear should be able to hear, Ghost launched herself into the air. J.D. let go of Molly and moved to protect his face, still stinging from his last encounter with the angry beast. Writhing, twisting in air, somehow she became more than a dog but not quite human. A flash of green mingled with the smell of sulfur filling the air as flames crackled around the figure of a beautiful woman, a beautiful woman with the face of an avenging angel.

Charlie reacted violently. He knew this woman! He heard her voice as he held his axe higher, poised but frozen in time, seconds ticking but not occurring.

Charlie, I loved you. He shook his head. She was dead. She was Eliza, but Eliza was dead. But it was Eliza, he was sure of it. Eliza, after all this time, his beautiful lost love. *Kill him, Charlie. Kill him.*

He turned to find the source of the voice speaking softly, ever so softly, from inside his head. He wished he could put his axe down. His skull was full of bees; he could hear them buzzing loudly, growing in decibels and volume, screaming to get out. *Kill him, Charlie. Kill him. He's going to kill your daughter. Kill him.* He had a daughter?

Molly moved backward, seeing her mommy leap from the body of her friend Ghost. Her tears turned to silver drops of blessed rain, washing her fear way. She curled up close to the cool wall of the cave, waiting for the flames to disappear and her mommy to emerge victorious to comfort her.

He had a daughter. Charlie could see that now. The child hugging the cave wall in front of him was the image of his mother; not Irish like his dad, but dark, with deep hazel eyes.

You have to kill him, Charlie. Kill him for me. Kill him for her. Kill him for your little son. He forgot Verbena as images of Eliza's husband flooded his mind. These were scenes he had never witnessed and he realized he was seeing the past through Eliza's tortured blue eyes.

Her last night had been so sad. He felt the whip descend on bare buttocks. It was Eliza's flesh, but it felt like his. He heard her screams as if they emerged from his own throat; begging J.D. to tell her, just let her know before she died.

"Tell me what you did with my son, my baby boy that you took away from me. Tell me where he is. Please, tell me he's safe."

"Ask your master, Beelzebub, what he did with that mewing little bastard," was J.D.'s only reply to her plea.

Naked and shivering, he watched as a caricature of the man wallowing in the dirt took the green silken belt of a kimono out of a suitcase and threw it across an open beam of the rustic slave cabin. Charlie could feel Eliza's last breath as she twisted and turned, hanging from the beam, and he felt her neck snap as if his own head had been wrenched from its neck.

It was all wrong. This had happened to her, not to him. Tears streamed down his face as he realized what she had suffered as a direct result of his desertion. She had suffered and died in the same little cabin where they so often had made tender love, the same little cabin he left only an hour before.

Eliza, forgive me. I never knew. He turned to look at the man he suddenly realized must have been her husband, who now rolled in the dirt, screaming his horror and pain.

"Eliza, you whore! It hurts!" J.D. covered his head with his hands and tried to avoid looking at the fearsome demon whose melding features leered at him, running and melting with the heat. She undulated with flames that seared his skin and laughed and screeched at him.

Kill him, Charlie. Lift the axe, Charlie.

As he stared at J.D, he felt his vision shift out of his body, again experiencing memories taken from the mind of another. He was in a room looking at not one, but two babies, both wrapped in a blanket next to Eliza, who reached toward him, weakly. There was a girl and a boy! He was the father of twins! But he wasn't happy, he was angry. He felt himself kick Eliza and send her spinning across the hard plank floor. How could he hurt her like that? What was wrong?

Next he felt himself pick the boy baby up by his feet and carry him out of the cabin, the infant struggling and fighting to get free.

The baby had bright red hair, just like his when he was little. Momentarily regaining control, he tried to push Eliza's loathsome husband, the ugly creature groveling in the dirt before him, out of his mind.

Kill him, Charlie. See his evil? Feel his evil? He gagged, wanted to free himself, but the horror wasn't over.

Once again he felt himself become the evil creature, and he walked along the dirt path leading to the river. Tears poured down Charlie's cheeks as he realized what must happen next. Shaking with fury, he felt as the creature possessing his soul plunged the infant into the river and he watched as it sputtered and struggled to breathe, kicking and flailing its tiny arms hopelessly. He heard the tiny little yelps sputtering and felt the child go limp as the tiny baby lost its battle to survive. Mercifully, another voice surfaced, pulling him away from the horrible events of long ago and he looked down at J.D., the monster who had committed the horrible crime he had just witnessed, now rolling in filth on the cave floor.

Look how he cowers! He's not brave now! It's time, Charlie.

The bees reached a crescendo in his head. He lifted the fireman's tool high over his shoulder and with a loud bellow plunged it through John Duke Parson's demented brain, passing straight through, cleaving his skull like the splitting of a grapefruit, neatly leaving even halves on the reddening dirt of the cave. He heard laughter now.

It came from the dog. The shrill noise frying the inside of his brain came from the white animal in front of him. It backed, and he followed it, holding his axe in front of him like a crucifix designed to protect him from the hound of Hell. Down the corridor they moved, Ghost growling and snarling, until he reached the boulder he'd placed to block the exit.

The animal looked at him with its lips drawn back, gums pink and teeth shining, backed up against the boulder and unable to move any further. Its blue eyes burned into his and he felt it crawl inside his head.

Goodbye, little dog. Say goodbye, puppy.

Lifting the axe one more time, he summoned every ounce of energy left in his body and brought the axe down on the dog and the boulder both. The flat end of the axe glanced off the frail body of the now-whimpering canine and split the sandy boulder into a hundred clumps of dirt. A simple white cloth dropped from the cave wall, and sparkling like pearls, a tiny set of human bones tumbled onto the earth outside, shining cleanly under the blue spring sky.

"Now!" Li screamed, and Verbena and the entire clan eased around Charlie, who stood, stunned, half-blocking the exit, looking at the chaos around him, blood still dripping from the axe held in his now immobile, hands. Within seconds, the entire group was outside and as far away from the mess as they could get and not leave the area. They gathered next to the river and waited, and after a few seconds of surveying the scene, the confused avenger returned to the darkness of the cave.

While they huddled together, staring at the little skeleton and the mangled dog, Charlie got very busy inside. First, he pocketed the shiny set of car keys he found in the dead man's jacket, smiling as he saw the cute little license plate key chain holder on one end. With any luck at all, it would be in the parking lot and all he would need to do would be to match the car with the keys. Somehow, he knew it wouldn't be difficult. It was a shame that he had ruined the man's head, but it felt good to reduce Eliza's murderer into a thousand little parts. And her murderer he was, he'd seen in the last few minutes before he took the man apart. He was Eliza's murderer and the killer of his little boy, his child, one of the two she'd birthed of his–his twins–his son murdered, and poor little Molly, his daughter, treated so badly.

Right now the best thing he could do for his daughter would be to stay alive and out of police custody, but what a mess he'd made. Maybe if he cleaned things up, they wouldn't be able to recognize J.D. and come after him. It wouldn't hurt to take as many of the pieces with him as he could. Scraping together all of the fragments of his former rival that he could find, he tucked them into Verbena's pretty birthday tablecloth. J.D., although useless, would go with him, as much of him as he could carry anyway, and he would dispose of him in a manner befitting the animal that he had been. His Eliza would be proud of him now.

I failed her, but I won't fail my daughter. Someday I'll make things right for her. Someday I'll make up to her all the years that we lost.

Finally, he felt like Eliza forgave him, even though now, after all these years, he realized that she died because he'd let her down. He wasn't there. It was J.D. who waited for her in the cabin instead, and she'd never had a chance. Looking backward one last time, he lifted the tablecloth onto one shoulder and cradled the axe in his arms. The trick would be to get all this into the trunk of the right car and not be seen, but he knew Eliza would help him. He could feel her guidance even now as he slipped quietly away.

Happy to still be alive, Verbena and her little crowd of boys watched from their vantage point near the river, all of the children except one; that is, all of the children except Mickey.

Verbena could never quite remember what happened inside of the cave, but she and the children would never forget their last view of Mickey, his mother, Eliza, and Ghost. Crying, she watched as the dog crept toward the scattered little bones, whining piteously, finally lying motionless beside them, nose touching the tiny skull. Mickey, too, was drawn to the little skeleton by an invisible power beyond even his enhanced senses, and suddenly he sat by them, touching them, stroking them gently, oblivious to the dying dog only inches away.

Explaining what came next was always very difficult for Verbena. A slight mist emerged from the human remains, and it curled around the tiny baby bones, cradling them, and then it enveloped Mickey, but he didn't seem to notice it at all. Suddenly, her eyes were drawn to the sky and whirling, turning, dancing in the light breeze, an adult skeleton appeared, propelled toward them from nowhere, its spinning bones kicking up dust and dirt as it hovered above them. Verbena couldn't take her eyes off of it, but Fox tugged on her sleeve, forcing her attention elsewhere.

"Look, Beeny, look!" The tiny set of bones danced, too, now. Little femurs outstretched, it reached for the larger skeleton, which dipped and after a second's hesitation, flew down to scoop the little body up and to cradle it in its long-empty arms.

"Mother?" Mickey questioned. As soon as the two strange relics had touched, he'd felt uncontrollably drawn to them. He had never known a mother and he was not familiar with any of the emotions that washed over him, but he knew that he had a sense of belonging he had never felt before, not even as a member of the clan of boys he had nurtured. This was different; this was a love and acceptance he had never known could exist, this was someone to watch over him.

Startled, Verbena watched as the child she had known approached the spinning dervish. The mist surrounded him, and soon he stood in the middle of the bones transfixed, his mouth open and eyes huge, green emeralds in his tiny face. No longer angry, Molly's angel, dressed in white, emerged from the vision and reached to touch her Mickey, who had faded until he was almost transparent. Reaching out to him, she pulled him to her, running her fingers through his red curls. No longer needed, the bones lost their energy and they tumbled to the ground, taking their place by Ghost's motionless body.

Mickey? My baby? My little son? Look at you! You're so beautiful! Exactly like I always pictured you! You are my magic-Mickey, my little Irish imp, so like your father. I always knew you would look just like this! I've found you, at last. Molly and Tessie moved toward the beautiful voice, but the apparition motioned for them to stay back.

The bare area in front of the river by the cave glimmered with light. Finally, arms wrapped around each other, mother and child disappeared into the sunlight together, turning and weaving like a sparkling funnel cloud, until they reached a point about two hundred feet above the little group.

From this position so high above them, the angel turned and smiled, then pointed toward the dark cave. Briefly her face darkened, and as they watched, a spark flew from the tip of her outstretched fingers and the hill beneath her exploded into a thousand small pieces, ricocheting around them harmlessly, rocking the air with a tremendous resounding boom, spewing smoke and dirt everywhere. When they looked again, she and Mickey were gone and only the limp body of the dead dog and the two skeletons remained.

"Will we ever see Mickey again?" Barnes asked, hiding his face behind his hands. He was bawling, but he didn't want anyone else to see it.

"No, honey. Mickey is gone to a place where he will be happy and at peace with his mother." Verbena sobbed too, wrapping her arms around her boys as tightly as she could.

So many things made sense to her now. Why Mickey never spoke. Why he appeared and disappeared at will. The tears pouring down her face were happy ones, happy for him and happy for them all, happy that they were allowed to see the reunion. For some reason Verbena turned to watch Molly, who sat in the still-circling dust near the bones with her arms around her little sister. Both children were covered with red dirt, streaks running down their faces where tears adhered the grit to their cheeks and foreheads. Tessie smiled and reached toward the sky, but Molly sobbed. Suddenly her tears stopped and a strange look crossed her face, briefly but visibly.

If that is what you want, Mother. I'll tell them the truth. I'll take care of Tessie. I love you. Thank you for my daddy. Holding Tessie as tightly as she could, she buried her mud-streaked face in the child's sunny hair.

"Where is Father?" Tessie suddenly asked. "Was he in the cave? I thought I heard him call me and I came, but he wasn't here." Horrified, Molly stifled a cry. No matter what her mother wanted, she knew she couldn't tell Tessie the truth.

"No, Tessie," she told her softly, "he's gone now. He wants us to live with Miss Anna. He told me to tell you that he wants us to be happy with Miss Anna." Tessie smiled and snuggled into Molly's arms.

Meanwhile, Charlie found the correct car in the first space, and although the area was crawling with police, they all poured into the woods, racing toward the site of the tremendous explosion that had just shattered the early evening peace. No one gave him or the car a second glance. The hot time in the old town was over for the night.

Chapter Forty-Three

Homes At Last

As the sun poured through the flowering trees, it was easy to count the gravestones in the small cemetery, eighteen in all. Three new stones lay flat next to two new gaping holes. Two small coffins rested next to Eliza's grave, and the small group gathered, dressed in their Sunday best.

"Eliza Duparte Parsons. Born 10-31-1954. Died 10-31-1975. May God bless those he has joined together at last."

Anna read the message from Eliza's new headstone solemnly for Tessie and Molly, one girl tucked under each arm. Slightly behind them, Verbena moved forward to look at the shiny new marble, pulling Freddy and Barnes with her, with Lionel and Harry beside her looking very adult in their first real grownup suits.

"Your mother was very young when she died, Molly, and very beautiful." They all smiled, remembering their last look at her as she disappeared into the sky.

"And my brother was so good to me." Molly missed her funny little Mickey as much as she did her mother.

"You're lucky you got a chance to know what he would have been like." None of them questioned what they now knew to be true. Mickey was Eliza's vision; a child who grew out of her restless dreams, but just as Molly was flesh and bone reality, a child of her mother and father, Mickey, too, was a faithful representation of all that he would have been had he not been murdered as an infant. Too many things could never be explained, and even Tessie knew instinctively not to try.

"Your brother was so smart and so funny." Verbena leaned down and hugged Molly. "He loved you very much. Ask any of the boys, they can tell you." Molly looked from face to face, and they each nodded agreement. Freddy bobbed his little face up and down, Barnes' chubby lips posed a silent yes, and Lionel's serious features delivered a verbal message for them all.

"We adopted you. A long time ago, we all agreed that you were to be our Princess, so now you are our sister. Mickey would have wanted that."

"And anything you want, we'll do for you," Harry added eagerly, hoping she would demand something of him. Molly felt a warm glow start with her toes and move all the way through her body. Was this what being loved felt like? She could get used to that! Not only did the boys all love her, but her mother had told her that she had a daddy, too; one that would love her and take care of her some day. She smiled at that secret, a secret she would always keep.

"Now, everyone, get in position, it's time for the ceremony!" Carrie, dressed in a bright spring-pink suit and Sunday straw hat, pulled the Cokesbury Prayer book out from under her left arm.

"This Easter Sunday, we gather together to rededicate these spirits to the Lord and to thank him for the wonderful future he has given us. We thank you for the love this mother felt for her children, even after death, and for the time you allowed this child to be a part of us on earth, and the wonderful love with which you blessed this simple dog, who cared for these children and protected them to the best of her ability. We thank you that we are now able to place these earthly remains in their final resting place, and we trust you to gather them to yourself and bathe them in your peace and love, for eternity."

Tears slid down Molly's face, but she didn't know if she cried because she was sad, or because she was happy.

"They've earned their peace, and we want to leave them in it. Thank you for making it possible." Fidgeting, Tessie pulled on Anna's skirt.

"Miss Anna!" she whispered. "Is my momma in that box now?" Anna wanted to be truthful to the child, and she suspected that the vision of her mother that she had seen on the day the bones were found at the cave had confused her.

"Was she here when we used to come see her?" Anna wasn't sure how to answer her, but gave it a try.

"Her spirit is with you, angel. She's always loved you, so her spirit was here." The little girl was persistent.

"Can she see me now?" A few feet away, three shadowy figures pulled back a little, behind the gate.

"Do you think they can see us?" The boy wasn't much smaller than the little woman, and all three of them were almost invisible in the bright sun that shone right through them. The woman smiled and placed one hand on the boy's shoulder, the other on the head of the big white dog.

"No. They can't see us anymore. Our job is done." Gently, the woman stroked the translucent child's faded red hair.

Verbena rubbed her eyes as they lowered each casket into the ground in turn, and the gravedigger began to spade earth into the first hole.

"We'll be back later to bring the flowers and see the stones in place," Anna told the old man as he went about his work.

"Back to the mansion to start the painting!" It was amazing how fast walls, flooring and roof were restored when the townspeople decided that this would be the first Group Home for Disturbed Children in the State of Alabama. Verbena couldn't believe her luck in being chosen to be the group mom for her boys. When restored, the mansion would only be a small part of what it had been, but it would be their home. Even Pryor Akins managed a little smile when the recompense for his loss far exceeded the worth of the furnishings and possessions he actually owned. The only one still unhappy was A. E. Beaufort, and no one worried about him.

"First, hamburgers and ice cream for all!" Anna led the Sicily bunch out the gate of the cemetery and toward Bob's Hamburger Heaven. As the happy troupe left, the three waiting behind the gate vanished also. Turning, they faded away into thin air, gone as if they'd never existed.

A few miles away, Sheriff Bobby Cox examined his notes; still as puzzled as he was on the day that the events took place. He couldn't make heads or tails out of this case; nothing added up. Only Molly admitted to being a witness to any of the events inside the cave, and that made no sense at all, since they were all in there when someone got hacked to death by an axe. At least that was what the little girl told him, and he knew J.D. went into that cave. How else could the little girls have gotten to the scene and been standing there wide-eyed when he and the boys arrived?

"What happened?" he asked them all, but only Molly answered. The rest of them stared at him wide-eyed and speechless.

"My daddy killed the evil man, with the axe," Molly told him.

"Is that true?" he asked, but the rest of them just looked at him. "Where is your daddy now?" he asked.

"In Atlanta," she told him. "He was scared, so he went to Atlanta." No matter how many times he questioned them, the story stayed the same. No one had any idea why someone would destroy the old mansion with a mortar stolen from the armory. And no one could figure out why the cave exploded. Maybe rolling that boulder around opened up a gas pocket and somehow it'd ignited? As unlikely as it seemed, it was the only explanation he found possible.

One other strange story came out of the afternoon, a tale from an old man walking by the Duparte Graveyard about the same time as the events were taking place in Sicily, a story that Sheriff Cox found as unbelievable as everything else that took place that day.

"I was just out for my walk, like I take every day, and the sky got real dark, like a big storm, but it was sunny before. I was looking in the graveyard and the ground starting shaking and dirt flew everywhere. I kinda sat down and covered my eyes for a second and I heard a noise like the shattering of a thousand glass windows, all at once. When I looked back up, there was pieces of headstone everywhere, just like someone or something done blowed it up and bones jumped up, right out of that empty hole over there, flew over my head and disappeared. I was lucky the damn thing didn't hit me."

Bobby Cox shook his head. Somehow nothing amazed him anymore. He remembered the investigation of Eliza's death because he was a young officer then, and he was the one sent to fill out the reports. The entire accident had been strange. No mother of two children sneaks out in the middle of the night in her nightclothes to ride someone else's wild horse, especially not Eliza.

He'd gone to school a few years ahead of her, and she'd never liked any of that horsemanship stuff so many of the girls loved. In fact, she was terrified of horses. He remembered being sadder that they destroyed that beautiful animal than he had been for Parsons and his white-trash wife. He never would figure out that family. Nuts, all of them.

He had no idea how Eliza's bones had gotten to the cave on the day of the explosions, or where the little bones from the infant they found at the cave originated, but he was relieved when Verbena insisted they belonged in the Duparte Family Cemetery. For some reason he would never understand, Verbena insisted that Eliza had an extra kid they never knew about. It was fine with him if they wanted to give the lost baby a Christian burial. There must have been some reason why Parsons was interested in that cave.

That J.D. was a true maniac and they needed to lock him up before he hurt someone, he supposed,but it was hard to get excited about hunting down a man who gotten rid of a three-time serial murderer for them. He was all for giving him a head start and couldn't see wasting precious county manpower chasing him all the way to Atlanta.

"Son of a bitch already done his community service," Bobby muttered. He never would have figured J.D. for being strong enough to pick up one of those fireman's special axes like the one they found in the parking lot not long after the cave disintegrated. He guessed he must have lifted a few car engines during all that time he was a mechanic at Ned's Service Station though, because the blood on that axe indicated that someone bit the dust big time. Plenty of fingerprints, but too smudged to tell just whose they were.

A Smokey actually stopped the Cadillac halfway to Atlanta. The Highway Patrolman wanted to cite the driver for littering, but the car stank so badly he waved the driver on before running a make on the tags. It was only later he realized it was the vehicle sought by authorities in Beaufort County, Alabama. The driver claimed she'd just bought the car and that its former driver had left a cooler full of fish bait in the trunk.

"One foul smelling cooler full of shit and one seriously ugly broad," the report read. According to the deputy, she'd been tossing the pieces of fish bait out of the driver's window one piece at a time, but he didn't wait to issue her a ticket.

Far away, in a suburb of Atlanta, Charlie examined the only parts of J.D. that remained, a pair of beautifully shaped hands, fingers delicately tapered and the nails clean and manicured. They taxidermied nicely, hardly any browning at all, and he was pleased with his work. Smiling, he placed them on the shelf by the sheriff, his fat wife, and Homer. He and his friends were safe at last, and he couldn't wait to get to his job at the beauty parlor, where he washed all the ladies' hands before the manicurist did their nails. She promised him that she would teach him how to do them soon, and he would be applying the coats of color, layer by layer.

Someday he would go back to Beaufort Falls as Charlie and claim his kid, but right now he would be safer as Charlene. The apartment was tiny, but he could afford it on his salary earned assisting the stylists and sweeping the shop. Turning to face the new full-length mirror, he straightened his hose.

"Yes, Siree, Charlene is styling now!" he told his friends, the Heads.

It's ME! Ink Press
offers you a preview of
Mari Sloan's cosmic sequel
To BEAUFORT FALLS,
ROAD TRIP

Coming in 2009

Beaufort Falls

From ROAD TRIP

Busted

"Cleaning up the past will always clear out the future."
Chinese Fortune Cookie

It was a small sound, the scurrying of tiny feet, but Molly almost dropped her magazine. It wouldn't do to get caught hiding in the woods behind her house on a school day. Satisfied it was a false alarm, she settled back into her reading.

"Anyone can be a star," her favorite film idol announced. "Anyone can. All you need to do is to be in the right place, at the right time, and for me the right place was here!" Molly stared longingly at the huge block lettered Hollywood sign so conspicuously behind the shoulders of the perky blonde teen, in the full-page picture that illustrated her dreams. *Damn!* She heard noises again and this time there was no mistaking the dry shuffling of leaves. Someone was coming her direction along the little path that led to her secret hideaway. Quickly, she scanned her brain for clues. Not a child. School wouldn't be out for another two hours. As far as she knew she was the only child in Beaufort Falls that braved the scandal of being caught skipping. Not another kid for miles around had her spunk, or her ability to push buttons when needed. She knew that no one from school was looking for her. Most of her teachers were just glad to have a day off. Even if she hadn't streaked her dark hair with bright purple, her last stunt established her reputation as insane.

But now she could hear dirt moving again so she moved quickly to wedge her long body, and her secret cache of forbidden reading material, into the dirt crevice behind the large river oak, carefully scattering the leafy debris behind her to eliminate any clues as to her position. By easing the leaves aside on a low hanging branch, she was able to see into the little clearing. Just in time, too. She resisted the urge to shudder as a tall man stepped into the open, pausing to look in her direction, almost as if he could see her. Broad shoulders, completely bald, he looked familiar but she knew that she hadn't seen him in Beaufort Falls any time recently. He had the look of an out-of-towner, but what would someone not from Beaufort Falls be doing in the woods behind a private subdivision? What could he be searching for in her little retreat? Maybe he was a surveyor, or a wild life specialist, but why was he behind her house? Almost afraid to breathe she winced as a fly brushed across her nose, and he paused to look in her direction again.

She could be my daughter, Charlie thought, his heart racing with excitement. *She could be my Molly.* Peering into the dense brush he wondered how he could approach her without frightening her. *Such a wild little thing, how can I tell her that she belongs to me, with me, her Father?* After following her for a week he was certain of two things. The dark-haired child was the right age to be Molly, and she was not the least bit happy with Beaufort Falls. Who knew what she might have been told about him if she knew anything about him at all? *The last time she saw me I was waving an axe,* he remembered. *She might even think I'm dead. I've spent the last eight years as someone else. I hope everyone in this pathetic little town thinks I'm pushing up daisies in the old slave cave.* There had to be some reason why no one ever came looking for him. *I don't want to scare her and I know she's hiding from me. How can I get her to come out?* Perplexed, he found a place to sit on an old log, but as he reached to brush it off before settling in to see if she would eventually surface, he disturbed the deserted timber's current resident.

Tail erect and screeching wildly, the angry squirrel leaped toward the intruder's right hand. Charlie hopped backwards, sliding on the thick mulch and hitting the ground with a loud thud. Gales of laughter erupted from the adjacent tree. The man didn't look so dangerous sprawled on his rear across the path.

Oh shit! Cover blown. Sheepishly Molly crawled out of her hiding place, putting as much distance as she could between herself and the stranger.

"If you touch me I'll scream so loud your ears will pop!" Her would be attacker moaned piteously as the indignant squirrel scurried off. "Are you hurt?" She felt a little sorry that she'd laughed at him.

"Mainly my pride," Charlie admitted, "but I could have sprained my wrist. It really hurts!"

"Let me see that. What are you doing out here anyway?" She found she was more curious than scared.

"Hunting."

"With what?" She didn't see a rifle, a bow and arrow, or even a camera. "For what?"

Jesus, how could I come up with anything that lame? Molly was backing away from him again. She was going to run from him in a second and this was the most private opportunity he'd had so far to approach the funny, long-legged imp who most likely was his kid. She was such a beautiful girl and looked so like the old photograph that was all he had left of his Mother.

"You're Molly, aren't you?"

"What's it to you?" The man was starting to scare her again but she needed to get around him to make the break for home. Best to placate him. She began inching toward him, gradually easing toward his right side. "Yes, I'm Molly. Why?" It was odd that he knew her name. She couldn't remember meeting him.

"I'm looking for a kid named Molly."

This was getting way out of hand. Who was this man? Frozen, she focused on his face and a thousand memories came rushing back of the one day she tried very hard to forget, the day she expected to die in the cave by the river. J. D. was never her father, could her father be this man?

Horrified, she stared at his strong shoulders and she could picture them swinging the big axe. What did he want with her now? Once again she felt the paralyzing fear as she had cowered almost underneath a monster and the man she now knew was her stepfather, once again feeling the wet spray of warm blood across her neck as the pieces of her stepfather's head smacked the side of the cave wall. Quickly, she searched for the horrible weapon, but this man's hands were empty, nervously clasped together as he stood quietly in front of her.

"I won't hurt you." *She's going to run. She'll run and then she'll never let me get near her again.* He could tell that she remembered him by the terror in her eyes. *Please Molly. Please don't run. I can't tell her I'm her father. She may not know. She would be really afraid if she knew. Think! Fast, before she flies out of here.* "I've...I've got a message for you," but it was too late. She shoved him roughly as she flew by him on the narrow path and he had no choice but to let her go.

"It was a good dream while it lasted," he muttered sadly as he made his way back to the street. Why should she ever trust him? What could he do to prove to his child that she would never see him harm another creature? Overwhelmed, he sat down on the curb in front of her house, cradling his head in his hands.

Molly watched him from the shaded window. This was the only chance she had to get the answers to the questions that disturbed her days, and haunted her nights. If he left, she would never know, never, ever, know. If he killed her at least she would die somebody, not just an odd fledgling stuck in a nest of beautiful songbirds. She had to know. Taking a deep breath she opened the front door and went out to face her future.

Beaufort Falls

About the Author

Born into a Georgia family of eccentrics and visionaries, Mari Sloan carries her heritage of storytelling from the Deep South to the hills of Southern California, where she shares a home with her writer husband and a black Maine Coon cat. She works locally, and is always the one who knows where the bodies are buried. On a good day, she will tell you.

"I put my heart and my soul into my work, and have lost my mind in the process."

Vincent Van Gogh

Printed in the United States
103164LV00003B/46-66/A